UNTOUCHABLE

by

Lindsay Delagair

This book is a work of fiction. Names, characters, places, and incidents are the product of the author's imagination or are used fictitiously. Any resemblance to actual events, locales, or persons, living or dead is coincidental.

DEDICATION

To family and friends that have
(sometimes unwittingly)
sparked my imagination.

.

Understanding love gives you inner strength.
Inner strength gives you real courage.
Real courage gives you the power for true change.

~ Lindsay Delagair ~

ACKNOWLEDGMENTS

Jan Ayola – Editing Assistance
Dr. Crystal Herold – Editing Assistance
Loridia Urquiza – French Assistance

PROLOGUE

He pushed the money across the table. "Are you sure you can handle this assignment? It's different from what you usually do."

"I can handle it."

"You realize you're going to have to get close."

"Yeah, I know. No shot from across the parking lot."

"That's not what I mean."

"I know, I know. This one is all about trust."

"People tend to get attached to those who trust them. I've seen entire plans ruined because someone couldn't pull the trigger."

He slowly thumbed through the money. "I've never botched a job and I don't plan on starting now. When will I get the other two-hundred thousand?"

A cell phone slid across the table. "This is our only contact. You call me when the job is finished and I'll tell you where to get the rest of the money."

He studied the cell phone for a moment. "So who is she really? This is a little more cloak and dagger than usual." The question was being ignored. He knew better than to repeat it.

"Did you have any problems getting the papers?"

"I never have problems with paperwork. You know that."

"Just making sure. Your associates are the best in the business, but one never knows when a tie might get cut."

"No, not even if I wanted to. It's just too lucrative to switch careers now."

"How long?"

"How long will it take? Depends on how trustworthy I look."

"You have at least six weeks. If it isn't finished by then—well, I guess I'll assume you couldn't do it. In any case, someone will finish the job—and you. No hard feelings, but with fifty-thousand dollars down, someone's gotta pay for it."

The top of the gun was pulled back to chamber a bullet. "Like I said, I can handle it."

CHAPTER ONE

I pulled my little blue Volkswagen into the school parking lot and turned off the engine, but left it on accessory so I could sing a little bit longer. Jewels, the varsity cheer captain, was waving furiously to me from her little Kia. She began to dance in her seat as the base from her stereo became loud enough to pummel me through steel and glass. She motioned for me to come over and join the fun.

I really didn't feel like getting my eardrums smashed this morning, but you don't turn down Jewels when she wants something. With that, I unplugged my iPod and slipped it into the pocket of my hoodie and gave her the signal like, "Hang on a minute, I'm getting there!"

"Hey!" I shouted as I opened the door and tried to slip into the passenger's seat. The force of the music was so hard on my chest that it literally felt like an invisible pair of hands pushing me back, warning me not to come closer. I saw her lips move, but I couldn't make out what she said. "Jewels, turn it down! I can't hear you!" I yelled into the base-reeking void.

She cocked her head slightly sideways as she wrinkled her little Barbie nose. Her hand went straight for the volume and turned it down. "Wha—What'd you say?"

"You know you are going to be deaf by the time you hit twenty," I warned, sliding into the seat. "And, your dad would flip if he caught you playing the radio that loud,"

She threw her head back like some little demon-possessed monster and laughed, "He hasn't got a clue! Why do you think I park next to you every day? He thinks you're the one with the bad taste in music."

"Ah, that's just great, Jewels. I listen to Christian rock and he thinks I'm into K-fed. No wonder he gives me the evil eye during lunch."

"Don't be stupid, Leese. He's the principal; he gives everyone the 'evil eye,'" she said, making quotation marks in the air. "He just does that so everyone will think he's mean and tough and that way they won't get out of line."

"Yeah, I'm a real dangerous…"

"Oh, Momma!" Jewels exclaimed, cutting me off and jerking on my arm.

"Ouch! Jewels—you've got my hair, Jewels!" But I could see by the look on her face she hadn't heard a word. I followed her eyes to where a guy was climbing out of a black 370Z two rows over from us. With all the muscle he had, he really didn't look like someone who should be called a student. He was dressed in blue jeans and a Hollister shirt, neither of which had an inch to spare. He reached back into the car and pulled out a folder of papers and glanced around as if he had no clue where he was going.

"OMG!" Jewels sputtered, "He *must* be new."

"Jewels, people don't normally talk text language."

She was still ignoring me. "Come on! We've got to go show Mr. Hunk where the *office is.*" She sang out the last two words.

"No, no thanks. I'm not going to be late for class to get the latest guy you are drooling over to the office."

She looked up quickly into her rear-view mirror. "I'm not drooling—am I?" She wiped the corners of her perfectly lip-glossed lips and smiled. "You're a stick-in-the-mud! See ya later." And with that she practically skipped across the parking lot to meet Mr. Hunk, or whatever his name would turn out to be. I knew I'd meet up with them later because once Jewels sank her claws into a guy, she didn't let go easily.

By the time I'd finished AP English, Psych II, and Macro Economics, I was starving and ready to dive into a grilled chicken salad. I had forgotten about Jewels chasing after Mr. Hunk until I stepped into the cafeteria. There she was, parading around with what's-his-face on her arm, going to each of her friends (which amounted to the majority of the cafeteria) and making introductions. I had no desire to meet this guy before my stomach met a salad. I pulled my long brown hair from the pony tail holder and brought it around to cover the side of my face.

"Hey, Lee…"

"Shhh!" I motioned Kevin to keep quiet as I stepped into the lunch line. He looked perplexed until I mouthed the word, "Jewels."

"Oh," he said with complete understanding.

I had the first mouthful of ranch covered, mouth-watering Romaine and whatever it was that the school passed off as grilled chicken ready to put between my lips when I heard Jewels say, "There you are!"

I paused mid-bite and then slowly lowered the fork. Taking a deep breath, I looked up to see her beaming a huge smile and standing beside Mr. Hunk. Oh, yes, with closer inspection he was exactly that. He looked like a jock; tall, broad shoulders, muscled arms and definitely some six-pack abs hidden under that brown and blue striped shirt. He smiled as I quickly wiped the drop of dressing that had made it to my lip before the interruption.

"Evan Lewis, this is Annalisa McKinnis, but we just call her Leese. Leese, this is Evan. He's new," she added with that little quiver to her voice that told me she was barely keeping her enthusiasm under control. "Leese is new, too," she went on. "Not really new like you, but she started at the beginning of the school year. She moved here from…" Her voice trailed as I realized she had forgotten where I told her I was from.

I wanted to blurt out Palm Beach, but I had to remember that subject was taboo.

"Alabama," I said, putting out my hand.

"Really?" He took my hand into his warm, firm grip. "What part? I have family in Alabama."

I withdrew my hand. "Nor—northern," I stammered. "Birmingham," I added for a pinch more credibility.

"Yeah, that's where my uncle lives. Where in Birmingham are you from?"

"Jewels are you going to let Evan eat, or are you going to parade him around the cafeteria the whole lunch period?" I dodged.

She glanced down at her watch, "Wow, we only have about ten minutes left. Are you hungry, Evan?"

"Sure. Are you getting something?"

"Yeah, I was going to get a shake." She started to pull him toward the dwindling line, but he slipped out of her grasp and went for his wallet instead.

He flipped out a ten and flashed a devastating smile. "No sense in both of us being in line. Would you mind grabbing me a burger?"

"Oh—sure," she fumbled, clearly unhappy with the prospect of leaving him alone even if it was only for a few minutes.

"Unless you want me to…" he motioned toward the line.

"Oh, no, no, that's okay. I'll be right back."

Evan sat across from me and continued where he'd left off. "You don't talk like an Alabamian. Where in Birmingham did you say?"

"Ah, Miss McKinnis," came a commanding voice.

I smiled at Evan because I was never quite so glad for the principal to approach. "Mr. Lykman," I said, turning around in the chair to face him. "Did you meet…"

"Yes, I did. Jewels brought him by my office this morning." But his tone indicated that he wasn't going to be distracted by small talk.

I knew what he wanted to discuss. Bring it on, I thought. This has got to be better than making up stuff about Birmingham, Alabama, which I know nothing about.

"I also heard your stereo this morning *all the way from the parking lot to the main office*. You do know there is a noise ordinance in the city limits, right?"

"Yeah, I'm sorry about that. I accidently turned the volume the wrong direction and before I could turn it down, I saw Jewels rocking out to my music and…"

He let a sound escape that was similar to someone blowing an annoying fly away from their mouth. "Don't make a habit of it. You might find Officer Martin in the parking lot one morning."

"Yes, sir," I mumbled as I finally placed my forkful of salad into my mouth. The bell would be ringing in a few minutes and I was still starving. Cute guy and principal watching or not, I was going to eat. Besides, how many questions can someone throw at you when you are stuffing your face?

"Hey, Dad," Jewels interrupted, as she placed the foil wrapped burger in front of Evan. "Is it too late for Evan to try out for spring football?"

"No, that's okay Jewels. I really don't..." Evan started to say.

Principal Lykman finally smiled because other than intimidating students, football was his focus. "You certainly look like you could do some damage on the field, Mr. Lewis. Did you play ball for Dawson High School?"

"Ah—no, sir. I was into weightlifting." It was Evan's turn to look uncomfortable.

I couldn't figure out why. Could this possibly be the one guy on the planet that didn't like football? Surely he had played some rough sports. He had a scar above his right eyebrow and another across his sculpted chin. I glanced at his hands and realized that his knuckles had taken a beating, or more appropriately, given a beating a few times. Surely this guy had played some kind of contact sport.

"Well, you should try out anyway," Mr. Lykman continued. "You have the right build for it." He slapped Evan on the shoulder. "I'll talk to Coach Cleveland and we'll look over your grades from Dawson."

"Ah, I really..."

"Great!" Jewels chimed in. "Now Daddy, leave us alone so we can eat before the bell." Then she gave her 'I like getting everything I want' smile and said, "Unless you want to give us late lunch passes?"

Mr. Lykman's face hardened. "No. Eat. You've got two minutes left." He glanced down at his watch and then walked away.

"Thanks Jewels," I whispered as soon as her dad was out of earshot. "I've been basically told that the resource officer will be waiting for *my* music to get too loud in the parking lot."

"That was you?" Evan said with genuine surprise.

I gave a fake smile, "No, it was Jewels. I'm just the scapegoat."

"Leese is the Christian rock singer. I'm the rapper girl," she said with a wink and a peace-out hand sign.

"You sing?"

I simply nodded, as Jewels continued.

"Yeah, Leese is really good. I got to listen to her at one of her Wednesday night Christian jam sessions..."

"It's called youth group, Jewels," I corrected.

7

"Well, anyway, I told her she should like try out for American Idol, but she won't do it."

"Why not?"

I smiled at him and shrugged, "I guess because I don't like attention; I'm an introvert at heart." This was a straight-faced lie, because I actually used to like the lime-light before my life went nuts.

"So why did you take the blame for Jewels?" The whole concept of taking blame for someone else seemed to confuse him.

"It doesn't matter," I shrugged. "One of these days she isn't going to have me to park beside and then she'll be busted."

"Why? Are you leaving?"

I looked into those dark green eyes and wondered why the seriousness to the question. He was handsome, but I was sworn to secrecy and I wasn't about to babble things to this guy I barely knew.

"No. I mean, you know, like I might be absent one day."

The ear-splitting bell rang above the cafeteria noise and would (hopefully) end my uncomfortable conversation.

"What class are you going to?" He asked me as Jewels grabbed his left arm and started pulling him toward the door.

"French," I smiled, completely confident that it was a class that anyone looking that tough would never be enrolled in.

"Me, too," he grinned as he laced his free arm through mine.

Jewels wasn't happy when she had to turn loose of him as we rounded the bend to the foreign language wing. "Well," she sighed, "I've got to go to English. What's your schedule like for tomorrow?"

He fumbled in his pocket for the pink paper and then handed it to her. "You tell me. The schedule here is crazy."

"It's not that hard to get used to," I said, glancing over at his classes. "You have even and odd days, but every day you have first period. Today is even; one, two, four and six, and tomorrow is odd; one, three, five and seven."

"All right! We've got P.E. together tomorrow," Jewels responded, never getting the point that he was as confused about the even/odd days as I was when I started. She looked up beaming, "If I don't see you after school today, I'll catch you in Government tomorrow morning. Bye!" And she took off down the hall, grabbing the arm of one of the football players as she went.

Evan raised his eyebrows. "So, does Jewels have a boyfriend?"

I couldn't help but laugh. "Well, I guess she has several. You just happen to be the FOTM right now."

"FOTM?" He questioned as he held open the door for me to French class.

"Yeah, you know, the 'flavor of the month.'"

"Oh, okay, I get it. I just wanted to make sure I wasn't going to have some pissed off guy waiting for me in the parking lot."

"No, I don't think that's going to happen, but if it did," I paused, checking out the biceps as he handed the teacher his schedule. "I think you could handle yourself."

"Damn right," he responded and then became aware that he was standing in front of a teacher.

My mouth gapped open and I felt the flush of embarrassment color my cheeks.

Mrs. Knoosh's eyebrows knitted together in a scowl. "I'll not have any of that talk in my classroom, Mr. Lewis. I suppose you'll be starting your first day with a referral."

"Je suis désolé, Madame," he replied in French.

"Ah," she sighed, breaking out in a big smile and clapping her hands together. "Parlez-vous français?"

"Oui, Madame—depuis que je suis un garçon," he smiled.

"Avez vous habité en France?" By this point she was beaming, evidently forgetting altogether his verbal blunder when he came into the classroom.

"Non. Je suis de la Nouvelle-Orléans."

"Ah, oui—Nouvelle-Orléans. Je suis heureuse de vous rencontrer, Monsieur Lewis."

"Merci," he responded in his flawlessly executed and accented French.

"Annalisa," she said turning to me, "Since Mr. Lewis is new perhaps you would be a good influence." Her eyes cut quickly back to Evan, "Asseyez-vous dans le fauteuil à côté de Annalisa."

With that, Evan suddenly looked very pleased. "Merci beaucoup."

I was a third year French student so I understood most of what they were saying, but I was still in shock that Evan was apparently so good at it.

"Wow!" I said quietly as we took our seats and the majority of the heads began turning back to face the teacher. "You certainly surprised me."

"Why? Don't I look like someone who could speak another language?"

"No, because she didn't write you up for cussing." I couldn't help but snicker just a little because I really didn't think he looked like someone that could speak another language, but I wasn't going to let him off that easy, especially since he was evidently off the hook for his slip of the tongue.

He gave me this really sexy smile and raised one eyebrow, "They don't call it the language of love for nothing."

"Ah!" I smacked him lightly on the shoulder with the textbook. "Page 148, s'il vous plaît, Monsieur."

We spent the rest of class conjugating verbs, but I have to admit he did most the conjugating before I could open my mouth. It seemed to please him that he could run circles around me in French.

Ten minutes before the bell, Mrs. Knoosh said we were allowed free time to talk quietly.

"So what do you do after school?" Evan asked, turning in his chair to face me. I stared at him for a minute just taking in the handsome lines of his face, his dark brown hair had that hand-tousled look like instead of combing it, he just ran his fingers through it. His green eyes sparkled from beneath long black lashes, set against a creamy, but not quite tan face. I still wanted to ask about the two scars, but figured it wasn't very polite. For just a moment, I had forgotten all my troubles and secrets, and I was just a high school girl talking with a cute guy.

"Hello? Earth to Leese," he said, waving a hand in front of my eyes.

"Umm—sorry, I wasn't paying attention. What did you say?"

"What do you do after school? Do you want to go hang out somewhere? I haven't seen much of the town since I got here yesterday, but I'm guessing you have a McDonalds or some kind of place like that for a quick bite."

Reality snagged me back to the problems in my life. "I—I can't. I've got tons of home work and I have to babysit my little sister until my—my aunt and uncle get home. But," I added. "There are a couple McDonalds close by, up on Fairview and one down in the historic district on Cervantes."

"You're kidding, right? You can't stop to get something before you go home?"

"No, afraid not. But," and it was killing me to say this, "I'm sure Jewels would be thrilled to show you around town." Jewels had a half dozen guys wrapped around her little pinky and I was getting ready to add another one to her collection.

He honestly looked dejected as he closed his textbook. "Yeah, but going with Jewels doesn't help me get to know you, does it?"

The way he said it gave me a tingle; this guy is interested in me. I had made some male friends while here at PHS, but they were easy to keep just as friends. I made it a point to never give out the signals that would lead a boy to assume that I was looking for anything else. I was used to the attention from the cute guys at my old school, but then again they knew who I was which always left me wondering what it was that they were really interested in. Here I didn't have my Porsche or my designer clothes to scream out to everyone, "Hey, I'm somebody." Instead everything about me had been toned down so that no attention would be drawn to me. Yet this guy didn't seem to care that I was wearing Wal-Mart off-the-rack, or the fact that I wasn't dripping in jewelry.

I tried a smile, but it was weak. "Jewels is more interesting, I'm sure."

"Definitely not. I spent first and third period with her and I can tell you she is extremely shallow—nice, of course, but nothing more than ankle-deep. You on the other hand, I get the feeling have a whole ocean available."

I rolled my eyes, but all the while my pulse was picking up the pace. "Not me," I said, trying to sound convincing. "I'm an ankle-deeper one, too." And then, thankfully, the bell rang.

He leaned over and whispered in my ear, "Liar."

In that instant I realized he had on cologne. It was very faint, like he'd put it on yesterday and only a little remained, but it was awesome. Without a conscious thought, I closed my eyes and inhaled. What was it? Expensive and very masculine, but I couldn't think of the name. When I opened my eyes he was smiling and still just a little bit too close. I grabbed my books and made a bee-line for the door.

"Hey, wait up." I heard him call. "Don't I even get to walk you to your car?"

I didn't slow down, but it only took him a moment to catch up with me.

"Do you always bolt for the door at the last bell?"

"You aren't going to turn out to be some kind of stalker, are you?" I said with feigned terseness as I struggled to keep from smiling.

He didn't answer as we dodged through the crowded halls and headed outside. He still wasn't talking as we came out into the sun-filled mayhem of teenagers going either toward the bus line or the parking lot. I was starting to think I had actually hurt his feelings when I snuck a quick glance at his face. He caught me looking.

"Maybe," was all he said.

I pulled out my key as we got close to my VW. Even though it wasn't new, I had to retain just a little bit of the freedom that I once took for granted.

"Maybe what? You have a little bit of stalker in you?" I managed to put a tiny bit of a teasing edge back into my voice, but on the inside I felt like it was pointless. There was no way that I was going to get involved with a guy in Pensacola when my whole life was a couple hundred miles away.

"VW Bug. Cool. Whoa, I am impressed," he added as I opened my door and toss my books to the passenger's side.

"It's five years old," I retorted, sitting down in the driver's seat. "Nothing impressive about that, not like that gorgeous Z you have sitting over there."

He reached over me and wiggled the shifter. "No, I don't mean your car. I mean that it's a stick."

"Oh," was all I could manage as he had put himself practically in my face to reach inside. He must have sensed that I was a little uncomfortable over the lack of personal space because he backed off to an almost respectable distance as he simply leaned toward me from the door frame.

"Most chicks can't drive stick," he finished.

"My first car was an..." Oops. I'd said a little too much. How many cars could a seventeen year old girl have been through? "I mean this is my first car—and, yep," I said waving my hand over the shifter like some ditsy game show hostess, "It's a stick."

"Mines a stick," he smiled. "You could actually drive it sometime, if you'd like. If you think you can handle it."

I was trying to keep the smirk from rising to my lips. I wanted to tell him that I'd been trained in an evasive driving school that specialized in survival, stunt and anti-terrorist driving tactics. I wanted to see him plastered to his passenger's seat when I dropped the gears and spun his car a hundred and eighty degrees and then smoked his tires off as I reached speeds that were hardly legal for the Autobahn. I sighed as I thought about my gun-metal Porsche 911 sitting in storage on the other coast. "No, I don't think I could handle it," I finally said.

"Hi, guys!" came a welcomed voice from behind Evan, and I knew I'd soon be released from this uncomfortable moment. Jewels had found us.

"Hey, Jewels," I laughed, glad for once to have her bouncy presence. "Evan was asking me where he could grab a bite."

"Nah, that's okay, I..." he started to say, clearly uncomfortable that he was getting ready to be put back into her grasp.

"Nonsense," Jewels said with a dismissive wave of her perfectly manicured hand. "I'm meeting Kevin, Carlie, Nate and Natasha at Sonic in like 10 minutes. You can follow me or..." Her eyes suddenly lit up as she considered what she had watched Mr. Hunk crawl out of this morning, "I could ride with you and then you could drop me back off here at school."

"I don't know," he began. "Do you think you could talk Leese into joining us?"

I gave him a blistering stare.

"Ah," she sighed. "I only wish. Leese is the gotta-do-my-homework-babysitter-extraordinaire. I have a hard enough time just getting her to go out with us on the weekends."

Ah, crap! I watched the grin spread across his face.

"So, you do have a life. I just have to wait for the weekend, huh?"

I had a feeling that this was payback for returning him to Jewels clutches. If I could have only slipped my fingers around her dainty throat, I would have choked her. All I could think was that she should have waited to ask me if I had any interest in this guy *before* mentioning weekends.

"Yeah," she continued, oblivious to the look of discomfort on my face. "There is a group of us going to the movies Friday night. Wanna come?"

"And you're going?" He asked, looking down at me.

I wanted to say, 'I *was*' instead of 'I am' but then actually avoiding him would have been way too apparent. "Yeah," I sighed. "Unless the earth falls apart first."

His hand slapped the roof of my car, "Great, I'm in for Friday night!"

Jewels let out a squeal of delight.

I honestly don't think she cared so much about the fact that he only seemed interested in whether I was going or not. She was the type of person who liked to surround herself with the cool or gorgeous people from school. Yeah, he was right—she was shallow. I started my car and told them goodbye.

I stopped by the grocery store to grab milk, bread and cat food for Beverly, my aunt-for-show. And then I headed over to the elementary school to pickup my six-year-old sister, Kimmy. The pickup line for car riders was long, as usual. I sat there inching my way forward every few moments, but the whole time I was thinking about Evan. I kept thinking about driving his car and seeing the surprise on his face. I chuckled to myself, but realized I needed a new game plan for tomorrow. I needed to act like I had no interest in him. I would have to be the stick-in-the-mud that Jewels had called me earlier this morning. I'd have to be more than a stick-in-the-mud—I'd have to be just plain old mud. I sighed as I made my decision for tomorrow; no makeup. Yeah, that should do it.

The car door opened and Kimmy jumped in with her Hello Kitty backpack in hand.

"Have a good day," Ms. Brenderson said as she prepared to shut the door. "And don't forget," she added, pulling it open again. "Wear your seat belt." She did that every day, and every time Kimmy would laugh.

She buckled her seat belt as I check my side mirror for an opening to pull out. "So did you have a good day, kiddo?"

"Oh, yes," and she began rattling off everything she did in her first-grade classroom. I was listening, kind of. I couldn't help it though when my mind would drift back to the smell of his cologne, the way he reached into my car, and the smile on his face when he knew I was going out Friday night.

"Snap out of it, Leese," I said aloud.

"Snap out of what?" Kimmy questioned.

"Sorry, Kimmy. I was just thinking about someone from my school."

"A boy?" she asked with a funny little lilt to her voice.

"No, of course not." And here I thought she was too young to figure that out.

"I bet it's a boy. It's okay, Leese. You can like a boy if you want to. I like Michael Peters. He's in my class. I think about him all the time, too."

I looked at her and she looked at me, and then we both began to giggle.

"Is he cute?" I questioned with exaggerated interest.

"Oh, yes. He's seven and he's missing his front teeth, but I still want to kiss him!"

"Kimmy!" I didn't have to fake the shock. "You don't go around kissing boys."

"Sure you do, Leese. Don't you watch TV?"

"Apparently not the same shows that you do, young lady," I said as I pulled into the driveway.

"Oh, come on, Leese: Snow White, Beauty and the Beast, The Little Mermaid—they all kiss the boys they love."

I frowned for a moment, considering that even though they were cartoons, she was right; it was all about one great kiss. "I guess, but you should wait until you're older. You might not even like Mike what's-his-name next year." For that matter, I was thinking we might not even be here next year, but I didn't want to get her hopes up about going home or dash them about leaving her friends.

"Peters," she said as she trudged up the front steps. "It's okay, Leese. I'm just livin' my life." She sounded like some mini-scholar who dispensed wisdom to every dumb teenager that walked by. My eyes began to sting as the tears filled my bottom lashes; that was mom's line. She raised us with the motto to always live your life, don't just go through it.

"Life," I remembered her saying, "is a daily experience. God gives us a fresh chance every morning to discover what's out there. I hope when you grow old, God willing, you'll look back and say, thanks for the memories, instead of saying wait, let me go back. I was just getting by. Let me go back and re-do it. This is a one-shot deal."

I put away the small amount of groceries while mopping the tears off my face. I thought I was past all the sobbing and pain, but just five little words reminded me that I wasn't living my life. I was stuck here because Mom started freaking out with the idea that someone was trying to hurt us, or worse. Ever since her dad took his life two years ago, she had become convinced that it wasn't suicide and that someone was after our money. She started having trouble sleeping, then, when she did sleep, she'd wake screaming from nightmares. Dad was at his wits end when she started saying that Kimmy and I had to go some place safe. We had to go away until whoever it was that was doing this to our family was caught. The problem was that as far as I could tell there wasn't anyone doing anything to our family—Mom was losing her sanity.

Then, last July, our yacht which was docked in the backyard in the intercoastal waterway, caught fire, and she snapped. She called Matt and Beverly. They had all gone to college together at Florida State University and were still close friends. I think they were the only friends that weren't stinking rich. Somehow that equated to being safe in Mom's book. She asked if they could take us in until things got back to normal. And, of course, with a generous cash offer to cover any needs we might have, they said yes. I truly think Matt and Bev would have let us come live with them even if Mom couldn't spare a nickel, but Beverly said with the economy going the way it was, she was certainly grateful to put some extra money in the bank.

I checked on Kimmy. She was seated at the dining room table working on her vocabulary words. "Need any help?" I asked, my voice still filled with sadness.

"Nope, I'm fine." She sat there with her pencil in hand, the tip of her tongue poking out the right side of her mouth and her feet swinging back and forth below the chair. She didn't seem to notice the tone of my voice and I wasn't going to bring her down by crying in front of her.

"I'm going to start my homework. You can watch TV when you're done, okay?"

"Okay, Leese." She never looked up, but just kept working to write her words neatly.

Moments like today I was glad that I'd taken honors and AP courses. I had plenty of homework to keep my mind off everything, especially things like Evan. He would just complicate my life, and it certainly didn't need any more complications.

Matt arrived home first from work. He was an environmental engineer, but there wasn't enough work to keep him with the firm that he'd been with since he got out of college seven years ago, so for the last year and a half he'd been working with a survey company. The problem was that there wasn't much happening in the commercial or residential real estate business either, so the need for surveys had dropped dramatically. I could tell he was worried, but I also knew that Mom's monetary gift would keep them from losing their home, and probably leave enough room to supplement their incomes for at least a year.

He walked through the door, setting his dirty work boots in the foyer. I had grabbed him a cold coke from the fridge and had just popped the top when he looked up at me.

"Hey, Leese." He gave a little groan as he leaned backward with his hands on his hips trying to crack his back. "Oh, thanks," he said, reaching for the coke.

"Tired, Matt?"

He made a nasal "Uh-huh," as he slugged down the soda. Within moments he handed me back the empty can and then let out a huge burp.

"That's gross, Matt," I yelled as he marched down the hallway.

"Can't help it, kid," he shouted back. "You give me a coke and you know I'll burp. I'm going to jump in the shower before Bev gets in." The bedroom door closed and reopened a moment later as he peeked down the hallway. "Would you mind throwing the lasagna in the microwave, Leese? At least that will be done when Bev gets home."

I had already set the frozen lasagna out and had the same idea, so I said, "Sure," and kept working. I set the timer for 22 minutes and went to help Kimmy clean up her mess in the dining room. Bev pulled in just as the timer went off. It didn't take long before I heard Matt Junior's little footsteps running into the house. I jumped out from the dining room archway just in time to scare him.

"Boo!"

He squealed with delight and turned to run back to Beverly. "Mama," he called.

"Matt-Moo," Kimmy crooned from behind the living room couch, "Come find me." And the game began. Every afternoon she played hide-and-seek with Matt Junior. He never seemed to grow tired of looking for her, even though the living room was small and there weren't many places for her to hide.

Bev tossed a salad while I warmed a couple cans of green beans, and dinner was done. One thing I had to admit was that it was nice to be around so much normalcy in life. Back in Palm Beach, we were always on the go. Dinner together was usually at a restaurant between lessons. Mom kept us involved all the time doing something. Kimmy had taken swimming lessons before she could even walk. Then there were dance, singing, and art lessons. I had taken dance, singing, piano, and baton.

Before I turned fifteen, Mom bought me a Jaguar convertible and sent me to evasive driving school. It just wasn't sporty enough, and I couldn't do some of the cool things with it that a car with a manual transmission could offer, so when I got my restricted license, I bought my Porsche.

My driving trainer, Tony Dix, got special permission (amazing what money can buy) to let me try out my new car on the Daytona speedway. What a thrill that was! I could accelerate from zero to sixty in just over four seconds, and could reach one-ninety on the straightaway.

The last lesson Tony had taught me was my choice. He asked if there was anything left that I'd like to learn, and I remembered a move I saw on TV a couple times where the person would do a quarter-spin and slide into a parallel parking space at about thirty miles per hour. He thought that was hilarious, but said sure he could teach me. I spent two days learning it and one day perfecting it. The only thing he made me promise was that I'd never try it out in downtown Palm Beach! Reluctantly, I agreed.

I had been in martial arts since the week after grandpa died and had earned a black-belt after a year. I was working toward my second black belt when Mom pulled the plug on our almost-fairy-tale life and sent us here. It was like doing two hundred miles-per-hour and then slamming on the brakes full force. Here it was

Normalsville, USA. I got a VW bug, a cheap cell phone, a department store wardrobe, and a new last name. My only luxury that I was allowed to keep was a special pre-paid Visa with a hundred grand in the account.

The weird part was that I never hated being sent here. I mean, you know, I cried a lot at first, but that was mainly because I didn't know what was going on back home. Being normal took a little getting used to, but in a way it was cool. I made friends, real friends because I had nothing else to impress them with, and that felt good.

CHAPTER TWO

The next morning, I showered and dressed for school, but skipped putting on my makeup. That was hard. It was like I was walking around naked—outside.

I pulled into the parking lot at 7:40, which was extremely late for me. I figured if I only had five minutes to get to class, then no one would be waiting. Wrong. Jewels and Evan were talking beside his car when I pulled in. "Great," I muttered as I opened my car door.

"What happened to you?" Jewels started in. "The bell is going to ring in like five minutes." She turned to Evan, "Leese is *never* late."

"Sorry. My alarm didn't go off." My story shouldn't be too hard to believe. Without my makeup on, I know I looked the part. I started walking toward the school and let the two of them catch up to me.

"You look different today," Evan noted as he got beside me.

"Yeah, you know there's no time for makeup when you're in a hurry."

He laughed. "Actually, I've never been so short on time that I couldn't put my makeup on."

I slapped his shoulder. "Jerk! You guys don't know how lucky you have it; no makeup, no panty hose, no bra…" I stopped myself, realizing I was going the wrong direction with this conversation.

He just chuckled.

"I'd rather be late," Jewels added.

"Well, in any case, what I was going to say was that you look really good today," Evan grinned.

"Yeah, right," I scoffed.

"Leese, you can pull off the no-make-up thing," Jewels tossed out. "I mean you've got the complexion for it, but me…" She let her sentence trail off, evidently remembering that there was a guy in this trio.

I turned toward the English wing, "I've got to go. Bye, guys." When I glanced back I saw that Evan had started to follow me until Jewels grab his arm and said, "This way, silly."

I made it through the classroom door two seconds before the bell. I took my seat next to Kevin and gave him a nudge. "What page?" I whispered. Mr. Shultz had already told everyone where to turn, and I was, for once, lost.

"Three-fifty-two; *The Raven*." He flipped his book on edge as if I was some dolt who needed a visual.

"Got it. Thanks." We had been studying the biography of Edgar Allan Poe and this was going to be the first work of his that we would dive into. I enjoyed the biography even though it was rather depressing, but he reminded me of myself in that he ended up living with someone else after his mother died. An uncontrolled shiver ran through my spine as I thought about my mom. Robert, my step-dad, would make it through this, but was Mom really losing it? I felt the need to say a prayer for her. For a moment, I closed my eyes and asked God to keep her safely tucked in the palm of His hand.

"Ms. McKinnis," Mr. Shultz spoke, breaking me from my private thoughts. "Would you be so kind as to start us off with reading *The Raven*."

I only nodded, and began reading for the class. My mood this morning was perfect for this assignment and my tone complimented the flowing poetry. Ten full minutes of being dramatic in front of the class and I was ready to slip down into my seat and disappear.

Second period, Kevin and Carlie and I had gym, so we walked together and talked about what was playing Friday night that we wanted to see. I always got a good laugh watching these two together. They were, to me anyway, the ultimate odd couple. Kevin was a 15-year-old brainniac who had the classic heavy-rimmed glasses, was fairly short and usually looked like he had slept in his clothes. Carlie was an eighteen-year-old senior, with flawlessly long, tan limbs, naturally blonde hair and a face that would piss off a Barbie-doll. Her plans after high school included a summer trip to do a photo shoot at the Ford Modeling headquarters in New York. Then it was back to Florida to start at FSU in the fall. Why FSU and not stay in New York? She was crazy about goofy little Kevin.

I was sure that once Evan got a look at Carlie with those 'good-grief-how-long-are-they' legs, he would forget all about me.

Carlie and I met Jewels as we turned down the hallway leading to the girl's locker room. "Coach said we get to run track today," she chimed.

"Cool," Carlie and I responded at the same time. Track meant it was basically a free day. We'd all go outside and walk, not run, at least once around the track for credit, and then it was hit the bleachers for some impromptu tanning.

I practically lived in the pool every spare minute in Palm Beach and my tan had been natural, even and perfect, but there was no pool at Matt and Bev's.

The guys were already running the track as the girls emerged from the gym. I could see Evan's broad shoulders and muscled arms standing out like a beacon in the throng of guys. I sighed, and then suddenly I wanted to run the track—really run the track, no walking. I bolted.

"Hey!" Jewels yelled, trying to catch me. "What are you doing? I thought we'd talk."

Today was too perfect for moping along and talking. I could smell the gulf in the stiff breeze that was blowing from the south and I suddenly didn't care about all my worries and problems. "I'm just livin' my life," I yelled back and kept going. I knew I wasn't going to catch the guys, not that I couldn't have poured on the steam and caught them—I felt like a gazelle today—but I preferred the view from behind. Ooh-la-la!

It was a quarter-mile around the track and I was winded by the time I'd completed the circle. Evan was standing around with the guys as I ran past. It wasn't that I planned to run the circle twice, but I didn't want to talk with him. I decided to catch up with the girls who were only about a third of the way around. I hadn't gone far when I heard a runner coming up behind me.

"Slow down a little, Leese," I heard Evan call out.

I just laughed, which took some of my air supply, so I slowed and he caught me.

"Let me guess," he said as he pulled beside me, "Track team, right?"

I was still laughing which continued to slow my pace. "Nah, it just feels really good to be alive right now." He didn't say anything and we were more than halfway to the girls. "My mom says," I continued, "to enjoy life, because there are no re-dos." I couldn't help but smile at him.

"That's pretty profound for someone who can't even go out for a burger after school," he quipped.

"Cholesterol is bad for you," I retorted and then (and only heaven knows why) I smacked his belly and took off twice as fast. Dang, that boy had some rock hard abs!

He reached me as I dodged through the girls to get to where Jewels and Carlie were talking.

"You're gonna get it," he threatened.

I grabbed Carlie and Jewels by the arms, "Safe!" I shouted, "I'm safe, you can't touch me when I'm around my friends."

He gave me an odd look and then shook his head.

Jewels looked at me like I'd lost my mind. "Ah! What is this all about?"

"She hit me," Evan blurted out before I could answer.

"It was a tap!" I defended. "Anyway I think it hurt my hand more than it hurt you."

Jewels looked at Carlie and raised an eyebrow; Carlie smiled back at her.

"Nah, it's not like that guys," I said, reading their minds. "We're just horsing around."

"Sure," they said in unison.

"I'm going to get some sun," I snapped, uncomfortable with them looking at us as if we were a couple.

I took off running and finished my second lap. Evan hadn't followed me, which suited me just fine. I didn't really want anything to do with him even if I was acting like an idiot that did.

I found a quiet section of bleachers and stretched out in the glorious Florida sunshine.

"Hey," I heard a quiet voice. I looked up and Kevin had come down to where I was.

"Hey, Kev—what's up?"

"You don't think Carlie likes the new guy, do you?"

I turned my head and squinted in the sunshine to see that Evan, Jewels and Carlie were still walking. Was I worried? Sure I was. Was I going to tell Kevin that? Absolutely not.

"Kev, Carlie is nuts about you. He may have the build, but you've got the brains and Carlie, well, she really likes brains." I glanced up at him and then reached over and squeezed his hand. "Don't worry."

Within a few minutes I heard the metallic sound of more people tromping up the bleachers. I also heard Jewels rattling on about needing a new dance routine for the cheerleading team. I didn't open my eyes, but I heard Kevin sigh so I knew Carlie was close. Then a shadow crossed my face and simply stayed there. "Pardon me," I said, eyes still closed. "But someone is blocking my rays." No response and nothing moved. I could hear some giggling a few benches over. Annoyed, I finally opened my eyes and there was Evan standing over me. I started to speak, but he beat me to it.

"Sunshine is bad for you," he smirked, then acted like he was going to pop me on the stomach. I tighten my muscles waiting for the sting but I refused to flinch. His fingers snapped at the air only inches away from my exposed belly. Exposed belly?

"Oh, crap," I blurted out, suddenly sitting up right. I pulled my shirt down and embarrassment filled my cheeks as I realized I'd been laying there with it hiked to my rib cage.

He just laughed and sat down beside me. "So you live with your aunt and uncle in the historic district?" It was a question, but he sounded like he knew the answer. That was when I realized why he stayed back with Jewels and Carlie.

"You really do have a touch of stalker in you," I snapped.

"You mentioned you're mom when we were on the track—is she..."

"Yeah, she's alive if that's what you were going to ask. She and my dad are having some problems." This wasn't a complete fabrication, but I left it sounding like marital problems instead of life-or-death problems.

"In Alabama, right?"

I think my face was a blank for a moment, then the illusion returned. "Yup, Alabammy." I tried a horrible impression of an Alabama accent.

He started to speak and I figured it was going to be more questions about Alabama. I really didn't want him to figure out I was a liar.

"So," I interjected quickly, "Who do you live with?"

"Myself."

That was a revelation. "Really? All by yourself? But how did you register if...."

"Eighteen," he answered my unfinished question. "I'm an adult, I can register myself."

"But you're only a junior?"

"My birthday is in November, so I started late."

"Where are your parents?"

"New Orleans," was his short response. It only took me a second to recall his conversation with Mrs. Knoosh from the day prior.

"What's in Pensacola then? Family, friends...?"

"You," he smiled.

That sent a tingle to the pit of my stomach. "Ha, ha, very funny. What did you do, close your eyes and stick your finger on a map and just show up?"

"Nah, I wanted something different and my family used to vacation here a lot. We have a house out on Gulf Breeze, so I decided why not? And here I am."

"Time to head back inside," Coach yelled. The unified groan came up from the bleachers. "Let's go, ladies and gentleman, move out! Lewis," coach called as we exited the bleachers, but Evan just kept walking beside me. "Lewis," coach called a second time.

"Uh, I think coach wants to speak to you," I nudged Evan's arm. He looked at me blankly. "Your last name is Lewis isn't..."

"Oh!" The recognition flashed on his face and he turned around. I guess he was a little deeper into our conversation than I thought. My pace slowed as I heard coach saying he'd like to see him tryout for spring football. Evan turned him down flat and then caught up with me.

"Not in to football, huh?"

"Nope," was the short response.

"What sport are you into?"

"Does *every* guy have to be in a sport?"

"I guess I should rephrase that then; what sport were you into?"

He had this annoyed-puzzled look on his face.

"Okay, you have a scar above your eye, one on your chin, I think I see a nasty one just under…" My fingers were reaching for the cuff of his tee-shirt when he grabbed my hand.

"Don't."

"Sorry, I didn't mean to be nosey," I said softly. He was still holding my hand and his touch was hot and firm. He started to let go, but I held on and turned his hand over, "Even your knuckles are scarred. I'm guessing you either used to be into football or you've picked a lot of fights with guys bigger than you."

At this he smiled broadly, "A few." Then he continued, taking back his hand, "Dumbbell."

"Excuse me!" I couldn't keep the ire out of my reply.

He pointed to the scar above his eyebrow, "I hit myself with a dumbbell."

"Oh—I—okay," I stammered.

"You didn't think I was calling you a dumbbell, did you?" He started laughing because he knew from the look on my face that he guessed correctly. "Barbell," he said pointing to his chin.

My eyes were drawn to the faint pink tail of a scar that was peeking out from under the edge of his sleeve.

"You don't want to know," he grumbled, catching the drift of my sight.

"Or you don't want to tell me." I looked away as I came to the point where I was about to turn off to go to the girls locker room. "But I can guess."

"Really? And just what would that guess be?" He blocked me from going around the corner with one strong arm stretched out to the wall at about the height of my shoulder.

I pursed my lips as if I wasn't going to say, then I smiled wickedly. "Gunshot," I blurted.

His lips parted slightly, his eyes were wide and a look of total surprised filled his face.

"And probably from the last girl you were stalking!" I gave a light laugh and watched the humor come back to his expression.

"You're good," he said with a nod of his head.

I dodged quickly, slipping under his arm and headed for the locker room. I didn't look back, but I knew he stood there and watched me the whole way.

Fifth period I had Chemistry Honors and then it was on to lunch. Carlie and Natasha had made it to the cafeteria first and were saving space for our lunch group. Jewels was in line with Brent Rushford, quarterback for the football team. Kevin was just a little ways behind them, but I didn't see Evan. I had just gotten into the line when someone put a pair of hot hands on my hips. I turned, ready to slap whoever, but I looked up and there was Evan. My hand was already poised to strike so he let go and backed off.

"Whoa, Momma—quick reflexes."

"Just don't grab me like that again, okay?" I really liked him and flirting with him was like second nature, but I didn't want him to have the wrong impression. In fact, I was hoping by this point he wouldn't have had any impression about me. I was hoping he would have been interested in Jewels, Carlie, or anyone but me. It just seemed that I couldn't back off. It was weird but I felt drawn to him even when I was trying to convince myself to leave him alone.

He winced at the inflection of my voice, "Hey, I'm sorry, I wasn't trying to… Ah, I didn't mean to…"

"I'm sorry, Evan." I was ready to cut the strings that we had started forming for the last two days. As much as I liked him, I just couldn't keep up the façade of being someone I wasn't. It wasn't fair to either one of us. "You shouldn't have to apologize. I think I've been sending out the wrong signals."

"I thought your signals were great," he smiled sweetly, trying to get me in tease mode again.

I shook my head and sighed. "I'm not looking for a boyfriend. I *am* a stick-in-the-mud and there are like six-hundred girls in this school that would be a lot more fun to be around besides me."

"I just have one question," he said as we grabbed our lunch trays. "Where's Leese? I think I actually saw her out on the track about an hour and a half ago."

"That was just a moment of me being stupid. I'm not like that." I reached out and put a salad on my tray. "At least not here, anyway," I muttered. I grabbed a drink and headed for the table. I was on the verge of tears, but I wasn't going to be a total freak and break out sobbing. I was ready to leave my tray and head for the nearest exit if the first tear rolled down my face.

He sat across from me and never said another word. I think it was because he knew I was getting ready to start bawling. I wanted him to believe I was an idiot and, so far, I think it was working. The lunch bell rang as I twisted my way through the thickest part of the crowd and headed down to the math wing. I walked through the door and went straight to Mr. Lucas's desk. I was his teacher's aide and he kept a list on his desk of those who needed help. I walked over and looked down and couldn't believe what I saw.

"Evan Lewis? You've got to be kidding?"

"No," Mr. Lucas stated with surprise, "You know him? He's new."

"Yeah, I know him," I said with a little too much irritation to my voice.

"His transfer grades were low in math so I figured you could work with him to get him up to speed, unless you don't want to, of course."

A pink piece of paper was tossed onto the teacher's desk. I looked up and there was Evan staring at me. I wondered how much he had heard, but from the look in his eyes it was enough to hurt. "No, that's fine," I sighed grabbing an extra textbook. "Where do you want him to sit?"

Mr. Lucas handed back the schedule to Evan. "Welcome to Algebra II, Evan. I'm Mr. Lucas," he held out his hand and Evan shook it in silence. "I guess you know Annalisa."

He only nodded.

"She's going to catch you up on what the class has been doing since January. Sit at the study table in the back of the room and after a few sessions with her, we'll move you to a permanent seat." He walked past me and went straight to the back of the room.

I've got to be all business, I kept telling myself. No more teasing, no more staring at his face or looking into his emerald eyes, and no more chit-chat, all business. I opened the book and began with factoring equations. "Do you remember how to do any of this?" I asked blankly.

"I hate math." He sounded nothing like the guy I met yesterday. He kept looking around the room, not paying attention as I tried to show him how to work the problem. He fidgeted and leaned back away from me in his chair. Wow! I had done too good of a job of turning him off. If anything, he acted totally pissed to be sitting there beside me.

I got what I wanted, so why couldn't I be at least semi-happy about it? A lump rose up in my throat, and audible bubbles fought to struggle through it.

He reached across me and closed the textbook.

"I wasn't finished," I rebutted with the half copied problem.

"I am," he said with a threatening growl. He got up and walked to the front of the room, grabbed a green pass from Mr. Lucas and went out the door. I sat there for at least two or three minutes just trying to absorb what happened.

He must think I'm a total jerk. I wondered at that moment if he would even stay at Pensacola High? A sickening knot began to form in my stomach as I thought about him quitting high school and never getting a degree because some stupid little girl ruined it for him. I worked with two other students before the last bell, but I don't know how much good it did them because I just couldn't get my head back into algebra.

I was slow finishing up after the bell. I collected the scattered textbooks and stacked them neatly, put away the calculators and wiped off the board. I was stalling because I didn't want to face him or Jewels in the parking lot, but I had to leave because I'd be late getting Kimmy if I didn't go pretty soon.

I was right about the parking lot. Only a couple cars remained as I walked to my bug. I put down my books and fished out a tissue from my purse. Alone in my car it would be okay to let a few tears fall. Tissue in hand, I turned the key in the ignition. The most amazing thing happened: absolutely nothing. "No way," I said out loud. "Crap!" I checked the stick and made sure it was in neutral, still nothing. I pushed in the clutch and put the car in first gear; no response from the engine. This can't be happening. I'm going to be late getting Kimmy. I've got to call the elementary school. I've got to call Bev or Matt. "This day sucks!" I said as I slammed my forearm into the door panel.

I had just taken my cell phone out of my purse when a knock on my window made me jump. There was Evan standing outside my car. I hadn't heard him pull in behind me.

He opened my door as I quickly dried my face. "Hey, Leese, what's wrong?" His tone was smooth and soothing.

"I—I—don't know. My car won't start and I've got to get my little sister from school." I got out and stared at my little blue bug like I was seeing it for the first time.

"Did you leave your lights on?"

"No, I don't think so." But I leaned back inside just to make sure. Nope, my lights had been off.

"When do you have to get your sister? How far is it?"

I glanced down at my cell phone. "I've got to be there in the next ten to fifteen minutes, but…" Frustration and emotion choked my throat and clouded my thinking.

"Come on, I'll give you a ride," he said softly. There was no hint that we'd just had a blowup in math class an hour ago. I started to take a step toward his car, but I knew that neither Bev, nor Mom would be pleased to know I'd accepted his offer.

"I—I can't."

"What?" he smiled. "Come on, it will only take us a few minutes and then you and your sister will be home. I'll come back and see what I can do to get your car started."

I wanted to say yes, but I was here in Pensacola because my parents were worried about my safety. I didn't know Evan. I wanted to think I knew him, but, to be real with myself, I'd barely just met him. It would be like stepping out on the main drag and sticking out my thumb.

I opened my phone and started dialing.

"What are you doing?" he asked, stunned that I was turning down his offer. He reached for my phone and I pulled away and backed up to my car.

"I have to call Kimmy's school," I said without looking into his stare. And that was what he was doing; he was staring at me so hard it was giving me goose bumps. I was relieved to hear someone's voice on the other end of the line. "Hi, this is Kimmy McKinneses' sister. I'm having car trouble. Could you have Kimmy wait for me in the office? Thank you. Yes, I'll call if I'm going to be much later. Thanks again." I hit the end button and began dialing the next number when Evan reached out and took the phone from my trembling hand.

"Give me that back," I demanded, trying to sound authoritative instead of afraid.

"The only thing I'll give you is a ride. Come on," he said, grabbing my wrist.

My martial arts training was not forgotten as I twisted his arm and jerked myself free. And then I saw it; anger written all over his face. His eyes had narrowed and his mouth was not much more than a tight line. His chest seemed to heave and every muscle and vein looked as if they had doubled in size, suddenly he looked like a giant.

As scared as I was at that moment, I heard the sound of something familiar. We both looked up to see the custodian heading toward us on his golf cart. Evan took a deep breath and some of the angry red that had filled his face disappeared.

"I just wanted to help, Leese." He tossed back my phone, got in his car and was gone.

My knees were trembling as Mr. Garvey pulled up beside my car. "Are you having some trouble?" He questioned, but he kept looking toward where Evan's car was speeding from the lot.

"Yeah, actually my car won't start. It's completely dead and I've got to get to the elementary."

"Let me take a look," he offered with a knowing smile. "I've got jumper cables in my cart, if we need them." He lifted the hood and peered inside. "Here's your problem," he showed me, as he lifted a cable in the air. "Your positive terminal cable popped off." He wiggled it back down on the post and told me to try cranking the car. I slid the key into the ignition. My hands were still trembling as I turned it and my car cranked.

He slammed the hood, "There you go, young lady."

"Thank you, Mr. Garvey. You don't know how much I appreciate your help." I was angry at myself for forgetting everything Tony Dix had taught me about what to look for when your car was... I swallowed hard. Cables don't just pop off. Someone had tampered with my car! The face that came immediately to mind was Evan. But why? No, it just couldn't have been him. I rolled up my windows and locked my doors as I gathered my thoughts. There was no one else around but I was terrified. "Stupid girl," I chided myself. "You're going to flip-out like Mom if you don't watch it!" I slammed my car into first gear and took off.

I didn't sleep well that night. I kept waking up about every hour and thinking about the events of my day. I wondered what would have happened if I had accepted Evan's ride? Would we have sat outside on the porch swing and enjoyed the evening together? Would Bev and Matt have said they liked him? Would I have made it home at all? I closed my eyes and could see myself as a lifeless corpse lying in a field somewhere. When I finally did sleep, I dreamed that Kimmy was crying over a coffin. I expected to see Mom lying inside it, but when I got next to her and looked down, the body was my own.

CHAPTER THREE

Jewels' car was in the lot as always, but she wasn't there. Evan's car was there, and I could see that someone was in the driver's seat. I parked a little further away than necessary and did something that I hadn't done since moving to Pensacola. I locked my car doors. My hood was locked down, but, as I recalled Tony's words, I knew there was plenty that could be done to a vehicle from the exterior.

I hadn't taken ten steps when Evan opened his door and got out. "Leese," he called my name softly, but I just kept walking. He caught up to me but kept his distance. "I'm sorry," he said as he jammed his hands down into his pockets. "I was a real jerk toward you yesterday."

My heart was crumbling at the sincerity of his words. I looked over at him and realized that he looked about as rough as I felt. "Tough night last night?" I questioned.

"Yeah," he responded. "I almost went home."

That stopped me in my tracks. I suddenly felt very foolish for believing he could have damaged my car. "Evan, I've got a problem with you." I watched his eyebrows go up. "I—I like you, but I don't want to."

"Any particular reason why you don't want to like me?" he shrugged.

"Yeah—because—I'm—I'm a liar and I absolutely hate it."

"*You're a liar*? About what?" His voice sounded strained.

"I wish I could tell you, but I can't. All I can say is that I hope we can still be friends when this is over with because I really do like you."

His hand slipped out of his pocket and wrapped around my shoulder in one fluid movement. He gave me a warm squeeze, saying it was okay. That was all it took for the tears to pour down my cheeks.

"I'm sorry," I muttered as I fished for a tissue. His other arm wrapped around me and I suddenly found myself with my face buried against his warm chest. I felt his hand reach up and stroke my hair over and over. I liked being in his arms, it felt safe. "I was such a jerk to you. I don't know how you can forgive me."

He pushed me back a little and looked at me. "I was just as much of a jerk as you were. I guess I can forgive you because I really like you, too," he smiled.

We resumed walking and he kept one arm draped over my shoulders. It felt like heaven, but once again I figured this was taking a step closer to what I'd been trying to avoid from the beginning. I stopped and stepped away from him, turning back toward Jewels' car. "Hey, have you seen Jewels this morning? She almost always waits for me."

His face spread into a wide grin. "I have bad news for you."

My heart skipped a beat, yet I was puzzled by the smile.

"I'm not the FOTM anymore."

It took a second for it to click in my head. "A new guy?"

"Yeah, he climbed out of that '78 Trans Am Firebird. She totally lost it. It was like she didn't even hear me."

I started laughing as I told him she had done the same thing when he appeared a few days ago. "She almost ripped my arm out of the socket," I said, faking a still sore shoulder.

"Me too," he chuckled, rubbing his arm.

I made a point to stay out of arms reach. Not that I wanted to, but I knew I had to.

I walked into English class and found, to my surprise, a new guy standing at Mr. Shultz's desk. Well, I could certainly see what set Jewels off, besides his cool car. This guy must have been at least 6'3" with a thin but muscled build. His hair was jet-black, which left me wondering if it could possibly be dyed because I'd never seen hair truly that black. He was wearing an equally black tee-shirt and blue jeans. His left arm had a barb-wire tattoo around his bicep, a smaller tattoo at his wrist and, as far as I could see, his right arm had a large colorful tattoo. My first thought was that when he turned around he would have piercings all over his face, but to my shock when he turned around all he had was a diamond stud in one ear and the most electrifying blue eyes on the planet. Once again, I figured they couldn't be natural, they had to be contacts, but they were gorgeous. I was expecting to see a leather jacket slung over one arm, because he had this whole tough-guy, James Dean thing going on.

He looked right at me and flashed an impressive white smile. I blushed and looked away trying to remember that it isn't polite to stare.

Kevin gave a little groan beside me, "Not you too," he whispered.

I wondered what he meant until I looked over at Carlie. She was all googly-eyed and flushed with color as she stared at the new guy. Poor, Kev.

The new guy walked to the seat behind me and slid in quietly.

"Hi," he said leaning forward, "I'm Ryan."

I turned and noticed he had offered his hand. I took it awkwardly and smiled, "Annalisa," I tried to say it quietly enough not to cause Mr. Schultz to look our way. I turned back around and grabbed my book, hoping to lose myself in a little Poe.

"All right," Mr. Schultz began, "We left off yesterday with Annalisa's beautiful reading of *The Raven*..."

I slid down slightly in my seat.

"Today we are going to break into groups of two or three. I want you to discuss symbolism in the poem. Don't be afraid to be daring. I need at least five paragraphs by the end of class."

I looked to Kevin and he had already grabbed Carlie and, even though she was looking toward Ryan, she settled in beside Kevin. Before I could say, "I'll work with you two," I felt a tap on my shoulder.

"So Annalisa, you do a *beautiful* reading of Poe?" He was looking up at me through some wisps of black hair that had fallen forward.

I rolled my eyes and shrugged, "I was in a strange mood yesterday; strange works for Poe."

He swept the hair back with his hand and gave a little grin, "Really? How's the mood this morning? If it's still strange, you could give me a reading before we start."

"No," I refused a little too quickly. "Maybe I'm a little depressed, but nothing strange today." All I could think was that there was no way I was going to read poetry to this guy, especially not with everyone listening to a personal performance.

"I think Poe wrote most of his best works while depressed. Are you sure you don't want to read?"

"Symbolism," I stated, ignoring his question. "What did the raven symbolize?"

"So why are you depressed? Did you break up with your boyfriend?"

"Evan's not my boyfriend," I retorted.

"Who's Evan?"

"Ah! That is none of your business."

"You're the one who mentioned his name," he said, clearly enjoying my frustration.

"I think the Raven symbolized his broken heart for Lenore," answering my own question.

He didn't say anything at first; he just leaned closer to me. I responded by leaning the other way.

"One more thing and then we can study. It's a simple yes or no question."

"Fine." I crossed my arms and waited.

He gave me that 'come closer' signal with his index finger as he lowered his head and leaned forward.

I knew whatever was going to come out of his mouth would be quiet, so (like an idiot) I bent forward to hear him.

He spoke so quietly that I couldn't understand. "What," I whispered back. Our faces were now inches apart.

"Do—you—have—a—boyfriend?

The partial smile fell off my face.

"It's just a yes or no question," he reminded me.

"Why?" I wasn't going to give him the satisfaction of providing an answer.

"You have a sexy voice, a beautiful face, I love long hair and—well, you're kinda funny. Do you want to go out with me?"

That hit me like a bomb. I wondered if he could possibly know my financial status, because that sounded like a Palm Beach pickup line. He was going to make it impossible to do the Poe assignment. "What are your plans after high school graduation?"

He seemed to like my odd response. "I'll be in the air force academy."

"Can you flunk high school and still get into the academy?"

His mouth closed and opened again. "Huh?"

"This is an AP class and we have an assignment. Got it?"

"It represents his hopes and dreams for the future being destroyed." He caved.

I grabbed my pen and finally found my smile.

After thirty minutes of intensely scrutinizing *The Raven*, I felt we'd done a good job. He had different opinions about the poem than I did, but that was okay because Mr. Schultz said he wanted uniqueness not a consensus. The only problem was that I was mentally exhausted, because keeping Ryan at bay and on task was like a tough game of chess.

I was looking forward to going to psych class just so I could relax. The only good thing was that it had been challenging enough to keep me from thinking about my problems at home, Evan, or even the mystery of what had happened to my car yesterday.

The bell rang and I wearily rose from my seat.

"Hey," Ryan said, catching my arm. "Can you tell me how to get to 3-101?"

I snatched the schedule from his hands and looked at it in disbelief; he had Psych II next.

I survived psych, but only due to the fact that the two available seats were nowhere near mine. He had the nerve to ask a couple people if they would trade seats so he could sit beside me, but Doctor Moss overheard and informed Ryan that the seats in her class were assigned; no one would be moving.

Although we didn't have our next class together, I knew we'd have the same lunch period. If I were lucky, I'd get there before him and our table would be full.

Evan actually met me at the cafeteria door and asked me if I was doing better. He was being impossibly sweet today, so different from his attitude yesterday afternoon. I told him yes, but that I was honestly so tired that I had dozed off in my economics class. I'm sure he figured my exhaustion was due to my restless night last night (which was a big reason). But what he didn't know was that I'd burned the last of my energy fending my 'I'm not looking for a boyfriend,' attitude against Ryan's onslaught first period. To tell the truth, I don't think Ryan was used to a girl turning him down. They probably all melted like butter in his hands, so I'm sure I was an oddity.

Evan and I went through the line and sat at the usual table. Kevin, Carlie, and Natasha were already in place. Jewels usually flitted around the room, doing her social-butterfly routine, but not today. It was starting to bother me that I hadn't seen her, but I shouldn't have worried because she had simply been out Ryan hunting. She came through the doors with him on her arm like she was showing off a new piece of jewelry. I started to duck my head behind Evan's shoulder, which was more than adequate to hide me, but it was too late, he spotted me. I thought Jewels would spend most of the period making introductions, but apparently Ryan had other plans as they reached our table in record time.

"Hey everybody," Jewels bubbled over. "This is Ryan Faultz. Ryan, this is Natasha Green, and…"

"Kevin and Carlie, right?" Ryan beat Jewels to the intro. "They're in my English class," he added.

"Oh," Jewels said, suddenly making the connection, "Then you must know Leese."

I watched his lips turn at the corners in a slow smile, "No, I don't know *Leese*…"

I thought for a moment he was going to be cool about the fact that I was sitting beside a guy with twice his muscle mass and a protective stare, but I should have known better.

"But I do know the lovely Annalisa. We have chemistry…" he paused.

What the crap was he talking about! My eyes went large as I gave him the 'I'd really like to slap you' stare. Everyone, including Jewels, was silent for a split second.

Out of the corner of my eye I could see Evan set down his sandwich, brush his palms together once, and push himself away from the table.

"And English, psych, and P.E. together," he finished.

I gave a little sigh of relief; he was talking about our schedules.

Evan was already in motion, standing up and reaching out toward Ryan.

"And this is Evan Lewis," Jewels finished, apparently relieved that it was going to be a hand shake and not a punch.

"Oh, so you're Evan," Ryan said, as he accepted the hand shake. "Annalisa mentioned you during English."

"Really?" Evan got a strange expression, and then glanced at me.

I was waiting for the rest of it. Surely Ryan was going to say that Evan's name was mentioned in the same sentence as 'not my boyfriend,' but to my disbelief he left that tidbit out.

"I'm going to get something to eat," Ryan said as he motioned toward the line. "Jewels?"

"No, I'm just going to grab a diet coke from the machine." She turned loose of his arm, but let her fingers trail down his colorful tattoo. "You go ahead."

Ryan was still waiting in line by the time Jewels settled beside me on the bench. "Can you believe it?" she asked, but didn't wait for anyone to respond. "It's like the gods are dropping good looking guys from the sky! First Evan and now Ryan—who's going to enroll tomorrow? Brad Pitt?"

I almost choked on my sandwich, "Jewels he's like in his forties."

"Closer to fifty," Kevin added.

"Who cares!" was Jewels' response. "He could be ninety as long as he still looks twentyish."

"That's gross, Jewels." I looked at Evan and he had this funny smirk on his face. I knew it had to be because Jewels had just classed him in a league with Brad Pitt.

Ryan was tolerable through lunch although he kept looking over at me. Every time he did, Evan would stare at him until he looked away. Finally, Jewels started asking him about his tattoos and that seemed to stop the 'look, stare, glare,' competition.

"I really want to get a tattoo," Jewels was saying. "But Daddy would kill me."

"Don't do that, Jewels," Kevin began. "They aren't safe."

"Yes they are," Ryan countered.

"No," Kevin went on, undeterred. "Some of the inks have metals in them. You can't have MRI's or…"

"Wrong, little guy," Ryan cut him off. "I've had an MRI and there was no problem over my tattoos."

I watched Carlie's face darken with anger; she didn't like him belittling Kevin.

Oops. I realized some of his gorgeousness just dimmed in her eyes. Good, maybe Kevin wouldn't have anything to worry about in a while. Well, that was as long as Ryan kept making stupid remarks like the last one.

Kevin adjusted his glasses and sat up straighter and taller. I knew what was coming when Kev did that; he was getting ready to unleash that brain that Carlie loved so much. "There are lawsuits in the courts right now over tattoo ink companies exposing their customers to chemicals that cause cancer and birth defects."

Ryan waved him off like Kevin had no idea what he was talking about. Kevin grew taller for the moment as he continued, "Lead is one of the biggest problems. Then you have elements that make up the colored inks, like on your forearm. Let's see, you'll find traces of titanium, aluminum, antimony, selenium, beryllium chromium, cobalt, nickel and, oh yeah, my personal favorite, arsenic. Tell me who'd want that under their skin!"

"What do you do, dude, like read encyclopedias all day or something?" Ryan was directing his question to Kevin, but he looked at Carlie and gave her a wink and a smile.

I was right. His charm hit her like an arrow against a steel shield as it bounced off harmlessly.

"I was going to get a small tattoo," Carlie began. "Just a rose on my lower back, so Kevin did some research for me. Besides finding out that a lot of the inks aren't safe, he also discovered that about a fourth of the people tattooed later regret that they did it."

"Well, that and what Carlie's mom calls a girl's tattoo..." Kevin let his statement fade as he looked to Carlie to see if it was okay to finish or not.

"A tramp stamp?" Ryan inserted.

Carlie rolled her eyes, but glumly nodded to confirm the remark.

All this time, I'd been looking to see what exactly was on Ryan's large tattoo. I could make out a skull and a sword, something that looked like wings, but I couldn't make out the small inscription. I reached over without much thought and rotated his arm by the wrist to get a better view. The tattoo was extremely intricate, but as I was studying it, he rolled his arm back before I could read the inscription.

"What does it say?" I asked, realizing that I was still holding his arm and he seemed to be enjoying the touch of my hand. I withdrew when I looked up into the disconcerting blue gaze.

"Come sit over here by me and I'll show you."

Now there was no way I was going to go sit beside 'oh-yeah-I'm-a-hot-guy,' and I think Evan knew that, but I had the distinct feeling that Ryan was getting ready to meet the angry side of Evan in a few seconds. I could feel his body begin to stiffen beside me and I remembered the way he looked yesterday as his anger reached a boiling point.

"Born to kill," Evan said rather calmly for someone who was about to turn into the incredible hulk. "Am I right?" he asked. "I've seen one similar."

"Yeah, that's right." But the way Ryan said it, it was more like a challenge than an answer.

Evan just laughed. But then he looked at Ryan and their eyes seemed to lock on each other; all the joking dropped from his face, "So how many have you killed?"

Ryan, as was the whole table, was silent for a few seconds. "Ask me that after I get out of the Air Force," he finally replied.

Again the whole group was silent as the reality of what he was saying sunk in, the only exception being Evan who was chuckling to himself.

"Well," I said, trying to break the tension at the table, "I'm getting a big tattoo this weekend; a cross on each arm and one right in the middle of my chest," I said looking down at my tee-shirt as I drew a giant cross with my fingers. They all still looked so serious. "I'm kidding guys! Come on lighten up." I bumped my shoulder into Evan's arm and giggled.

"No, you don't need any tattoos, Leese," he smiled. "They are permanent, but if you do have them removed, it's really painful and leaves a scar."

"Really?" I asked, "How many have you had removed?"

"None," he answered with a serious tone.

I could see Ryan looking him over, "You don't have a tattoo, do you?"

I was positive that there were no tattoos on Evan's very hunky body, but to my utter shock he replied, one.

"Where," I demanded a little too forcefully.

"You can't see it." He sounded like he regretted having mentioned it.

"But where is it?" I asked a little nicer than my previous demand.

Ryan was snickering. "I bet I can guess where it's at." He paid no attention to the peril he was putting himself in by pissing off Evan. "Across your heart, am I right?"

Evan broke into an unusual smile; it was purely sadistic like he would derive a lot of pleasure out of snapping Ryan's neck.

"I bet you have a girl's name tattooed on it," Ryan continued his suicide speech.

At this Evan lost the killer façade and started to genuinely laugh.

"What's so funny? Is he right?" I asked.

"Yeah, sure, he's right," Evan shook his head and went back to eating his lunch.

"That," Kevin spoke up quickly, "Is why a quarter of the people regret getting a tattoo! They put someone's name in it and then they break up." He was being dead serious, but it was just so completely funny the way he blurted it out that everyone began to laugh.

I was glad the tension had finally broken, but I was still curious. I turned my face toward Evan, letting my hair provide a curtain from the other prying eyes at the table. "What was her name?" I whispered dolefully. Just as I finished getting the words out, the bell rang. Everyone else was getting up, but I was still looking at him for a reply.

"You're serious? You really want to know?"

I couldn't help myself as I nodded. He looked at me and gave a sigh then he leaned toward my ear. I inhaled and there was that scintillating scent that I'd smelled in French class. His mouth was so close to my ear that I could feel his warm breath. It tickled, but there was no way I was pulling back until I heard the answer that I didn't honestly want to know.

"Mother," he whispered.

"Ah," was all I could get out as I realized he was probably teasing me, but before I could react, he kissed my cheek and bolted from the table.

There would be no need to dash after him and smack him for what he had done. He couldn't escape me; we both had French class in a few minutes and he'd be cornered. It would, of course, be difficult to show that I was angry with him, when I couldn't get the stupid smile off my face.

By the time I strolled into French, I'd given up the idea of being mean to him. I was resigning myself to the idea that he liked me as much as I did him. I just couldn't figure how this could possibly work out. I didn't see any real danger in revealing a little bit of myself to Evan, but it couldn't be a full disclosure until Mom was no longer paranoid. If she began to come to her senses, she'd want her daughters home. How would I feel if I had to look into those deep green eyes and explain that I was leaving? Maybe I could convince Mom and Dad to let me stay in Pensacola for my senior year. That would only work if they didn't realize a boy was involved. Then I would be lying again.

Mrs. Knoosh had decided to give a pop quiz so there would be no talking for the first half hour. The test was more difficult than I expected. I think what made it more disconcerting was that I could hear Evan's pencil marking the paper at a rapid pace while I felt like I was trudging through beach sand.

The final forty-five minutes were spent watching a French film. When the lights came up, we had ten minutes before the bell.

"I was thinking," Evan began. "I know you have to pick up your sister and baby-sit, but wouldn't your aunt and uncle be okay with you going out for a little while in the evening? We could go to the mall or drive the beach." He must have thought that no rebuttal over the kiss on the cheek was going to entitle him to a date.

"I already have plans for tonight, but you could join me, if you want." I realized that I had taken him by surprise. He was prepared for an argument instead of an invitation, but I could see the suspicion also.

"It's Wednesday," I added, but saw no kind of comprehension on his face. "It's church tonight."

"Oh," he replied. Using one syllable and just two letters he was able to convey his discomfort with the thought of church.

My heart dropped like a rock. I loved church, especially my Wednesday night youth group. What if he was against church or even a belief in God for that matter? That could be a stumbling block even bigger than my reason for being in Pensacola. "It's okay," I offered, trying to give him an easy out. "You don't have to…"

"No, it's just, well, it's been a while since I was in church."

Relief washed over me. "You'll probably like it, if you like music. We have a band and you'll know a couple of the kids from here."

"I won't have to sing, will I?" With that question the discomfort came back to his face.

"Not unless you volunteer," I teased.

The bell rang and we started for the parking lot. "So is this like a date-date?" he asked and proceeded to place his arm around my shoulder.

"No, it's church. It's not a date." I removed his arm from my shoulder. "Don't think, Mr. Lewis, that I've forgotten what you pulled in the cafeteria, and I don't let strange boys do that."

"Hum—I see. Well, how many boys that weren't strange have you let do that?"

"*All* boys are strange," I countered.

"Don't tell me you've never been kissed." There was a genuine amount of surprise in his voice.

"I have," I said obstinately. I unlocked my car and climbed inside. He didn't walk away, he just stood there.

"How old were you?" he asked. "And relatives don't count."

I was going to try to answer this honestly, but I grew up being very sure of myself and didn't feel the need to validate my ego by getting male attention. "I got it," I finally said. "Jimmy Levito."

He looked mildly entertained as he leaned toward me from my window, "How old were you?" he repeated.

There are times when I don't like honesty. "I—I was nine. No, wait. I was ten. It was at my fifth grade dance and he kissed me when we were on the dance floor."

"And," he prodded.

"And what?"

"Was it on the lips?"

"It would have been if I hadn't turned my face," I retorted.

"What happened after he *tried* to kiss you?" He was making sure that I knew it didn't count as an actual kiss.

I took a deep breath, annoyed that he had to have the whole truth. "I punched him. I think I may have broken his nose," I finished miserably.

His warm hand reached for my chin and tenderly turned my face toward his. It felt as if my resistance crumbled to dust. "So if I kiss you here," he said letting his thumb gently brush across my lips. "I'll be the first guy to *really* kiss you?"

I looked deeply into those distressing green eyes and replied, "If you survive it. I am a black belt, after all."

His face lit up as if I had just handed him a present. "You're not serious, are you?"

"Yes, I am. Don't test me."

"You know I think you're the funniest mystery I've ever tried to unravel."

I didn't say anything, but I grabbed a piece of paper from my binder and scribbled down my address and handed it to him.

He looked pleased, but still mystified.

"For church tonight," I clarified. "You did say you wanted to come, right? You do like music, don't you?"

"Yeah—yeah sure; AC/DC, Led Zeppelin, Metallica," He looked at my shocked expression and laughed. "What time do you want me to show? Is this the address of the church or your house?"

"Six-thirty, and that is my home address. Bev and Matt will want to meet you first."

There was an expression on his face that I simply couldn't read. I didn't know if it was pleasure or pain, but it bothered me. It reminded me of his face yesterday when he was trying to get me to accept a ride from him, but then he smiled and said he'd see me at six-thirty.

At six-twenty five, a sleek, black 370Z pulled into the crowded driveway at Bev and Matt's. I smiled and waved from the porch swing as he stepped out onto the concrete. He motioned me toward his car, and I shook my head while motioning him to the porch.

He gave a little grimace as he approached, "I really have to do this 'meet your parents' thing?"

"Aunt and Uncle," I reminded him. "And yes you do."

I opened the door and walked inside with my reluctant prisoner in tow. Kimmy was the first to meet us and she seemed very surprised when she saw him.

"Hi," she said shyly. "I'm Kimberly. I'm Leese's sister."

He smiled and put his hand out. "Hi Kim, I'm Evan. You're just as pretty as your sister."

She giggled and her cheeks pinked as she finished shaking his hand. Matt Junior came toddling down the hallway, apparently having gleefully escaped from getting his hair combed. He stopped short at the sight of the big stranger standing in his foyer.

"Kimmy," Bev called from her bedroom, "Would you bring him back here, please?"

Kimmy started toward him and he turned and began his short-legged, waddle-run back toward his parent's bedroom. "MA MA!" he yelled, excited that Kimmy was chasing him.

"Come on in," I said, pulling him into the living room.

I heard Kimmy down the hallway very excitedly announce, "Leese's boyfriend is here!"

I wanted to cover my face and hide. I'd told her he was just a friend from school, but I guess that equated to a boyfriend in her book. I didn't have to look at his face; I could feel the smile on it without a visual.

"So where's your room?" he asked in a quiet voice.

"Right there." I pointed to the double-doors leading from the living room. Bev and Matt had a three bedroom home, but when we moved in with them, Bev decided that a teenager really needed a little privacy. Kimmy got the third bedroom and they turned their den into my room. I told them they didn't have to do that, but they insisted that it was no problem especially since Matt wasn't with his engineering firm anymore, he didn't need it as an office. And, I had to admit that I was used to having my own room, but the thing I missed the most from home was having my own bathroom. Bev and Matt had a private bath off the master suite, but Kimmy and I had to share the other. That had taken some getting used to.

I was a little mortified when he headed into my room. It wasn't that it was a mess, except the fact that the den didn't have a closet so I did have a few things hanging on an open rack, my clothes were picked up and my bed was made, but I didn't expect him to just stroll right in there. What would Matt and Bev think if they came out and we were in there? I stood at the doors and tried to coax him back out, but he ignored me as he looked over some sketch books that I had open.

"Very nice," he mouthed silently as he picked up a cherry-blossom water color that I had been working on. He pointed to me and then back to the painting. I nodded, still nervous that he was walking around my room. He came to a stop beside my bed and his hand was reaching for something. My heart all but stopped when I realized it was a picture of my family—my real family. I wanted to go in there and snatch it from his grasp and tell him to get out of my room, but I think he realized that my feet wouldn't carry me into that private space while he occupied it. I heard Matt and Bev coming down the hall so I motioned for him to get out of there and then I headed for the couch. He emerged a moment later, seating himself beside me just in time as they came around the corner.

I couldn't help but see the surprise on Matt's face when he got a look at Evan. I stood quickly, "Matt this is Evan Lewis. Evan this is my Uncle Matt McKinnis."

Matt was a slender 5'10" so he looked kind of shrimpy as he shook Evan's hand. "Hi, Evan. I thought Leese said you were a junior, but you've got to be a senior, right?"

"No, Sir. I'm a junior, I just take after my dad, size wise."

"Wow, you could have fooled me. I don't think you'd have any trouble passing yourself off as someone in their twenties."

"This is my aunt Beverly," I continued.

"Hi Evan, it's really nice to meet you."

"Thanks, it's nice to meet you both. So which one of you is actually related to Leese? I can't pick out the family resemblance."

"Oh—me," Bev answered before Matt could speak. "I'm Nadia's sister."

"Nadia?" Evan questioned.

"My mom," I answered and then moved on to the final introduction, "And this is Matt Junior," I said sweeping him off the floor and growling into his exposed neck. He burst into tiny peals of laughter as I nuzzled against his baby-scented skin. I put him back down on the floor as it was clear that he wasn't familiar enough with Evan to permit him to come too close.

"So are we ready?" Matt asked, looking a little uncomfortable.

I watched Evan's eyebrows raise and I realized that he hadn't understood that this was a family event, not an opportunity to go out on our own. He shot a quick glance my direction. "Yeah, sure. I'll take—do you want to ride with me?"

"I do!" Kimmy quickly volunteered.

"Oh, I'm sorry Kimmy, there are only two seats in my car," he said apologetically.

"That's okay," she answered, "Leese can ride with Matt and Bev."

"No," Bev laughed, "I think Leese should ride with her—her friend."

"Aah! No fair," Kimmy whined. I was hoping she wasn't getting ready to pitch one of her fits. She was normally well tempered, but every once in a while she could be an average six year old.

Evan shrugged, "I don't mi…"

I quickly shook my head no, to stop him from saying what would encourage her begging. My biggest worry wasn't that I wouldn't get to ride with him, but that she might get her way and then he would be free to ask her plenty of questions about our lives—our real lives that is.

"*Please*," Kimmy emphasized, batting her eyes.

"That's okay, we'll ride in my car," I said, ending the awkward moment.

Evans mouth opened to rebut, but Matt quickly replied, "Great, I'm glad that's settled. Now, let's go before we're late."

As we filed out the door, I whispered in Kimmy's ear to remind her that people didn't know why we were living in Pensacola and, for Mom's sake, we had to keep it that way. She nodded solemnly.

It was a short ride to church, barely enough time for him to ask many questions. I walked Kimmy to her class as Matt and Bev took Matt junior to nursery and then we met in the fellowship hall where the band was warming up. We normally had about forty to fifty people in our music worship, and that included the two youth pastors and the younger adults like Matt and Bev, but tonight it seemed extra crowded as everyone said their hellos. Then the lights dimmed and the band fired up. Everyone started clapping and yelling as the music got louder. I looked over and noticed that Evan was smiling, but I could tell he was still uncomfortable as people started to show their enthusiasm. Pastor Shawn got on stage and opened us in prayer and then introduced the first singer. Mike Hendry, a senior from PHS started off the night with some Matthew West hits. He was finishing up his last song as I squeezed Evan's arm and smiled, "My turn."

"You're going to sing?" He knew Jewels said that I sang Christian rock, but I don't think he expected to hear me. "Cool," he said turning loose of my arm and walking closer to the stage.

I could feel the glow coming over my face. Singing was one of my favorite things. I wasn't vain, but I was glad that it was something that I could do really well. I just felt so free when I sang. It was like the world and all its problems completely vanished and all that remained was the ability to make people happy.

"Hey, everybody! How about a little Natalie Grant tonight?"

The shouts and cheers began as I turned to the band. "Let's start with *I Will Not Be Moved*."

That got a big smile; they really enjoyed a challenge.

The spotlight came on and the first steady hum came from the keyboardist as I gripped the mic in one hand and the mic stand in the other. Then the electric guitars and the drums kicked into high gear as the music pulsed through my veins. And that is when the music seemed to take over and the performance began. I had it nailed down as well as if I were Natalie Grant herself. I could see the sea of heads bobbing up and down as they jumped and danced to the beat. "...I will make mistakes, I will face heartaches" I sang. "But I will not be moved..." All the while Evan's stare was intent and he seemed oblivious to the throng moving to the beat and surrounding him. As the music died, the cheers and shouts rose, I watched him put his fingers between his lips and let out a loud whistle and then began to clap.

"One more. One more," was the chant coming from the group.

"All right, one more." I turned to the band, "*Perfect People*, can you guys do that one?" They all nodded and I turned once again to face my audience. I lowered my gaze to the floor as the slow and steady beat began. This song didn't start like the more rocking melody I'd just sung, but it quickly became one of my favorites because of the silky strands of the music and the desperate and soulful sounds of the words as they flowed. "Never let 'em see you when you're breaking, never let 'em see you when you fall...Tell the world you've got it all together, never let them see what's underneath..."

He seemed mesmerized.

I usually look around at the faces in the crowd, but I couldn't take my eyes from his as I continued to pour out my soul into the song. "There is no such thing as a perfect life. Come as you are, broken and scarred, lift up your heart; be amazed and be changed by your perfect God." The look on his face was telling me that this song was hitting him where he lived, but I actually chose it because I felt it helped to tell my own story. Yet, as I sang, I knew the words were digging deep into his flesh, "He knows where you are and where you've been and you never have to go there again." The look on his face was heart shattering, but it only gave me more fuel to pour onto the fire in my performance. The song ended and I hopped off the stage.

"Great job," Bev was yelling at me over the din. I smiled and grabbed his arm as we moved away from the stage.

"So how'd you like it?" I asked as the next person began to sing. "Was it better than your Led Zeppelin?" The back of the room would be the only place where I knew we would be able to hear each other, but he didn't say anything. I looked at him and suddenly knew why. His eyes had this unusual quality to them, and I understood at that moment just how much impact the song had made. I didn't push the conversation; I just went to the table where the drinks were sitting out and poured us each a coke.

We listened to another two songs when he finally turned to me and said, "Jewels was right."

"About what?" I took a sip of my drink.

"You should try out for American Idol, or something. You've got a lot of talent."

The evening seemed to end too quickly and I knew I wasn't ready to say good-night. He asked me if I'd sit with him in his car for a little while before he left. Bev and Matt were okay with it, although Matt distinctly mentioned *not* leaving. It was funny to hear him take that fatherly tone with me, but I whole-heartedly agreed that I wasn't going any further than the driveway.

He opened the passenger door and I slid down in the kid-soft leather seat. I was amazed that I liked the interior even better than my Porsche, but I was sure I could blow him away in a race. "This is gorgeous," I told him as he lowered himself into the driver's seat. "What's under the hood?"

"An engine," he smirked.

"Very funny…"

"Annalisa," he spoke my full name causing me to go silent. "Who are these people?"

I hadn't expected that question. "Wha—I don't understand what you…"

"Yes, you do. You told me you were a liar this morning, and I'm starting to feel like your whole life here in Pensacola is just some kind of fake front. And don't tell me they're your aunt and uncle."

"They—they are," I began to stammer.

"Really? Then how come Beverly said she's your mother's sister?"

"She is," I said feeling completely vulnerable to his prying words. I suddenly didn't sound confident at all. "She's my aunt."

"What's your name? You're real name. Don't say McKinnis because that's Matt's last name. Unless your mother married Matt's brother, there is no way you guys have the same last name."

It suddenly dawned on me the flaw in the name. Matt would have had to have said he was my uncle on my father's side for it to have worked. Unfortunately, Beverly had been too anxious to answer his question and had volunteered herself as my aunt. I thought about trying to say that Matt's brother was my dad, but I knew there was no way it would fly at this point.

The tears welled up, distorting my vision. Tonight had been a mistake. My hand reached for the door handle.

"Don't go, Leese—please, I'm sorry," he said, grabbing my arm. "I just want to know who this girl is that I'm…" He left the sentence unfinished. Just the hint that he was falling for me stung worse than the tears.

"I can't tell you very much, my parents would kill me."

"Tell me what you can," came the simple reply.

"My family isn't from Alabama, but I'm guessing you've figured that out, too." I didn't look at him, I just kept talking. "They aren't having marital problems, my mom—my mom," I began to sob, "is slipping off the deep end." I didn't have a tissue so I was using the sleeve of my hoodie to dry my tears. "My grandpa committed suicide two years ago, but she thinks someone killed him." I looked into his face with a pleading stare, "She thinks someone is going to try to kill me and Kimmy, so she sent us here to keep us safe."

His arms wrapped around me as I began to shiver. It wasn't that cold tonight but it suddenly felt like it was twenty degrees as I cried my eyes out. "I can't tell anyone, I mean it would be like what was the purpose of coming here if everyone knows who I am?"

"Who are you?" he repeated in a whisper against my hair.

"I can't tell you, but my real first name is Annalisa."

"Why would someone want to hurt you?" he coaxed gently.

"My—my family has money. A lot of money," I finished with a hard swallow. "I guess someone might be trying to get to it through us. Evan, all this has got to remain quiet. You can't tell anyone, please."

"There is no way I'd say anything about it," he said tucking a loose lock of hair behind my ear. "I just want to be someone you can trust, someone you can be alone with and feel safe."

I couldn't tell him that I wanted that more than anything, but I wasn't there yet. I still didn't know much about him and sitting in the driveway was as alone with him as I could possibly venture.

"I've got to get inside." I wiped my eyes and hoped I hadn't just smeared mascara all over my face.

He flipped down the passenger's sun visor and opened the vanity mirror on the back. "You might want to fix that first," he said with a grin.

I looked up and sure enough I had two black streaks under my eyes. "Ugh! I don't know why I put on makeup tonight. If I'm going to keep bawling like this, I've got to get waterproof mascara," I said, carefully wiping away the traces that I'd been crying.

"You look beautiful without it so don't put it on for my benefit." He turned my face toward him.

When he leaned forward, I knew he was going to try to kiss me. His face was so close, but I simply couldn't.

"Evan, I'm not ready for this." I couldn't keep the quiver from my voice.

He studied me for a moment and finally said, "un baiser sur la joue?"

I smiled weakly, my resolve crumpled up in a pile on the floor, "Oui, a kiss on the cheek would be fine."

His cheek pressed to mine for a moment and then his lips brushed softly against the same place he had kissed earlier that day. "Good-night, Annalisa."

CHAPTER FOUR

Thursday morning I woke early, excited that I would see Evan's face in a little while. What I felt had been a disastrous ending last night now seemed much more appropriate. I came to the realization that I liked it better to have fewer secrets between Evan and me. I made it to the parking lot almost twenty minutes early. Sitting there with my doors unlocked and my concerns forgotten from what seemed like eons ago, I sang full blast to my music. I definitely had cranked the volume a little high so when the tap came on my passenger's window, I expected to see Officer Martin; instead, it was Ryan Faultz.

He opened the door and moved my books before I could refuse his non-existent invitation to sit in my car. "Wow, great music. Was that you singing?"

I turned the volume down to where it was barely audible and crossed my arms, glaring at my intruder. "Do you always just barge in on people?"

He leaned his head back against the head rest. "You are an awesome singer. What was the name of that song you sang last night? Something about I will not be moved? Is that a personal motto?" And then he crossed his arms, copying me.

My mouth was open but nothing was coming out.

"Yeah, Nate and Natasha asked me if I'd like to come. They said you'd be there, but I never expected to hear you sing. And, by the way, that guy who isn't your boyfriend was looking at you last night like you *are* his girlfriend."

"You were at my church?" I questioned, still amazed that I hadn't seen him there—he wasn't the kind of guy who should be able to blend into the scenery.

"Yeah, and we drove right past your house, too. You looked kind of cozy sitting with him in his car."

I wanted to call him a stalker, but the words just wouldn't come out of my mouth. I usually used that line in teasing, but I was getting the strange feeling that it might not be a joke with this guy.

"Ah, come on, Annalisa. Lighten up. I just wanted to know if you really had a boyfriend or not. You could have just told me."

"Evan is just ah—a really good friend," I finally managed to get out. "He just started here on Monday. I don't know him any better than I know you, but," I added with anger clear in my voice, "at least he has more manners!"

I heard the purr of the Nissan's engine as Evan pulled up on the driver's side of my car. He looked at me and Ryan sitting together, and I could see the anger fill his face.

"You'd better get out," I warned.

Ryan gave a half grin, "He doesn't scare me, but he does look dangerous. You be careful now," he said as he opened the passenger's door. "Good manners don't automatically mean good intentions." Then he turned as Evan was approaching my door and said something quietly that I couldn't quite make out, but a shiver ran through me as I thought it sounded like something about locking my hood. How could he have known anything about that?

Evan opened my door. "Is he bothering you?"

I heard Ryan laugh, which did nothing for cooling the anger on Evan's face. I saw the look and I knew Evan was getting ready to walk away from me and go after him.

I put my hand on his arm, which stopped him before he could move. "Hey, no—it's okay. He just heard my stereo and came over to listen for a few minutes."

One eyebrow went up on his face asking a question without words.

"No," I answered, "I didn't invite him, but it's okay."

Jewels pulled in right behind Evan and must have had an idea what was going on. "Hey, guys," she said cautiously. "What's up?"

But behind his back she motioned me to head in with Evan and then she pointed to Ryan and back to herself to let me know she bring him along separately.

"Let's get going." I tugged Evan's arm, "I've—I've got to stop by the office this morning."

He didn't say anything at first, but when we were almost out of hearing distance, he growled, "I don't like that guy."

I didn't have anything to do in the office when I started my morning until Ryan made that comment, and I now had a burning question for the registrar.

"I've got to see Mrs. Jones about one of my grades," I lied—I hated to do that, but if I was right, he would likely go back out in the parking lot and beat Ryan into a pile of crap. He sat in the lobby, still trying to get his temper under control when I slipped around the corner to her office.

"Hey, Mrs. Jones, do you have a minute?"

She looked up from behind a stack of folders on her desk, "Sure, come on in. Annalisa, right?"

"Yes. I was wondering about the new student that started yesterday, Ryan Faultz."

"Oh, yes, nice boy, but a little odd—don't tell him I said that," she said with a wink.

"No, I won't, but I was wondering was yesterday his first day being on campus?"

"No, he was here most of Tuesday afternoon getting registered. Why?"

"I just thought he looked familiar." I started to go out her door and then an afterthought hit me. "He is from Florida, right?"

"Umm—I think he's from," she picked up one of her manila folders and glanced inside, "West Palm Beach."

I froze in place.

"Are you okay, Honey? You look a little pale."

"I'm f—fine," but the whole while I felt like throwing up.

Evan didn't want me to go to class when he saw how sick I looked. "I'll drive you home—your car," trying to squelch any objections. "I'll walk back."

"That's like six miles, Evan. I'll be fine, honestly." I turned for the English wing. I would have to get through three periods with Ryan today, English, P.E. and Chemistry. P.E. wouldn't be so bad because I had a feeling he wouldn't get too close to me with Evan at my side. Who knew where he'd be sitting during chemistry. The only thing I was becoming keenly aware of was that Ryan was on campus the day my battery cable had been pulled from my car and now I knew he was from my hometown. I was trying to calm my shaking nerves as I walked into English. He was already there, but he wasn't looking up as I walked into the room. He was drawing something on a sheet of notebook paper and didn't notice me until I took my seat.

"Evan leaves you alone long enough to go to class, huh?"

I ignored the remark and took out my textbook.

"Today we are going to take up the period with Poe-etry," Mr. Shultz said with a smile. "We have a great collection to work from and we will see how many we can read today. Tonight you are going to do a little poetry of your own. I want at least one poem in Poe's macabre style. I'll choose from the best and we will have another poetry reading on Monday, but it will be your poetry, not Poe's. Take a look in the textbook and raise your hand as soon as you've selected a poem and we will begin."

I heard a noise behind me and then, "Mr. Faultz, what would you like to read?"

"Annabell Lee," he answered.

"Very good, begin whenever you're ready. When he's done, I'll expect someone else's hand to go up. You have the floor, Ryan."

He took a few steps forward as if he were heading to the front of the classroom and then stopped short just past my desk and turned around and began reading the poem. He was very good at being a dramatic reader, but the way he recited it gave me the creeps. Every time he said the name Annabell Lee, he drew out the Anna longer than the rest of the name. I never looked up, but it felt like his eyes were locked on me during the whole reading. The poem wasn't that long and he eventually sat down, to the applause from the other students, and then the next person rose and began.

"Was that as good as your Raven?" he whispered.

I nodded, but refused to turn toward him. He said nothing for the rest of the period, but every once in a while I could feel my hair being moved and I knew he was playing with it.

There was no sense in trying to avoid a conversation with him when the bell rang because I knew he'd be stuck to me like glue so I might as well try to get some answers. I picked up my books, ignoring that he put out his arm as an offering to carry them.

"That's okay," I refused.

"Why don't you have a book bag like everyone else?"

"I don't know, I guess because there are only four classes a day instead of seven so that's not too much to carry."

"True, but why won't you let me carry your books for you?"

I rolled my eyes.

"Are you that afraid that Evan will get mad and try to beat me up?" He gave a sardonic laugh.

"I don't think it would be a matter of trying. I think if you get too pushy he might—or I might." It was supposed to come out threatening, but it sounded hollow.

"You? Would you jump in and sacrifice yourself if it looked like he was getting the worst end of things, too?

I nodded.

"Very tough," he smirked. "But not the wisest thing to do; jumping on a guy that is. Some guys don't follow the rules about never hitting a lady."

"I might turn out to surprise you. How about you? Do you follow that rule or is everything fair game in love and war?"

"I love how you talk," he said, breaking off my train of thought. "You aren't a drama-queen, but yet you leave the drama up to the person listening. Very clever."

"Why are you in Pensacola?" I blurted.

"I told you, I'm joining the Air Force after high school, remember? Eglin is practically next door."

"A lot of guys join and get assigned to Eglin, but that doesn't mean they all move here first."

"True, but they may not have all the opportunities that I have."

"Like what?"

"Money," he answered, looking away from me.

"Why do you even want to go into the military? You don't seem the type?"

We turned the corner for the locker rooms. He gave a slow smile, "It's the only legal way to kill someone."

That sent a chill down my spine. "Why would you want to do that?" I looked him in those ice cold blue eyes with as much courage as I possessed.

"Everyone has their reasons behind what motivates them—mine are private." He turned and headed toward the guy's locker room.

I felt someone grab my arm, Jewels was standing there.

"Hey, you know I don't think that is a very good idea after this morning, unless you want to see them get in a fight."

"No, I don't."

"Good because I like Ryan, and I don't want to see him get that perfect nose of his broken."

"I think he's dangerous, Jewels. Don't try to get too close to him."

"Ha!" She laughed. "You're a fine one to talk. Evan is like a ticking time bomb and you are warning me that Ryan is dangerous? I think Ryan talks a good game, but Evan *is* a good game. And, girlfriend, Evan really likes you."

"You think so?" I felt he did too, but I didn't know it was that apparent to others.

"Oh, yes. You seem to be the only topic he cares to discuss when you aren't around."

I was trying to hold back the smile that felt like it was going to tear my face apart if I didn't let it out.

"It's kinda creepy though. Definitely stalkish," she added.

"Please, if there is a stalker here, it's Ryan. Do you know he was at my youth group last night and I never saw him? And then he said he went by my house and saw me and Evan sitting in his car?"

"That is cree…ooh, how was the car?"

"Jewels," I laughed, "You are impossible."

Evan was good through gym and, just as I predicted, he stayed close by me. Ryan (with a little help from Jewels) stayed away.

Chemistry wasn't so bad because Ryan couldn't sit near me. When the final bell rang, I was out of the room before anyone else and headed for my car. I beat Evan, Ryan, and Jewels. I was aching to see Evan before I left, if for no other reason than to look at his face and know that he was now closer to me than even my best friend, Jewels. Yet, I was afraid of the implications of falling for someone. I'd been friends with several guys and thought I liked a couple of them, but it was nothing like I felt when I was near him.

I found myself imagining what it would be like to kiss him, really kiss him. But that terrified me to the core. It was like some deep, dark emotional chasm that I might fall into and be irreversibly lost. I'd seen it a lot last year as girls I have known all my life suddenly took notice of particular guys and then BAM! It was like they were from another planet and all they could talk about would be how they could spend every waking moment with these guys they'd fallen for. That to me was scary—like turning zombie scary.

CHAPTER FIVE

The parking lot topic for Friday, besides the weekend, was what we were going to agree to go see tonight at the movies. There were thirteen of us that stood around after school, discussing the options. With the exception of Evan and me, most of the girls wanted to see the latest romance, and the guys were out for guns and guts. Neither he nor I had a preference.

They finally decided on the latest scary thriller which was a little of both. I was certain that I could have told them the plot before seeing it; guy meets girl, killer enters scene, blood-guts-gore, killer is vanquished, guy gets girl, killer not really dead, end of movie. It was definitely not something I would have picked, but for the sake of the group reaching a consensus *before* I was late picking up Kimmy, I caved. The showing for 7:15 was agreed upon and the group broke up.

"Great, I'll see you at the movies," I told Evan as I prepared to crank up and leave.

"Whoa, wait a minute. We're going together. I'm picking you up at your house. I'd like to talk you into dinner, too. You pick the place."

"Evan, I'm used to driving. It's like a control thing, I guess, but I like being able to head home when I want to. The group sometimes decides to do other things that I don't like doing."

"You are really worried about this being an actual date, aren't you?"

"N—no. I told you, I'm used to driving…"

"Fine then," he seemed to relent, but then continued, "I'll pick you up at 6:45 *and* you can drive my car. Fair enough?"

I wanted to tell him that it was not fair enough, because he was making it hard for me to weasel out of. "I keep the keys," I retorted, hoping he'd give me an excuse to say no.

"Fine."

"No dinner though. I'm eating before I leave the house."

"Fine, but a snack after the movie, *if* you are willing, won't be out of the question."

"Fine," I replied, mimicking his short response.

"And, you are my date tonight, got it?"

I opened my mouth and sat there like an idiot. He reached in and pushed my chin up to close my mute argument.

"You will be my date tonight. End of discussion," he turned away and got in his car, smiling the whole time. He was gone as the word, "Fine," finally came out of my mouth.

"What's my curfew tonight? Ten or eleven o'clock?" I asked Matt. I purposely asked him because Bev was too lenient on me. Matt had this whole 'dad' thing going on lately so I was likely to get an early end to my night if he made the decision.

"I don't think you have a curfew for the nights without school the next day," he seemed confused. "Besides most seventeen-year-olds don't like curfews, do they?"

"I do," I beamed, hopeful that he would take a hint.

"Leese, that is exactly why I trust your judgment. You know your limits. I don't want you to make it too late, but I won't be mad if it's one in the morning. Just be safe, okay? God knows your mom couldn't handle the stress if anything happened to you."

I knew that was true. Mom was so fragile right now that the tiniest thing might put her in the mental ward. I didn't want to be that 'tiny' thing—that's why I was here.

At 6:45 sharp, I heard the sound that sent my heart racing; Evan had pulled in.

I walked out on the porch to see him standing beside the open driver's door.

"Do I need to come in?" He asked.

"No, they've already met you, so they're cool about tonight." I walked carefully toward the vehicle. It was a very distinct threshold I was getting ready to cross over. There was still something about him that caused me to be afraid, but I was to the point where my curiosity and desire to be close to him were slightly more overpowering. But, one wrong move on his part and the balance would quickly shift.

I put out my hand.

He smiled. "You know this isn't your bug. The handling is different, it's not a four speed, it's six."

I never changed the slight smile I wore on my face as I extended my hand.

"You're sure you can handle it?" He looked worried for once.

I opened and closed my palm to signal that I was growing impatient. "I drive and I hold the keys, all night." I reminded him.

He resigned with a sigh and carefully placed the keys in my palm.

I slid into the driver seat as he walked around to the other side. I put the key in the ignition and pressed down the clutch. "Are you ready?" I asked him, still wearing my barely visible smile.

"Please, don't wreck my car," he whined softly.

My smile got bigger, "You'd better put on your seat belt."

He obeyed, but the worried look intensified.

I turned the key and the engine purred quietly to life. I left it in neutral and revved the engine, watching the tachometer move smoothly to the right and back down.

"You're not in gear," he pointed out. He must have thought I was trying to make the car move.

"I know that, silly. I'm just getting a feel for it." I put the car in reverse and backed carefully into the street, then dropped it in first gear and took off in a flawlessly smooth motion. "I love the instrument panel," I said as I worked my way through the gears. I could see out of the corner of my eye that he was starting to breathe again. "How hard have you pushed it?" I looked over, hoping that his knuckles would soon get a little color back in them from gripping the seat so tightly. "The transmission is tight." I continued my one-sided conversation. "Well that's odd," I muttered.

"What? What's wrong?"

"If you stay this quiet the whole time I'm driving, then tonight is gonna be a cinch!" I started to laugh. "Evan, I can handle your car."

"Just not the owner," he said, finally relaxing in the seat and letting the color return to his knuckles.

That was when it dawned on me that it might have been better to have him gripping the seat in terror.

We pulled up to the light where the two-lane road turned into four. As I sat there waiting for the light to change, the sound of a classic engine came roaring up beside me. It was Ryan and Jewels with Nate and Natasha in the back seat. They pulled up with big grins on their faces until they saw who was in the driver's seat.

"Ah, crap," Evan muttered.

"What? It's not cool to let a chick drive your car?"

Ryan revved his engine making the car lurch slightly forward, "You wanna run it, Leese?"

"Don't—don't listen to him," Evan said in a way that clearly showed he was worried.

"Drag racing is dangerous."

"Good girl…"

At that moment the light changed and I dropped the Nissan's gas pedal to the floor as the tires peeled out on the asphalt. I heard something come out of Evan's mouth that didn't bear repeating. I worked easily through the gears as I left Ryan and his muscle car screaming to try catching me.

"Leese! Slow down!" Evan yelled out over the high pitched whine of the Nissan's motor. I checked my speed. I was close to 100 miles per hour so I backed off, down shifting gradually until I stopped a quarter mile away at the next traffic light. "Wha—what happened to 'drag racing is dangerous'?"

I looked over at him and smiled sweetly, "Oh, please Evan. It's only a race if it's at least close—did you see how far back there I left him?"

The Trans Am pulled beside me, "Very funny, Leese—you didn't say you were gonna race," Ryan yelled.

I acted like I couldn't hear him. Once again he began to dump the fuel into his four barrel carburetor, his car jumping up and down with the need to move forward. I looked over, and I don't know what came over me, but I winked at him.

"No, Leese!" Evan warned, "I'm gonna take my keys back!"

I looked into those angry green eyes and then wound the tight little engine into a frenzy.

The light changed and the Trans Am tore off the line in a stinking cloud of blue-white rubber smoke. I just smiled as I gently nudged the car forward and proceeded at a normal pace.

"Good," he began, "At least you finally got some sense..." Then I saw the smile break out on his face as he realized why I didn't tear down the street. Ryan was being pulled to the curb by a Pensacola police officer. "You saw the cop, didn't you?"

"Yeah, I saw the cop. I hope they let Ryan off with a warning—he couldn't have gotten up too much speed by the time they pulled him."

"I hope he gets a ticket," he muttered. "That's what he gets for encouraging you."

"Be nice," I scolded. But he gave a merciless laugh, and I knew he was hoping that it was a big, fat ticket.

"Don't race my car, anymore," he added. "But, you did a good job—just don't do it again."

"I'll be good," I replied sweetly as I pulled into the movie theater parking lot.

He reached for the keys, but I clenched them in my hand, "Nope. All night, remember?"

"No racing, *remember*." He looked serious and then he smiled. "Come on, Danica Patrick. Let's go get our tickets."

Kevin, Carlie, and a few others were in line when we walked inside. We got our tickets and then Evan insisted that we couldn't see a movie without popcorn. He was at the concession counter about to finish up, and I was seated in the lobby when Ryan, Jewels, Nate, and Natasha came through the doors.

Jewels spotted me and dashed over, grabbing my arm. "You got to drive his car?" she squealed, though she knew the answer because she'd seen me. "That was so cool the way you took off the first time."

"Did Ryan get a ticket? Is he mad?" I figured it was better to get these answers before Evan came back.

Jewels gave a big smile and shook her head, "Nah, I talked the cop out of it."

"How did you do that?" I said, stifling a laugh.

"I told the officer, 'Oh please don't be mad at him, I just asked him if he'd show me how to make the tires smoke,'" and then she gave this really fake bat-your-lashes thing and put a sweet smile on her face.

"That worked?" I asked in disbelief.

"Well, yeah. The speed limit was forty-five and Ryan had only hit fifty when he saw the cop. But the cop said he could give him a ticket for an 'uncontrolled start' or something like that, so I begged for forgiveness; it worked. And, I don't think he's mad actually," she added. "Although he says he could have beat you if he'd known what you were going to do on the first stretch."

"Jewels, I could have taken him the second time too, but I saw the cop."

She giggled. "I believe you. Just don't tell Ryan that. I don't want that sizzling male ego to be too damaged by my best friend."

Evan made it to where I was sitting, carrying two bottled waters and a medium popcorn. "Hey, Jewels," he acknowledged her, but then looked to me. "Let's go ahead and get our seats before the good ones are all gone."

Ryan and the others had just come around the corner, and I realized that he was trying to get me moving before they got to where we were. "All right, see you inside, Jewels. Bye."

We went down the long hallway to the appropriate theater number and slipped quietly through the door. The room was already darkened as the previews played. He turned and started up the stairs to the upper rows of seats. I was a sit-in-the-center kind of girl, but evidently he liked the very top row. I asked him why so high when we settled in our comfortable chairs. He seemed mildly annoyed that I hadn't figured that part out, then he tapped the wall behind our heads and simply said there'd be no 'jerk' sitting behind us. I translated jerk into Ryan.

It didn't take long for the whole group to migrate toward the upper rows. The movie began and the theater became darker than before. Not long after the opening credits and the boy meets girl part, the killer axed off one of her friends. I jumped unintentionally—why did I agree to watch this? Yikes! There went another teenager. I hadn't realized the grip I had on the arm rest until Evan pried my hand free and put it in his. Only for a moment, my mind was distracted from the flying body parts on screen as he held my hand and gently stroked my forearm with his fingers. It was warm and safe and almost melodic enough to make me drift into comfort. NUTS! A kid had been gutted on screen.

Thirty minutes later I was so wound up that I felt like one of those Halloween cats with its back arched, claws out, and every hair standing up on its body. That was when I realized I was nearly in Evan's lap. Every time the hero or heroine would back up near a dark place in an alley or hallway, I'd duck my face against his neck and grip his shoulder. Once or twice, I thought I heard him chuckle—I don't know how he could have found anything funny in all of this!

Finally the climactic scene arrived. Would she live? Would he save her in time? I knew the answers in my head, but my nerves were unconvinced. It appeared he was getting into the scene as well because at this point he had both his arms wrapped around me and my head rested against his cheek. Aah! Finally the killer was down, surely to vanish before the end scene, but I didn't care. The pair had survived the onslaught and he finally told her he loved her—kiss— missing killer—the end. Whew! I could finally take a breath and relax.

"You can let me go now," I whispered as the credits rolled.

There was a hint of a smile at the corner of his lips, but he didn't budge.

I pushed myself gently out of his embrace and that was when I saw it. In all the gripping, clawing and fright, I had pushed the sleeve of his tee-shirt almost to the top of his shoulder. I hadn't meant to expose the scar that he was so sensitive about, but I gasped when I saw it. I'd never seen a bullet wound, but I knew that's what it had to be.

Quickly, he pulled down the sleeve and gave me a steely look.

I wanted to say I was sorry and that I hadn't done it on purpose, but the words wouldn't form.

Everyone trudged out to the lobby. It was a few minutes after nine and they were making plans. The mall was open until ten, but by the time we would arrive there, it wouldn't be long before we'd have to leave. Someone suggested pizza, but after all the blood and guts earlier, there weren't many interested in that idea. Then it was down to billiards at Cooties, bowling at the AMF, or cruise out to the beach for a campfire. The whole campfire thing sounded just a little too romantic for my taste, but it seemed to interest everyone else.

Skeeter, one of the boys in our group, had a key for the West Beach park gate. His mother was a park ranger, and he was privileged to have it as long as he never took people out there that did stupid things like drinking or vandalizing park property. "We can't get loud," he warned.

"I don't want to go," I whispered to Evan.

He was still looking a little gruff over the business of me seeing his scar. "Why not? It's early. What time did your..." he pause and dropped his voice lower so that he wouldn't be heard. "...friends say you have to be home?"

It stung a little hearing him say it that way. He was reminding me of my secrets, the same way I had reminded him about the secret he kept under his sleeve. The difference was that mine was completely unintentional.

"I—I don't have a set time."

"Good, then you can go to the beach. Don't worry, Leese," he spoke, quieter than before, "With all your friends around, you'll be safe." And he just stared at me with those unnerving eyes.

I wondered, though my face felt expressionless, why he said it that way? Once again he was making me afraid of him.

"Leese," Jewels called over the lobby noise, "Are you guys in?"

"Yeah, I guess. But just for a little while."

Five vehicles, practically in train formation, headed out toward the bridge. I was in the back of the line. My fleeting joy over driving his sports car had evaporated, and I wasn't about to get near Ryan at the front of the line because I knew there would be another challenge.

He seemed pleased that I wasn't enjoying the drive as much as the one on the way to the theater. He looked relaxed in the seat as he stared out the window watching the bridge lights go by. I studied him in the moments that I knew he wasn't looking. Matt had been right, he could have easily passed for someone in their twenties, not just because of the well developed sinuous sinew that ran from his neckline to his finger tips and places I hadn't seen, but only were alluded to beneath his form fitted clothes, but also by his maturity. The other guys his age were usually more immature and less deliberate. There was something about him that was very deliberate, almost the point of being driven, and it seemed to be staying close to me.

My hand reached up for his stereo system. He didn't notice the movement at first until I switched the controls from navigation to show the stereo options.

"You know how to work that?"

I ignored the question and was getting ready to search for my kind of music when I remembered I could bring up the previously played songs on one of these. My heart skipped a beat when I saw that it was the Natalie Grant song *Perfect People* that I had sung Wednesday night. I was ready to replay it when his hand stopped mine.

"Don't."

"But you must have liked it…" I started to rebut.

"I wanted to compare you to the original, that's all."

I moved further down the previously played list, surprised that he had played the other song I had sung as well. Then I hit Evan's music. He hadn't lied to me. It was all heavy metal. I recognized a lot of them. I flicked to what was most recent just before my music and clicked play. *Welcome to the Jungle,* by Guns n' Roses began to pump through the Bose sound system like shock waves through water.

A smile curled onto his face.

I pushed the button for the windows to roll down, letting the salted air in and the music out. The list read like a bad boys dream. There was *Paranoid* by Black Sabbath (which had been played numerous times), *Smells like Teen Spirit by Nirvana, Enter The Sandman* by Metallica,…

"Ah," escaped my lips before I could stop it.

His brow furrowed as he looked at me, "What?"

"One of my favorites," I exclaimed.

I could tell by the look on his face that there was no way he figured I'd have found something in his playlist that was one of my favorites. He looked at the screen, "*Twilight Zone* by Golden Earring? I don't believe that."

"Oh yes, Baby," I said with an almost iniquitous change in tone. "This song reminds me of eight minutes of shear heaven." I hit the play button and gave it more volume. I knew every word and I could see it stunned him. I dropped the gears and pulled into the passing lane.

His eyes got bigger as he realized that I was getting ready to take the lead from Ryan. "Leeeese!" came the warning, but it was too late as we flew passed the line of cars.

I just kept singing, eyes on the road, hands on the wheel. I knew where we were headed and I left the pack in the dust. I weaved through the tight streets and headed for the dead end at the beach. The look on his face changed as he listened and watched my facial expressions. The big finish was coming and I was charged like a bolt of lightning to do something I hadn't done in almost two years. Daytona was back in my mind like some happy drug. The final approach to the park ended in a large round cul-de-sac turn around just before the big iron bar that blocked the visitors from entering at night. I could see on approach that the circle was empty. I dropped the shifter one more time, looked at Evan and said, "Hold on."

He didn't have time to rebut or tell me no, all he could do was grip the door with one hand and brace against the dash with the other. It was brake, shift, steer and we spun three-hundred and sixty degrees into the circle.

"Wow!" I practically screamed out as the smoke and dust began to clear.

"What is wrong with you? You could have killed us both!" He had my right arm in a grip so hard that it was painful, but I still managed to reach over with my left and turn off the music.

"Ow, ow, ow," I was saying about the power of his hold, but yet I was trying to laugh too, "I'm sorry, but I've done it before—at Daytona."

He let go, realizing he'd put a nasty red mark on my skin. "Daytona?"

"Yeah, you know the race track." I said rubbing my arm. "I told you my family had money…" I let it drift off hoping he'd get an idea of what I was talking about. "I was allowed to drive for the length of one song. *Twilight Zone* is eight minutes long—it was what I picked."

"This isn't Daytona," he growled.

Just then the headlights of the other cars came into view as they filed into the circle. I was still trying to get the mark to disappear from my skin while Skeeter was unlocking the gate.

He reached over, all the anger had dissipated from his eyes as he gently stroked my upper arm. "I'm really sorry about that." His voice was so low and choked that I could barely hear him.

I gave a braver-than-I-felt smile and replied that it was okay, but I'd need my jacket to cover it up.

He reached behind the seat and handed it to me, apologizing once more.

"I guess I deserved it," I muttered.

"No," he said, his hand turning my face toward him. "You didn't deserve to get hurt." He let a little grin come out from behind the pain filled expression. "I—I just wish you'd have mentioned your weakness for fast cars and bad music, *before* I convinced you to drive."

The gate was open and everyone drove down the winding shell road, through the dark tangle of pines that led to the beach area. We parked next to the pavilion as Skeeter unlocked the rental shack and pulled out beach chairs for everyone. Evan, Nate, and Ryan gathered pieces of wood and tossed them into the big round fire pit and, after a short while, we had a nice crackling blaze.

Some sat around the fire while others wandered down to the water's edge. It was just a little bit nippy in the March air, so my jacket actually felt good and the fire was a perfect complement to the night. Ryan and Jewels were into a pretty deep conversation so I didn't have any worries about him and Evan causing friction. Kev and Carlie were beside us, Kevin having vaulted into an explanation about the special effects from the movie. Evan looked over and asked if I'd like to walk to the water. There were other people there so I felt it was safe. Once we were far enough away, he asked me what I'd driven on the speedway. I grinned and looked down at my feet trudging through the sand.

"Your VW isn't your first car, is it?" He sounded fairly sure of my answer.

Now I had to decide how much to say. I'd told him my family had money, but I never said how much. I knew his family must also have money, simply because most teenagers don't have a brand new forty-five-thousand dollar car to drive, so would it matter to him? "I'll tell you, but on one condition." I stopped walking and looked up, my hair getting tousled by the wind. He took both hands and tucked the fluttering strands behind my ears.

"What?"

"You're getting information about me, but I know almost nothing about you."

The smile slowly faded from his face, "There isn't much to tell." He turned and continued walking toward the water.

"I still want to know more about you."

He rubbed the hidden scar on his arm. "You may not like what you hear. Tell me about your car—your real car."

I was assuming that was as close to a yes as I was going to get. We reached the place where the loose sand became compacted and I lowered myself to sit with my knees drawn up to my chest and my arms wrapped around them. He followed suit, putting himself hip to hip with me.

"Before I turned old enough to get my restricted, my mom bought me a Jaguar—so I could learn how to drive," I added.

He let out something that sounded like a half laugh, "Nice first car to learn in."

"Yeah, but it was an automatic and the kind of driving school I attended…" I let my words fall into nothingness.

"Not your average driving school, I take it?"

"No, not at all. And, if I was going to learn how to do some of the more—more challenging moves, I needed a manual transmission and a faster car."

"Daddy to the rescue, right? You talked your dad into something sportier than what your mother bought?"

"No—Dad thought I was too young to have a car. So I bought myself a Porsche 911."

He got a funny look on his face as he stared at me. "That explains your driving."

"I wanted to at least see what it could do."

"*At least*," he mused.

"So my driving instructor got special permission for me to try it out on the speedway. There was nothing going on there so I had some privacy. Tony said I could try my favorite moves and then I could run it flat-out on the track, but only for the length of one…"

"Song," he finished for me. "So how fast did it go?"

I was trying my best to be humble at that moment, but I could remember the thrill of nearly unchecked speed. "I ran mostly about one-fifty, one-sixty, but I got it up to one-ninety before I lost my nerve."

"I don't believe that," he said rather nonchalantly.

"It's the truth! I really did run on Daytona," I insisted

"Oh, I believe that. I can't believe you lost your nerve."

"I'm not a big risk taker…" I started to say, when he burst into laughter and rolled back on to the sand.

"What?" I stretched out on the sand as well, rolling to my side to face him. It was cold and slightly damp, but it was worth it to get a good view of the genuine happy look on his face.

"You are not a risk taker? I saw the speedometer in town and I just went three-sixty with you on a sand covered beach parking lot, and…" He went quiet.

"And, what?" I prodded.

He reached up and touched my arm where he'd tried to snap it off earlier. Even though the touch was soft, my arm was still painful, and I had to bite my tongue to keep from crying out. "You're here with me," he answered.

"So you're saying you are a big risk?" I pried. It was time to find out more about the guy who was magnetizing my heart, drawing me to his steel façade.

I reached over and touched the scarred shoulder through his tee-shirt. I thought I felt him shudder under my fingers. "I didn't realize I'd guessed this right that day at gym—I just hope I was wrong about it being a girl you were stalking."

"No, it wasn't a girl."

"Do you mind?" I asked as I started to lift his sleeve.

"Would you be satisfied if I said no?"

"I already know what's there. I just don't know the story behind it."

He nodded slowly, giving me permission to look at the disfigurement on an otherwise perfect arm. I pushed the sleeve upward, exposing his shoulder in the moonlight. I could see the pink tail of the scar where the bullet must have grazed before piercing through the muscle. He had closed his eyes as I inspected the place on his arm, his breathing deep and quiet as my fingers traced from the tail to the rounded indention. It dawned on me that it must have traveled completely through and exited along the triceps, so I carefully felt the back side of his arm with my free hand. Once again

I found a scar, but it wasn't quite as rounded as the one on the front. He flinched as my fingers brushed the marred skin. "Does it still hurt?" I asked, surprised that what appeared to be an old wound might still be sensitive.

His eyes opened. "No, I'm just not used to having someone touch it."

"How did it happen?"

Indecision was so clear on his face I could almost watch the internal struggle as he weighed what he wanted to tell me.

"If it's not the truth," I added quietly, "I don't want to know."

His eyes closed again. "You're a fine one to add that little disclosure—I don't even know your last name."

That remark stung. "But—but, I can't..." Stupid emotions! I sat upright and wrapped my arms around my legs once again. I couldn't continue the conversation if I couldn't control my feelings. I wasn't one of those 'I'll cry to get what I want,' kind of girls, and it infuriated me when I could do little to stop the tears from appearing every time my feelings bruised.

He sat up, brushing the sand from my back. "My car seats are never going to forgive me for this," he said as he continued wiping me off.

My chin was resting on my knees at this point and I was starting to gain a little composure.

"I was in a fight with someone," he said hoarsely. "I had him down on the floor when he pulled a gun and shot me through the arm."

"You could have been killed," I said, clearly shaken at the truth of what he was revealing, and I was certain this was the truthful version.

"I thought I was dead when that gun when off," he admitted. "It didn't hurt as much as it burned like he'd slammed a piece of red-hot steel through me. My ear was in so much pain, I thought the bullet had gone through my head." He looked at me and could tell I didn't understand. "The sound of the gun going off that close ruptured my eardrum."

"What happened after he shot you? Did he leave you there or was he sorry..."

He gave a gruff sound like a strangled laugh. "Yeah, he was sorry he did it," he said tersely, "when I got finished with him."

"What did you do?" I was asking, but I wasn't really certain I wanted to know the outcome. he turned to me with those eyes. Those eyes that I knew were dark green, but out here away from any lights they just looked like deep black pools.

"I killed him, Leese."

My heart seemed to stutter to a hard stop and then took off a million-miles-an-hour. He just told me he actually killed someone. My mouth had become so dry that it was as if I had grabbed a cup of beach sand and filled it. I was struggling for anything to say, but I could only think of one thing. "Did you have to go to jail?"

"No," was his abrupt answer.

All I could think was that it must have been self-defense. That would have been the only logical solution to have kept him out of jail.

"Now you understand why I said you were taking a risk being with me." The way he said it was utterly somber.

"Evan, you aren't going to shoot me," I said as if he had slipped a mental cog.

He was expressionless.

"Unless I wreck your car tonight," I added, trying hard to get away from the subject that I'd brought up.

That broke the void stare and he laughed, "Actually, I think I'd just make you pay for it. You could do that, right?"

I grimaced, "Yeeeah, I could—unless you would take my Porsche in trade?"

"That would be quite a deal." He seemed to be considering it. "Mine was forty-three thousand. How much was yours?"

I winced a little, "A hundred and thirty-eight."

"Barring you killing us both, have fun driving my car tonight," he said with an enormous grin.

CHAPTER SIX

By a quarter to midnight everyone was ready to go home. We doused the fire and put the chairs back into the building. Then we cleaned the area well enough that no one would ever be the wiser that we had been there. Ryan led the way, once again, but this time I was second in our train, as we drove back up to the gate. But, to everyone's surprise, the gate was blocked by an older Buick that had pulled in sideways. A pickup truck and another older car were also in the circle and a group of six men and two women stood around leaning against the vehicles drinking. They looked mildly surprise to see a group driving out of the woods.

Ryan leaned his head out and yelled, "Hey, buddy. Would you mind moving your car so we can pull out?

The tallest of the group sat down his beer on the bumper of the pickup and gave a fake smile holding up one finger as if to say to give him a minute. He climbed into the car as one of the other men approached and spoke to him. The Buick pulled away from the gate and continued around the large circle stopping on the opposite side blocking the road out.

"Well, that's stupid," I muttered. "How does he expect us to get out?"

Evan began to stiffen in the seat, "That isn't good."

Skeeter came up from the car behind us and hurried to unlock the gate. The remaining five guys that had been standing around drinking began moving toward the car that was now blocking the exit. Ryan pulled through and over to the left, I pulled to the right, allowing Carlie and Bethanne to come up in the middle and Andrew bringing up the rear.

My training with Tony Dix was starting to yell in the back of my head, but this scenario wasn't anything I expected to encounter. The road behind me was of no use since it dead-ended into the beach. The large rocks on either side of the roadway blocked me from making use of the shoulder around the Buick. The only other option, if this should turn bad was using the car as a battering ram. The problem was the car I needed to be in would have been the Buick because Evan's little Nissan would hardly stand up against the clunky metal beast. I swallowed as I considered, by the time this night was over, I might actually need to get the keys to my Porsche to replace Evan's car.

With everyone in the circle, Skeeter locked the gate and hurried to the car he was riding in. Ryan and the guy from the Buick were standing there talking when Evan opened his car door.

I reached for his arm. "Don't get out. That's what they want."

"Sit still, Leese. It might be nothing." But the sound of his voice clearly told me he really didn't think this was going to turn out to be nothing.

I could see Nate crawling out of the back seat of the Trans Am. His tall black frame caused the other men to slow their walk toward Ryan. Then as Evan came into the picture, it appeared the men almost stopped their approach. I rolled down the window, listening to what was being said. The guy from the Buick sounded friendly enough. He was talking about Ryan's car, saying he'd really like a peek under the hood. Ryan was politely refusing saying everyone in our group was tired and we were on our way home. But the guy just kept talking.

"That's a bunch of good-looking women you *boys* got with you tonight," I heard one of the men say as he sauntered up to the budding group.

I could see Carlie in her little Suzuki Sidekick, her eyes wide and panicky. Jewels simply looked annoyed. I couldn't see Natasha. Bethanne, in her Saturn with Skeeter and Lori, all looked upset (I had a feeling Skeeter was more upset with the fact that these idiots had scattered beer cans around the parking lot), Andrew was climbing out of his Dodge Dakota much to the dismay of his girlfriend, Tina.

Then I heard one of the drunk women, yell, "Whoohoo, look at them pretty little boys."

There were six men that looked like they attended barroom brawls for relaxation, next to our six high school guys. Kevin had opened the door to the Suzuki and was wisely standing there and not approaching the group. Andrew, a senior, slim built and wiry, was making his way toward them, while Skeeter, a junior but no bigger than Kevin, approached the group half way. The only threatening ones were Nate, a medium built, 6'2" ball player, Ryan a well-built 6'3" and then there was Evan who was the only truly menacing guy on our side. Just over 6' tall he had at least twice the muscle mass with broad shoulders and sculpted, thick biceps. So for all intensive purposes it was a two to one ratio, in favor of the other men.

I heard Evan say, "Just move your car, man." And then the voices began to escalate. I looked up in the rearview mirror and saw the drunken women bothering Tina as she sat in Andrew's truck, but I noticed she'd prudently locked the doors. I looked back just in time to see one guy put his hand on Ryan's chest and the melee was on.

I simply couldn't believe what was happening before my eyes. I'd never seen something like this in real life. This was only supposed to happen on television. My heart instantaneously began to pound, and the blood rushed so hard in my body that it was like a great roaring in my ears. I could hear myself yelling, "NO!" as if my shouting was going to interrupt what was happening and then suddenly I was standing outside Evan's car. It was as if the motion to open his car door and step out was so automatic that I didn't even know I'd done it.

Ryan had thrown the first punch when the guy pushed him, sending the man staggering only to come charging back. Evan wasted no time in taking out the guy closest to him with a tremendous punch that was so loud, I could hear the crack of his fist on flesh and bone from where I stood. The guy went to the ground and never moved. Evan had knocked him out cold and was on to the next one. Nate had stepped up beside Ryan in an apparent attempt to stop the fight, but one of the other guys jumped him and they were rolling on the asphalt, punching and kicking. The largest guy in the group was now fighting with Evan, but Evan clearly out-skilled him.

That's when the other two guys in the group jumped Evan. When he suddenly became outnumbered, Andrew and Skeeter didn't need any other provocation to join the brawl and they were running toward the group.

I was in motion, but before I moved two steps, I heard a screeching behind me. I turned to see that the two women had Kevin up against the Suzuki, yelling, "Give me your wallet!"

Carlie was screaming for them to leave him alone and in my peripheral vision I could see that Jewels was out of Ryan's car and heading toward them. Tina was out of the truck and also moving toward the new battle that was erupting in the center of the parking lot. Everything was happening so fast. We were only seconds into this battle, but yet my mind was clearly separating every piece as it occurred. The second woman whirled around, fists clenched, as I came rushing up. She took several steps in my direction when the realization crossed her face that I wasn't stopping. I knew that the momentum of my entire body was a huge force. She didn't even have time to swing as I hit her with my forearm and shoulder in her chest. She was knocked, breathlessly, into the back of the Suzuki and then hit the ground.

The other woman turned from Kevin to me. My hands went up and my body automatically assumed the fighting stance I'd learned in martial arts. I knew this was no sparring match, and the other person would not be aiming just to make contact. I'd have to remember what I'd been taught to do in this situation; hold nothing back.

The other girls had almost reached me when Kevin jumped on the woman's back, wrapping his whole arm around her throat in a choke hold and held on for dear life. She was reaching back scratching and clawing, knocking his glasses to the pavement, but she was rapidly running out of air as she went down to her knees and then almost face down rolling and thrashing to try to get Kevin off her back. It was no use—that boy had a tiger by the tail and he wasn't about to turn loose until she passed out. Her eyes began to flutter as she stopped flailing.

Tina was yelling that it was enough, "Don't choke her to death!" she screamed.

But I knew better. If Kevin was to let her go at that moment, she'd come up swinging. "Hang on Kevin," I commanded. "Don't let go until she's out." Tina was still shouting as I grabbed the first woman that I'd knocked senseless. She was trying to stagger to her feet when I kicked her back to the pavement and rolled her over in one quick movement. I pulled her arm into a sharp "V" behind her back and twisted her wrist and palm so that it almost touched her spine. "Hold her," I ordered Tina. "Here," I said, showing her how I expected her to hold the arm. "If she moves, just pull her hand upward; trust me, she'll stop."

Kevin's woman was completely out at this point and I quickly positioned her arm the same as the first woman's. "Jewels," I yelled. "Hold this," I said indicating the woman's arm. I repeated my instructions. I looked up at the faces around me and then glanced toward the two other vehicles. "Bethanne, see if their keys are in their cars; throw them in the woods." She gave me a nod and then I was headed toward the men.

I could hear the shouts behind me to stop, but I was no longer in control of my sense of direction. It was like I was being pulled to the main fight. Nate had given his opponent enough of a battle that the guy was backing off. Ryan had gotten the upper hand on the man who had started the entire thing, and that guy was crawling back into the Buick. Ryan, Skeeter and Andrew jumped in to pull the three guys off Evan. As they gave Evan a seconds worth of breathing room, he was able to deliver the same powerful punch that knocked out his first victim—down went another guy from a tremendous blow. One of the men took off running into the woods, and that only left one and he quickly realized what his fate would be if he kept fighting, so he backed away toward the guy that had given up fighting against Nate.

I was amongst the group of men by that point when I saw it.

"Evan, look-out!" I screamed as I watched in terror. The guy from the Buick whirled around with a knife and charged toward him.

It wasn't conscious, but everyone in the group seemed to back up, leaving Evan and this obscenity-shouting man facing each other. The guy charged, swinging for Evan's body. There was a slash, but then as the arm was extended, Evan grabbed the guy's wrist. Evan's knee came up as the wrist was slammed down, causing the knife to fall from his hand and hit the pavement. He had the guy's arm in an unnatural position as he brought the full force of his strength down and a sickening crack was heard. The man screamed in pain and then crumpled to the ground. He had broken the man's arm at the elbow.

That was when I heard the sound of a car cranking. Kevin had slipped around the back side of the Buick and crawled through and cranked the car. He backed it a few feet and then put it in drive, crashing it among the big rocks on the shoulder. The sound of tires popping and metal crunching as it came to a stop was gratifying. Kevin jumped out the passenger's side and yelled for everyone to get moving.

Evan was at my side pushing me toward his car. I went automatically for the driver's door and he didn't try to stop me. He bailed into the passenger's side and we were moving. Ryan had driven out in front of me, then Carlie as she picked up Kevin. I fell into line, but looked into my rearview to make sure Bethanne and Andrew were following.

Ryan drove to the base of the big bridge about two miles away and pulled over under the street lamps by the fishing pier. It was a chance to make sure everyone was okay, ending the adrenaline rush of what had happened.

Jewels came running toward me and I met her half way. She gave me an excited hug. "That was freaking wild! You were like BANG! And that woman went down! And Kevin, oh my god, Kevin was like freaking wrestle mania!"

"Calm down, Jewels," I laughed. Suddenly, my nerves were giving way and I felt giddy and jelly-legged.

"I hope they aren't following us," Natasha was saying.

"No way," Bethanne chimed in. "I pitched their keys. They'll never find them in the dark."

Everyone was talking at once, replaying what they had seen. Evan's name was clearly coming out of the conversation as the hero for snapping that guy's arm and knocking out two others.

He didn't get out, but Ryan came around and gave him one of those arm-wrestling kind of handshakes.

"Awesome job, my man," Ryan was saying. "I think we're gonna have to get you one of these 'born to kill' tattoos."

He smiled mildly, "No, that's okay. I don't want them to know what's coming."

It took Ryan a split-second and then he laughed, "Yeah, you're probably right."

I was doing a quick damage assessment. Kevin had a couple scratches, but his glasses had survived. Nate had some road-rash where he'd been down on the pavement, but nothing serious. Ryan had a bruise darkening around one eye and a bloody and swollen lip, but (to Jewel's relief, I'm sure) his nose wasn't damaged. Skeeter and Andrew looked fine. I sat back down in the car with the door open, still listening to the jumble of voices as everyone spoke at once. I looked over at Evan, and saw surprise written all over his face.

"What?" I asked as I surmised his injuries. He had several bruised places on his face and his lips were swollen, those scarred knuckles of his were bloody and ripped open, but it was how he was looking at me that had me worried. "What?" I repeated.

"You were in the fight?"

It evidently hadn't occurred to him that while he was trying to do the incredible hulk with three guys on his back that I had gotten involved.

"Well, yeah—those women jumped Kevin and I had to do something," I sounded as if I was defending my actions, but I didn't think it should be necessary.

He closed his eyes for a moment, "How'd you do?" he finally asked.

"I knocked one out and Kevin knocked out the other."

"Kevin?" he questioned, reopening his eyes and looking at me as if I wasn't serious.

"Yeah, he jumped on her back and got her in the sleeper hold."

A big grin spread across his face, I could tell he was visualizing it. But then he frowned and looked serious again. "What were you doing near the men?"

"I thought—I mean, you had—there were three guys on you! I couldn't just stay back…"

"You should have," he snapped, his eyes suddenly livid and very alert. "People like that don't play around. You could have been hurt." He paused and suddenly looked very pained. "Or killed."

"You could have been hurt or killed," I rebutted. "What was I supposed to do? Let that happen?"

He looked at me very succinctly, "That would have been better."

I could feel my eyelids peel back as I looked at him and shook my head. "Evan Lewis, that was stupid! If you haven't noticed, I have reasons why I couldn't let that happen."

"There are reasons why you should," he whispered and looked away.

"Well, I didn't have to fight one of the guys," I continued, ignoring his idiotic statement.

He turned back, his face filled with some emotion I couldn't describe, "But you would have, wouldn't you?"

My own emotions were knotted up about throat level, ready any second to overflow. "I—I *really* like you, Evan, more than anyone I've ever met. I couldn't stand by and watch you take on three guys."

His face was turning pale and a moment of agony filled his eyes. "We've got to go," he whispered hoarsely.

I looked at the rest of the group and it was obvious that everyone had decided it was time to head home. I said my good-byes, but at Evan's urging, I waited until the last of the vehicles got on the bridge and started driving away.

"I need you to drive me to my house, Leese."

I cringed inwardly, going to his house at one in the morning, alone just the two of us was way up there on my list of 'not-good-ideas.' "I don't think that's…"

"That's fine then—let's get you home…" His face was becoming whiter.

His right arm move slightly, and that's when I saw the fresh red blood.

"Oh my god, Evan! You're bleeding!" I grabbed at his black tee-shirt, seeing the slice in the fabric. The material was wet and when I turned my hand over it was stained with blood. "I've got to get you to a hospital," I said grabbing the shifter.

"Leese," he responded firmly, holding my hand in an iron grip. "I'm not going to a hospital."

"Oh, yes you…"

"*Annalisa*," he stressed, not allowing me to engage the car. "Take me to my house and I'll see how bad it is."

"It's bad enough. You're bleeding all over the place."

"I don't think it's too deep. My lungs are fine," he said, assessing his wounds. "Please," he finally crooned. "I *need* to go home."

"Okay," I agreed, "But if it's bad, you're going to either let me take you to the hospital or call an ambulance."

I could tell by the look he was giving me that there was no way he was going to the hospital, so when he agreed, I knew he was lying.

"Turn left. My house is on the island."

I pulled into a drive that led down to a house on the beach. It was a single story Mediterranean-style home. He pulled out a clicker from the glove box and the garage opened and the light came on. It was a triple-car garage, but was completely devoid of anything inside. I drove in cautiously, but I couldn't control my pulse when he hit the button for the door to close behind us. At that moment, I was scared—truly scared. It wasn't the wound on his side that had me frightened, but somehow I had the feeling this is what he had been working toward all along. He and I were utterly and completely alone together.

My hands were shaking as I turned off the key and went around the car to help him out. He already had the door open and I could see the pained expression on his face as he tried to stand. "Come on," I whispered, slipping myself underneath his arm. He winced, but then I felt his weight as he leaned on me for help.

He unlocked the door to the house, and we stepped into the dark interior.

"Light switch—your side," he croaked.

I felt the wall until I touched the panel and the lights came on. The house was large and beautiful. We were walking into the area by the kitchen, and beyond that it opened into a great room. I could see a pool just outside the sliding doors. He put his keys on the granite counter top and was guiding me toward the hallway. Another light switch and I could see we were entering the master bedroom. I had this urge to slip out from under his arm and run, but I couldn't do that to him. As much as I felt the need for self-preservation at that moment, I knew he needed me.

Through the bedroom and into the master bath and I found the light switch. As we were bathed in florescent lights, I looked up into the face staring back at me in the mirror—it was of someone who was terrified.

He let loose of my shoulder and grabbed a large black shaving case on the counter, unzipped it, and spilt the contents onto the vanity. It wasn't what I expected to see. There were hypodermics, small vials, needles and stitching thread, a scalpel, scissors, alcohol and betadine pads, gauze wrap, pads and tape.

"Jeez," I uttered without thinking. "Does this happen often to you?"

He gave a bitter laugh and looked at me in the mirror. "Go wait in the living room."

"No, I can help…"

"Absolutely not," he snapped, but then winced again in pain. I could tell he didn't want to take his right arm away from his side.

"Evan, you've got to let me help. You can barely stand up," I said, gently pushing him to sit on the edge of the tub. He tried to resist but realized it would be easier if he sat down.

I started to grasp his shirt, but he stoutly refused. "Leave!" He growled out the words so deeply that it sounded more like an animal than a human.

I went down to my knees in front of him, grabbing the scissors as I did. "That tee-shirt is going to have to be cut off," I whispered.

His hand gripped mine, stopping me from what I was intent on doing. "I can't let you do this," he replied, softer this time with less growl.

I looked at him for at least two or three seconds, just staring into that handsome face so filled with pain, anger and what appeared to be out-right fright. There was something he didn't want me to see, and I had a feeling it wasn't the cut on his side.

"Evan," I said in a whisper, "You're gonna pass out in about two minutes if you try to do this yourself—then I'm just going to come right back in here and do it anyway. So you can either be conscious and let me help, or you can be out and let me help. It's your choice."

He swallowed hard and released my hand. I pondered for a moment the best way to cut the shirt and then I realized I had to cut from the neckline out to the end of each sleeve to get it to drop and then once right up the center and he'd be out of it. My hand worked quickly to cut through the fabric, and within a matter of moments I was peeling it carefully from around his waist. I gave a gasp as the shirt hit the floor.

The slice was about six inches long and appeared deepest toward the front. It wasn't the gash that took my breath away, and neither was it the fact that his chest, abs and arms were so beautiful that I could have cried, but it was the other marks on his body that held me nearly frozen. He had a second gunshot scar along his left side, numerous scars that looked similar to the one he'd just obtained, and then I saw the tattoo. I must have looked like a wide-eyed child as my gaze met his. My fingers came up without thought as I reached out and touched the image of a chain and lock piercing across his heart with the word 'Untouchable' inscribed above it.

His hand met my fingers and held them there against his chest as he tried to say something that wouldn't come out. Then he raised my hand to his mouth, closed his eyes and kissed my finger tips.

Had it been any other situation, I think I would have been locked in the trance as he held my hand to his mouth. But no matter what questions, and worse, no matter what answers I got out of him tonight, I had to help him.

I pulled away gently and dampened a washcloth. He didn't say anything as I cleaned his side, wiping away the blood. Then I grabbed the betadine swabs and washed the edges of the wound. "I—I can't do stitches," I remarked softly. The slice had quit bleeding and seemed to be trying to congeal. He stood slowly and looked in the mirror.

"We'll use the glue," he stated pointing to one of the small tubes on the counter. "Then we'll bandage and tape it. Just do it exactly the way I tell you. And, Leese," he said, causing me to look up at him. "Don't glue yourself to me." And then he smiled and sat back down. It was the first hint of humor I'd heard in a while.

"Yeah, I can see where that could get awkward." It felt good to finally smile.

He explained how to match the edges of the wound and hold them carefully together as the glue was applied. It was amazing to see how quickly the glue held. It only took about two minutes for me to seal the cut. He then had me wipe it off again with antibacterial, place a thin strip of gauze over the slice and then he tore off and handed me three inch strips of tape to place vertically along the cut as he explained that the glue wasn't really meant for such deep wounds, but it would work as long as the tape was able to keep the skin from stretching. Then it was a larger amount of gauze and then the wider tape around the perimeter to finish the job.

He stood up, still wincing a little in discomfort, but his face looked like it had more color than when I began. I started picking up all the medical supplies and placing them back into the bag.

"You don't have to do that," he whispered warmly against my hair.

I was facing the sink as he stood beside me close enough to feel the heat coming from his bare chest. I looked into the mirror and realized that I was standing next to a man—there was no boy in him. His sleek arms reached out and wrapped around me, his mouth sought my neck as he began to kiss and caress my throat and shoulders.

"Stay with me tonight, Leese," came words so hot and determined they felt as if they had the power to actually take hold of me.

I couldn't think, though I know there were words tumbling around inside my head. By this point he turned me to face him as he pulled me hard against himself. His mouth moving toward mine, his fingers twining like lace at the sides of my waist and the only thing I could hear was the slamming of my heart against my chest.

"N—n—no..." I was struggling to pull away, but his grip increased. "Stop it, Evan! I've got to go home."

The more I resisted, the stronger he became. His right hand came up to the base of my throat and was beginning to tighten. I wasn't able to take in a breath. I knew how to stop him, but I didn't want to do it; just one hit to the bandage on his right side and I'd be free. And then it happened. As I tried to free myself, my body went totally limp and he had to struggle to keep me from hitting the floor. My eyes fluttered. I could see the pain on his face as he tried to lower me slowly. There was a blackness that was blocking my sight and then nothing.

When I came to, he was seated on the floor beside me, holding me. "Leese? Leese? Snap out of it. Are you okay?"

I blinked a few times, not really sure where I was.

"Leese, say something," he pleaded.

"I want to go home," I mumbled.

He took a deep breath and then moved the hair away from my face. "You scared the crap out of me."

"What happened?" I asked, the fright of what occurred before everything went black returned.

"I guess you passed-out, fainted—geez, you just went down like a rock. I thought I—I thought I killed you." His face was contorted as if he was really torn at the moment as to what to do.

The tears came up without any warning and spilled down my temples. "Please, Evan—don't hurt me, please. Please, take me home."

"How did you know I was going to hurt you?" he asked, his fingers caressing my face as he held my head up with his left hand.

"Because, for a minute, you weren't Evan," I sobbed. I pushed myself up on my elbows, forcing myself to get some function back in my legs. I rose from the floor and he rose with me.

"This is crazy." He was shaking his head like he couldn't believe what had just happened. He walked into the bedroom, opened the dresser and grabbed a button down the front shirt. Then he went back to the dresser and slowly opened the top drawer. He reached inside but never withdrew his hand. He just kept shaking his head.

"Evan?"

He ignored me.

I slipped quickly from the bathroom and headed for the door.

"Where do you think you're going?" He didn't sound anything like the guy I knew.

"I'm going home." My voice was quivering yet confident.

"I can't take you home," he said, still standing at the dresser.

"Then I'll walk," I stated and I stepped out from the room. The walk turned to a run as I entered the great room. Which way? The garage door was closed and I could see a keyed dead-bolt on the front door. It was either out through the pool area, which I didn't know where I'd end up, or grab his keys and try for the front door before he caught me. I dashed to the counter where he'd set his keys. I'd just wrapped my fingers around them when he stepped into the great room.

He was straightening his collar and buttoning the shirt so nonchalantly, he looked like he was getting ready for a dinner date. He looked at me and smiled, "You aren't going anywhere."

And that was when the idea hit me. I turned and grabbed the door to the garage. I could hear the sound of him as he started to run for me from across the room. I slammed the door and fumbled my way to the car in the darkness. I found the handle and the light inside came on just as the door to the kitchen opened, sending a shaft of light into the void. I jumped inside and hit the automatic door locks. Opening the glove box and scattering the contents, I pressed the button to open the garage. The lights in the garage came on as the door began to rise.

He was at the driver's door as I struggled to make the key fit in the ignition.

"OPEN THE DOOR, LEESE!"

The car cranked. I saw his fist draw back getting ready to smash out the window when I found reverse and burned the tires backwards out the not fully open garage door. I heard the roof of the car scrape, but I didn't care. I floored it backwards until I hit the road. Spinning at a forty-five degree angle, I hit all six gears within six seconds and was traveling more than seventy miles per hour.

I crossed the bridge, sobbing and crying, feeling like my heart had been ripped completely out of my chest. What was wrong with him? What was wrong with me? Did I do something to turn him into an animal? What was going to happen? Would he get a taxi and be at my house soon? Dear God in heaven, I cried, he knows too much about me. I may have just become that little thing that would send my mother over the edge.

It was two thirty in the morning as I cut the lights and parked on the street just before the driveway to Matt and Bev's house. I looked at myself in the rearview mirror and realized I was a wreck. I didn't know if anyone was waiting up for me, but I couldn't go in like this. I dug for my small purse in all the clutter that had fallen from the glove compartment. I found it and opened it up on the passenger's seat, searching for my hair brush. I quickly pulled it through my hair, grabbed a tissue and dabbed my eyes, wiping away the mascara. I moved past my wallet and cell phone to find my tinted lip gloss in the bottom of my bag. I put a little on and checked myself in the mirror one more time. My eyes were still wild, like I'd been on drugs.

"Calm down, Leese," I said aloud. "Pull it together and get inside." I was grabbing up my things when something caught my eye. It was the registration slip for Evan's car. I picked it up and stared at it recognizing something was wrong. The registration was for a Nissan 370Z, but it wasn't registered to Evan Lewis. It belonged to a Micah Gavarreen. The car didn't belong to him? No wonder he was so concerned about me wrecking it.

Headlights turned onto our street and my heart felt like it instantly exploded. I ducked in the seat, fully expecting the car to stop and I would be trapped, but to my relief, it continued and turned left at the next corner.

I had dug around so much in my purse that I couldn't find my house keys. I finally turned it over and they tumbled out. I quickly stuffed my purse full and stepped out into the street. There was a light on in the living room. I tip-toed up the steps and slowly unlocked the door; no one was waiting. I locked the door and slipped off my shoes as I moved silently to my room. I set everything down, feeling like I could finally take a breath—a real breath—one where my lungs actually moved.

I needed a shower badly, but it was like one of those stupid horror movies coming back to mind. Do you take a shower when you are being chased by a deranged killer? I was sure that Evan wasn't a deranged killer, but I had definitely done something tonight to cause his male libido to replace his brain.

I felt the urge to double check that I had locked the front door, and then the urge to check the back door. I was really starting to feel like I was flipping out. Every door was locked. I peeked on Kimmy and she was sleeping peacefully. I went back to my room to get my pajamas and my towel. I couldn't put my clothes in the bathroom hamper because my jacket and shirt both had blood on them—that would freak out Bev, for sure. I would undress in my room and then wash my clothes tomorrow—or throw them away if the blood didn't come out.

I started to undress when I decided my window blinds could be closed just a little bit tighter, but when I went to pull the chain I noticed my window lock was open. I never opened these windows. How did one of my windows get unlocked? My mind drifted back to what seemed like an eternity ago when Evan was walking around in my room. Would he have done that? I locked the window, my head beginning to pound from all the questions. I undressed and headed for the shower.

CHAPTER SEVEN

I overslept the next morning. I didn't dream about the fight, but I did dream about the way Evan's body looked as he stood next to me in just his jeans. I dreamed that I didn't tell him no. I didn't stop him before his mouth tried to meet mine. I told him, in my dream, that I was so very much in love with him. And then all I remember from the dream was his refusal to take me home. The way he looked at me as he buttoned his shirt. The last image I had was of his fist hurling toward the driver's window, but this time smashing through it. I sat straight up in bed, gasping for air.

I glanced at the clock and it was almost ten. I moaned and rubbed my temples as if I could drive the tired cotton clouds out of my muddled brain.

"Hey, sleepy head," Bev said, poking her face into my room. "I heard you rolling around so I figured it was okay to come in."

"Yeah, sure that's fine. I can't believe I slept so late."

She smiled and came into the room and sat on the edge of my bed. I drew up my knees and went to put my arms around them when I winced in pain. That was when I remembered how hard Evan had grabbed my right arm. Thank goodness my pajamas were long sleeved.

"So did you guys have fun?"

"It was alright. The movie was awful, though." I said shaking my head. "We went out to West Beach for a little while afterward." I added it so that she wouldn't, hopefully, continue to ask questions.

"Evan seems like a sweet guy," she grinned. "So do you think this is going to bloom into something serious?"

"Wow, didn't expect that question, Bev," I dodged.

"Well, he is really handsome."

"Yeah," I rolled my eyes. "He is definitely that. But..." I looked down, picking at my fingernails.

"What?"

"What if Mom says to come home? What then?"

"You could work that out, Leese. I'm sure you could still see each other, and..."

"On weekends? I won't be here at school anymore. Senior year will be West Palm Beach—and," I said, suddenly remembering one of the biggest factors. "He'll know I lied about everything—everything other than my first name!"

Bev reached out touching my face lightly, "If he's the right guy for you then that part won't matter." She got off the bed and headed to the door, then turned back.

"I'm going to the grocery store in about fifteen or twenty minutes. You want to come?"

"Sure," I said, rolling out of bed. "Just give me a couple minutes to get dressed."

I closed my doors and peeled off my pajamas, "Oh, crap!" I said a little too loudly.

"You okay?" Bev called from the living room.

"Yeah, I—uh—stepped on my—shoe and twisted my ankle a little, that's all." That was a load of baloney. I had just taken off my top and got a good look at my arm in the daylight. That was scary. It was deep purple and greenish with a yellowed rim—and it was big. I recalled the sound of the guy getting his elbow broken, and I swallowed as it occurred to me that he could have just as easily broken my arm.

I grabbed a pair of shorts and a tank top, then I slipped on a button up the front over-shirt, but left it unbuttoned. I pulled my hair into a pony-tail and put some lip gloss on my chapped lips.

We walked outside into a picture-perfect Florida Saturday morning. I buckled Matt Junior in the back seat beside Kimmy, then climbed into the front. Bev was backing down the driveway when I remembered that Evan's car would be sitting out there in the road. I was trying to come up with a believable excuse for why it should be there, but my mind was a total blank. Bev was cutting her wheels to the right and I was afraid she might back into it.

"Bev, you need to be careful..." but as she backed out I was shocked to see the car was gone.

"Huh?"

"Oh, never mind. I—I thought I saw a car coming."

We went around the grocery store collecting the items from her list and then we finally made it to check out. I had picked up a few things for myself, shampoo, a couple magazines and a vitamin-water. She checked out and then waited patiently for me to pay for my items.

"That will be twenty-three-ninety-five."

I opened my purse and looked where my small wallet should have been. I moved my brush, phone, gum, keys, change purse, lip gloss. "Oh no," I cried out in disbelief.

"What's wrong, Leese? Don't you have your wallet?"

I just stood there looking for what wasn't in my purse. "No, no, no—oh, I'm such an idiot!"

"Leese, it's okay," She said, stepping up to the counter to pay for my items. "You can pay me back when you find it."

"I must have dropped it in Evan's car." I pictured myself in the dark digging for my keys, dumping my purse. "Bev it's got my card inside—*my Visa card*," I said hoping she would understand the hundred thousand dollar problem.

"Oh," she responded, finally catching my drift. "That's okay, just call Evan and tell him to drop it by the house."

What was I going to tell her? Hey, sorry, I can't do that 'cause the guy went crazy on me last night and tried to keep me prisoner. He tried to punch out the window of his car to get me as I was stealing it. I scraped the roof of a car that really doesn't even belong to him on the garage doors at his house during my escape. Getting my Visa might not be so easy.

We loaded the groceries into her car and started the journey home. I was staring out the window, thinking about calling and canceling my card and having another reissued, as we passed a Pensacola police officer. I laughed to myself thinking about Ryan and his near ticket when I suddenly felt sick. My driver's license— my real driver's license was in my wallet. It had my Palm Beach address and the one thing that he was insistent to know, my real name. The last person I wanted to see today was Evan, but I had to get my wallet.

As soon as the groceries were put away, I told Bev I was going to take a ride over to his house. She smiled and told me to have fun. Kimmy begged to come, but I turned her down a little too gruffly and she went crying to her room.

I drove to the beach house. It looked really different in the daylight. It was a beautiful lot, right on the water with swaying palm trees and a manicured lawn. I still had his keys, keys to his car and house, but I didn't have a garage door opener. I rounded the drive and I could see the garage door was up. My heart fluttered in panic, but then I noticed that his car was missing.

I parked not far from the garage and climbed out of my bug. I could see the slight damage to the garage door where black paint was smeared.

Maybe he was home. Perhaps his car had been towed and he was stuck here without a vehicle—I moved closer to my car. "Stop being an idiot, Leese," I muttered. "Just ring the stupid doorbell!" I walked to the front of the house and rang the bell and then moved a few paces away. It was a strange mix of emotions rolling around inside me; I was scared to death, but I was also hungry to see his face. I wished last night had never happened and I wanted desperately to be near him with the assurance that he'd not go weird on me again.

Nothing happened. I rang the doorbell once more. I sighed, "He's probably just out spending your money, Leese—like at the Nissan dealership picking out a replacement."

The house key felt like hot lead in my hand. I could unlock the door and go inside. I could maybe find my wallet. I could go to his bedroom and find out what was in that dresser drawer that he kept fiddling with…

The sound of a vehicle shook me from my thoughts of larceny. I practically ran to my car, just in time for a red, Pontiac Solstice convertible to pull in behind me. The top was down and I could see a tousled head-full of dark brown, wavy hair behind a pair of Maui Jim sunglasses. Sheesh! He *is* out spending my money!

He climbed carefully out of the car, but he didn't appear surprised to see me standing there. His face was lightly bruised, his lip still swollen, and the way he was moving told me his side was hurting. That made last night suddenly real where only moments ago it seemed like some strange nightmare.

"New car already?" I said simply because I couldn't think of anything else.

"Well, when your Porsche wasn't in my driveway this morning, I figured I'd have to get something in the meantime."

I didn't hear even a hint of teasing in his voice and I couldn't come up with a response.

"It's a rental, Leese. My car is in the body shop—roof damage, you know."

My anger flared to life. "Well, if it hadn't been roof damage then it would have been in the shop for a new window!"

"What do you want?"

"I—I dropped my wallet in your car last night—I need it back."

One eyebrow went up behind the sunglasses. "Maybe you didn't drop it in my car."

"Where did you get the money for the rental? And the new sunglasses?" I knew the glasses alone were over three-hundred dollars and who knew how much it would cost to get a sports car as a rental.

He looked mildly annoyed. "I have plenty of money... Did you think I was stealing from you?"

My emotions were getting out of check. I couldn't start crying, I simply wouldn't allow it. I bit my bottom lip—hard. "Were you?"

"I don't need your money," he growled, grabbing my arm as if to put me in my car.

"Aaah," I cried out as the sharp pain shot through my bruised skin. The tears wouldn't stay down. These were a mix of emotional and physical tears. I wasn't sure right at the moment which hurt worse, my arm or the fact that he was angry with me. I turned my face so he wouldn't see.

He let go of my arm immediately, evidently remembering it was the same arm he'd grabbed last night. He rubbed my shoulder warmly as he apologized. "I'm sorry, Leese, I forgot about your arm. Is it that bad?" The question was filled with sincerity, but I couldn't turn to answer him. "Let me see it," he said, trying to slip my over-shirt off my shoulder.

"Just forget it," I snapped, still keeping my face turned away from his. "I just wanted my wallet back. I—I guess I'll just..." My hand was squeezing the door handle to my Bug, but he pushed it back shut with his free hand.

"Let me see your arm."

I stood there obstinately refusing to move. Once again he tried to lower my over-shirt, but this time I didn't resist. I was wondering how much longer I'd be able to resist anything he asked of me. I kept my face turned away as he slid it down past the hideous bruise.

"Oh, Leese—I'm so, so sorry. I never meant to do that." He pulled my over-shirt back up. "I have your wallet, it's in the house. Would you…"

"Don't ask me to come inside," I said stifling a sob. "I may be stupid once, but not twice."

"You aren't stupid, Leese. I've never had to work so hard to…"

That got my attention. Worked so hard to do what? I looked up at him and he took the opportunity to wipe my tears with his thumbs. "How do you feel about me?" I said it on an impulse, like if I hadn't let it out it would have ripped me apart like an alien. It took him completely off guard.

"You are very difficult for me," he paused. "I don't want to like you, but I'm finding that it gets more complicated every time I see you." Then he let a little hint of a smile play with his mouth, "So, turn-about is fair play, how do you feel about me?"

"You are very difficult for me," It was a mimic, but it was the truth. "I don't want to like you," I said, "but I'm finding that it gets more complicated every time I see you."

He nodded. "Good answer."

"What happened last night?"

"Well, let's see; we went to the movies, the beach, a brawl, and we played doctor in my house."

"You know that would be funny, if you didn't do a Jekyll and Hyde after I bandaged you up."

He nodded slowly. "I'm sorry. I was a little too pushy."

"Pushy?" I stated in disbelief, "You were going to *make* me stay here."

"I asked the first time," he corrected.

"Wait a minute, if you ask a girl to spend the night with you and then, when she says no, you decide to keep her anyway, that's okay?" His mouth opened, but I wasn't finished. "If those guys last night had kicked the crap out of you and said, 'Hey baby, wanna stay with us?' and I said no, it would have been okay for them to do whatever they wanted because they asked first?"

I could see the anger boil up under his skin, his neck muscles starting to flex. "No. Of course not. I wasn't going to let those guys get to you last night, and you practically offered yourself by walking right into the fight!"

"I wasn't going to stand by and let them kill you!"

"Why not! I'm nothing to you, just some guy from school you're stringing along."

"You're not just some guy. You're the guy I'm crazy about! You're the guy I think about before I go to sleep, you're there in my dreams, and you're the one I think about when I wake up. I didn't want to come here today, but besides my wallet, I felt like I needed to—no, I take that back—I had to see your face. I had to know you were all right. I was wishing I wasn't so stubborn, because all I could dream about last night was changing my answer when you asked me to stay."

All his temper vanished, and his gaze softened. "You wanted to stay?"

"I still do, but if you're the one, then I want you to be the only one. I've got to know you're always going to be there for me, not just for the night. But none of this can happen, not until I know who you are. You're just about as fake as me." That was when things suddenly became so clear it was like waking up and realizing your whole life was just a dream. "Oh, my God," I blurted, hating myself for bringing God into an exclamation, but it was so shocking—He wasn't Evan Lewis. He *was* a fake just like me. My hand covered my mouth to literally keep myself from saying the word, "Micah."

I could see the expression of bewilderment on his face as he wondered what I'd just concluded.

"I've gotta go." I was clutching my stomach and feeling like I could hurl at any second.

"You're shaking like a leaf," he said, trying to block me once again from getting into my car. "What is it, Leese? Something just changed; I can see it in your face."

"Please..." I wanted to say Evan, but the word just wouldn't come out. I was afraid to say what I just realized. What would he do? I had to know the truth, at least about one thing. If I was wrong, he would think I was out of my mind. But, if I was right, I might never see the light of day again.

"You're not getting ready to pass out on me again, are you?" He asked. "You almost ripped out your handy glue work when I had to keep you from smacking the floor, and I don't think this concrete is any softer."

"My mom was right, wasn't she?" I asked, trying to keep my voice from quivering, but I was trembling so hard my teeth were about to chatter.

He still had the bewildered expression, but then something clicked and his eyes changed.

I had to ask. I had to know. "Did you come here to kill me?"

He just stared. The sunglasses were slowly removed. "You're going to come inside. I think the sun is affecting your brain." He wore only the faintest smile, but the humor was as void as his eyes.

I had hope, for just a moment. Now I knew how Mom must feel when dad looks at her like she's off her rocker, the way I look at her, the way Bev and Matt must think of her. But he still hadn't answered my question. "If I come inside, are you going to kill me?"

His hand reached for my arm automatically, and, as I braced for the pain, he changed and took hold of my left arm. Why? I wondered. It would be so much easier to make me do what he wanted if he'd just grab for the bruise, but he was trying not to hurt me. There was Evan in him somewhere. This was the guy who was falling for me; but the guy I was falling for was tucked away inside a killer. By now his grip had tightened and he had me off balance enough that I had to step toward the house.

"Let go, Evan, Please."

His grip lightened, but he still held on.

"If I'm going back in there with you, then I'll walk in on my own."

"Why don't you fight me?" His voice was almost pleading. "My side is hurting pretty bad, I think you can get away—just like last night—just don't come back this time."

"Will you have to come after me?"

"Yes," he whispered.

"Is my sister part of this, too?"

He reached down cupping my face to make certain I paid attention to his answer, "No—Kimmy was never in danger from me. For some reason, you're the only target."

It was strange to feel such complete relief in knowing the truth, and that I was the only one who was going to die.

"If you didn't do—if you don't do what you're hired to do, what happens?"

His body leaned in front of me against the car, once again he was getting close to me, close enough that I could feel the warmth and smell the cologne. His face was serene, but his eyes were filled with anguish and indecision.

"Tell me," I asked, and then did something I had never done. I slowly reached my trembling hand out to rest gently against his side, just below the bandage. I watched as he braced himself, thinking it was my ploy to get away. He was waiting for me to hit him, but I couldn't. I just wanted to touch him and know he was still real and this wasn't all just some dream that had gone terribly wrong.

"Someone else will take my place and you'll be dead." His voice was almost mournful.

"And you? Do they let you just walk away from a—a job?" Those words sounded so cold and calculated. It wasn't murder for some people; it was simply a job.

"No—I took the down payment."

"So do you just give the money back? They'll let you do that, right?"

I could see he wanted to tell me the truth, but he stubbornly refused to open is mouth.

"They'll kill you, too, won't they?" I didn't know who 'they' were, but I could see the answer in his eyes.

I took a step back from him as he turned loose of my arm. He was giving me a chance to run, but I stepped around him and walked to his front door.

"Leese, what are you doing?"

I ignored him. I pushed the key into the lock and walked inside. He was following me, telling me to get out and leave. I kept my pace steady as I headed for his bedroom. I knew what was in that dresser now. I pulled open the drawer that he'd been in last night. This was real and I couldn't believe it. Lying there in an open case was a large, dark handgun.

I only knew a little about guns, but I could plainly see that the clip was in the handle and I was certain it was loaded. I lifted it out, careful to keep my fingers away from the trigger, and turned around. I expected that he would be standing right there waiting to snatch it from my hands, but he wasn't. He was standing in the doorway, arms braced against each side of the door frame, his face pained and pale, and he was perfectly still. He was giving me the best shot possible.

I walked toward him, the gun butt clenched in both my hands but pointed to the floor. When I was no more than five feet from him, he told me to stop.

"You can't miss from there—and if you get any closer, I *will* take it away from you."

I hadn't realized until that moment that the tears were spilling down my cheeks. I walked right up to him and turned the gun sideways and put it against his chest. "Take it," I choked. "You'll make sure it doesn't hurt, right?"

His eyes were wide with disbelief, but his hand was trained to go for the gun.

The next thing I knew, I was against the bedroom wall. He had me by the throat and the gun was at my temple. I kept my eyes shut. I didn't want my last memory of him to be the look on his face when he pulled the trigger.

"What the hell is wrong with you?!" He snarled, his grip getting tighter on my throat. "Don't you realize that this is what I do? I don't get involved—I don't fall in love—I don't care if someone lives or dies—I do what I'm paid to do! Why didn't you just shoot me and end this?"

I swallowed, but it was difficult with his hand so tight on my throat. My eyes opened, they felt like they were about to bulge out of my head. I couldn't take much more of this. I would simply pass out and never know what happened. Then his grip relaxed and I could get some air.

"Tell me why you didn't shoot me?" But this time it sounded like a plea.

"If you let me go, someone else will step in. Maybe that person won't care if Kimmy, or Bev or Matt or Matt Junior is in the way—maybe it's better this way," I said, trying to keep my quivering lips from pulling down at the corners. "And, I don't want someone to kill *you* because of *me*." I'd never seen a more confused look on someone's face in my life, and then he seemed to snap out of it.

"I have to kill you," he stated, using the full press of his body to hold me to the wall, "But—I have to have you first, Leese."

His mouth was moving toward mine, but my face turned away. "You're going to have to shoot me," I replied, a certain amount of bravado still clinging to my moral fiber. "The only man that is going to have me will be the one who loves me." My fingers were formed into claws, and I pressed them to his bandaged side to let him know the fight was getting ready to happen.

"What does it matter? You're ready to die and you said you wanted to say yes last night, say yes now. Tell me you want me," he breathed the words against my neck.

"Last night, I was hoping it was love. Not this way—if you're looking for a rape victim, you've found the wrong girl."

The word rape must have taken the fire completely out of him. He didn't want to force me into anything, and he was apparently having trouble coming to grips with the fact that I'd give him permission to kill me, but not to violate my body. He knew he couldn't make me do it by threatening to kill me—I'd already agreed to that—but it seemed he desperately wanted me to need him enough to willingly give him the living part of myself, not just to offer my death.

"Will you tell me something?" I asked as the gun returned to my temple and the void returned to his eyes. "Who paid you? Who wants me dead? And why this way? Why didn't you just find me that first day and walk up to me and shoot me?"

He released me slowly and lowered the gun. "This business isn't always about knowing who's flipping the bill. Matter of fact, it's rare to know who is really behind the money when it's a complicated hit."

"Why was I complicated?"

"You really want to do this, don't you? You want to discuss how you're supposed to die?"

I could only nod.

He took a deep breath and turned his back to me. He went to the dresser and put the gun away, "I was given six weeks to get this job done. I guess it won't hurt to talk to you about it."

"Six weeks?" I said in disbelief. What kind of mental case would need someone to get so close to me? Did they want me to fall in love and then have that person murder me? I knew if I had spent another five weeks with Evan, I would be so deeply in love—and no matter what he said about his job or the fact that his heart was supposed to be untouchable, I knew he would have fallen.

"Let's go out by the pool and have a drink," he said, sounding like a good host—at the Bate's motel.

We sat on the patio, the waves lapping at the shoreline and the sun sparkling off the pool. It would have been perfect under other circumstances. He brought out a tray with coke, glasses of ice and a bottle of rum. The rum was something I didn't expect. He set it down, getting ready to uncap it; I was suddenly so scared.

"Please—please no alcohol."

He shrugged his shoulders, uncapped the bottle and moved to his glass.

"For either one of us," I pleaded.

He looked up at me, his hand frozen in place. "I'm not eighteen, Leese."

"I don't care, please, please don't."

"You aren't afraid when I hold a gun to your head, but you're terrified if we drink?"

"Drinking makes people do things they never intended to do. If you're going to put a bullet in me, you'll have to do it sober."

"Well, then, maybe you should drink," his hand shifting the bottle to my glass.

"No, I might try to kill you—and you'd let me." I looked back into that handsome face. "I'd never forgive myself."

He put the cap back on and set the bottle down on the pool deck. "You are the strangest woman I've ever met." Then he opened a coke and poured it into our glasses.

"So tell me why so long? Why didn't they just pay you to get it over with?"

He laughed and leaned back against his chair.

"What's so funny?"

"I've never had to explain my job to my victim—it's ludicrous."

"So I'm weird, but you've figured that out."

He took a sip of his coke and began, "My job was to get you to go out with me, for people to see us together. I was supposed to get you to like me enough, that when you vanished, everyone would believe that you ran away with me."

"Why?"

"I don't know. It was supposed to cause a reaction somewhere. It would have been in the papers. I'm sure the story about what you were doing in Pensacola in the first place would have been all over the news. But," he said, setting down the glass and looking at me. "After a week or two, whenever they told me, your body was supposed to turn up. Evan Lewis would have been the guy with the blame, but he no longer exists."

"You didn't..." I swallowed, "You didn't kill the real Evan Lewis, did you?"

"No. He was a high school drop-out from Dawson High School in Georgia. His family moved to Lincoln, Nebraska and he was killed in a car accident a few weeks later."

"How did you take his identity? I mean, it can't be something simple to assume."

"You really are determined to learn all about me, aren't you?" he mused.

"Weird, remember?"

"My whole family is involved in the criminal 'underworld'," he said, making quotation marks in the air. "My mother is a master at forgery, records, and documents. Whatever is out there, she can find it, copy it, alter it; she's extremely good at what she does, an artist actually. She put the records together for me to register as Evan Lewis, and she made sure that the school still thought they were viable."

I didn't understand; evidently he saw that.

"She made sure Dawson wouldn't refuse a records transfer because they had knowledge that he was dead. Then she made some changes so that no trail would connect me to the real owner of this identity. I'm him; at least until I do something stupid like kill a girl from Pensacola high school."

"So you're Evan Lewis while I'm still alive?"

"Yeah, except for my car which I'm assuming you read the registration. I have two, the fake one is in my wallet, but I'd forgotten about the other one until this morning. That was a stupid mistake and I don't usually make mistakes."

"Really?" Now it was my turn to laugh a little.

"What?"

"You've evidently been shot twice and cut more than once. Don't they count as mistakes?"

"No, just occupational hazards. The guy who shot my shoulder for example was the body guard for my target. He never left the guy's side and it was supposed to be a close range shot, so I had to deal with him after I made my target."

"You talk like a target isn't something human." I couldn't keep the sadness out of my voice—I was his target.

"It's not, not for me anyway. My dad taught me my trade when I was fourteen. He was waiting to see if I could be completely detached, just like he and my brother. That's why we get the big money—we don't get involved, we just get the job done."

"But I was different," I whispered.

"Yeah. You're my first civilian."

"Civilian? You mean you do this in other countries?"

"No," he gave a bitter laugh and tried to explain, "In my business we call a civilian someone that isn't part of, or involved in, a crime or a crime family. You're an innocent," he sighed catching my sight. "Like someone being bumped for insurance money. My family doesn't usually do that. Even we consider that dirty money, but they needed someone that was professional and could pass for your age."

"How much am I worth to you?"

"You *were* worth two-hundred and fifty thousand until this morning."

"Were? What changed?"

He reached into the pocket of his jeans and produced my wallet; he'd had it on him the whole time.

"I only had your fake last name. I think that was one reason I couldn't take my chances and simply kill you, I didn't know who you really were—Miss. Winslett. You weren't kidding about being rich." He placed my wallet on the table and I picked it up as he continued. "I called my contact this morning and told them the price was going up to a million."

I held my wallet and stared at it. "Does more money make it easier for you?"

He got up, still holding his coke and walked to the edge of the pool. "Not this time," he faintly replied.

An idea was taking shape inside me. I had no clue if he'd even consider it, but I had to try. I had to know who was behind the plan to get me killed.

"We still have five weeks," I said, following him to where his back was turned to me. "I want to hire you."

He turned around, eyes wide open. "You want me to kill someone?"

"No, and if I had my way, you'd never kill another soul, but I want you to help me figure out who is behind the money. I've got to know who is doing this and why."

"I'm no detective, Leese," he started to rebut.

"Yeah and you're no idiot either. You have connections. You know how this all works. I know you can do this for me."

"What are you offering in trade?"

I didn't like the way he was looking at me and if he wasn't a killer with a gun in the other room, I'd have slapped his face. I opened my wallet and pulled out my Visa. "Did you check my balance?"

"Ninety-eight-thousand-four-hundred-something."

"That sounds about right." I was trying not to act surprised that he had actually checked what was on the card. "If I throw in the title to my Porsche, that's almost a quarter million—the original going price for my life—but I want my five weeks."

"And at the end of the five weeks?" he questioned.

"Do what you have to," I stated firmly. "I just want whoever is doing this to my family stopped."

That tiny grin that liked to play with the edges of his mouth was starting to form, "We'll have to make it look like everything is going as planned. They could be watching me and I don't want this botched."

"You mean I have to look like I'm falling for you?"

He wrapped his arm around my shoulder and pulled me close, kissing my forehead. "You've got to be my girl—just like you're falling."

"On one condition." Although I knew I wasn't in a very good position to make demands. But, I wrapped my arm around his waist to see if this would work. "You don't go crazy on me like last night or in the bedroom. You'll be a perfect gentleman."

"You're going to make this job tough on me aren't you?"

"I hope so," I said, resting my face against his chest. "Hard enough to change your mind."

"Don't plan for it," he chided me.

I tipped my face up and, to his surprise, kissed his cheek. "I'll see you tomorrow."

"Tomorrow?" he questioned with clear curiosity.

"Yes. Be at my house by nine-fifteen. We have church."

"I don't think…"

"My *boyfriend* would go with me," I reminded him. "And besides, I don't think you'll burst into flames or anything like that."

"I don't know," he quipped, "Tomorrow is supposed to be stormy and lightening is a distinct possibility. But I'll be at your house at six tonight."

"For what?"

"Dinner. My *girlfriend* would go out with me on Saturday night—some place nice."

I smiled. "Fine, I'll see you tonight. Just remember your promise."

He sighed and turned me loose.

I needed to go home. I had a lot of work to do before my 'date' tonight.

I got home around one o'clock. I had to get on the computer and print out some things I wanted him to go over. I had determined that he was going to remain Evan in my book. Besides, he wouldn't go back to being himself until I was dead, and then it wouldn't matter to me anyway. There were newspaper articles about my grandfather's death, names and information about our family and some friends. And of course, there was the matter of family history on both sides.

It was almost three p.m. when I finished. Just in time. Kimmy and I called home, every Saturday at three. It was a chance to talk with our parents, catch up on what was going on in Palm Beach and listen to Mom's latest suspicions about what was happening. I really owed her an apology, but I didn't want to give her more to worry about. If I was lucky, Evan would discover what was going on, and I'd expose it to the police before anyone else in my family was hurt.

I tried the house phone, but there was no answer. That wasn't unusual. They could have been out at the pool or out for lunch. Maybe Mom even felt good enough to go out shopping. I tried her cell, but it went to voicemail after a few rings. Next was Dad's. It rang once and he picked up.

"Hey Dad," I said, relieved to have someone answer. "Where's Mom? I tried her cell phone."

"She's right here, Leese, but she isn't feeling so good right now; she's lying down."

"Oh, I don't want to wake her if she's sleeping..."

"No, she's not asleep, yet, but she's kind of groggy. She didn't get too much sleep last night. You know how that is. She heard a hundred sounds in the night and stayed up until almost dawn, so she took a sleeping pill."

I didn't like the idea of Mom taking pills. She was one of those people who wouldn't take an aspirin for a headache, much less a sleeping pill. I heard her in the background asking if it was me on the phone. She sounded far away and woozy. And then I could hear the sound of the phone being passed to her.

"Hey, Honey," she slurred. "How are my girls?"

"We're okay, Mom. What happened? You didn't get any sleep last night?"

"Leese, becareful..." she ran it together. "...make sure your doors and windows are locked."

That sent a chill down my spine as I remember the unlocked window in my room. Could someone be doing the same thing to Mom, going around and unlocking things just to freak her out? "I do, Mom. I check every night before I go to bed. Kimmy wants to say hi, hold on?"

Kimmy was jumping up and down, anxious to have her turn. She got a funny look on her face though when she finally got on the phone. She wanted to know if Mom was okay because her voice was different. Eventually Dad got on the line and she talked with him for about ten minutes telling him all about her week at school. And then I heard her say something I didn't expect,

"...and Leese's got a *boyfriend!*"

"Kimmy!" I scolded, "I was supposed to get to tell that if *I* wanted to."

She stuck her tongue out at me and continued her conversation. She was telling Dad all about Evan; he was big and strong and handsome and he has a cool car, but that I wouldn't let her ride in it (the tongue stuck out at me again). She finally said her goodbyes and returned the phone to me.

Well, that should be a fun act to follow. I took a deep breath and put it to my ear. "Hey,"

"So you have a boyfriend, huh?" he asked with a chuckle.

"He's just a friend from school who happens to be male, that's all."

"Yeah, I know how those things end up. First he's a friend, and then a boyfriend, and then it's 'Daddy, I want a big wedding, please,'" he laughed.

"Let's not start planning my wedding right now. I think I'm still warming up to the boyfriend idea."

"Have fun, Leese. You're only young for a little while."

I held in a bitter laugh; that thought was too literal.

"Tell Mom that we both love her when she wakes up. Maybe you guys should go for a short vacation to a hotel or something so she can get some rest at night."

"She'd never go for that," he said honestly.

"Yeah, I know. Bye, Dad. Love you."

And the call ended.

A few minutes before six p.m, the red Pontiac pulled into the drive. Matt was a little surprised as he looked out the window.

"Wasn't his car black the last time he was here?"

"This one's a rental. He got a scratch on the Z last night so it's in the shop."

"Gee, that must be nice. I wonder what kind of insurance company he has?"

He had said we were going someplace nice tonight and I figured it wouldn't hurt for me to look wonderful. But I had to be careful that the balance was 'wow, she's beautiful,' but not quite 'wow, she's sexy.' I didn't want to end up having to punch him in the side and ruin our deal.

I wore my black mini skirt, with a snug black spaghetti string tank and my light weight black Roxy jacket—besides being a little cool tonight, I needed something to cover my arm. I finished it off with black high heels. I wore a little more make up than usual and used my red lip gloss to give me a punch of color. My long hair was loose, but I brought a couple pony-tail holders in case he had the top down. The only jewelry I wore was my simple silver stud earrings and my silver cross necklace. I was a little worried at first I might have this whole, 'going to my own funeral' kind of look, but when I checked the mirror, I just looked very polished (even if it was a low-budget outfit). I slipped my iPod into my pocket, grabbed my purse and headed out the door.

The reaction I got from him was very good. The mouth was slightly open and then he remembered his manners and ran around to the other side of the car to let me in. I thought about asking if I could drive, but I looked down and saw the car was an automatic. I settled comfortably into the plush seat and figured I might as well relax. I had five weeks left and I was going to enjoy them.

He wore black tailored dress slacks and a white button up the front dress shirt. He wasn't going to go so far as a tie, and I liked it better anyway because he left the top two buttons undone. Tonight he definitely didn't look his fake age.

He didn't say anything as we backed out and headed down toward the waterfront. I noticed his car had an iPod hookup, which I had been hoping it did, so I took mine out of my pocket and plugged it in. Jeremy Camp's, *Lay Down My Pride* filled the air. He was frowning at the lyrics, but I didn't care. It had been one of my favorite songs before I met him. I couldn't help it now if some of the words had become a little bit prophetic. The next song was another Jeremy Camp, *Take my Life*, and it was part way through as we pulled into Skopelos. He appeared relieved to have it turned off.

"Did you pick that music out especially for tonight?" he asked as he placed his hand on my lower back and guided me into the restaurant.

"No, I had it on random play. But, if you want to be honest, all my favorites might make you uncomfortable."

"Lewis," he said to the maitre d as we approached.

"Right this way, Mr. Lewis." She took us to a table outside on the patio. There was a light breeze blowing and the sun would be setting in an hour. She took our drink order and left us alone.

"So why would I *not* like most of your music?" he continued, leaning back in his chair.

"Well, I guess because most of my music is about surrender, change, sacrifice and love. You know the heartfelt stuff that would make a hitman puke," I added with a smile. "It really bothers you, doesn't it? I mean like the song I sang, *Perfect People*, that got to you, and don't say it didn't. I was there. I saw your eyes."

"I just have different taste that's all. And, if it pleases you in some sadistic way, yeah, you threw a couple darts when you sang it."

"It does please me," I admitted.

The waitress was back with our drinks and asked if we'd like an appetizer. Evan suggested the bacon wrapped scallops, and I said that was one of my favorites so it was fine with me. As soon as she walked away, I could see he was dying to ask, "Why?"

"If I can hit you with a consciousness dart then that heart of yours isn't as off limits as you think." I lifted my drink as if in toast. "Here's to darts."

"Annalisa," he said, refusing to lift his glass. "Don't go through these next weeks thinking you're playing a game with someone who can change."

"Everyone can change, Evan, but that's not why I hired you." I opened my purse and pulled out the folded papers that I had run off from the computer. You have work to do for me and time is of the essence, right?"

He gave me an annoyed breath, as he took the papers from my hand. He didn't say anything, but I could see his brow furrow as he read the article about my grandfather.

"My mom suspected, not long after he died that it wasn't suicide. There were too many things in his life that brought him pleasure to just throw it all away."

"It says that your grandmother died of cancer the previous year. That certainly sounds like a reason for depression."

"He loved her and he was crushed, but he was back on the road to recovery. He had been on a couple dates just the month before they found him in the garage. He had a small amount of barbiturates in his system when they did the toxicology reports—he didn't take any medications and there weren't any in the house."

"Leese, if he was planning on ending his life, he might have purchased just a few. It doesn't mean he had to have a bottleful."

"But why take it before getting into his truck and turning the engine on? The exhaust alone would have knocked him out, right?"

"Not necessarily. Maybe he was afraid that he'd get sick from the carbon monoxide and give up before finishing the job."

"He wasn't that kind of man. He had almost a billion dollars in banks all over the United States. He was making business deals up to the day before he died. Why make deals if you're planning to die." Wow. I hadn't realized how deep that statement was until I had uttered it.

He gave me an odd look from across the table.

The waitress returned with our appetizer, took our orders and then left us alone once again. The sky was starting to cloud up to the south, and I found myself hoping it wouldn't fill before we got to see the sunset.

"Can you find out if someone was paid to get rid of him? I know it was two years ago, but I would think, in your circles, taking out a billionaire would be…"

"Like taking you out," he finished.

I frowned, "No, that's not what I meant. But don't they like have some kind of hall of fame for whoever bags the person worth the most bucks?" I was being an ass at this point, but I didn't like the comparison he made when he mentioned me.

He ignored my remark, "Who is going to benefit the most by getting rid of you?" he asked. "Do you have a will?"

"No, I'm like my mom in that regard; I think it's morbid."

"Wait a minute. Do you mean to tell me your mother has no will? This says she was your grandfather's only child. People with that much money have wills."

I gave a half-laugh, "Grandpa had a will, but my mom is only thirty-five…"

"Age has nothing to do with it. She's worth a fortune if he left everything to her."

"She and I," I corrected, but he looked confused by the way I stated it. "He left everything to her, and I'm the alternate or whatever they call the person second in line."

"What about Kimmy and your dad?"

"Kimmy was only four when grandpa died. His will was made a year before she was born and he evidently never changed it. Mom and I were the sole benefactors."

"How does your dad fit into this?"

"Robert is my step-dad—don't give me that face, he's like a real dad to me."

He flipped through the paperwork and looked at what I had concerning Robert's family.

"You'll notice," I said as I watched him read, "He comes from a wealthy family, too. Maybe not as wealthy as Mom's, but they had millions."

"I'll look these over tonight and do some research." He tucked them into his pocket as the main course arrived.

"So what now?" I asked. "I don't know what to say to you now that my premonitions about you were right."

That got an odd look. "Premonitions?"

"I had a very distinct feeling that you were trying hard to get me alone with you."

"Leese, do you ever really look in the mirror? What guy wouldn't want to be alone with you?"

I enjoyed the compliment, but yet it was hollow. "Isn't there more than a guy just wanting to sack a girl?"

He smiled, "Men are shallow."

"Be honest with me about something, really honest."

"I'll try," he said cautiously.

"Haven't you ever, I mean in your entire life, felt like you could love someone?"

He appeared to be struggling with what he wanted to say, but finally resigned himself to a simple, "No."

"How about you? Other than the fact that you've never been kissed, hasn't there been someone that made you want to abandon your morals?"

Wow! This was going to be a hard one to get through. "You know I put on mascara tonight, right? That question for me is pretty emotional."

He handed me his dinner napkin, "Tell me about him."

This big lump rose up in my throat and just sat there blocking any intelligible sounds. I dabbed my eyes a couple times and looked down at the dinner that had been appetizing only seconds earlier. "I can't eat if you're going to make me do this."

"All right, dinner first, you pick the topic of discussion."

"Tell me about yourself and your family," I blurted. "And don't give me that line about 'if I told you, I'd have to kill you' because we both know I'm already there."

I spent the rest of the evening learning what he would permit me to know about his family. They were from New Orleans. That much had been true to form from his school persona. He was of a French/Italian descent. He was fluent in the French language (which I already knew) and Italian (which I didn't know) and had an older sister and brother. What was a surprise was that his sister was a police chief somewhere in Louisiana. I thought there was some glimmer of hope for his family to have at least one redeeming member, but he told me no.

"Working with the police is the death knell for a mobster, but it is actually a pretty honored position to be a ranking officer who is in the family. She's the person that keeps up with potential problems before they occur and keeps us one step ahead of prison."

With dinner finished, we watched the sunset and then took a short walk on the beach.

"You know for someone who has never fallen for anyone, you certainly know how to set the mood," I laughed lightly as he closed the car door behind me.

He walked around and sat down. "Top down for a little while?"

"It's only like seven or eight minutes to Matt and Bev's. It almost isn't worth it for such a short drive."

He reached in his pocket and pulled out a tissue and gave it to me.

"Where did you get this and why are you handing it to me?"

"I grabbed it from the hostess station on the way out of the restaurant. I'll drive until you can finish answering my question."

I was momentarily blank and then I remembered what he'd said he wanted to know. "It doesn't matter anyway—nothing is going to matter in a few weeks." I couldn't look at him anymore.

"All I want is for you to tell me about him."

"This is stupid," I remarked, using his stolen tissue.

"I'm curious, that's all."

"You really want to know?" How about a picture, too?" I stated, opening my purse.

He was somber, but he nodded.

I reached into the side compartment and pulled out the small two-by-three and handed it to him. I watched the expression on his face as he turned it over and stared.

"It's you, you idiot." I said softly, reaching with trembling fingers to take back my mirror.

"You'd have to be crazy," he replied, still holding on to my hand. "Don't you understand what kind of person I am?"

"I know who you've sold yourself to be, but I don't believe it. And you're right. I'm starting to think I'm more wacked right now than my mom, but I can't help how I feel."

"Then why do you want me to follow the gentleman act? Let me at least kiss you, Leese." He leaned across the seat, "Don't you want me to kiss you?"

"Kiss me just before the end, so I won't care what's about to happen."

"You don't mean that," he said in disbelief.

"I've thought about it ever since I figured this whole thing out earlier today and, if you give such stupid things as last requests, that's what I want."

He slumped back into the driver's seat and just sat there staring at the dashboard. Finally, his hand reached over and turned the key. Without another word he took me home.

As I turned to get out of the car, I reminded him to be back at nine-fifteen in the morning. He never said yes or no or anything for that matter. He just waited for me to shut the door and then he nodded once and backed out.

CHAPTER EIGHT

The next morning was, as the weatherman predicted, overcast and stormy. Bev and Matt were not ready by the time Evan arrived, but they urged me to go ahead and they would meet us there later. I found it extremely funny that the lightening began popping just before we got to church. He gave me a nervous look as we opened the car doors and ran for cover.

We stopped under the church overhang and the sky opened up and the rain began pouring down. "Wow, that was close," I remarked.

"The rain or the lightening?" He still looked worried.

"You survived this last Wednesday. I think you can make it through today. Just remember three things if you *should* burst into flames."

"What?" He asked impatiently, holding the door open for me to the main foyer.

"Stop, drop, and roll," I laughed.

"Amusing, Leese, very amusing." But he wasn't smiling.

My Sunday morning youth group was tiny compared to Wednesday nights. There were only about a dozen or so teens. I honestly think Evan would have been more comfortable had it been a large group so he could manage that feeling of getting lost in the crowd. Pastor Shawn seemed glad that I had returned with my visitor from Wednesday night, but I got that same feeling from him that I did from Matt; he thought Evan was a little older than the others.

One of the guys that played in the mid-week band had brought his acoustical guitar and Shawn asked me if I'd start us off with a song.

"Tell me what you can play, I can probably sing it."

He looked up at me through a mop of disarrayed dirty-blonde hair and smiled, "I just learned all the cords and riffs for *Cry out to Jesus*. Do you know the words?"

"Sure," I smiled. I wondered how Evan's conscious was going to handle the lyrics. I couldn't help the fact that something inside him was waking up through music. I'm sure it was an uncomfortable feeling with everything he had done in his life, but I felt like the pain was a good sign that the guy I liked was in there somewhere.

Surprisingly, he smiled as I sang. He was leaning forward in his chair, his forearms resting on his knees and his hands clasped. I guess that was what made him so good at what he did; no one would suspect what was underneath the pretense.

When the song ended, I took my place next to him and waited for Shawn to begin his lesson on the conversion of Saul to Paul. Every sentence was another dart. I gripped the inside of my lower lip with my teeth to restrain the smile.

We met up with Matt and Bev on the walk from Sunday school to the main sanctuary. We sat a few rows back to the left of the podium.

Bev, grinning, leaned over and looked at us, "You two look so cute together."

He looked over at me and gave me a quick, double-rise of the eyebrows and then leaned back and put his arm around my shoulders. I should have felt like the little pig that was invited to dinner by the big bad wolf, especially since he told me this was the image he was paid to create, but I was too comfortable to care. And then the pastor asked the congregation to stand and open the hymnals—a look of shear panic crossed Evan's face.

"You said I didn't have to sing!" he fiercely whispered in my ear.

"That was Wednesday. Everybody sings on Sunday morning." The way he looked at me made me really glad that he didn't carry his gun on him.

The song was *I'll Fly Away*, and I didn't expect that he would actually sing, but after the first chorus, I could hear a soft rumble beside me. Although I loved the song, I lowered my volume and listened carefully; he actually had a wonderful voice. I could feel myself flushing with color as his sexy base became clearer. We sat down and I looked at him with a purposeful open mouth and then had to fan myself to cool off. He was stone faced.

He was either actually listening to the sermon or he was very good at being immobile for an extended period of time. After church, he asked me to go with him for lunch and I agreed. This whole business of being alone and close with him had gone from frightening to something I craved. I wasn't going to change my mind regarding my virtue, but I simply had a need to be with him. Maybe the old saying about keeping your friends close and your enemies closer came about because your enemies could sometimes be more interesting.

The rain was long over with and the sun was trying to peek out from the straggly gray clouds so I wasn't surprised when we got in the car and he pressed the button for the top to come down.

Kimmy hadn't realized the car was a convertible and I heard her cry out when she saw it, "I want to go with them!"

He looked at me and asked if I would mind letting her come along.

I didn't have to debate the question whether it was safe or not, I was certain that there was no danger posed to her by him. Bev and Matt agreed to let her come with us and she happily climbed into the back seat and buckled up.

"All right, Kimmy, do you have a favorite place to eat?"

"Of course I do," she answered smugly. "Chuck E. Cheese."

He looked at me strangely, "What's a Chucky Cheese?"

"You've never dined at the famous Chuck E. Cheese? Wow, you haven't lived." I heard Kimmy burst out giggling. "Head up one-ten to I-ten and I'll show you where it's at. You're really in for a treat; I hoped we've dressed up enough." By this point Kimmy's giggles had turned to shrieks of laughter.

He glanced at me as we pulled out on to the street, "She certainly seems excited."

"Oh, you haven't seen anything yet."

We pulled into a packed lot at Chuck E. Cheese and headed inside. As soon as the doors opened and the sounds of hordes of overly excited children reached his ears, he looked at me and scowled.

I shrugged my shoulders, "You never ask a six-year-old where they want to go eat."

"I'll remember that," he said, his level of discomfort rising.

We found a booth in the back corner and he placed the order for pizza and then seated himself across from Kimmy and me.

"Leese, can I get some tokens and play before we eat?"

"Yeah sure," I said opening my purse and then realizing I didn't have any money. Before I could tell her that I couldn't buy her tokens, Evan had my wallet pressed into my hand.

"You dropped that in my car," he smoothly inserted.

"Oh—I—I wondered where that went." I lied.

With Kimmy happily occupied by a big cup of tokens, I returned to the table and tried to hand it back to him.

"No, you keep it. I'm guessing you don't carry cash."

"I don't, but I owe you."

"Not now. And besides, you've had that card I imagine about seven months and you haven't gone on any obvious spending binges."

I put the card into my wallet and sat back down. "Did you find anything out last night?"

"Some, but I'm waiting on more information, and I didn't think you'd want to discuss this with Kimmy around."

I waved my palms into the obviously empty space beside me, "She won't be back until I go get her, and with all the noise in here no one is going to hear anything you say; matter of fact I'll be lucky if I can hear what you say."

He must have taken that line as an invitation. He smiled and switched sides, slipping in beside me and placing his arm around me.

"The people here don't know us," I reminded him.

"That's okay," he said, squeezing me a little tighter. "I did find out some things about your step-dad." The smile faded from his face, replaced with seriousness. "Has he mentioned anything about the fact that his business and fortune have been dwindling for the last three years?"

This was a complete surprise. Robert never indicated that he had any money problems. I knew if he had, Mom would have quickly volunteered funds to help him out, but I also knew that Robert was an intensely independent and somewhat narcissistic person.

"Never," I shook my head. "He doesn't discuss his business." I felt the need to give a little clarification on our relationship. "Robert has always treated me just like I was his own. Mom was seventeen when she made a bad judgment and nine months later I was born and the man she'd fallen for was nowhere to be found."

"That explains a lot," he said quietly.

I rolled my eyes, "My decisions are my own and I'm not going to let someone else make them for me. Anyway," I sighed. "Robert came on the scene about a year later, and within two years they were married. He's been the only father I've ever known."

"Well, Robert has lost millions in the stock market and his father's boat business is heading for bankruptcy. He has been relying heavily on his business partners, but I don't know if he'll be able to pull away from this with anything left in his or their pockets. Did he and your mother have a pre-nup?"

"I don't know. They never mentioned it, but why would they?"

"I've got my—an associate, pulling records. Rich people try their hardest to hide their personal information, but she is the best in the business."

"It's okay, you can say it's your mother."

"Not in this business. You keep everyone anonymous."

"I hate the way you call it a business." I was simply being truthful.

"That's what it is, Leese—unfortunately, it's a *big* business."

"So will you be reporting my one and a quarter million dollar pay off on your income taxes?"

"You'd be surprised at what the government looks the other way on as long as you pay the taxes. That's my dad's specialty. He used to do hits, until he discovered he was better at creatively paying the government. Now he has a thriving business doing that for others."

"So you think that Robert might be the person who wants me killed?"

He nodded slowly.

"It doesn't make sense. What does he benefit by killing me? Mom has the control of the money. If I'm dead she still has control. If she's dead, I have control. He's not in the picture—unless he's going to kill us both—but he's got to know that would be too suspicious and he'd get caught."

"I have a theory, but I'm going to wait until I get copies of your grandfather's will, any pre-nup that can be found, and any will your mother might have that you don't know about. I'm also waiting for some information on his business partners."

"And you said you weren't a detective," I teased.

"I'll admit you were right that this is exactly in my line of work so it really isn't too difficult."

"See, you could get a real job…"

"What I do is a real job, just not a legal one."

"You'd at least sleep better at night," I huffed.

He took a breath and then a sip of his drink, "I sleep just fine."

"Will you be sleeping fine in five weeks? Never mind," I added quickly, "Please, don't answer that."

The waitress delivered our pizza to the table and vanished. He just kept looking at me, evidently contemplating a response. I gave him a gentle nudge, "I've got to go get Kimmy."

After we had our pizza, I challenged him to a game of skeeball and then promptly kicked his butt. I was interested in what his attitude would be, but he ended up showing me he could be a gracious loser.

Once back at Matt and Bev's, I wanted to find some reason to continue our time together, but school was in the morning. Kimmy ran into the house as we said our goodbyes.

"You will be at school tomorrow, right?" Suddenly I had some irrational fear that since I knew what he was, the cover of school might not be needed.

He reached out and touched my cheek lightly. "Of course I will. Can't say that I'm enjoying repeating high school, but…"

"Yeah, I know, it's your job."

"No, I was going to say it's bearable with you there. The other girls are—well, they act their age. You on the other hand are mature like no one I've ever met."

"You know that's a question that I haven't asked you; how old are you, really?"

"Do you want to try to guess?" he smirked.

I was afraid to try, afraid to actually know, but I was the one who asked. "I'd rather not."

"Twenty-three." The smirk became a mild smile. He put the car in reverse and pulled out.

CHAPTER NINE

Monday morning found me sitting in the school parking lot trying to understand how I could be going through normal functions knowing that my life had been turned completely upside down only days prior. I listened to my music, trying to gleam some hope for my situation.

Jewels pulled in after me, rapping away to music too loud with a huge smile on her face. Once again, she was trying to get me to come over and sit with her. I put my fingers to my ears and made a face as if I were in pain. She rolled her eyes and turned down the volume. I gave her the thumbs up signal and opened my car door. She reached over and pushed her passenger's door open, but before either of us could speak, the sound of tires screeching at the far end of the parking lot could be heard. I looked up and could see Ryan's Trans Am racing against a red Pontiac convertible.

"Idiot boys!" I snapped.

Jewels opened her door and stood on the car's frame to get a better view. When she saw Ryan's car she began to scream and cheer for him to win against his opponent. Without his little Z, Evan had lost the advantage of a faster engine, a manual transmission, and a lighter weight. Now the race was equalized. All I could think was that both of them were flying at break-neck speed and were either going to wreck or, if seen by administration, officer Martin would have a field day writing tickets.

It was too close to call as they both braked for the turn to take them to where Jewels and I were watching wide-eyed. Ryan had the inside lane and took the advantage to cut Evan off as he made the turn. Ryan's bumper missed Evan's front fender by inches. They pulled into the parking spaces on either side of us. It was only then that Jewels realized who was driving the convertible.

"Ah! Where did you get this?"

Her excitement seemed to steal Ryan's victory thunder as she ran to Evan's passenger's door and opened it to get a better view of the interior.

As Jewels babbled on about how cool the car was, Ryan decided to reclaim his bragging rights by draping his arms around me. "Leese!" he said far too loudly for the tiny distance to my ear. "How's my ninja girl?"

"Get off me, Ryan." I was trying to make sure he didn't grab my still very bruised arm hidden under my over-shirt.

Jewels paid no mind to Ryan, but Evan was out of the car and standing next to us in an instant. Just as I was slipping from Ryan's grasp, Evan's arm wrapped firmly around me and pulled me to his side. I was hoping that I wouldn't turn into the object of a macho tug-of-war.

Jewels finally turned her attention toward us and asked again, "Where did you get the car, Evan?"

"It's a rental," he finally answered, but was still glaring at Ryan.

"Rental?" Ryan asked with a laugh, "What'd you do; wipe out you're Z?"

"No, it got a…"

"I scratched up the roof," I interjected.

"Oh," Ryan said, clearly confused as to how I managed that feat.

Evan leaned into me and placed a warm, slow kiss on my cheek—right there in front of both of them! "But it's okay, I forgive you." I was without the ability to speak, and apparently so were Jewels and Ryan. "Come on, Baby," he crooned to me. "We don't want to be late."

I might as well have been a mindless zombie at that point because he literally had to turn me and point me toward the school. "You—you guys are lucky Officer Martin wasn't in the parking lot!" I got it out, but it was horribly delayed.

He walked me all the way to my English classroom doorway. Ryan went on in, somewhat disgusted by the whole affair. Evan smiled broadly as he watched him walk past.

"You are pouring on the whole boyfriend thing a little thick, aren't you?" I ground out my quiet words.

"What?" he said innocently.

"You are going to make them think we've..." I growled again, "You're gonna ruin my reputation, so back off a little!"

He smiled and left.

I took my seat in front of Ryan and it didn't take him long before he leaned close to my back and whispered, "Just what exactly happened after we left you guys Saturday night?"

I crossed my arms and stared at the white board, "Not what he's trying to make you think!"

Mr. Schultz began the class with the poems he had decided should be read for his Poe-etry contest. "Annalisa, I believe your poem was my favorite. Would you please recite yours first?"

He handed me back my poem. A large, red 'A' marked across the top. I had written this on Thursday, but it now suited me so well that I didn't even need to look.

"Insanity," I began. "Oh sweet insanity, your hands are very cold. You take my mind and twist it, bend it until it's old. You started small within my mind, like a child within the womb; then grew into an ugly thing with laughter rich, a deadly ring. I hear you inside laughing, and it rips at my soul, looking for an opening to take my body whole. Please, oh please, leave me now with the damage that you've done. Don't continue to eat away—it's futile, you've won."

"Now that," Mr. Schultz commented as the class reaction died down, "is something Poe would have been proud of."

He moved on to the next person. The chair behind me creaked lightly. Once again Ryan was whispering at my back; his voice blending with the iniquitous words of the next poem. "You might as well replace Evan's name for the word insanity if you keep dating him."

What he said infuriated me, but for the rest of the period my mind couldn't help but to rearrange the words of my Insanity to suit what was really going to happen between Evan and me—and unfortunately, no matter how I tried, the last four words stayed the same.

After an hour of poems about mental incapacity, dead lovers, tortured minds and words from the grave, my mood was as bruised as my arm. Ryan, on the other hand, was as happy as if we had been doing Browning instead of Poe. He followed along beside me down the hallway that led to gym expounding what made for 'good' bad poetry.

"You must have a little Goth in you—and, do you dye your hair that color?" I'd never have asked such a question had I been in a better frame of mind. But it didn't alter his mood, it only seemed to encourage him because I was willingly making conversation.

"Actually, my hair is black, just not black enough to suit me, so, to answer your question, yes I do. But my eyes are all me—no contacts; everyone usually asks me that first."

"So are you and Jewels getting serious at all?" I was hoping he'd say yes and then I'd have no reason to feel an odd sense of guilt over talking with him. If Evan were watching, I'd want to be able to tell him that Ryan and I were discussing her.

"She is a lot of fun, but I don't think she could be loyal to one guy. It may take her a decade or so before she reaches that level. For instance, I could tell her today that you and I were going on a date and she'd probably ask if she could bring someone along and make it a double."

I tried hard not to laugh and spoil my rotten mood, but he was absolutely correct, and I couldn't stop the smile that covered my face. He gave me a surprised look as he turned to go to the boys' locker room. It didn't dawn on me until I was slipping on my gym shorts that he may have taken my smile as having to do with he and I going on a date instead of the honesty about Jewels.

I left my tank and over-shirt on for gym because I certainly couldn't take it off in the dressing area. I just hoped my deodorant would make it through the day.

Coach was organizing us for a soccer match, but I didn't want to add any more sore spots to my body, so I opted for the four-laps-around-the-track alternative. Evan told coach he'd pulled a side muscle over the weekend and he too would opt to walk the track. A few others did likewise but most of the class stayed on the field.

He put his arm around me, but I was too mentally exhausted at this point to care what anyone thought. I leaned my head against his shoulder and we moved at a slow pace. I'm sure we looked quite cozy to the onlookers, but he actually spent most of the period telling me about additional information he was getting about my step-dad and his business partners.

"So you think some of their business is a front for criminals?" I could hardly believe what he was telling me that Robert had been dabbling in.

"It's not what I think, it's what I know. This is how they've managed to stay afloat, but if he doesn't get some capital back in the company pretty soon, he might find himself to be the one with the contract."

"And this is your best guess? Robert is the person that's doing this to me and Mom?"

"I got something else late last night," he added, glancing around to make sure none of the others were near us. "My associate found a copy of a pre-nup. Your parents had agreed to keep all funds completely separate. I think at the time, he felt his wealth might exceed hers and he didn't want your mom to get her hands on it. You were specifically mentioned as being her only benefactor. It isn't a will, but the courts will follow it in lieu of a will. If your mom doesn't make a will and include Kimmy in it, your da—I mean, Robert, will be out of luck. Talk about a back fire."

My stomach rolled at the knowledge that there was a very strong chance that he was right; the man I called 'Dad' had a good reason for getting rid of me. Could he be trying to rattle Mom so bad that she would make out a will? If she did, she'd leave everything to Kimmy and I. With me out of the picture, and Kimmy being a minor, he could gain access to the money.

"Are you okay?" He asked as I digested the reality of what he'd told me.

I took a deep breath and looked up at the sky, shaking my head no, but the tears wouldn't come. "I can't even cry; I feel so empty inside, like it doesn't matter to me anymore—nothing matters."

A look of pain so vivid crossed his face that I thought he'd done something to his side. "What's wrong? Did something just tear open?" I glanced at his tee-shirt for any signs of bleeding.

"No," he said quietly, "I was just thinking that you sound like me now. I hope I'm not turning you emotionless."

"You have more emotions than you give yourself credit for," I told him. "If you didn't, I wouldn't have been able to read that on your face just now."

"This could get ironic; the hitman gets emotional and the victim goes cold." He gave a light laugh, but the seriousness stayed with him.

"Maybe that's why God brought you here," I sighed.

"You really believe that, don't you? Not the part about God, I know He exists, but about everything being according to His plan."

"Yes, I do. Why? What do you think about God?"

"I believe He created us and put us here, but everything is a simple matter of chance. We make our own decisions and then, someday, we'll answer for them." He glanced at me and then looked back to the track.

"But you *can* change," I insisted.

Coach's whistle blew.

He turned to me, his eyes getting that void look to them again. "In five weeks, I'm going to put a bullet in you. I've been on a path straight to hell for the last seven years and even though this feels good to me right now, I'd rather go back to feeling nothing at all."

He left me standing there as he walked away. Within a few moments Jewels and Natasha were flanking my sides begging to know the scoop between Evan and me.

I ignored them both and went inside.

Ryan was waiting for me outside the locker room. It didn't totally surprise me, after all our next class was Chemistry Honors, so I half expected he would walk with me. What did surprise me was that he was quiet most of the way. Just before we went through the doors into class he stopped me. "You know, Leese, if you were dating me you'd at least be smiling instead of looking suicidal."

I swallowed, "I don't look suicidal." My argument was weak and I knew it.

I followed him to the lab coat rack, thrust mine on and then went to stand and fume by my table.

"Okay. Today we are going to pit the boys against the girls," Mr. Chester began. "I want everyone to come up and get an empty soda bottle, a nail and a balloon, then find a partner of the opposite sex."

I inwardly groaned; I'd had enough of the opposite sex.

I went forward to get my supplies. Ryan was waiting at my table when I turned around. "I want a different partner." No one paid me any attention and Ryan only smiled.

The experiment was simple, the guys stuffed the balloon into their bottle, peeling the top of the balloon down and over the bottle's threads and then they were instructed to try to blow up the balloon. I enjoyed watching Ryan's pitiful efforts as his face turned red and then he stopped because his ears were aching.

The girls were instructed to fill their bottles first with water, cap it and then take the nail and pierce a hole near the bottom of the bottle. We emptied the bottles and then did the same thing as the boys, stuffing our balloons inside and attempting to blow them up. To my amazement the balloon inflated easily. What was even cooler was the fact the when you covered up the nail hole with your finger and took your mouth away from the top of the bottle, the balloon remained inflated.

As we were all ooing and aahing over the results, he told the boys to repeat the same thing with their bottles. The experiment was completed and we spent the remainder of the period listening to him explain the principals of air. He also showed us a large clear vacuum chamber with a rock and a feather. Once the air was removed and a vacuum created inside the cylinder, we watched in amazement as both objects fell at the same rate of speed when he turned the chamber over.

Ryan was still playing with his bottle and balloon as class was ending. He'd blow it up, put his finger over the hole and observe the balloon staying inflated, then move his finger and watch it deflate. I was starting to wonder just how many times he would do this before getting tired of the amazing little trick.

"I wonder," he whispered as Mr. Chester continued to speak. He reached in front of me to the sink in our table and turned the water on very slowly. He had his balloon inflated and was keeping his finger over the hole as the water ran inside the balloon.

"I don't think that's a good idea, R…"

But before I could finish my statement, Mr. Chester noticed what Ryan was doing.

"Mr. Faultz! Don't…"

It was too late. Being caught in his own private science experiment, Ryan's hand slipped down the bottle, uncovering the nail hole. The water shot up dousing my head, our table and he even managed to hit Mr. Chester before the balloon emptied.

"You stupid ass!" came out before I could shut my big mouth. The entire class roared with laughter.

Mr. Chester stood there staring at the two of us. Finally, he gave a steely smile and went on to explain how the air rushing into the bottom of the bottle caused the water to shoot out of the balloon.

The bell rang, but he stopped us. "Well, you two have a choice. You can both get referrals…"

"What did I do? He's the one who squirted *both* of us!" I snapped.

"Miss McKinnis, you are correct about his experiment, but what came out of your mouth was inappropriate. So, if you'll allow me to finish." He stood there waiting for me to respond.

"Fine, I'll be quiet."

"As I was saying, I know you both have lunch right now, but in lieu of referrals, I'll allow cleaning up the mess to serve as your punishment. Agreed?"

"Yes, sir," Ryan said moving to where the mop was kept.

I only nodded and went for the stack of paper towels to dry off the counter.

"Very good. I'm going to lunch and when the two of you have cleaned this up, you may go also."

As soon as he was out the classroom door, I went to smack Ryan but he dodged my hand.

"Come on Leese, I'm sorry," he was backing up with his hands up in the air. "I didn't know it was going to do that."

If I chased him, we would surely end up with an even bigger mess, so I resigned myself to go back to drying the table, and my hair, and my face, and the front of my shirt. I even had a little on my jeans. Fortunately for me though, my lab coat had taken the brunt of it.

"Let me help," Ryan offered when he saw that I was trying to peel off the wet coat.

He grabbed it by the collar and pulled it down and off behind me. "What the crap?" I heard him exclaim.

And that's when I realized what he'd done. He had grabbed the collar of my over-shirt with the lab coat and removed them both. My face flushed with embarrassment as I jerked my over-shirt out of the coat and away from his hand.

"I—I hurt my arm in the fight Saturday night, that's all," I lied.

"No, no you wait just a minute." His voice had become hard and commanding, all the teasing disappeared. "Annalisa, I saw you hit that woman and you did it with your left side."

I was surprised that in all the commotion he had seen my battle. Then he reached out and carefully placed his hand around the bruised skin. It was an almost perfect, large hand print.

"That son-of-a-bitch!"

"Ryan, stop! It wasn't his fault."

"He did this to you? I'm surprised he didn't break it like he did that guy's elbow! I'm gonna kill him!"

At this point I was trembling all over. I didn't want him to confront Evan, and I was afraid that I wouldn't be able to calm him down if he got out of the classroom. "Please, please," I said stepping directly into his path, pushing my five-foot, eight inch frame into his. "Please, don't do this. Let me explain." I was trying to keep the tears back, but I could feel them building up on my lower lashes.

His face was flushed and his eyes were wide with anger. "I told you he was dangerous! I didn't think he was that stupid though."

"Please believe me, he didn't mean to do this. He feels awful about…"

"He should!" He snapped.

The tears had finally started to fall.

He seemed to calm immediately. "Hey, it's okay, I'm sorry. I don't want you to cry." His arm wrapped around me but that only seemed to open the flood gates wider.

We must have stood there for two or three minutes as I tried to gain my composure. I couldn't tell him all the stress I was under or anything that was going on—that, I was certain, would put him in danger if he challenged Evan, but I needed an emotional release.

He sat me down on a lab stool and handed me tissue, after tissue as I got myself under control. He finally must have felt that I was holding it together, so he asked me to tell him exactly what happened.

A million stories raced through my head. But the only one that was going to work was the truth. "Remember how I passed everyone on the bridge?" I said snuffling back a tear.

"Yeah, you scared the hell out of all of us," he gave a little laugh.

"I got to the circle before any of you and—well, I learned how to spin a car three-sixty when I was fifteen," I glanced up to see the look of surprise on his face. "Evan didn't know what I was going to do and I was feeling a little crazy."

"*You* were the one who made those marks in the parking lot?"

"Yeah, I spun out the car and kind of freaked him out. He didn't mean to grip my arm so hard and he really did feel bad about it afterwards. Please don't start anything with him over it, okay?"

He still had a perturbed look on his face, but he finally broke into a grin. "Would you like to drive my car?"

I choked out a laugh and smacked his shoulder. "It's a thrill-junkies' wildest ride if you put me behind the wheel."

"*Anytime*," he stated with emphasis, "you want a walk on the wild side, my vehicle is available—and I won't freak."

I thanked him for his offer and put my damp over-shirt back on. "So we're cool, right? You aren't going to get to the cafeteria and flip on me are you?"

"I'll be fine, but if he ever lays a hand on you and does mean it, I'm gonna hurt that boy."

We headed down to the cafeteria with only about ten minutes left in the lunch period. Just before opening the cafeteria door for me, he paused. "Do you really, really like him? You're sure you don't want me to kick his…"

"Ryan!" I stopped him. "Yes, I really do like him, and *please* be good."

Every head at our regular table snapped our direction when we came through the door. I was looking a bit like a drowned rat and Ryan still had that, 'I'd like to choke someone,' expression on his face. Evan was on his feet and moving toward us. Ryan had promised me he would be good, but he must have not been able to resist clipping shoulders as they passed each other. Thankfully, Evan seemed more concerned about what had happened to me than Ryan's challenge. With any luck, he'd just think that was left over male ego from this morning's race.

"Where have you been? And what," he said letting a handful of my wet hair slip through is fingers, "happened? You're soaked."

"I had to stay after and clean up in chemistry class. Ryan had a little accident with a water balloon."

"If he had the accident, then why did you have to stay after and clean up?" He was already starting to look Ryan's direction and the visual challenge was beginning.

"I—I called him an—I cussed in class," I said dejectedly.

"*You* cussed?" he mused.

I only nodded.

"Good girl," he said as we sat down at the table, his warm arm wrapping around my damp, chilly shoulders.

"Don't call me good for doing that. I almost got a referral."

I could tell he was trying hard to hold in the laughter. He pushed his salad toward me, "I saved you half. Hurry up and eat; the bell is gonna ring any minute."

He and Ryan began their usual staring competition. I ignored them and simply followed orders because I was starving. Six bites down and one sip of coke, and the bell rang.

Once we made it to math class and took our seats at the back table, Evan lean toward me and whispered that he wanted to know what really happened in chemistry.

"I told you," I tried to say it calmly.

"Leese, he was looking at me like he could kill me—and, I mean really kill me."

"He saw my arm," I finally admitted. "He was trying to help me get off my wet lab coat, but he got my over-shirt, too. Can we talk about it later, please?"

He was staring intently at me and then it was as if he flew right into me. He and I went sprawling across the classroom floor, the chairs and table going every which way. My head went back hard but it was cradled in his hand, keeping me from hitting the terrazzo. I heard two loud cracks and glass shattering, everyone was screaming and diving for the floor. I laid there trying to make sense of what was happening, but Evan wouldn't let me up. I was covered by his body and he had my head pulled into his chest.

"Crawl for the door!" he yelled, half dragging me and half allowing me to move on my own.

People were still shrieking and cowering as we reached the door and pushed it open; others began to follow. Once in the hallway, he pushed me against the wall, frantically looking me over. "Are you okay? Were you hit?"

"I—I—I don't know what—what just happened?" It was as if my body had gone in to convulsions from shaking so hard. I looked at myself, realizing I was whole. "I'm—I'm okay," I finally managed to say.

The P.A. system went off as Principal Lykman's voice came over and urgently told everyone we were going to immediate lock-down. The teachers were instructed to move the students to safety and lock the doors.

There was a small teacher's lounge not far away, and I could see Evan's mind working as he looked at the door. "In there, no exterior windows—come on." We moved into the darkened room, the only light coming from the glass panel in the door.

I was still shaking as he held on to me, yet as frightened as I was, I felt safe and warm.

"I still don't understand what happened. One minute we're talking and then you got this incredible look on your face and we were on the floor. Were those shots?"

His eyes were wild as if his whole body was running on years of instinct and training. "You were talking to me when I saw the red bead hit your shirt. This would have been really hard to explain if it had been someone's laser pointer instead of a laser sight, but there was no time to wonder that at the moment.

I know my eyes batted several times before I could process what he'd just said. "You mean there is another one, someone else like you after me?"

"Just be quiet and lean against me. I'll find out what's going on." He pulled his cell phone from his pocket, he always carried it, but I had never seen him use it. "Damn it," he muttered. "There isn't any signal in here."

"What are we…"

"Shhh, don't talk," he whispered as soothingly as possible. "We'll wait here until they give the all clear and then we're out of here."

I laid my head against his chest and listened to the rapid beating of his heart. I closed my eyes and began praying.

Within an hour, an announcement was made for the student body and faculty to calmly proceed to the gymnasium. We stepped into the hallway. Police were everywhere, and there was yellow tape around our math classroom entrance. He was pulling me left as I was going right toward the room.

"No!"

"Wait, give me a second," I pleaded.

He was still moving me the opposite direction when I pulled from his grip and approached one of the officers.

"Young lady, you are supposed to be going to the gym. You're not allowed…"

"Please, that's my classroom. My purse is on the floor…"

"You'll have to wait…"

"I can't go home, no car keys, house keys, my—my medication for—epilepsy." I lied, but I was still so shaken that he probably thought I was on the verge of a seizure.

"Oh—okay, what does it look like?"

I pointed just past the tape line. "There, the small black leather one, by the orange chair."

He ducked under the tape and quickly retrieved it.

"Thank you so much," I said grabbing my bag and turning to Evan. "Let's go."

He wrapped his arm around me as we headed toward the gym. "Very nice job, but you should have told me you were epileptic." He smiled.

I looked at him and rolled my eyes. "Aren't we leaving?"

"Not yet, you'd stand out like a big bulls-eye if we were the only ones in the parking lot. We're getting a change of clothes."

"I don't under…"

"If the shooter is anywhere around, he is looking for you in your yellow top and white over-shirt, with blue jeans. We'll get you into the girl's locker room, and I want you to put on your gym clothes. I'll try to do the same." We rounded the bend to find the gym hallway was packed with students. He moved me like a chess piece until he got me to the girls locker room door which was, fortunately, unlocked. "If you can make it to the boys' locker room door, wait for me there. If they make you go in the gym, I'll come in through the west doors. Keep watching them until you see me."

I nodded and slipped into the locker room. I didn't think I'd ever be able to get my stupid combination lock undone, but finally it gave way. I pulled on my shorts and tee-shirt when I remembered my arm and put my over-shirt back on. The counselors and office staff were moving everyone into the gymnasium. I tried to slip around them undetected, but it didn't work and I was sent into the throng of nervous students.

Within minutes, Evan came through the west doors. He was frowning as I walked up to him. "No over-shirt," he stated firmly.

"But my arm..."

"It doesn't matter, take it off. Do it now. And here," he said, handing me a ball cap. "As soon as they release us, put up your hair."

I cringed as I removed my over-shirt and tossed it onto the bleachers. "What now?"

"We wait, but we've got to work out a ride."

"My bug..."

"Out of the question. I don't know how long this person has been watching you, but I'm sure they know that you drive that bug and probably what your boyfriend drives, too, so we can't use my car either."

He looked around the gym and then grabbed my good arm, "Come on."

I could hear Jewels before I actually saw her, but Evan must have found her by looking for the tall guy with extremely black hair.

"I need to talk to you two," he said as we walked up behind them.

Ryan turned first, a look of confusion and shock as he seemed to appraise the fact that we were in the wrong clothes. Then his eyes darted to my arm and then back to Evan's face. "What do you want?" he growled.

"Leese needs your help."

That took me by surprise as much as Ryan. Evan reached over and grabbed Jewels hand, "I need a couple minutes to talk."

"OMG! Leese, what happened to your arm?" She said as Evan was pulling her along. The four of us proceeded toward the storage room door where the floor mats were kept. The door was locked but no one was back in that dim, small alcove.

Jewels was still babbling when Evan got her attention by taking her chin in his hand and turning her face toward him. "Jewels, you know what happened just a little bit ago, right?" I think he was trying to see what rumor was traveling around school. Only the twenty-five students in Mr. Lucas's algebra class had the first hand knowledge.

"Yeah, someone was shooting at the school."

"They weren't shooting at the school," He began. "They almost shot Leese."

Ryan's face went dark, "What the hell are you talking about?"

"It's true, Ryan," I said, reaching out and placing my hand on his forearm, trying to cool the furious look that seemed to take over. "Just before the shots hit, Evan saw the laser dot on my chest. He knocked me to the floor a split second before the windows blew out."

"But why?"

"I don't know, but I've got to get her out of here as soon as we're released. She can't use her car, and probably not mine either."

"What do you want us to do?" Jewels suddenly seemed calm and ready to help in any way possible.

"Jewels, I need your car for a little while. You and Leese ride with Ryan—take her anywhere except home."

I started to object, but he silenced me.

"I'll meet you guys at five o'clock at the diner by the Car Star body shop." Then he turned to me, "I want you to call Bev and Matt, tell them to pick up Kimmy but not to go home for any reason."

I opened my mouth to speak, but he stopped me again. "It's imperative they don't go there. Tell them to wait for us at the Holiday Inn where we got on one-ten yesterday. Call them now, if you've got signal." I started digging for my phone as I listened to the rest of his instructions. "As soon as they say we can go, you two drive up here to the gym." Then he turned to Jewels, "Leave your car running, and get in with Ryan."

I got a hold of Bev, and she said the news of the shooting at school was already on television. I told her I was fine, but Mom wasn't crazy after all. She agreed that she would get Kimmy and they would meet me where I asked. "Whatever you do, Bev, don't go home."

Ten minutes later they released bus riders. Another ten minutes passed and they release drivers and riders. Walkers would have to wait for family to pick them up.

I waited with Evan at the gym doors, knowing that my world was changing and I could do nothing to stop it.

Ryan pulled up first with Jewels behind him. She got out and hopped into the backseat of his car, leaving the passenger's door open. I had my hand on the crash bar, when Evan leaned forward pulling me against him, his face nuzzling into my hair next to my ear.

"You can tell them whatever you need to about yourself, but nothing about me. I'm going to take you somewhere safe, but they can't have any information or even suspicions. Do you understand?"

I nodded, but a deep kind of fear was now pulsing through my body. I would be leaving soon with someone who didn't exist. I kept remembering his words that day at his home, 'you're supposed to runaway with me.' Had this been part of the plan all along? There would be witnesses that knew I had done exactly that. I looked back into his face, the face that I hungered for, the face that made my heart find new rhythms, the last face I knew I would see before my life ended.

He pulled slightly away to look into my eyes as he repeated, "Absolutely nothing." His lips softly found their way to my temple for a brief moment, "I'll see you at five o'clock."

I was too numb to respond as I tucked my hair under the cap and ran out to the waiting vehicle. We pulled away and I looked back just in time to see him close the door to Jewels' little Kia and take off.

I had barely snapped my seat belt in place when Ryan demanded to know what was going on. Jewels was talking over him, asking why anyone would try to shoot me. Ryan was cutting her off and asking if Evan had anything to do with this. The questions were coming at me so rapidly they were like a chorus of confusion. But, the first thing out of my mouth, silenced them both, "I'm not who you think I am." The only noise that remained was the steady drone of Ryan's engine.

CHAPTER TEN

"My name isn't Annalisa McKinnis and I'm not from Alabama. I'm Annalisa Winslett from…"

"Winslett? Like the Palm Beach Winsletts?"

"Yeah, I guess you and I are from the same town," I said barely louder than the sound of the car.

Jewels kept talking, but Ryan just looked too stunned for words. I turned to her, "My family has a lot of money. My sister and I were sent here too keep us safe, somewhere where no one was supposed to know who we were."

"Keep you safe from who?" She asked looking more confused than when I began.

"Someone wants me dead." The words were so familiar to me now I didn't even flinch when I uttered them.

"Dead? But wouldn't you be worth more if they like kidnapped you or something?"

"Not when it's someone in my own family." I turned my face to the window, waiting for the sting in my eyes to subside.

I felt Ryan's warm hand slip into my own and grip it firmly. "So is Evan your bodyguard or something?"

"He couldn't be," Jewels inserted. "He's only been here a week."

Ryan ignored her, "Is he?"

The thought was almost enough to cause me to laugh. Wow! Bodyguard had a whole new meaning to me at that moment. My body was what he needed to earn his million dollars, it's just the living part of me would be missing.

"No, he's just a friend."

Ryan shot me a disturbed look.

"But, he put himself in the way of a bullet a little while ago to keep me safe." I finished, hoping this would be enough for him.

"Yeah, I guess you're right. He seems really intent on helping you. I just hope it's not for the money." He kept glancing back at my arm.

I knew what he was thinking; if Evan had discovered how much money I was worth, then he might be using me. He was so close to being right in the worst way.

"No," I tried to squelch his fear. "He—he's really trying to help." I swallowed, wondering how convincing that sounded.

He squeezed my hand tighter and then pulled into the theater parking lot. "This is the only place I can think of where you aren't out where someone can see you. We're a block away from the diner and we've got almost two hours to kill," Ryan stated and then reconsidered his poor choice of words. "Sorry."

"It's okay. I need some quiet time."

"What do you guys wanna see?" Jewels asked it as if this were any other trip to the movies.

He gave a weird chuckle as he turned to look at her, "Whatever is playing right now."

When we walked inside and looked at the movie schedules, one movie had started only five minutes ago and the next closest had a thirty minute wait. "Great," Ryan mumbled as he bought our tickets. "It's a freaking love story."

I sat in the dark theater trying to sort out my jumbled emotions, feelings and fears. It was so surreal to be watching the couple on screen as they displayed their need for each other; bedroom shadows, twisted sheets, glimpses of bare skin and the words 'I love you,' being uttered. Everyone wants to find that one person that God planned for them before the foundation of time. Everyone wants to be someone's treasured possession. I wondered how the person I was hopelessly drawn to could be that second half of myself if his heart was untouchable.

I looked at Ryan's face as the sounds of the two lovers increased on screen. He was so far beyond the stage of discomfort that he almost looked to be in pain. Jewels was drawn in with rapt attention, her lips slightly moving as if she could feel the lover's kiss on her own mouth. Then the pace of the movie changed and they were trying to save each other from the tragic fate that I knew was coming. A gunshot on screen made me jump so hard that I shook the row of chairs. Ryan immediately grasped for my hand. It was over. She was lying there lifeless as he cried over her. She had sacrificed herself to save him. The theater lights came up.

"Well!" Ryan stated, his voice thick with sarcasm and repulse, "I guess I did a real good job getting your mind off your troubles."

I wanted to tell him it was okay. I wanted to let him know not to beat himself up over the luck of the draw on the movie, but I couldn't speak. The vision was just too fresh. All I could do was to squeeze his hand and hope that he knew I didn't blame him for the choice.

It was 4:40 when we left for the diner. I had been in the dark theater and felt so safe, but now sitting in the diner, windows on three sides, I felt like a target in one of those carnival arcades. What made it worse was that my friends were here with me and apparently whoever this new killer was, he didn't care about who got hurt in the process. My heart jumped to a faster beat as I saw a little white Kia pull into the lot.

There was something about him when he got out of her car. He had on his stonewash jeans, but other than that he was different. The tennis shoes were gone, replaced with an expensive pair of what appeared to be Italian leather, a white dress shirt half buttoned, over a white cotton tank replaced his tee-shirt. He was wearing his Maui Jim sunglasses and his hair looked as if it had been gelled and then his fingers run through it. I now noticed the lighter, more golden tips in his dark brown hair instead of before when it had been worn dry.

He looked like some kind of guy right off the movie screen; he looked like a hitman—the kind that made women want to throw themselves in front of him. I'd seen guys dress this way plenty of times, but they were the social elite that I was used to. They were men with money. That was when it struck me that he made a fortune doing his job, and I was his next paycheck.

"*Is that Evan?*" Jewels said in a funny pitch.

I guess I wasn't seeing things. He actually looked that good. I wanted to tell her no, he was no longer Evan; the man who had come to get me was Micah, but that name was taboo.

When he came into the restaurant, every female head (and a few of the male ones) turned to look at him. My legs were suddenly jelly as I could see that his eyes were focused on me as he approached the table.

"I've got a problem," was all he said as he seated himself beside me, but now looking at Ryan.

"I figured that when I first met you." Ryan thrust a barb into Evan's ego.

He ignored the remark and continued, "My Z isn't ready from the shop across the street. I need a car..."

Jewels started to speak (I think at that moment she'd have offered him anything she possessed, her car being the least of it).

He continued, "A fast car."

He reached down and pulled out his wallet, then removed a small stack of one-hundred dollar bills. "Can I pay you to let me use your Trans Am? I'll give you the keys to my Z. It'll be ready on Wednesday."

Ryan seemed to be assessing the new and improved Evan in front of him. I could tell he didn't like him any better than the old version. "I don't want your money." He reached into his pocket and produced the keys to his car, but did not hand them to him, but to me. "I'll let Leese use my car, but I get a few minutes *alone* to speak with her. You and Jewels wait outside."

He looked extremely tense at this request, but he reluctantly handed Ryan the keys to the Z as he asked Jewels to follow him outside. She was more than happy to comply.

Ryan kept looking at me, but he waited until they were out the door before he spoke. "You've got to tell me what's going on. I'm not stupid, Leese, something here isn't right. If he's eighteen then I'm forty-five."

"Ryan, I told you, he's..."

"Yeah, yeah, I know what you told me, but it's what you aren't telling me that's scaring the hell out of me."

"I'll be okay." That was the most pitifully weak line I think I'd ever used.

"Promise me something. Just because he looks like—like that," he pointed out the window. "Don't let him talk you into sleeping with him."

"*Ryan!*" I said a little too loudly. "I'm not that kind of girl."

"I know you aren't, but he *is* that kind of guy—I'm telling you, I can see it written all over him. And, well, I don't really care about the car, I just want you to be safe, but I'm okay if, when this is all over, *you* bring it back."

"I'll find a way to get your car back to you."

"Then you have to promise me one more thing if you take my car." He was smiling broadly at this point so I was a little concerned as to what the one thing might be. "You bring back the car and I get one date. You get to drive and show me what you've got—three-sixty or whatever."

My lips had begun to tremble because I knew I wasn't going to ever make it back once I left. "I've got someone who wants me dead—I don't know if…"

"Stop, right there. We're not going with dismal possibilities; I'm counting on you being a survivor. So is it a date?"

I swallowed, but the lump remained. "Yeah, it's a date."

We got up and went outside. I gave Evan the keys because he needed to open the trunk. He moved a long, wide, hard gray case from the Kia that appeared to be heavy, two duffle bags and a smaller case. I knew that case and I knew what was in it. I really felt like I could pass out. My knees started to buckle and Ryan was the one to catch me.

"Whoa, Leese, you're gonna be okay. Keep it together."

Evan quickly opened the car door and Ryan passed me off to him. I felt Evan's arm around my back as his other came up underneath me, scooping me off the ground and placing me gently in the bucket seat. He slammed the trunk and went around to the driver's door, firing up the Trans Am. Jewels came to my open door and gave me a teary good-bye, and then Ryan was kneeling beside me.

"Remember your promise," he said softly. He pulled me into his arms and held on tightly. I heard Evan give the engine a little more gas to signal he wanted Ryan to turn loose of me. We were letting go of each other, when suddenly Ryan's face was right there next to mine. I saw it coming and I was barely quick enough to avoid the kiss he intended to put on my lips, but missed, getting it just off to the right. I could see Evan's reaction through the corner of my eye and I knew it was time to go.

"Bye, Ryan," I silently mouthed as he closed the door and we backed out of the lot.

He pointed the car toward one-ten, his fist gripping the wheel as if it was trying to get away. "What did he make you promise?" He asked, trying to reign in his temper.

"It doesn't matter," I mumbled, watching the town of Pensacola evaporate to a memory.

"It does matter, promises matter. You're the one person who I thought would agree with that." It sounded as if the temper was cooling.

"He asked me not to sleep with you and..."

he laughed before I could finish. "And you promised him you wouldn't." It should have been a question, but he didn't phrase it as if it was one.

"I told him I wasn't that kind of girl."

This was greeted by a long moment of silence. When he spoke again, all the temper was absent and his voice was soft, "I know that. I can't believe he didn't."

"Good-grief, Evan," I blurted, "Did you notice how many heads you turned in that little diner?" He seemed surprised, but I had trouble believing the honesty of it. "Is this how you look all the time? I mean, I thought you were a hunk before, but..."

He smiled slowly. "Before, I was trying to look like an eighteen-year-old boy."

"Well you certainly don't look like one now! I don't know what Matt's gonna say when he sees you, but I'm sure it'll get a similar reaction."

"You aren't going to see him," he spoke those words incredibly low, but he might have just as well screamed them at me for the volume at which my brain amplified them.

"What?" You said to have them wait at the motel? You said..."

"We can't chance it. You're right, Matt may decide that you can't leave with me and that would be very bad."

"NO! YOU TAKE ME THERE! I WANT TO SAY GOODBYE—I WANT TO..." I was yelling at the top of my lungs.

My hands balled into fists punching at his shoulder, trying to hit his side, but he kept protecting it with his arm.

I didn't notice that he had pulled off to the side of the road until I felt both of his hands on me. The steel grip holding my shoulders, refusing to let me get a good swing. He was shaking me and saying something that I refused to hear.

"I've got to say goodbye to Kimmy!" I finally sobbed out. "Please, I'll go with you and you can kill me tonight if you want, but I—I have to say goodbye."

"Leese, I'm sorry, I really am. Whoever this is doesn't care who gets in the way."

His words were starting to prick at my consciousness.

"Just a goodbye; it's all I want."

"Listen to me, please. If we go there and they decide you can't leave with me, what will happen? Tell me, Leese."

"I—I guess we'd stay at—at the motel until..."

"Don't you think whoever is after you knows that? If you're there, they're in danger—all of them. Do you understand now why we can't take that chance? I was afraid to leave them without protection. I called the police and told them what was going on. I know the police are at the motel right now. It's their only chance to stay safe until this person figures out you're no longer around."

The steel grip softened as what he said registered. He pulled me against him and I let the pain and anguish flow out of me. There would be no chance to tell them goodbye, and I knew I'd never see my little sister again.

"Is that why you almost collapsed at the car? Do you really think," he whispered, stroking my hair as I began to calm, "that I'm planning to kill you tonight?"

I pulled away and kept my face down, trying to wipe away the tears. "'When I saw your gun case, I... You have what you wanted. All you had to do was to get me to leave with you. I'm here and everyone knows I left with you willingly."

He tipped my chin upward, "Leese, you hired me, too."

"I know, but..." My eyes went to the cell phone in his shirt pocket. I put my hand on it and he clasped his hand over mine and slowly took it away from the phone. "Tell me what you've learned. I know you called someone."

He slumped back in his seat, his hand going up to grip his temples and then gliding back into his hair. "We need to get back on the road. We can talk on the way."

"I guess it doesn't matter, but where are we going?"

"Louisiana," he said and then turned the car back onto the asphalt.

"New Orleans?" I was asking, but I was pretty sure of the answer.

"We could have, but I decided some place quieter would be better." He changed the direction of the conversation. "You need to call Bev and tell her you're with me and that you're safe. I told the police to check their house. This kind of rogue isn't afraid to blow one up."

"Rogue?" I asked

"He isn't your normal hitman. He's the kind of guy that's messy, but it doesn't matter to him. He isn't paid to do a job by instructions; he's paid to simply get the job done."

"Why would someone pay you to set this up so carefully and then turn around and pay someone else to ruin everything?"

I'd seen that look on his face before; he didn't want to tell me.

"Please," was my single word request for him to go ahead and say it.

"Because it's two different people paying."

"So you're telling me that your contract is still good and his is good. It's just a matter of who kills me first?"

I could see that he swallowed before answering, "Yes."

"And you're also saying this guy probably wasn't hired by my— by Robert?"

"He definitely wasn't hired by the same person who is paying me. When my contact heard about the shooting, he called to find out from his contact if the plans had been cancelled, and that person said definitely not."

"But maybe this is some freak coincidence. Maybe this person just happened to pick our school and…"

"No, Leese. I already checked it out. In the circles I run in, word spreads."

"Don't stop. Tell me, Evan. Who is the other person?"

"I don't know who, but I do know it's a woman—and she wants you dead quickly."

I didn't know many adult females besides teachers and a few of Mom's friends. None of this was making sense any more. Things had become clear for a while when Evan found the information about Robert, but who was this new threat? A gentle touch on my arm shook me from my thoughts.

"Call Bev and tell her you're okay."

As hard as it had been for me to accept the fact that I wouldn't get the chance to say goodbye, it was even harder to convince Bev and Matt of the same thing. After nearly twenty minutes on the phone, I finally said they were just going to have to trust that I knew what I was doing. They put Kimmy on the phone and it felt like my heart was crumbling. I had to stay strong, no sobbing, no weeping, just be positive, even cheerful.

"Hey brat," I teased. "Are you enjoying the motel?"

"If they'll let me go swim!" she said with that tone that told me she was going to pitch a fit pretty soon.

"Well, I'm sure they'll let you eventually—if you're good," I added.

"I'll try," was her candid response. "When you get here, Leese, will you bring my swimsuit?"

"I—I won't be able to make it. I've got to go on a short trip so I may not see you for a while."

"During school?" she asked incredulously.

"Yeah, what luck, huh?" I was trying to keep our last moments together light and happy.

"Can I come?" she pleaded.

"Not this time, squirt—this is business." There was a long pause as she must have considered what business I might possibly be doing. She knew her father was away all the time on business, but never Mom or me. "But I love you. And, *please* be good for Bev and Matt."

"Okay," she relented and then she told me that she loved me too and the line went dead.

I knew I had to make one more call. I dialed my mother's cell phone. This time she answered quickly. The first thing I said was, "Mom, I'm okay."

She was really upset. She was saying she wanted us home right now.

"Mom, you always said I had a good head on my shoulders. I need you to believe that right now."

"I do believe that, Honey, but..."

"Mom, I'm not coming home." She started babbling right away, but I had to stop her, she had to focus on what I was saying. "Please, Mom, trust me. I'll get this figured out; then no one will do this to our family again."

She was still upset, but within a few minutes she began to accept that I might actually know what I was doing. That was the great thing about my mother; she had faith in me.

"Dad wants to talk to you, Honey, hold on."

I didn't know if I was that good of an actress. I didn't know if the words would come and if they did, could I make them sound genuine?

"Leese, what's going on?"

I felt as if I could now discern the fakeness in his voice and it infuriated me. "I—I'm okay, Dad."

"Where are you and who's with you?"

I wondered how he would respond to a tidbit of information. "It's okay, I'm with a good friend from school."

He paused for a millisecond, "The boy you like?"

"Yeah, but it's okay, he's really trustworthy. He'll keep me safe until this blows over."

"Call us when you can. We trust you, Leese."

It was as if I could hear the tinge of excitement in his words, 'Yes, go with him. It's exactly what I wanted you to do.'

"I'll try. I—I love you." I couldn't quite get those words out without a small stumble. I closed the phone.

Evan reached over and rubbed my arm gently, "You did good. Do you think you could get a little sleep?"

"I'm exhausted but, no, I'm too keyed up."

"Close your eyes and try."

It made me wonder if he didn't want me to see where we were going. I leaned the seat back slightly, opened my purse and pulled out my iPod, put in my ear buds and closed my eyes. Every fiber within me began to relax as the sounds that had been holding my life together lately began to course through me. His fingers stroked along my arm gently as the rhythm of the engine lulled me into sleep.

I woke a few hours later as I felt the car slow and pull off the main highway. It was dark now. I sat up straighter and was surprised to see we were pulling into a super Wal-Mart. "What are we doing here?" I yawned before I could stop myself.

"You don't have any other clothes and we need to get fuel. I know this isn't exactly high fashion, but it'll do for now."

"Yeah, that sounds good, these gym clothes kinda stink," I said, lifting the tee-shirt to give it a sniff.

We walked around as I picked up several tops, a few pairs of jeans, a couple skirts, a pair of black flats, sandals, flip flops, and then I turned the buggy down the lingerie aisle and watched his face for a hint of discomfort; all he did was look at me and give a slow smile. I grabbed a couple packs of cotton, low-rise string bikinis and then two extra bras. I gave a disappointed sigh as I moved toward the night-clothes.

"What's wrong?" he asked, slightly amused that I didn't shake him by dragging him through the 'unmentionables' aisle.

I looked at him and rolled my eyes, "I'd kill right now for a Victoria's Secret."

The smile got bigger. "You like Victoria's Secret?"

"They just fit better, that's all. That and they have a bigger selection."

I picked out something to sleep in and then headed for cosmetics. The only time I actually managed to embarrass him was when I went down the feminine aisle. Within two seconds he vanished.

I started pushing our cart toward check out when he mentioned I'd need to get a swimsuit.

"Why?"

"Well, you still have nearly five weeks left, and I have a *big* pool."

If I hadn't asked for a kiss as my last request, I would have planted one on him right then and there. If ever there were a little glimmer of heaven in the pits of my despair, it was hearing that he had a pool. I grabbed two bathing suits, and, beaming a big smile, headed back toward check-out.

"You realize," I said, pulling the visa out of my purse, "I'm actually spending your money."

"No," he replied quickly, taking the visa from my hand and dropping it back into my open bag. "I'm paying for this." He pulled out his wallet as the cashier told him the three-hundred and seventy-eight dollar total. Four one-hundred dollar bills hit the counter.

I started to rebut, until I saw the look he was giving me that said he'd explain as soon as we were out of the cashier's hearing.

We walked out the automatic doors and he looked at me, "Don't use your visa. That's one of the easiest ways for someone to track you down. People that use those things might as well rent a billboard and write their address and phone number on it."

"But then that means that I actually don't have any money." I was uncomfortable with that feeling. Even when I was just little Miss McKinnis, I had money. I just didn't go crazy with it.

He noticed the distressed look on my face. "Don't worry, I have more than you can spend."

"Don't be so sure," I smiled with a haughty attitude. "Given the proper places, I bet I could put a serious dent in your finances."

We were almost to the car, but he stopped anyway and turned me to face him. "I know you come from big spenders, but I could put you on a private jet tonight, fly us to Paris for a shopping trip down Champs Elysées, then have the jet fly us to Hong Kong to finish off our day on Causeway Bay. We could return to the States and stop at the Porsche dealership and pick you out a new 911 and that day wouldn't put a dent in my finances."

There was only one thing that I could possibly even think of to respond to that, "Good grief, how many people have you killed?"

His face went dark and he moved forward and unlocked the trunk of the car. "Did it ever occur to you that I might make money in legal ways, too?"

I felt like a jerk for my momentary lapse of humanity and humility. He only agreed to be a gentleman for my purchased five weeks of life; I never specified that he had to be kind to me. And, for all intensive purposes, he had been kind to me.

"I'm sorry. I didn't mean to come across like an arrogant, spoiled brat. That's not me. I guess I'm..."

He sighed as his hand slipped softly around the left side of my face, his thumb caressing my cheek, "Leese, don't apologize. Under the current circumstances, I'm surprised you're even civil to me. I only wish..."

I was so involved in the moment that I didn't realize he'd stopped talking. I was looking into that striking face, feeling the warmth of his hand and the nearness of his muscled body, and I forgot almost everything else. And then the words, 'I only wish,' came back into focus.

"What do you wish?" I asked softly, my hands finding a resting place on his waist.

"Why couldn't I have met you some other way?"

"God does everything for a reason, but you have no idea how much I wish the same thing." He started to pull away from me, but for once I was the one who didn't want to let go. "Micah," I whispered, surprising him since he knew I refused to call him by his real name. "If my life could go back to normal right now, just by having never met you, I wouldn't do it."

His head was shaking side to side slightly as his arms pulled me into his embrace, "You're killing me, Leese. I never thought my job could be this hard."

I couldn't stay in his arms; if I kept wanting to be near him, if I kept telling him how I felt about him, I *was* going to get him killed.

I pulled back and turned away. "We'd better get going."

We continued on I-10 through New Orleans. He was talking about his favorite restaurants in the French Quarter. Since I was in my gym clothes and I wasn't changing with him in the car, I declined his offer to try one tonight. He also had a few casinos that he wanted me to try, but I pointedly reminded him that I wouldn't be eighteen for another three months; I wasn't legal. He gave a light laugh and told me he'd have his mother make me a Louisiana (or any other state I wanted) driver's license and I could be any age I desired.

"We have a house in the historic district on St. Charles. If you want, I can pull in, I'm sure she's still up." He wasn't teasing.

"No," I said, feeling uncomfortable. "Let's just get where we're going."

We left the bright lights of the city and continued along the interstate for about twenty minutes. He took an exit onto a two lane highway that wound around back into the darkness for another ten to fifteen minutes, finally making an abrupt right down a long and winding drive. I was actually starting to get scared because it seemed we were driving into the woods. That was an unsettling thought, but around another bend in the drive, a beautiful two story plantation style home came into view. Its front columns illuminated, but even if they hadn't been, the house was in a clearing and bathed in moonlight. Sitting in the circle drive was a silver Mercedes S550.

"Wow—this is…"

"Why is Mom here?" he stated with amazement. He had told me she was back in New Orleans, so this was evidently a surprise for him, and a very uncomfortable surprise for me.

He pulled the car around to the back to a long garage with triple bays, but he didn't open the doors. Instead, he parked outside. He grabbed the Wal-Mart bags. We came in through the back, past the manicured hedges around an enormous pool, complete with a rock waterfall, and built in Jacuzzi and up onto a house length back porch and then through the kitchen door. Immediately I smelled something wonderful. We continued through the gourmet kitchen and into what appeared to be a family room, only very masculine in every detail.

"Mère?" He called out in French.

A very beautiful woman with shoulder-length dark haired pulled back into a pony-tail was coming down the hallway. I couldn't help but stare at her. She was probably about fifty, with a long slender nose and prominent cheek bones and a slightly wide mouth set against flawlessly creamy skin. It wasn't until she was close to me that I noticed the same deep green eyes I'd been staring into for the last seven days.

"Micah, I was wondering when you would get in. I thought you said you'd be in around eight-thirty?"

"I'm sorry, Mom, we had to make a stop," he said lifting the Wal-Mart bags slightly and promptly setting them down next to a large leather recliner.

"Annalisa Winslett, this is my mother, Celeste Gavarreen."

"Hello," I said extending my hand.

She grasped it warmly in both of hers. "Hello, Annalisa, it's nice to meet you."

"Mom, what are you doing here? I thought you'd be in New Orleans?"

She released my hand, turned and gave him a surprised look, "Well, you said you would be bringing company and I knew it would be fairly late, so I decided to come make you some dinner and get the house ready."

"You didn't have to do that," he said, sounding younger by the minute.

"I know I didn't have to, but I wanted to—and I wanted to meet your guest."

My face felt as if it instantly flamed red. She knew what I was to him and I wasn't exactly a guest. I was his target.

"I hope you like chicken parmigiana, Annalisa."

"Oh, yes I do. I smelled it when we came in the house. Just the aroma alone is wonderful. Please, call me Leese."

"Wonderful, Leese, I'll show you where you can wash up." Then, turning to him with a very large smile, she said, "Elle est une très belle jeune femme, Micah."

My face flushed with color again, and I could see the embarrassment hit him as well.

"Ah, Mom, she speaks French."

"Oh—that's a wonderful surprise." But if it embarrassed her that she just told him she thought I was beautiful, it never made it to her cheeks.

She showed me to the downstairs bathroom so I could clean up before the meal, and he took my bags to a bedroom just down the hall on the left.

I thought at first it would be awkward having her here, but I actually felt relieved that we weren't alone in the house. The meal was wonderful. She had cooked everything from scratch, fresh chicken breasts, mozzarella, with a very thick and rich tomato sauce. She steamed wild rice and made a wilted spinach salad with bacon dressing and cut a loaf of French bread. I hadn't realized just how hungry I was until I began to eat.

She joined us for the meal, saying that she was getting ready to head back to New Orleans as soon as we were finished.

"You should stay, Mom. It's too late for you to drive back now."

"It's only a quarter to eleven and..."

"Mom, it's too late. Sleep here and head back tomorrow. Besides, I might talk you into cooking breakfast."

She and I both gave a small laugh.

"That sounds more like my son." Her wide mouth pulling back into a sweet smile. "I'm already ahead of you. If you'd looked in the fridge, you'd see I brought you some croissants from the bakery, honey butter and a big bowl of cut fruit."

He leaned over and kissed her cheek. "Thank you."

"Now," she stated, "If I'm staying the night, we can break out a bottle of good red wine. Leese, would you like a glass?"

"Oh—no—no thank you, I don't drink. I was actually kind of tired. I was going to take a bath and get some sleep." That wasn't exactly the truth. I'd had a pretty good nap earlier in the car, but I felt it was time to excuse myself from their 'family' time.

"You don't want a swim?" He asked with a surprised expression.

"No, not tonight, but if you hear something splashing around out there in the morning, that'll be me."

"Good night, Leese," Celeste said softly, "We'll see you in the morning."

Whew! That meant that she had definitely decided to stay the night.

I walked down the long hallway that led to the bedroom where he had placed my bags. I closed the door and began removing the items, tearing off tags and stickers as I did. I folded everything with the exception of the night clothes and placed them inside the ornate large dresser. All the toiletries, I gathered and placed in the bathroom, glad that the room was a suite and I didn't have to go out of the room to take a bath.

I really liked the bathroom; it reminded me of home. I had planned to sink into the garden tub and let the jets pound against my bucket-seat-for-four-hours body, but I changed my mind and decided to go with the faster route and take a shower. It didn't matter anyway because the shower was just as luxurious as the bath. It was a rain shower and water poured from the walls and ceiling, washing away my horrific day.

I wrapped my hair and dried off, then slipped on the cotton top and shorts I picked out for nightwear. I was certain, after all the time I had spent in the shower, they would have gone to bed. I slipped out of my room and went quietly down the hall. I just wanted to sneak into the kitchen and find something to drink before going to sleep, but as I got closer I heard low voices. He and his mother were still in the family room and they were talking very quietly. Now, I know all the remarks that are made about eavesdropping and it wasn't something I wanted to do, but I couldn't move, I had to listen because the conversation was all about me.

I could see them sitting by the fireplace, each of them with a glass of wine and they were very close.

"…Son, this isn't going to turn out well. I saw the way you were looking at her, and I'm afraid you aren't going to be able to do what you *have* to do."

"I know my job, Mom. You don't have to tell me. It's just that I was given a total of six weeks and I didn't expect her to hire me to find out what was going on."

"I know you want to help her, but you're getting too close to this one. No one is going to come after you if you don't finish what she asked you to do—but, Micah, D'Angelo won't hesitate for one second to send someone after you if he thinks you've quit."

It was quiet for a moment and then he spoke even lower than before, "But what if it's wrong this time?"

"You knew when you took this job that it was a civilian, and even worse, you knew it was a young woman."

"I just never expected…"

I couldn't hear what he said as his voice trailed off.

"I think you should at least talk to David."

"No!" His voice rang out clear on that note, and then lowered again. "You've got to trust me that I can kill her when the time comes, but I'm going to solve this first."

As soon as he said that I felt the tears begin to flow. He wasn't going to forget what I asked him to do. He would figure out a way for me to prove what Robert was doing and stop him from taking everything away from my mother. I knew he would also try to find out about the mystery woman who decided I needed to die immediately. A jolt of fear surged through me; what if the person was Celeste? What if she knew he was struggling and decided to take matters into her own hands?

"David said he was coming out to see you sometime tomorrow anyway."

"No, Mom, I don't want him here. He won't understand why I can't finish this job until I do what she's paying me to do. If he gets in my way, I'll kill him." There was no emptiness to the threat.

I was completely frozen in place. What was going on and who was this David that Micah was threatening to kill?

"Don't do anything foolish. I'll stay tomorrow and I'll talk to him first. Micah, she's beautiful and I can see why this is so hard, but I'm afraid I'm going to lose my son—I can't lose you, Micah. Please, son…"

He set down his glass and wrapped his arms around her thin shoulders. I turned silently and returned to my room.

I laid there the rest of the night praying that God would show me the purpose of this test. I had decided there was a solution that would save Evan anymore anguish, but I knew it wasn't God's plan, it was my own and I knew it was wrong.

CHAPTER ELEVEN

I dozed off about an hour before dawn, but as soon as the sun began to color the eastern sky, I had to get up. I brushed my hair and quickly made one braid down the back. I slipped on my bathing suit and grabbed a robe from the bathroom. I needed a swim to clear my head. Last night had been one of the roughest yet, and I couldn't shake my thoughts just before I had fallen asleep.

The house was quiet and it appeared that I had made it up before anyone else. I walked into the kitchen, found a small glass, and poured myself some cranberry juice, opened the package of croissants and removed one. I wouldn't take time to butter or warm it, I'd just slip out onto the back porch and have a bite to eat, then jump into the pool. When I got to the door, I realized there was a problem; I stared at the blinking red light on the alarm panel. Before I could turn around to step back into the kitchen, a muscled arm reached around me and entered the code. I almost dropped my glass.

"Shhh," He whispered. "Let's not wake my mom."

That was when I realized he wasn't dressed—well, let's just say much less dressed than I'd ever seen him. All he was wearing was a pair of board shorts.

"How's the—your side?" I was trying desperately to come up with something.

He twisted slightly to look at the angry red line. "Your glue work is still holding," he said with a smile tugging at his mouth.

I remembered the night I had sealed the wound for him. The night I looked into the mirror and realized that he was no boy. The heat began to pulse up my neck and onto my face. I was like ice cream in July, melting rapidly. Suddenly my robe felt as if I had just pulled it out of a dryer. He noticed my momentary befuddlement.

"You shouldn't eat before you swim," he mused, pulling a piece off the croissant that I was holding and putting it in his mouth.

"Yeah, well you aren't supposed to scare the crap out of someone who's getting ready to go swimming either."

"Sorry. Come on. Let's go before we have company." With that he pushed open the door and I stepped outside.

We sat at the patio table sharing the bread and cranberry, which wasn't helping my problem with temperature.

"Time for a swim," he grinned, rising quickly and charging across the deck, diving in like a knife. He had done it so well, he barely made a splash. He motioned me to join him. I was about to remove the robe when I realized he wasn't swimming. He was at the edge of the pool treading water and staring intently at me.

"Look the other way," I finally hissed. "I can't take off the robe if you're watching."

"What does it matter? You're going to have to take it off to get in. Leese, I'm going to see you in your bathing suit eventually, take off the robe."

I'd never been self-conscious about wearing a bikini. I had never cared who was around when I had one on, but why was this so different? Why was it so hard to disrobe in front of him? I knew why and it went right back to the temperature issue. I couldn't stand there forever like an idiot, so I untied the knot and slipped it off, placing it on the back of the chair.

He was staring even harder, if that is actually possible. I walked around the deck to enter at the waterfall and he took off through the water trying to beat me there. I was quicker on land. I reached out my hand to feel the water. It was perfect; not too warm, but not freezing cold. I stepped under the fall. By this time he was waiting at the base for me to jump in. I went to the left of him and dove. He wasn't the only one who could execute a perfect dive. I came up on the other end of the pool, pleased to notice that it was deep almost all the way around. I turned to look for him and he came up right beside me.

"Good morning," he said, but his voice was thick and husky. His eyes were getting that wild look in them that told me he was having just as much trouble with seeing me in my suit as I had when I looked at him.

I could feel his hand coming to rest on my bare waist, the fingers gripping me and getting ready to pull me toward him.

"You—you promised," I spluttered. "A perfect gentleman."

The eyes never changed in intensity and he was getting closer.

"I'm getting out," I swam backward to get away from him, but he continued to advance.

"I know what I promised," he finally responded. "Just give me a minute to wish I hadn't agreed." He was closing in and I was almost to the pool wall. The panic on my face must have been apparent. "Don't get out, Leese. I won't touch you. I'll just watch you swim." He drew his hands back and held them both up to show his resolve, "But I want to tell you one thing." And then he drew very near, his cheek against my cheek as he whispered, "Vous êtes au-delà de la beauté."

I had never heard it spoken that way, but I translated it roughly to the effect that he felt I was beyond beautiful. Then I told him in French that he was a beautiful man and I swam away from him. He didn't bother me anymore. He did as he promised and only watched as I made laps in the pool. Fifty laps later, I was ready to get out and dry off. He was on a lounger by this point. He had brought out a few more croissants, the butter and fruit and had them on a table beside him. He was motioning me to join him. I dried my face and hair, ready to grab the robe when he asked me not to.

"It's a beautiful morning, plenty of sunshine. Don't put it on just yet."

It was starting to bother me because I knew what he was doing; he was purposely torturing himself. I didn't know if it was to see exactly how strong he was, or if it was punishment he was storing up in memory for when I was gone.

I sat down gingerly, picking up half a croissant and spreading a little honey-butter on it. "So your family must have several houses," I began.

"This is my house," he revealed. "Our family home is the one in the city. But they maintain one in Vegas, Chicago, New York and San Francisco, also."

I smiled, "My mom doesn't like that level of commitment; she's like the rental goddess." I rolled my eyes. "Except for our home in Palm Beach, we only have one other and it's on Maui."

"I like Hawaii, but we don't get too much business that takes us there."

"That doesn't surprise me," I laughed. "Great aesthetics give a kind of endorphin rush. Who wants to kill someone when their so happy?"

I watched a look of revelation cross his face. "That's what it is," he stated as if he had discovered the solution to a puzzle.

"Well, it's true. It has waterfalls and…"

"No, not the island," he stopped me. "That must be what I get when I'm close to you. I get an endorphin rush and it makes me feel," he paused, trying to find the right word, "odd."

I believed it was something much different happening, but perhaps it would be better if I led him to believe that was all it was. "Yeah and—and when I'm gone, you can go back to feeling normal."

A scowl crossed his face. "That's the problem. I didn't feel things before you came along. It's like you said that day on the track about living life; it feels like I haven't been until now. You know that can't be right," he remarked, his mind was back on the puzzle. "I've been around plenty of beautiful women. It can't be endorphins."

I took a big bite of the bread hoping I could come up with something profound before he figured out he might actually be falling in love with me. Love, for him anyway, would completely complicate his situation. As far as I was concerned, it was only making things clearer.

"If I wasn't around you so much, it would be easier for you— you know, when *that* time comes. Maybe I shouldn't be here. If you just rented me a place to stay for the next few weeks, you could finish solving my problem and then—well, it just might be easier, that's all."

He was still scowling and very much deep in thought, "I think I know who the woman is."

I swallowed and wondered if he'd come to the same conclusion as I had. That was a relationship I wouldn't want to see damaged through all of this. If he suspected her, how would that change the dynamics of his family? Dear God, I prayed, don't let him say her name.

"Mom..." he began.

My heart went to hyper-drive and I was opening my mouth to rebut, when he continued.

"...told me last night that she's been tracking his credit cards. There are a lot of hotel stays that..."

I shook my head immediately, "He travels on business all the time so there would be a lot of hotel entries."

"Leese, I know that, but I also know men. If we have to spend the night, alone, we don't rent the suite, we just get a room. Many times in the last several months his rentals have been suites. His dining is for two..."

"He has partners," I reminded him.

"Once again, if you'd let me finish, the quality of the restaurants has dramatically improved. It all points to a mistress."

"I just can't see it," I frowned. "I mean this whole business over the money is one thing, but my mother is beautiful." I watched the smile spread across his face. "And, besides that, Robert is just—well, he's plain."

"First of all, you are thinking about him in Dad mode again. You would have trouble understanding the attraction part. And, even if he is plain, money can make even the plainest of all look like prince charming."

"Well then you must have a double dose of prince charming," I gave a little laugh. "You got them both going on."

He smiled again. "Mom is starting to cross check the female partners. She'll find out if someone has charges that she can connect with his."

The sound of the kitchen door opening startled both of us from our conversation.

"I guessed I'd find you two out here. Discussing theories?" She glanced at me and I suddenly felt the need to put on the robe.

"Thank you for the breakfast," I said, rising and slipping the robe over my swimsuit. "I'm going to go change," I said turning to Evan.

"You don't have to leave on my account, Leese," his mother was starting to say when we all heard the sound of a car door and a male voice calling out Micah's name.

"Get in the house!" he ordered me. "Go now, Leese."

"Son, it's okay…"

"I said now!" he snapped, completely ignoring his mother.

Suddenly I had the feeling that I needed to run. I turned and flew through the kitchen door heading for the safety of my room. Yet, as I entered the protection of the hallway, I turned and watched through the family room windows to see who would appear by the pool. Within moments a man, fairly young but older than Evan, appeared. He was slightly taller, but had the same muscled build. His hair was lighter, but the face left no doubt about his identity.

I heard the name David, and I realized the person that he threatened to kill last night was his own brother. David kept glancing toward the house, making me uncomfortable as if he could see through walls. I decided to head to my room and dress.

I put on a pair of jeans and a tank top, brushed my damp hair and went ahead and put on my makeup. If I had to meet his brother, I might as well, hopefully, make a good impression. But I would wait in the bedroom until Evan came and told me it was safe. I kept replaying the fear in his voice when he told me to get in the house. It wasn't fear for himself; it was all for me.

I laid back on the bed, my hands folded across my stomach and my ankles crossed. It was quiet enough that I could almost doze, especially since I only got about an hour's worth of sleep before dawn. But then I heard the angry male voices rising, and the sound of a door slamming. I sat bolt upright as the argument became louder and the words became clearer. I could hear their mother trying to calm what was escalating, but she didn't appear to be having any effect.

David's words were like acid in my ears, filled with the worst vulgarity possible. He wanted to know what had gotten into Micah. Why did he bring me here, when I could now tell others where I had been? The shouting increased and I realized they were coming down the hallway. I thought about the fact that David could very well over-power him, especially since his side was exposed and his brother sounded like the type of person who would use that weakness against him.

Now I was feeling panic; trapped panic. I went to the window and turned the latch, pushing it open yet wondering if I should slip out. It wasn't far to the ground, perhaps six feet. I could easily make the jump, but should I? Where would I run? I didn't know this place.

The only thing I was wishing at the moment was that I had the keys to Ryan's car.

The bedroom doors swung open, smacking the walls, as the three of them entered the room.

I must have looked like some frightened animal caught in the roadway that didn't know which way to turn. I could see a small stream of blood coming from his side, apparently from trying to restrain his brother from getting to where I was. I knew the sting of the glue tearing and the wound trying to reopen must have been agonizing, but he showed no signs of pain. They both were terrifying to watch. These were two trained killers and the battle was only going to get worse.

David gave a contemptuous laugh when he saw me, "And now I see why we have a problem."

"There is no problem," Evan growled loudly. "She knows what's going to happen. She's just buying time…"

"Have you slept with her yet, little bro?"

I felt the color drain from my face.

"David!" his mother delivered with commanding authority. "I told you to drop it! This is Micah's job. He knows what he's…"

"You haven't, have you?" David continued looking from his face and then to mine. "That's the problem," he said, laughing and smacking his palm against his shoulder. It wasn't a light hit, but he was immobile like granite. "You need to do this thing and get it off your mind. She's playing with you, bro."

"Get out of my house," he ground out the words so deeply it was more like a rumble of distant thunder than a human voice.

"If she's too much for you, Micah, I can help you out."

It was as if I was watching a lit fuse disappear into a stick of dynamite. The explosion was getting ready to happen.

"Because if you can't shoot her…" He moved so fast. His hand had reached behind his back, and in one smooth motion was coming in front of him with a gun pointed my direction, "…I sure as hell can."

Evan was on top of him.

There was no time to think, I was outside on the ground running for my life. I heard a shot and my mind was crying out in terror wondering if I'd just lost Evan. Past the hedges and around the far end of the garage until I realized it was a long open run for the woods.

I glanced to the right and remembered what was in the back of the Trans Am. The doors were unlocked and I ripped the front seat forward, climbing into the rear, grabbing and pulling with all my might at the back seat to get it to come loose. It wouldn't budge, but then my fingers felt the latch and it came down hard. I reached in the darkness for the case that I knew was right on top. It had slid off center, but it was still there. I gripped it firmly and stumbled out of the car to the side away from the house and quickly opened the box. The clip was lying beside it. I didn't know exactly what to do, but I knew enough to slam it into the bottom of the handle.

I heard the sound of footsteps running from the back porch, and across the pool deck at break-neck speed. It would only be a matter of seconds before he reached me. My breathing was too loud and I was trembling so hard, it felt as if the gun would shake completely out of my hand. I put one palm around the grip, a finger on the trigger and the other palm under the butt of the gun to steady it. I could hear their mother screaming and more footsteps running toward the garage.

There was no more time to cower in fear, I stood and swung the gun toward the sound of the approaching person. It was David. His shoes slid across the asphalt as he came to a full stop. I could see he never expected to find me with a gun in my hands. Then Evan was through the bushes taking aim. Their mother wasn't far behind screaming for them to stop it. David's hands slowly went up. Evan's eyes were unrecognizable as I saw him prefect his aim.

"NO, MICAH, NO!" I heard Celeste yell. "Stop it now, or regret it forever!"

"Wow, I've got to admit, Bro," David spoke, ignoring the grave danger he was in. "You've found yourself a little wildcat."

"You're going to get in your car and leave right now! Don't come back here!" He spewed.

David turned slowly and began walking around toward an ice-blue BMW parked at the edge of the front circle. "I'm gonna want my gun back, Micah," he stated as if he wasn't concerned by the fact that it was still pointed his direction.

"You can get it from Mom," came the careful reply.

David continued to laugh and then opened the car door and turned to look at me.

I wasn't aware until that moment that I was still clutching the gun and pointing it his direction.

"Well, Annalisa, it was fun to have met you. I hope we can do this again—without my brother around."

"Leave!" Evan barked.

The car cranked and pulled away as I crumpled to the ground sobbing.

He was beside me, carefully removing the gun from my hands.

His mother was vehemently angry with him, rambling on about why this never should have come to this.

I wasn't hearing all she said as I looked at him. "Are you okay," I sobbed, my hand touching his bare chest and then moving toward his bloody side. "We've got to stop the bleeding," I continued, my hands still vibrating with fear as they slid across his skin.

"Leese, it's okay. It's only a small tear. I'll be fine. Are you okay? That was a hell of a jump and run you made." He was pulling me up onto my feet, looking me over. I could only nod.

That was when I noticed his mother had become silent.

She was just standing there, her eyes riveted on the two of us. She suddenly seemed to snap out of her abstraction and her line of sight went to his side. "Let's get you inside and clean that up," she finally said.

"It's not bad." Then he paused. "I'm sorry—about all of this, but I knew what he'd be like when he got here."

"I know," Celeste replied gently. "I know you don't believe it Micah, but he doesn't want to see you get..." she paused, looking at me, and considered her word carefully, "hurt."

I knew that wasn't it. He didn't want his little brother to get killed.

We went into the house. He insisted that he would clean and dress his own wound, leaving us standing in the family room as he went upstairs. I wanted to say something to her. I wanted some way to apologize, although I knew it wasn't my fault that this contract had been placed on my life. Yet, I needed to let her know how much I didn't want to hurt her son. I wanted so much to tell her that I was deeply in love with him, but I just stood there like a mute.

She turned, evidently seeing the distress on my face, and put an arm around me. "Sit with me, Leese," she asked, guiding me to the couch. She smoothed my hair and looked at me carefully, "You're in love with my son, aren't you?"

It was like a weight tumbled off my shoulders. It had been so apparent on my face that she knew the answer without doubt. I swallowed and then whispered, "More than I can say."

"Micah has never fallen in love with anyone. This life our family lives is very hard on my boys. What woman could understand a man with an empty heart? The problem is you've woken something inside him that he doesn't know how to handle. This is foreign ground for him, Leese. He's in love with you and it's going to destroy him one way or another."

"No," I began to sob again. "I won't let it. I just want to save my mom and my sister. When they're safe—I—I don't know what I'll do—but if he can't—if he can't... I'll do it myself before I'd let someone hurt him."

She wrapped her arms around me in a grip that was surprisingly similar to his steel embrace. "Good god, Leese, don't let him hear you say that. I'm going to help him clear up this mess. I only hope that we can find a way out, a way for *both* of you."

She had no idea how much I wanted that same dream. I wanted a way to come out of this together. Yet, it was only a dream; there would be no way the two of us would survive. He had said that he could complete his task at the end of our time together and, for his sake, I was now hoping he was right.

I could hear the sound of his footsteps moving down the stairs as the two of us straightened innocently and turned to him. His side was wiped clean and a fresh, small bandage covered the wound. "See, it wasn't that bad. It's mostly healed except that small spot on the end."

His mother rose and met him half-way. "I've got to head back to New Orleans and do some more research on Leese's situation. Do you need me to bring anything back for you? You're shelves and freezer are pretty well stocked, but you might need some fresh items."

"No, that's okay. I'm thinking I might take Leese down to the French Quarter for dinner tonight so if I need anything in town, I'll get it. I might stop by and show her the house, if you don't mind."

"Of course not. You know that would be fine." Then she seemed to reconsider, "Call first though, I want to be sure David isn't over. I think you two need a chance to cool off before you run into each other."

He kissed her cheek.

She told me good-bye and she was gone.

He closed the front door and returned to where I was seated in the family room.

Suddenly everything seemed a little different because we were alone.

He came over and sat down beside me on the love seat, his arm outstretched along the top of the cushions, his hand reaching out and feeling my hair.

"Leese, I want to do something…"

That sent a garden full of butterflies loose in my stomach. I could only look at him with expectation.

"You don't know much about guns, and if you get in another situation like this morning, I want you to know how to handle one."

The statement was an odd relief, but I still couldn't speak so I just nodded.

"How about you and I take a ride down to where I like to practice and I'll teach you."

I wanted to say yes, but I was honestly so exhausted, mentally, emotionally and physically that I needed some sleep. "Would it be okay, if we just took a breather for some rest before we go? I didn't sleep very much last night and…"

"Me neither," he added softly. "All right, it's only a little after nine, how about we take a few hours and then hit the range around noon?"

I nodded.

"You can relax. It's just you and me here now. I'm going to lock up the house and turn on the alarm. You'll be safe. David won't come back."

I went down the hallway into my room. The window was still open, so I pulled it shut and turned the lock. There was a bullet wedged in a hole in the wooden floor which was a too poignant reminder of my near catastrophic morning. I closed the blinds and drew the curtains, making the room blissfully dark. I didn't pull back the thick comforter on the bed. I just laid down and let my head come to rest on the pillow. I heard my bedroom door open, causing me to sit up quickly.

"I'm sorry, I'm just checking your window," he said as he crossed the floor.

"I locked it."

He looked anyway and then left me alone.

Once again, my head went down to the pillow. I don't know how long I slept, but when I rolled over I actually felt rested. I checked myself in the mirror and ran the brush through my hair before stepping out into the hallway to find him.

I could hear unusual metallic sounds and a sound that I was becoming, unfortunately keenly aware of, the chamber of a gun sliding and locking in place. I walked slowly, though for some odd reason, I wasn't afraid. I peeked into the family room, but saw no one. I followed the sound toward the large formal dining room, but when I looked around the corner I was shocked at what covered the table. He was there with his large, flat gray case from the car. It was open on the table revealing two rifles and four handguns. His black case was also open and he appeared to be cleaning his black pistol.

"Hey," I said softly. I certainly didn't want to startle someone with that much fire power.

"You weren't kidding about being tired," he said with an easy smile.

I yawned and stretched, "What time is it?

"A little after two. Are you ready to learn how to use one of these?"

I was back to nods only.

He slipped his thick shoulders into some type of double harness and placed a handgun securely in each holster. He placed one gun in his black case and added two boxes of bullets, closed it and looked up at me. "Come on." We went outside to the garage down to the last double stall on the end. He unlocked the handle and lifted the door.

"We're going on those?"

He smiled, "No, we're going on *one* of these—you're riding, I'm driving." He put a key into the ignition of a large green four-wheeler and backed it out.

"Why can't I drive one?" I asked, trying not to sound disappointed.

"Do you know how?" he asked, raising an eyebrow.

166

"Not really, but I'm a fast learner."

"No, not today. Besides, I don't want you to get crazy and get the notion to race me." The engine cranked with a steady, blub-blub-blub. He placed his black case in a rack on the front and sat down on the beast.

"No helmets?" I wondered out loud.

"We're just going to the back of my property. Climb on."

I didn't want him to know how excited I was, but I couldn't contain the large smile that emerged on my face. I straddled the seat close behind him and he showed me the pegs where my feet were supposed to rest. "How do I hang on?"

He didn't say anything but, even though I was behind him, I could see the cheek go back as the smile formed on his face. He reached for my hands, placing them around his waist. "Just don't touch my guns," he laughed.

"I'm not gonna touch your..." and the beast lurched into gear, causing me to grab him tighter.

He just kept laughing and we were off across the lawn. I'd ridden jet-skis before, and the feeling was similar, but I think it was even more enjoyable because I had a good reason for wrapping my arms around that marvelous waist. We took a trail through the woods and around a large lake to his personal gun range on the other side. The ride ended far too soon.

He wasn't kidding when he told me this was going to be a lesson. He was very thorough as a teacher, stressing over and over the issues of safety. He made me unload, check, reload, unload again, safety on, safety off, check the chamber, where's the target, where was I pointing the barrel when I wasn't pointing at the target, over and over again. I had a feeling I'd be able to do this tonight in my sleep.

"Have you ever actually fired a gun?" He finally asked as he was demonstrating how to load the shells properly into the clip.

"Does a starter's pistol count?"

He looked at me oddly and then, "No. And I don't know if I want to know what you were doing with one of those. This is a Glock-17 and it's what I'm going to have you shoot. You're going to have to pay attention to every detail I tell you because, if you don't, you're going to hurt your hand and you'll quit on me."

"I'll do what you ask, and I won't quit on you."

"Okay, we're just going with the basics of shooting the gun." He put a target on a pulley and sent it out into the range about ten yards away. "Stand with your legs about shoulder width apart, relax your knees slightly. Good. Without putting your finger on the trigger, grip the gun in your dominant hand and cup your weaker hand underneath and around your stronger. Keep your elbows slightly bent, but your wrist should feel locked in place. Use your weaker hand to come up and pull the loading mechanism backward, while pushing the gun forward with your stronger hand.

"You didn't pull the chamber all the way back, Leese." Then he pressed his body to the back of mine, his strong arms fitting perfectly over my own. He cupped my hand and chambered the bullet. Then his arms relaxed and slid back to my mid-forearms. "You'll chamber the next clip, okay?"

I nodded, afraid to breathe.

"Don't hold your breath, Baby. Take slow shallow breaths just before you fire. Remember how I told you to sight the gun. Aim for the chest on the target and use steady pressure to squeeze the trigger. Grip the gun firmly because it's gonna kick and you'll see a shell fly out the top, but that's okay. The kick only scares people; it doesn't really hurt that bad. Okay, Baby, squeeze the trigger."

My heart was running double-speed, but I didn't know if it was from the power of what I held in my hands or the power of who was holding me in his hands. I took careful aim and gently squeezed the trigger. The blast was deafening as I felt the sensation of the gun thrusting its self back into my hand like the sting of catching a baseball with no glove. The shell flew out the top, but I never flinched. I wasn't going to disappoint him; I wasn't going to quit until he told me I'd done it correctly.

"Good shot, Leese. You have sixteen more rounds. I want you to fire until the gun is empty. Count off your rounds in your head each time you squeeze the trigger. Don't forget your aim. Go!"

I squeezed the grip firmly and began unloading the magazine into the target. I wanted to stop after about three more rounds because I could feel my hand beginning to tingle, but I refused to quit. After the last bullet was expended, I pressed the clip release button and watched the empty clip fall to the small table in front of me. I checked my weapon and laid it down. I had those goofy little orange ear plugs in, but it didn't prevent the hard hum in my ears. "When will my ears stop ringing!" I said a little too loudly.

He was reeling back in the target and he smiled, "They'll stop in a little while." He gave a low whistle as he inspected my accuracy. "I don't think I did that well my first time shooting," he said approvingly. "Nice pattern."

They looked like holes in a piece of paper to me, but if he was impressed, I was happy.

He put a new target onto the pulley and sent it out further this time. "Okay, Baby, you're doing this one all on your own. I'm stepping back. Put in your new clip, chamber your first round and see how well you can do."

I liked it much better when he was standing right behind me with his arms wrapped around mine, but I was determined to prove that I was a good student. And besides that, every time he called me baby, I became more eager to please him. It was just the deep velvety way it rolled up from his chest, giving me goose-bumps with every utterance. I followed everything he had shown me exactly and managed to pull the mechanism back far enough this time to chamber my first round, I sighted carefully, took slow shallow breaths and away went seventeen rounds into the paper target.

Now, my hand was really vibrating and stinging, my palm and area between my thumb and index finger were red and sore. But, my teacher was pleased with my performance and, to be honest, I was pleased that I accomplished what I determined to do.

Then it was show-offs turn. His target was further away and he used two Glock-31 pistols drawn from his holsters at the same time, firing both guns simultaneously. He obliterated the paper target.

After our lesson was finished, we picked up all the items and climbed back on the four-wheeler.

"So," I said, leaning forward before he hit the key, "How long would it take for you to teach me to be as good as you?"

He frowned for the first time since we had begun our adventure. "You don't want to become as good as me." Some of the light heartedness of our afternoon dimmed. He cranked the four-wheeler and I slipped my hands around his waist, securely *below* his guns. All too soon we were back at the house.

He was putting the four-wheeler away, when I asked for another shooting lesson. His frown deepened, "I just want you to be able to protect yourself if you have to, Leese. I'm not trying to turn you into something bad."

"You aren't turning me into something bad," I rebutted. "I just want to learn more—I want to be able to fire two guns at once, like you do."

"You don't have the arms for that," he snapped. "How did you think I got these muscles?"

"You work out," I stated plainly.

"Yeah, I do. But most of my workouts are from holding two Glocks perfectly steady while shooting. You don't need to learn more."

"Isn't there a possibility that something might go wrong and I'll end up facing whoever the other person is alone?"

"The only way that will happen will be if he takes me out of the way first."

"But it could happen, and then I would need to know all the extra things you know, but didn't want to teach me. It would just be me with the knowledge to point and shoot." I wasn't going to let this rest. I wanted to know more.

"Leese, almost everything I know is about killing someone. I want you to know how to protect yourself, not how to murder another person. It's something you'll never need to use." His volume was rising and I could tell he would be angry with me in a matter of moments.

By this point we were standing next to the Trans Am, and I let my fingers trail down the hood as I continued. "Did you know that I can take this car and slide it into a parallel parking space at about thirty miles-per-hour? It's something I'll never need to do out in the real world, but I learned how to do it, and do it well."

"What's your point?" That temper was starting to pulse up his neckline.

"I'm never going to go out and purposely look for someone to kill, just like I'm never going to be looking for a parking space at thirty-miles-per-hour, but having the knowledge isn't bad. If this morning had been different and you hadn't taken that gun away from David, what would have happened if I had to face him?"

"He would have blown you away before you even knew what was happening." He sighed deeply, pulling me to him in those steel bands that he uses as arms and leaned his face next to my ear,

"Everything in my life—everything—is corrupt. I've only known one glimpse of innocence and that glimpse is you. I don't want to corrupt you. That's why I agreed to be a gentleman, and that's why I haven't grabbed that impetuous mouth of yours with my own and taught it how to respond to a man. I've never had to use as much strength in my entire life as I have in these last nine days."

"You aren't corrupting me," I whispered. "Everything happens for a reason. I just want to know more, but if you feel that strongly about not showing me, then I'll stop asking."

"I don't know, maybe you might get some crazy idea like trying to go after your step-father by yourself."

I think my face was one of utter revulsion, "I could never—I hate what he's doing but—but he was like my dad and he is Kimmy's dad. I couldn't take his life!"

He finally smiled, "That's my girl. That's what I needed to see and that's what I needed to hear. I'll teach you some more tomorrow. We've got dinner reservations tonight at Brennan's."

"You realize my wardrobe isn't high fashion?" I said, reminding him that I only had a limited amount of clothing.

"The dress code isn't strict, and I think you'll look perfect in whatever you put on."

We went in and got ready. I wore one of the gauzy calf-length skirts with a white, mid-sleeve cotton top. My bruise was still apparent, but it had lightened to the point that I could tell it would be gone in just a few more days. I pulled the top of my hair back into a pony-tail and left the rest loose. He, once again, had that natural chic look, which made it hard for me to think of him as Evan. I wondered when he would tell me to stop calling him by his false name, but he hadn't so far.

When it was time to leave, I walked to the Trans Am, but he headed to garage door number one, put in the key and turned the handle to open the door. "I thought we'd take something with a little more horsepower."

The door went up, and, even though it was under a car cover, I could tell it was a Corvette. When the cover was removed, it was a gleaming silver Corvette Z06. I know my eyes illuminated at that very moment and I said the first thing that came to my brain, "Can I drive?"

"No," was the merciless reply. "This has more horsepower than your Porsche and it goes from zero to sixty a full four-tenths of a second faster than your car."

I think I was salivating. I looked at him with a pleading glance. "Four weeks and five days of life left and you'd deny me a chance to drive your car?"

"That's not fair," he stated flatly.

I tried that bat-your-eyes thing that Jewels had shown me.

"NO!" He marched to the passenger's door and held it open for me.

I even considered tearing up to see if that would sway him, but that was just too mean, so I reluctantly slipped into the comfortable passenger's seat.

I was all ooh's and aah's as he brought the engine to life and backed out onto the drive.

He looked over at me for a long moment and finally said, "On the way home, but just for a little while."

I squealed; he laughed.

Dinner was delicious, but for me the dessert was the highlight. I've always liked Banana's Foster, but, according to the restaurant, they served the original recipe. It was, down to the very last bite, scrumptious.

He called his mother just as we were leaving the restaurant, but she told him that David had stopped by to see her and that tonight might not be a good time to come over.

He made one more stop at a small grocery store and purchased a few things such as eggs, bacon, sliced ham and turkey, bread, cheese and milk. I was trying to be patient, since he said I would be able to drive the car for a little while, but I was beginning to wonder when that would happen. Just as we got near the ramp for I-10, he pulled over and, somewhat reluctantly, switched places with me.

The car was incredibly responsive. Just the slightest touch and it was eager to break all known Louisiana speed laws. He pulled out a small radar detector from the glove box and plugged it into the power supply. "Just a little. This doesn't do anything if a cop is coming up from behind."

I smiled and carefully maneuvered around enough vehicles that I was certain I had no officers behind me. I only wanted a few seconds of unadulterated speed. As soon as I got a clear stretch in front of me and the radar showed no problems, I dropped the petal to the floor. I only held it for about seven fantastic seconds, but I was exceeding one-hundred and forty so I felt it was time to reign in the fun and go back to almost normal speed.

I could tell that he was no longer nervous to be a passenger when I drove. He evidently had come to accept that I could handle whatever had four tires and a steering wheel. He let me finish the drive home, which was fun because there were great curves in a few places and I got to feel the car's excellent road-hugging ability. My only mishap was that I over-shot the driveway to his house. He had become so comfortable that he had forgotten that I'd only entered that drive once before. Fortunately, there was no one behind us and I simply backed up.

CHAPTER TWELVE

Over the next several days, we fell into a happy routine. It was a morning swim, breakfast on the patio, out to the shooting range and several nights of dinner at home. I wasn't horrible in the kitchen; I just hadn't done that much cooking. He, surprisingly, was good in the kitchen, so between the two of us, we were managing a decent meal each night.

But it was the lessons on the shooting range that consumed most of our days. He showed me ways to make my body less of a target if I was under fire, how to flash sight a pistol so that I took less time to aim, remain accurate but greatly increased my speed from holster to firing position. I tried the double pistol firing and it was, as he told me it would be, extremely difficult because I didn't have enough muscle to keep the guns from wobbling wildly after each shot. I was determined to practice it, but I knew, should the time come, I'd best stick to two hands and one gun.

I asked him if we could make arrangements to have Ryan's car shipped back to Pensacola, but he told me to be patient. I didn't have Ryan's home address or phone, but I did have Jewels' number. He reminded me that the phones of my friends and pseudo-family might be under surveillance and we didn't want to tip anyone off to my location in Louisiana. My phone had died the morning after I arrived here because I didn't have the opportunity to get my phone charger from my bug or the one at Bev and Matt's house. I wanted to call my mother, but he said that was absolutely out of the question since we wanted Robert to at least believe his plan was working and we would eventually discover what he had been hoping to accomplish through my demise.

My only link to my mother would be to pray every night that she had enough trust and faith in me that she would know, in her heart, I was still alive.

When Friday came around, he had planned another evening in the French Quarter. He had decided I needed to try some authentic Creole food. We sat out by the pool discussing types of foods that we've tried, when his phone went off. I hadn't realized until that moment that it was the first time I had actually heard his house phone. An odd look crossed his face and then he went inside to answer it. I climbed back into the pool. I no longer had any inhibitions about being in my bikini because, after that first initial temptation of watching me in a bathing suit was under control for him, I had no more fear that he would get too enthused. I was also getting used to seeing him in his board shorts, showing off that beautiful physique for his only audience member.

The only thing that was bothering me in what was otherwise time spent in paradise was that there had been no more information coming in about who this woman was that had paid someone to kill me or, for that matter, no more information about Robert's motives for wanting me dead as well. I knew he was staying in contact with Celeste, but when I would ask, he would tell me that there had been no progress. There were times when I questioned whether he was being truthful or not. He was becoming much better at controlling his facial reactions around me. I could tell it was practiced control because, before, I could discern his emotions easily. My time was going by too quickly and although I was in friendly captivity, I knew that status was going to have to change at some point. Sometime in the next four weeks, he would have to call his contact and let him know the job had been completed.

I continued making laps in the pool, but it seemed he had been gone a long time for a conversation. I was becoming curious as to whether he was even on the phone at this point. I toweled off and grabbed my robe, deciding it would be better to go in and find out what was going on. But, as I opened the kitchen door, he hung up the phone.

"Everything okay? Was that about me?" There were no reasons to hide questions, but I had a distinct feeling from his expression that there might be a reason to hide answers.

"We've got a change of plans for dinner tonight," he responded tersely. "I'm going out for a little while. You'll need to stay inside. I'll turn on the alarm, you'll be safe."

"Why can't I go with you?" I asked feeling apprehensive over being left in the dark, as well as left behind.

He didn't answer. He just turned and headed for the stairs that led to his room on the upper floor.

I hadn't thought it wise to go up there before, but now I was right behind him. "Is there a reason I can't come?" I persisted.

"I'd just rather you didn't," he answered as he reached the top step and continued on.

I wasn't going to give in so easily. "I could come; you'd just rather I didn't."

He turned so sharply that we bumped into each other just before reaching his bedroom doors. "Are you coming inside while I dress?" His attitude was getting that sharp edge to it that told me he was preparing for an argument.

"No," I shot back, giving a little sharpness of my own. "I just want to be sure…"

He rolled his eyes toward the ceiling, letting me know he was getting exasperated quickly. "Sure of what, Leese?"

"You aren't going to—this isn't something…"

"Spit it out!" His patience finally snapped.

My eyes began to well at his harsh tone, "You aren't taking your stupid guns, are you?! This isn't some kind of fight with whoever is out there, is it?" I was saying my words too loudly, but my rising emotions were pushing my volume.

His whole body stopped tensing and he seemed to relax as he took my shoulders in his hands. "No, no, it's nothing like that. I'm sorry. I just didn't want to tell you that were having dinner tonight with—with my family."

There was a moment of stunned silence as I contemplated every possible connotation of the word family. "You mean like…"

"My parents and my brother and sister."

"David is going to be…" Then there was a moment of deeper understanding. "Your dad is going to be there?"

"Yeah, he wants to meet you."

I could plainly see this worried him, as if David wasn't a big enough worry on his own. I didn't know much about his father, but if he harbored a similar attitude toward me as David did this might be more like a last meal than a simple dinner.

"I've got to pick up a few things in town and then I'll be back." He was completely gentle once again.

"Are they coming here?" I questioned, the nervous feeling mounted.

"No, we're meeting at one of my dad's restaurants. I've got to get changed." He pushed open the double doors revealing a place I had not seen before.

"You're dad owns a restaurant? I followed inside, marveling at the simple but masculine design. His bed was on a black lacquered platform, against a floor to ceiling built-in headboard of dark padded silk squares. The dressers, armoires and nightstands were also a black lacquer and his bedding was a rich, deep green like his eyes. I sat gingerly on the bench at the foot of his bed watching him open drawers and pull out his clothes.

He looked at me, apparently surprised that I was making myself comfortable in his room, shook his head and went into his bathroom. I heard his damp swimming shorts hit the floor. "He owns several, as well as numerous other businesses. I told you what he was good at, and businesses are better than banks. I have several myself."

He returned to his bedroom, now dressed in his jeans and a button up shirt. He grabbed his shoes and joined me on the bench.

"You own a restaurant?"

"I own quite a few things that might surprise you. Although things have been quiet here recently, I'm usually, well, let's just say I'm usually much busier than I've been lately." He grabbed his wallet and keys from the night stand and then walked out of the room, expecting me to follow. He was halfway down the stairs as I exited the room.

"So what do I do while you're gone? Stay inside and watch television?"

He paused and turned, "Be good. I could unplug the house phones and take them with me, but I'm hoping by now you realize why you can't call Jewels, or Bev or especially your house. I'm doing my best to unravel what's going on."

I nodded. He knew how desperately I wanted to call my mother. Every day that passed without her having heard from me, increased her pain, anguish and worry. She probably was starting to suspect that something horrible had happened to me.

"Leese," he said pulling me from my troubled thoughts about Mom. "Please tell me you won't try to leave. You're safe here—for now. Promise me you'll be here when I get back."

"If I left," I said slowly, "I'd ruin everything for—for both of us. I'll be here."

He placed a warm hand on the back of my neck and kissed my cheek. It seemed to me, on the rare occasions now that he did this, each time his lips got closer to my mouth, closer to what would at some point become our final true kiss.

The alarm was set and I watched the silver Corvette vanish down the drive. I rambled around the house, exploring what I had felt uncomfortable to see before. The house was large, perhaps five or six thousand square feet. The downstairs consisted of the guest room which I stayed in, a formal living, formal dining, family room, kitchen and a media room. Upstairs just to the right was his bedroom, two additional suites and a large den also occupied the upper floor.

I hadn't seen inside the den before and was surprised that he left it unlocked. The big mahogany desk had a computer and a few files lying out. I shouldn't have looked, but I felt that if he had been concerned about what I would find he would have put the items away. I sat down in the thickly padded leather chair and open the first file. It was the dossier on Evan Lewis. Everything was there; birth certificate, social security card, driver's license, school records—and a complete history including a photo of the real Evan Lewis stapled to his middle school records. Wow, he was nothing like his imposter. He smiled from under a thick pile of strawberry blond hair, a splash of freckles across his face and crooked teeth.

The next file was thin, but the contents were shocking. It was about me. I looked at my school picture from earlier last fall. There was information on me as Annalisa McKinnis. My Pensacola address, phone number, even my class schedule was there. It was a short summary of my false self. No wonder he was concerned about who I really was—there just wasn't enough here to make a complete life for anyone. There were two dates hand-written in the folder, one was March 10th, the day before he started at Pensacola High School and the other was April 25th. It took me a second, but then I understood that I was looking at his deadline—a literal deadline for me.

I felt like Dorothy in the Wizard of Oz, trapped in the castle, watching the sand pour through the hourglass. I didn't have a brave trio out there trying to rescue me. I was here with the soldier that had vowed to take my life; the true villain was Robert and his mystery woman. Yet, kind as Evan had been to me, I was still his captive and he was still the executioner.

I tugged at his file drawers, wondering how many other lives I would view that he had taken, but the drawers were securely locked. I booted up his computer, expecting to meet a password roadblock, but to my surprise the guest account had not been removed. I couldn't get to his documents and records, but I could get to the programs and... I caught my breath, something I hadn't thought of doing that was now one simple click away; the internet.

My mind began to race. I couldn't call Mom, but most email accounts were untraceable. I could go to my email and send her a message. Robert had his own computer and they each had separate accounts so he would never see my message. I could tell her I was safe. I could tell her to be careful and not mention anything about me to him. I could tell her I was close to solving the mystery of who was torturing our family.

I was certain of one thing, he would be so angry if he knew what I was doing. I wasn't actually doing anything against his wishes. He never specified that I couldn't send email. I must have debated with myself for a solid ten minutes before I opened my email account and hit the word compose. When I was finished and had hit the send button, I was overcome with guilt. I turned off his computer and went downstairs to wait for him to come home. I would debate with myself if I would tell him what I'd done.

I must have dozed off on the couch, because when I woke he was seated beside me, gently shaking me. "Hey, sleepy head, time to get up and get ready."

"It's still early, isn't it?" I asked rubbing the tiredness from my eyes.

"It's a little after three. I bought you some things, I hope they fit. I need you to try them on."

Boy, now I really felt guilty about what I'd done. He comes home with presents and I was doing things behind his back. I looked at the bags scattered by the base of the couch. "Wow, if you were going shopping for me, you should have brought me along."

"There were a few places I was going that you couldn't go," he said sheepishly, glancing toward a bag that was off from the others.

My curiosity peaked but I went into the bag closest to me. "Stitch's jeans! Awesome," I exclaimed pulling out the item.

"It's a jean skirt," he corrected.

"How did you know my sizes?" I said, looking at the tag and seeing it was a zero.

"I was with you when you bought your items at Wal-Mart, remember?"

"Well, I love it. It's gorgeous! Nice hoodie, and, ooh, heels, too. I dug into the next bag and pulled out about a half dozen, assorted colors of spaghetti tanks, which I dearly loved wearing. There was a Victoria Secret's bag—I was excited, but quickly becoming concerned about this father of his I was supposed to meet. Why would my undergarments matter?

He must have seen the confusion on my face, "You needed one of their clear-strap bras to go with the tank tops, so…"

"You went into a ladies lingerie shop," I laughed. "I bet the sales girls were fighting over who was gonna get to wait on you!"

I could tell he was trying to keep a straight face, but the smile had already gripped the corners of his lips.

"Panties, too," I said, trying not to sound overly shocked. That was going above and beyond the call of duty for any man.

"The sales girl said you have to have something to match the bra. Who was I to argue over what a woman needs under her clothes?"

A smaller bag was from a jewelry store but I couldn't go further, I had to ask. "Why do I need to have all this stuff to meet your dad? He's not—he's not strange or something, is he?"

"My dad is a bit unusual, but not like you're thinking. He appreciates the finer things in life and he expects those around him to dress the part, but I got carried away. I started out just looking for the hoodie and before I knew it, I had filled the car."

It was true that I didn't have a jacket, and the last time we went out, I was cold, but it still didn't make much sense. "Why do I need a jacket?" This time I was really suspicious as to his motives.

He reached over for the large plain bag and pulled out a daintier single holster version of the shoulder harness he normally wore when we went shooting. "To cover this," he confessed.

"You're not gonna—I'm not carrying a gun to dinner!"

"It's just a precaution, Leese..."

"NO! I can't! I'll be a nervous wreck all night! Don't make me do this, please."

"Baby, David is gonna be there and even though I plan on staying between you and him all night, if he gets a couple drinks in him, he'll be worse than he was here."

"I can't shoot your brother!"

"I don't want you to, but I also don't want you to be defenseless." He was pleading with me now, but I just couldn't see me doing this.

"The gun is too—it's so big, someone will see it under my jacket. I'm not defenseless!" I exhorted, "I'm a black belt for crying-out-loud."

"Black belts don't stop bullets. The new gun I just bought for you is really small." He reached down into the same bag and brought out a gray container. "It's a Glock-26—a baby Glock—it holds ten rounds," he said opening the box.

Ten rounds! I had a feeling I was going to a gangster massacre instead of dinner. I looked at it and it was smaller than the Glock-17 he had taught me to shoot, but I knew it was still going to feel like a cannon strapped to my side. I wanted to cry. With all the shooting lessons I had begged for, I never dreamed he would expect me to carry a gun at some point.

"Let's at least get you dressed and have you try it on." He was giving me the most pathetic puppy-dog face, begging me to do what he wanted.

I grabbed the bags, leaving the gun and holster right where they were, and stomped off to the bedroom. I suddenly didn't feel so guilty about my one little email.

I took longer than usual to get dressed. The skirt was an ankle-length denim with a high front slit that fit like it had been made just for me. I picked out my top and tried on my new bra. I could hardly believe that he paid attention to my bra size as well as everything else. I'd have to remember that he had a nearly photographic memory. The black strapped stiletto heels made my legs look longer than they already were and brought out their shapeliness. After makeup and brushing my hair, I stood in front of the mirror surprised at how elegant I actually looked.

I hadn't opened the jewelry bag until I finished dressing, knowing that it would be hard to stay mad at him if there was something really beautiful inside. The first box revealed a pair of dazzling one carat diamond stud earrings set in white gold. The second box contained an inch long, white-gold cross with five diamonds in the center. Having him remember that I wore a silver cross when I was in Pensacola caused me to forgive him for the whole 'wear-a-gun-to-dinner' thing. The only problem now: I was back to feeling guilty again.

I walked down the hallway, stepping out in the living room where he was dressed and patiently waiting for me. I was surprised that he was wearing a suit. I thought it must be very important to him to impress his father, but it wasn't until he walked up to me and wrapped me in those glorious arms that I realized why he had on a suit. He was wearing his double holster and the jacket was simply a covering.

"You look amazing," he whispered.

With my heels on, I was as tall as him, so I was able to look directly into those intense eyes. "Well, my personal attendant did a marvelous job picking out my outfit," I teased. Then I took a long breath and pointed to my holster. "I suppose you wouldn't mind fitting that thing on me would you?"

He gave me a smoldering look that could melt steel.

At that moment he could have fitted me for full body armor and I wouldn't have cared.

He slipped the harness on me and fastened the clips to the waist of my skirt and then adjusted the buckles until it was as snug as second skin. He picked up the baby Glock and, reminding me it had a full clip, he secured it into the holster. I was right. It felt like I was wearing a cannon.

He held out my new cotton hoodie for me to put my arms through the sleeves. He lifted my hair carefully out of the jacket and turned me toward a nearby mirror. "You see," he said, standing close behind me. "No one will even know it's there."

"Except for me," I gave my weak rebuttal.

He reached around in front of me and carefully started the jacket's zipper, pulling it halfway up. "Don't undo that. I don't want you to lean forward and have someone get an accidental view of your baby."

"Well, I'd always said that someday I wanted a baby, but this isn't what I had in mind." We both looked into the mirror at that point, our eyes focused on the others. I hadn't meant for that to come out that way. I had been careful not to mention my hopes and dreams for my future in front of him because I knew I'd never reach them. But one tiny slip and his face was filled with anguish. It would be my life or his at the end. He knew what his refusal to kill me would mean, and then someone else would just finish the job he didn't do. It seemed much simpler to me now, the loss of one instead of two.

It was total silence the rest of the way to the restaurant. I brought my iPod and once again was finding comfort in my music. I needed comfort; my nerves were going wild. The restaurant was on the western end of New Orleans in what appeared to be an area filled with boutiques, shops, cafés and other restaurants.

We pulled in front of Giorgio's Italian Bar and Grill, but before he opened his car door, he finally turned to me to speak. "Don't call me Evan tonight." And that was all he said.

The restaurant was fuller than I expected and then I remembered it was Friday night.

The hostess looked up and smiled broadly when she saw him, and then gave a quick surprised glance at me. "Your father is in the back," she said over the din of the crowd.

He never smiled, nor slowed his pace, as if she hadn't been standing there at all. We worked our way past the tables and the bar, heading back to an area marked as the banquet room. It was immediately quieter as we entered the room. There were only four people in there. Celeste was the person who met us at the door. The other person I recognized was David; I gave an unintentional shudder when I saw him. She took my arm and brought me over to the table to where a handsome older, but heavyset man was seated. The man stood and gave me a surprisingly warm smile.

"Well, you must be, Annalisa, Micah's million dollar target."

The color drained immediately from my face. He not only said it out loud but, he said it as if it was no big deal. Even his sister showed no surprise at the remark. I glanced at Evan and I could see the pulse rising in his neck.

Celeste intervened, "Annalisa, this is my husband, Giorgio Gavarreen."

I offered my hand, but instead he grabbed me and gave me a kiss on the cheek. "You certainly are beautiful. I can see where this is going to be difficult for him."

I was trying to come up with some kind of response, but I was shocked.

"Have a seat," he said, pulling out a chair for me next to him. "I've already told my staff what to bring out for dinner. I hope you enjoy spicy food. We do a Creole/Italian blend."

"Yes," I managed to force out. "I—we were discussing that just this morning. I think I like food hotter than—Micah." I caught myself in the nick of time, I had almost said, Evan.

"Really?" He seemed surprised. "You seem like a cultured young lady. I would have thought the hottest thing you've ever handled might be a little black pepper."

"No," I said, finally smiling and realizing that however uncomfortable this had been at the start, he was simply being forthright because everyone in the room knew what was going on. Why act like everything was fine and I was just some date that his son had brought to meet the family? "I've got a soft spot for deep-fried, stuffed jalapenos."

He chuckled deeply. "Next thing you'll tell me is that you drive stock cars and swill down beer!"

Evan actually let a laugh slip on that one. Giorgio looked from him back to me. he gave me a small nod to let me know it was okay to be candid with his father. "No, not me. I don't drink, but I have driven the Daytona Speedway before."

"She can also," Evan interrupted, "Spin a car three-sixty and slide sideways into a parallel parking space at thirty-miles-an-hour."

David scoffed and leaned back in his chair.

This must have been the type of thing that his knew his father would enjoy learning.

"That I would like to see," his father remarked.

"I've got the Corvette out front, Dad. Would you like to take a ride with her—she's already had it over one-hundred and forty on the interstate."

"Micah Gavarreen, you're an idiot!" his sister began a tirade. "You've got a billionaire's daughter that half the nation is looking for right now, doing over a hundred miles an hour down the interstate! Just how deep of a pile of crap do you plan on putting yourself into? I might not be able to pull you out of this one!"

"Gwen!" Giorgio snapped, "You will learn to hold your tongue when you are around me, do you understand?"

She grumbled something unintelligible and then responded with a, "Yes, Sir."

"I have to admit, Micah, that doesn't sound like a smart thing to be doing," Giorgio said, turning back to look at the two of us.

"I—I used a radar detector and made sure no one was behind us—and it was only for a few seconds and then I backed off. I'm not trying to get Micah caught."

His sister rolled her eyes, and David laughed.

"You've got to tell me something, Annalisa," Giorgio began.

"Call me Leese, please," I said, putting my hand on his (which generated a big smile on his face).

"I've never seen someone, rich or poor, be comfortable with what you know is going to happen."

"That's because she's banking on him not pulling the trigger," David interjected.

Giorgio shot David a look that made the smile drop immediately from David's face.

"Micah isn't the bad guy here," I said slowly. "If it hadn't been him, then someone else would have taken the job, and I probably wouldn't be here right now."

"You got that right," David sneered.

"Son, if you open that mouth of yours again, I am personally going to close it for you! Do you understand?"

David nodded. Evidently the family was ruled by Giorgio and no one dared cross him.

"Go on," he urged.

"When I figured out what Micah was, he nearly killed me right then." I was still able to feel the Glock pressed to my temple. "I only asked him, since he was given six weeks, if he'd let me pay him for the other five weeks so that I could live long enough to figure out who's doing this to my family."

Giorgio nodded as if in deep thought. "You are a very unusual girl," he said softly.

"You don't know the half of it," Evan remarked.

Giorgio waited for the explanation.

"When she figured it out, she got to my gun first." Everyone in the room suddenly seemed very interested in what he was about to say. "She had the perfect shot, but, instead, she handed me the gun and asked me to make it painless. And, after she said she'd like to hire me, she helped me finish setting all this up."

"Kinky," David uttered with a smile.

I rolled my eyes, "It's not his fault, but I've got to help my mom and my sister."

"And now you're in love with him." Giorgio wasn't asking; he was stating it.

Evan jumped back slightly as if someone had shocked him. Evidently, Celeste had told her husband what she discovered when she had been at the house. I told him that I thought he was someone I could fall in love with back when we had our first dinner at the restaurant in Pensacola, but I'd never looked him in the eye and uttered those words. There was no way I could reveal how strongly I felt about him. I couldn't let him know he'd have to kill the one person that truly loved him.

"No! Absolutely not," I gave a nervous laugh. "I felt like I was falling for him when I thought he was eighteen, and Ev... Micah is really sweet, but he's too old for me. We're two different people, two different worlds," I lied harder than I've ever lied in my life. Now if my eyes didn't tear up and give me away, I could make it through this moment. Celeste knew the truth, but I was hoping she would understand why I was denying what I felt for him.

"Micah," his father looked at him. "How do you feel about this girl?"

"She's my mark, just a target, Dad. You know I've never screwed up a job."

Giorgio's hand reached up and gently patted Micah's face. "Good. So you're telling me I'm not getting ready to lose a son and start a war."

"What do you mean?" I asked before Evan could answer.

"Stupid little twit," David growled. "If someone whacks off Giorgio Gavarreen's son, there will be retaliation and then..."

"And then," Gwen interrupted. "All hell breaks loose."

Evan glared at them all, "If I walk out of this place right now and get blown away, I don't want anyone to…"

"Boy!" Giorgio snapped. "Don't tell me what to do if someone shoots you. An eye-for-an-eye just as the Bible says…"

"Forgiveness is what it really says," I spoke up, knowing that was not something that was done in this family; you do not interrupt the father. Giorgio turned to me, his face flushed with anger. I figured I'd better clarify before he opened his mouth to chastise me. "I've already forgiven Micah for what he has to do." That seemed to calm his father, but I had to continue. "But I couldn't have done that if God hadn't already shown forgiveness to me."

"You don't understand these matters," he stated, gripping my hand. "But you are a strong young woman and I truly believe you have forgiven him. I don't think I would have your type of strength."

The wait staff began filing into the room, bringing in the appetizers for the first round.

"We can talk later, right now we're going to eat" Giorgio stated as the dishes filled the table.

"What do you suggest I start with?" It wasn't hard to read whose ego at the table liked being stroked the best.

Giorgio smiled and I didn't have to ask after that. As each course came out, he told me what I should try—absolutely fascinated that I could handle the spicier dishes. We continued on this way all the way through to dessert. I felt bad for ignoring Evan most of the time, but he kept squeezing my hand under the table to let me know I was doing well by impressing his father.

David kept giving me nasty glances across the table, but when his father would look at him, the face would return to serene, until his father looked away.

Gwen, who I found out was the oldest sibling, was very interesting. Evan had told me she was as corrupt as the rest of them, but I got the distinct feeling that she wanted to see her baby brother get out of the family business before it killed him.

The table was cleared and I thanked my host for all the delicious food. Evan was rising, pulling the keys from his pocket, when Giorgio asked us to stay for a few drinks and enjoy some karaoke in the bar.

"Dad, if I drink then she has to drive home. I don't think Gwen has enough officers to catch us if Leese is behind the wheel."

"Who said you can't have a coke?" His father laughed. "I'm enjoying your—your friend's company."

It was nice to hear him refer to me as his son's friend and not his target.

"Would you like to sing?" Evan said turning to me.

"Oh, no, that's okay—I…"

"Does she sing well?" Giorgio asked.

"She could be a star, if she wanted to, Dad," he replied with an enormous smile.

"Then it's settled. You're singing for me, Leese." He was leaving no room for rebuttal.

"I don't know what to sing for him," I hissed at Evan as he was moving me up to the karaoke stage.

"I know exactly what you are going to sing. Get out your iPod. Benny," Evan yelled to the man in the karaoke booth. "Can you use music from one of these if you don't have it in your collection? You'll need to dub out the singers voice."

"Yeah, sure, I can handle that. Just show me which song."

He scrolled through my iPod and finally turned it toward me so I could see what he'd picked out. I had more than just Christian rock on it so I knew he could find something, but when I saw what he chose, I was stunned.

"You want me to sing *Perfect People—in a bar*?" I figured he had lost his mind. "And besides that—I—I thought this song was a little on the painful side for you last time?"

"I know my dad, Leese. He needs this song just as much as I did. Maybe someday there will be hope for my family, but it's got to start somewhere."

His encouragement filled me with the desire to illuminate some minds tonight. "Okay," I whispered, but before he walked away, I grabbed his arm and motioned him to lean his ear toward me. "The gun won't fall out of the holster if I'm dancing around with the mic will it?" I knew I couldn't be perfectly still when I was singing; I had to dance.

He kissed my cheek and laughed. "No, you're safe."

I took the stage as the music was ready to start and had a moment to intro my song. "This song is just to remind us that we've all made mistakes in our lives that scar us, but God accepts us as we are because there's no such thing as perfect people." I nodded and the music began. It wasn't hard to forget where I was. It might as well have been Wednesday night youth group for all I cared. I put my all into the song, hoping and praying that he was right; someday there would be hope for his family. As the song finished I was surprised that the crowd was just as responsive as if they had been in church. They were clapping and cheering and I could see Giorgio was nodding his head and Celeste was drying her eyes.

"That was wonderful," Gwen was saying as I came down from the small stage. I noticed that she had my iPod in hand and was going through all the songs that I had saved. "Do you know all these songs?"

"Yes, I do."

"I mean the words; can you sing anything that's on here?"

By this point Evan was standing beside me smiling. "Pick one Gwen; she can sing it."

"Sing this one then," she said turning the iPod toward me.

I knew the words, but there was no way I was singing that song with him in the room. "I—I can't sing that…"

He grabbed the iPod, "*Stupid Boy*? That's one I haven't heard."

"You said you could sing any song on here," Gwen continued. "Do you know the words or are you simply refusing to sing it?"

"Can you sing it, Leese?" He was giving me an intent stare.

"You—you won't like it," I mumbled, knowing it would break my heart to have him hear it.

"Sing it for me," he said, suddenly understanding that there was something in it that his sister wanted him to hear, and that I didn't.

Gwen took my arm and walked with me to the stage, but I wanted to know why. "Because," she began, "I've never seen my brother in a bigger mess than this. I'm seeing something different in him now that he's around you. I'm hoping when this is all over, he'll get out of Daddy's business, and the only way that's gonna happen is if you keep that little bit of a conscience you've woke-up inside him from going back to feeling nothing."

"This will break his heart," I whimpered, knowing I'd give the performance the same command as the last one. "I can't hold back when I sing."

"Yeah, well guess what? That will mean *he has a heart to break*."

I gave no intro, most of the audience knew the song, but it wasn't his kind of music.

"She was precious like a flower, she grew wild, wild but innocent, the perfect prayer in a desperate hour. She was everything beautiful and different..." I couldn't look at him as the haunting words filled every fiber of my body. I had to continue.

If Gwen was right maybe he'd decide after I was gone that he simply couldn't do this anymore. Maybe his heart would never go back to the void where it used to hide. "She laid her heart and soul right in your hands, and then you stole her every dream and crushed her plans...you stupid boy...now you've lost the only thing that ever made you feel alive...she loved me, she loved me. God please, just let her know I'm sorry..." When the song ended, it felt as if I had wielded a scalpel and slashed a wound right across his chest.

The applause and cheers were wild and I could hear people shouting out requests, but I couldn't go another step. I found the closest empty table and crumpled.

Gwen came and sat beside me, her hand rubbing my back. "You're even better than I thought," she said lightly. "I've never, and I mean *never* seen anyone get to him, until tonight."

I raised my head, tears in my eyes, "Where is he?"

"He left the room for a little bit, he'll be back. If he survives this, you're gonna leave the ugliest scar right across that stupid untouchable heart of his."

I didn't like the way she said, if he survives—God, let him survive this, I prayed silently.

Celeste and Giorgio came over and sat wordlessly. For the ones in the room who knew what was happening, the song had too much meaning; the exception being David who had been entertaining himself at the bar.

Evan came out of the men's room about ten minutes later. He had it together, but I could tell he was keeping it that way by a thread. He made it to the table and Gwen decided it best to leave us alone.

"Leese," Celeste said breaking the stillness, "I was trying to find the right time to talk to the two of you, but—well it might as well be now—I got the information I needed just before I came here tonight. We need to speak privately."

I looked to Evan. It was what I'd been waiting to hear, but I needed to see if he was okay first.

"Let's go back in the banquet room." He rose and offered me his hand.

Once we returned to the table in the quiet calm of that room, she began.

"Leese, do you know a Sharon Norton?"

"Sharon? She's one of Robert's associates. She's been to the house a couple times when we'd have business parties. She was always stuck up and rude to Mom and me. Why?"

"She is the one who is behind the second hit."

"I barely know her," I stated, clearly shocked that she was the threat.

"Well, unfortunately, she knows your step-father too well. I finally found the match in the records that have charges in the same areas on the same dates." I guess she could see I didn't understand so she produced a few sheets of paper from her purse. "These are hotel suites that he stayed in for the last six months. Look at her charges."

We began comparing the lists, and there were too many times they were in the same town on the same night making charges in the same city, too many to be a coincidence. Robert was having an affair and had been having it for quite some time.

"But this doesn't make sense. She is only about twenty-seven, twenty-eight, and she's a beautiful blonde. She could pick anyone, why Robert?"

"Money. He's the one with the access to your mother's money." Evan stated plainly.

"She also made a twenty-five thousand dollar withdrawal, just one day before someone tried to shoot you at the school. There's more," Celeste continued. "I recently got some new documents that show he started the process for gaining power of attorney over your mother's affairs."

"What! Mom is competent. He can't just step in and start taking over her money."

Giorgio put his hand on mine, "Look at his charge receipts for the last few months. He has been getting prescription medication from the pharmacy, the kind of things that could make anyone seem incompetent. We're pretty sure he's been drugging your mother, and, if you are out of the picture, he *will* be granted power of attorney."

"Can I use all of this to get him arrested?" I asked. My body was beginning to tremble with fury. How could he do this to the woman who had loved him for sixteen years? She would have done anything for the stupid bastard if he would have just asked.

Evan spoke before his parents could, "I think this is all circumstantial. We're going to need something more concrete. We could talk to Gwen for a little while. She could tell us what we'd need to stick the scum-bag in jail."

Celeste and Giorgio stayed behind as Evan and I headed to the bar. Gwen was arguing with David, but she grew quiet as we approached.

"I need to talk to you for a minute, Gwen."

She looked at him and then motioned to a nearby table.

We had barely sat down when David sauntered over. He had consumed several cocktails and appeared to be in a very good mood. "You, Miss Leese, are one hot singer, baby."

I could see the anger building in Evan's eyes. "Go away, David. You don't want to start your crap tonight."

"Ah, baby brother, you're just all pissed off 'cause little Miss Perfect here won't give you any." He winked at me.

"I'm going to knock you completely out if you don't shut up."

"You know I'm right," he continued, ignoring the danger. "If you'd just go ahead and get things done with her, you could blow her brains out no prob…"

I saw the arm come up, but to my shock he was going for what was in his jacket.

"NO!" I yelled, reaching to stop him.

Gwen realized the danger and got to his arm before I did. She had some amazing strength as she grabbed with both hands and pushed his arm to his chest and held it, "Don't do it, Micah," she pled as she held on for dear life. "Think about Mom and Dad—and Leese. You can't help her if you're in jail. He's just drunk. Ignore him."

He relaxed his arm slightly as David laughed.

Gwen cut her eyes to her foolish middle brother. "Go get us some cokes, Jackass," she ordered.

David gave her a salute, "Yes, Sir—chief Gavarreen!" He headed back to the bar.

"Never let him get to you, Micah. He's your best ally when he's sober and when the chips are down. You never know, he might find a way to help you straighten out this mess for Leese."

"Gwen, your mom has this figured out, but you've got to tell us what kind of evidence we need to prove what's going on and get my step-father put in prison."

We spent the next few minutes discussing what we knew was happening. By the time we were ready for her to explain what we needed to make the evidence stick, David had returned to the table with the drinks.

"Okay, hard liquor all around," he laughed. "Nah, I forgot this is the goody-two-shoes group—just cokes." He placed the glasses in front of us and sat down with another cocktail for himself.

"You've got to record him admitting to setting this up. We could have D'Angelo send someone to tell him there is a problem with the plan to kill Leese. Tell him she got away, anything to get him talking. If we can have Mom figure out what account he got the hit money from, then that would be a big nail in the coffin. As far as this woman goes, we've got some good evidence with her withdrawal, but we need to know who she hired. Maybe Daddy could call in a few favors."

"I don't think D'Angelo is going to cooperate. He gave me a lot of warning when I took this job, and he's been pretty edgy since I told him I've got her."

"I coouldd go, bro," David laughed at his slip of the tongue. "I'd beat the confession out of him!"

"That's not the right way to get a confession, bozo," Gwen stated, then went back to ignoring him.

We talked for another few minutes, but it was getting late and David was getting drunker so, for safety's sake, we said good-night to his family and headed for the car.

"Wow, is it warm out tonight or what?" I said unzipping my hoodie.

"Leese!" He scolded, "Don't take that off." Then he made a little gun with his fingers and reminded me why I couldn't.

We climbed into the Corvette and started the journey home, but I was so warm and uncomfortable, I couldn't stand it. I had turned his air conditioner on full blast, but I still felt like I was cooking from the inside out. "I've got to take this off," I whined.

"Yeah, put it on the floor by your feet. Unclasp the holster from your skirt and lay it down there with the jacket."

I obeyed but my hands felt clumsy as I fumbled with the clips and buckles.

His cell phone went off and scared us both. He answered and all he said was, "WHAT!" A string of obscenities followed as he pulled the car off the road into the grass. He snapped the phone shut and got out and ran around to my side of the car, jerking me out.

"What are you…"

"Leese, listen to me, you've got to throw-up! Do it now! David put something in your coke. Stick your finger down your throat and puke. DO IT NOW!"

He was forcing me to my knees, and all I could smell was exhaust, grass and dirt. My hands still weren't operating correctly, but I finally managed to get my finger down my throat and gag, over and over until the contents of my stomach rolled forward and spilt on the ground.

"Do it again," he ordered.

I got to a point where I had the dry heaves and he lifted me up and placed me in the car.

"Why did he do this to me?" I began to cry. I dug in my purse for a tissue and a mint. My mouth tasted awful and my throat added to the still smoldering feeling that was working its way through me. "I still don't feel very well—maybe I need to go to the hospital." The strangest sensations and emotions were pelting my brain.

He wasn't talking, but I did happen to glance at our speed and we were holding around a hundred miles per hour on the interstate. "Slow down, please, please, please—I don't want you to get pulled over."

I watched it decrease, ninety, eighty-five, eighty and then it stopped going down. "Please say something," I begged, my hand clutching his arm. I began to smell the cologne he was wearing, the feel of his muscles under his clothes. My free hand splayed across that broad chest feeling the rapid beat of his heart as he drove. I was becoming incensed at the idea that I couldn't get past his shirt to feel his skin. My fingers struggled against his buttons, managing one and then his hand came up and stopped me.

"I'll get you home, you'll be fine." His voice was soft and warm, like someone was wrapping me in a downy soft blanket.

"I don't feel right; I feel strange and warm. What did he do to me?" I knew that I wouldn't be able to understand him in a little while as my mind seemed to be drifting away. I struggled to keep focused.

"He put a drug in your drink, a strong drug that will make you do things—things someone like you would never do. He must have given you a hell of a lot of it, too. I can't believe it's still working on you."

He turned down the drive and made his way back to the house. I was still so warm, like I had been in the Jacuzzi for a very long time. He opened the car door and began walking me toward the patio, but the stilettos were making it impossible to keep going.

"Let me sit down and take these off. You unlock the door."

He walked away and I remember undoing the shoes and my hot feet finding the cool deck, but then something was at my ankles and I was kicking it away. I had to get in the water, I had to cool off. I heard his footsteps as he came back for me and then I heard him call my name, but it didn't matter at this point. I stood up and looked at him. His face was so handsome, his eyes so wide and his lips parted, but he wasn't making a sound. I looked down and noticed my clothes lying on the deck and then I remembered I wanted to swim.

He grabbed for me as I stumbled forward, but he wasn't quick enough and I was in the water. The feeling of the water on my skin was like ice; I was trying to swim but I couldn't make it to the top. That's when I felt a strong arm around my waist and I was being pulled to the surface. He was carrying me up the pool steps and I was clinging to his neck. He smelled so absolutely wonderful, I kept kissing the base of his throat, my fingers twinning through his wet hair. I needed him more than I felt I'd ever needed anything, more than air, more than a beating heart, more than life.

I felt the softness of my bed, but he was trying to leave me. I got up to follow him and he returned, trying to get me to be still.

"Please don't leave me," I begged.

He was saying he couldn't stay. He was saying something about a perfect gentleman. Every time he tried to leave me, I had to follow. He finally said he'd stay with me if I'd only stop. I wondered what he wanted me to stop? I knew his clothes were dripping wet and my fingers were trying to help him remove them. He kept repeating something about a perfect gentleman, be still, and he wasn't this strong.

I could taste the cologne by his ear, my mouth seeking his, but he was refusing me. My hands moving to forbidden places and then he was over me, holding my arms against my chest, his legs pinning my own. I was trying to taste his skin again, struggling to get free so I could touch him. It felt as if the struggle lasted for hours, I remembered saying that I wasn't going to tell him how much I loved him because I didn't want to hurt him. I was telling him my plans to save him from having to kill me. I finally gave up the struggle. Out of breath and tired, I could feel something warm running against my skin and the taste of tears that were not my own.

CHAPTER THIRTEEN

When I opened my eyes, it was daylight outside. My head throbbed and my mouth was dry. I could feel something heavy over my waist. I looked down it was his arm—and I was completely bare.

I don't remember screaming as much as I remember the sound of it. I scrambled, stumbled, tripped and tumbled away from the bed in a panic. He sat up, telling me to calm down, but I ran for the bathroom and slammed the door.

Thank God my robe was hanging there. I slipped it on shaking violently, trying to remember what happened.

"Leese, open the door, please."

"N-n-no," I shuddered. Then I was screaming and crying again.

"Please, Baby, *please* open the door."

"What did you—(I choked on a sob)—what did you do to me?"

"Please believe me; I didn't do anything to you. You've got to believe me. David gave you a lot of ecstasy in your coke last night. Please, open the door."

It was becoming clearer: the restaurant, his family, dinner, singing, talking about my step-father. The memories rushed back into my mind and the throbbing increased. I remembered him making me throw up.

"Please, open the door," he pleaded once more.

My fingers turned the lock and opened it slightly.

"Leese," he called to me softly, pushing the door further open.

"I feel sick," I mumbled. My empty stomach was rolling, but there was only acrid air coming up. I gagged and crawled toward the edge of the tub. I felt his warm hands supporting my waist, holding me until my stomach calmed.

"I'm okay now. Help me to the sink." My legs were wobbly as he lifted me to my feet. I was a wreck and I didn't want to look in the mirror. I swished mouthwash and spit it out, feeling the fresh burn in my mouth and sinuses. When I grabbed my brush, I finally looked at my reflection.

He was standing there watching me. He looked about as rough as I felt. His chest was bare and there were scratches on his skin. I saw what looked like bruises along his neckline, and then I remembered seeing something like that before on a friend that had made-out. They were hickies. His slacks from the night before were deeply crumpled from having been worn to bed wet. Yet, it was his face that disturbed me the most, the way he was looking at me. Just knowing what I'd done, remembering that I begged him to stay with me… More memories were rushing back and I knew I'd said the wrong things to him last night. His was the face of knowledge and that knowledge had crushed him.

The tears were coming; I couldn't hold them back. I tried to brush my hair. Doing something normal I hoped, would stop the emotions from taking over, but I couldn't do it. I dropped the brush to the counter and turned. I looked into that face and begged him to forgive me. I felt the wonderful arms as he cradled me and then swept me off the floor and returned me to the bed.

He was wiping away the tears from my cheeks and forcing back my lowered chin so that I had to look at him and see the pain I caused.

"You told me some things last night, Leese. We've got to talk."

"I'm so sorry. I never meant to hurt you."

"Stop apologizing, it wasn't your fault and, in a way, I'm glad it happened."

"Glad? How could you be…"

"Or I'd never known until it was too late. I want to hear you say it—sober and in the light of day, I want you to tell me what you told me last night."

"I can't. Please, don't make me do this. There's no reason to go through all this pain. It won't matter…"

"It matters to me," his voice becoming urgent.

"It's sadistic to go through this. It's bad enough what has to happen, but do we have to make it hurt this much?

"Tell me. I have to hear it." He wouldn't let me turn my face away.

I studied those eyes for a long moment and I could see the need, the deep longing and the pain to hear what he already knew. "I—I love you, Micah Gavarreen. I love you with all my heart." I had told him I wasn't going to call him by his real name, but he had to know that I loved him no matter who he was or what he'd done.

We simply held each other. I'd never felt anything so good as wrapping my arms around him, feeling his arms around me and finally getting to admit the truth that had been aching inside my heart for too long.

He relaxed his hold and pulled away, brushing the hair from my face as he did. "Go ahead and get dressed." He rose up and pulled the bedroom doors closed, leaving me alone.

I took my cotton gym shorts from the dresser, slipped on a tank and went out of the room to look for him. He was still upstairs. I noticed the alarm panel hadn't been set in all the commotion last night so I went out the back door onto the patio. There was something dark lying by one of the lounge chairs, and, as I approached, I realized it was the pile of my clothes from last night. I sat down, picking up the items and folding them slowly, placing them on the small table beside me. I couldn't believe it was all there right down to my undergarments. I had stripped outdoors.

I recalled the look when I turned and saw his face, the expression when he saw what I'd done. The look had been so gentle that I could almost reach out my fingers and touch the memory.

I felt the lounger sink down, and I knew he was beside me. My eyes were closed. The shirt I had worn last night folded tightly in my hands and pressed to my face. I could still smell the scents of the restaurant.

"You told me a lot of things last night," came his tender words. "You didn't hold anything back so I believe they were all true." He paused, his hand reaching over and rubbing softly between my shoulder blades. "Do you remember much of what you said?"

I nodded, still clutching the fabric tightly.

"You told me you were going to make this all easier for me—at the end." It sounded as if his throat had caught on the last words. "I don't want you to do anything. Do you understand me? Don't…"

"I didn't want you to have that memory," I whispered.

"Promise me—swear to me, by God, that you won't do anything like that." He was removing the shirt from my grasp, turning my shoulders toward him. "I can live with whatever I have to do, but I couldn't—I couldn't handle that. Innocence doesn't destroy innocence. Swear it to me, Leese. Make me the most honest promise you've ever made."

I looked at him and threw my arms around his neck, clinging against the rock solid frame. "I'm sorry, I didn't know you felt that way about it—I promise."

I held on a little longer, then let him go. "My head is about to split apart. Do you have some aspirin, Tylenol, anything that might help?"

He left for a few minutes and returned with a glass of cranberry and a couple aspirin. I forced them down, my stomach still trying to roll. "How did you know? Who called you?"

"Gwen. After we left, I guess David got to bragging that he had solved my problem. All he figured he had to do was turn you on and I'd never be able to say no. She was in a panic and she told me to make you throw up."

"But, I remember, you did get me to throw up. Why didn't it work?"

"My God, Leese, he must have given you enough to kill a horse."

"Would I have—I mean would an over-dose have been…"

"I think if Gwen hadn't called, you'd be dead or at least in a coma." Then I could see the anger flashing in his eyes, "I'd kill him right now if it hadn't ended up making you tell me what was going on. You told me something else last night."

I didn't know what else could have been more revealing than what we'd just been through so I could only look at him expectantly and wait to cringe.

"You broke the rules, Leese. You know I meant *no* contact, not just no phone calls."

Oh—yeah, that was a big cringe. "I'm—I was just afraid she would be going crazy by now…" My hands went up to rub my temples, "Why would anyone do this to themselves on purpose? I feel like a piece of crap!"

"Come on, let's get you back inside and out of the sun. He wrapped his arm around me and helped me navigate indoors. Instead of feeling better after the aspirin, I was feeling dizzier and weaker by the minute.

"Do you want to go to your room?"

"No, my sheets are damp. How about the couch for a little while?"

We went into the family room and I lay down, pulling the cushion securely under my aching head. I woke about two hours later, took a couple more aspirins and went back to sleep. It was one in the afternoon when he woke me up to get me to eat some lunch. I sat up slowly, taking the warm cup of soup from his hands. I sipped it, letting the salted broth trickle down my throat.

"Starting to feel better?"

"Yeah, just a little."

"Eat some bread with the soup," he said, offering some slices he had brought with him. "Something solid in your stomach is bound to help."

"Thank you," I said, setting the items down on the coffee table. "You're wel…"

"No, not about lunch, but thank you for not—last night would have been an easy excuse for you to abandon your promise."

"You have no idea how… Well, let's just say I found strength that I didn't think existed. You are," he paused. "You are a very, very beautiful woman—and really insistent when you want something badly enough."

I felt the blush cover me so completely, it was like a second wave of the drug was releasing in my system.

We sat there together for a little while listening to the sound of thunder in the distance. The sky had begun to cloud and I was certain that the rain would be here soon. He turned on the television, flipping it to a local news channel that played the weather report every ten minutes. We had just missed the report and would have to wait before we could see it.

My heart jumped to my throat as visions on the screen of something familiar began to play. It was a helicopter shot of a huge house on the water. I snatched the remote from his hand and hit the volume.

"…heiress to the Joseph Parkerson fortune was found this morning…"

Oh dear God, no! I was on my feet, my hand clamped over my gapping mouth, stifling a scream.

"…by her husband, after slitting her wrists in an attempted suicide. Mrs. Winslett has been distraught over the disappearance of her seventeen year old daughter, Annalisa. She was taken by ambulance to Columbia Hospital's psychiatric ward and has been listed as being in serious, but stable condition."

"I've gotta go home!" I cried, trying to push him out of my way. "I've gotta…"

"No, Leese, it's too dangerous."

"I DON'T CARE!" I screamed at him, "Mom needs me. I've got to go! You've got to let me go!" I was pushing, hitting and shoving as he struggled to get a handle on me. "MOVE!"

"NO!" He yelled it back so loud that he scared me. "You can't go there. You'll be walking right into a trap. Sharon Norton's man is going to find you and shoot you, run you off the road, or blow you up. It won't matter to him as long as you're dead!"

"I have to go. I'm as good as dead anyway. I'm just waiting here for my time to be up! I'd rather die in Palm Beach trying to help my mom than to wait here and torture both of us!"

"Please, Leese, I don't know enough about the other man. I've got to know more about what you're up against."

"I'm up against the wall, that's where I'm at. You've got for however long it takes to get from here to Palm Beach to learn what you can about him. I have to go to her. Please understand; *I have to go.*"

"I've got to pack," he relented with a sigh. "Get your things together. We'll take the Trans Am because I can't fit everything we need in the Vet."

I was ready in five minutes after having stuffed my items into a duffle bag that he had given me. It seemed that he was taking an eternity to get ready, and then I saw him coming down the stairs. He carried the long gray case, the black case and a single duffle. He set the alarm and locked the house as I stood impatiently by the car. I helped him load the trunk and was ready to go, but he told me I'd have to give him a minute. He opened the garage and parked the Vet inside and then immerged carrying my holster, Glock and jacket. The gun was secured in the trunk, and he tossed me the jacket and climbed into the driver's side as the familiar sound of a heavy metal machine filled my ears.

He was carrying both cell phones, his and the one that I knew he would use to let someone know my life was over. He opened his personal phone and began dialing.

"Mom, yeah, we saw it on the news, too. We're on our way to Palm Beach. Yes, I know, I know, but she has to get to her mother. Of course I understand. I need to talk to Dad. Please, just put him on the phone."

I could hear his breathing becoming controlled, as I realized he was preparing himself to speak to his father.

"Dad, I need a favor. I need you to pool all your contacts and resources and see if anyone knows who the rogue is. I just need to find out his M.O., anything that will give me an edge. Yes, Sir, I know that." There was another pause. "Yes, Sir, I will. And Dad, would you do me a favor and tell Gwen the stupid boy said thanks."

My heart panged against my chest at the memory of singing that song for him. I reached over as he snapped the cell phone shut and softly touched the back of his hand. "Thank you, for this I mean. I know it isn't going to be easy, but—well, thank you."

"How's the head feeling?"

"Still pretty bad. I think the adrenaline rush when I heard the news, cancelled out my aspirin."

"Well, it's an eight-hundred-mile ride, give or take fifty, so hopefully you'll feel better when we get there."

"How long do you think it's gonna take?"

"I'm doing the speed limit the whole way because I've got so much fire power in the trunk that we'd end up in jail for sure, maybe twelve to thirteen hours. We should get in town about two in the morning. But I know when you go to the hospital to see your mom, you're gonna get swarmed by police. You're still seventeen; Robert could make you come home with him, and that would be bad."

"Can I use your phone? If I can get a good lawyer to help me with an emergency emancipation, then he can't do that to me."

"Don't you have a lawyer?" he asked, seeming surprised.

"Sure, my family has lots of lawyers and they all work for Robert. Mom didn't have much use for them."

He just shook his head and reopened his phone, pressing a speed-dial key and putting it to his ear. "Hey Teri, this is Micah. Is Bill there? Bill, I've got a problem and I'm going to need your help."

I listened as he spoke with who I assumed was his lawyer. I thought it was a little scary that he keeps the guy's home number on speed dial, but I guess, in his line of work, an on-call attorney is essential. When he told this man that he had Annalisa Winslett in the car with him, I heard something very loud through the phone that sounded like obscenity. He never flinched as he continued telling his attorney that he needed an emergency emancipation and he wanted it before tomorrow morning. "Yes, that's what I said. Tell the judge it is a matter of her physical safety from her step-father."

When he finally closed the phone, he told me that his attorney was calling a close friend in Florida who would get it before a judge today. All we had to do was wait for the call letting us know if the judge would approve it.

By five thirty we were passing Pensacola on I-10, and a wave of melancholy swept over me as I wondered what everyone was doing on a Saturday afternoon. I could see their faces so vividly in my mind; Jewels, Kevin, Carlie, Nate, Natasha, they were all there, and of course there was no way to forget, Ryan. I could see him right now, driving the Z all over the place, having a good time, but yet wondering how I was doing.

He gave me a little smile, apparently noticing that I had drifted into a daydream. "Can you believe," he began. "It was a week ago today that you hired me?"

I smiled. That was one of those bitter-sweet memories. It was the day I went back to see someone that I knew was dangerous; the day I realized I was going to have a very short life span; the day that forever linked me to the person beside me. I simply squeezed his hand. Life was certainly turning out much different than I ever expected.

His attorney called and said they had taken care of the emancipation order, and as soon as we let him know where we would be staying, they would fax a copy to us.

His estimate had been correct. It was two in the morning when we reached the northern edge of Palm Beach county. I was back here under the worst possible circumstances, yet I couldn't deny that there was an innate feeling in coming home. He turned off I-95 and headed toward the beaches.

"Where are we going?" I asked. The idea of where we could stay for the night hadn't occurred to me until now.

"I reserved us a cottage on the beach before we left," he said with a slow smile. "We'll be about twenty minutes from the hospital, but I didn't want us to be too close, just in case."

We pulled into the small motel and he went to the office to pick up the key. He returned and drove into the interior courtyard all the way to the back against the inlet. He grabbed our duffels and locked up the car. The sky was overcast and the stars and moon remained hidden leaving the path to the door dark.

"I can't see a thing," I whispered, holding on to the back of his shirt.

"Hang on, we're almost in." With that the door to the cottage gave way and we stepped into the void that smelled like beach sand, sunscreen and fresh linens. He found a small table lamp and turned it on. We were standing in the living room, but it was also combined with a dining and kitchen area. It was one of those shabby chic type of arrangements, but tastefully done.

I walked toward the large, sliding glass doors to the rear of the unit and turned to a doorway on the left, found a light switch, and discovered a large bedroom—with *one* large bed. I sat down my duffel and went back to the other room and looked at the furniture. It was an intimate type of setting with a loveseat and two wing chairs with ottomans. He had dropped his bag and was in the kitchen putting the drinks we had purchased from our last fuel stop into the refrigerator.

"What's wrong?" He asked after studying my face.

"I call the wing chairs," I answered trying to sound enthused.

He gave me an odd look. "It's a two bedroom unit, Leese."

I shrugged my shoulders and gestured to the single doorway leading off from the main room.

The eyebrows went up as he caught my unspoken meaning, "There are at least two beds then, right?" But he was already in motion toward the room to see for himself.

He was only gone for a few seconds, but in that tiny space of time, I had turned one chair to face the other and was pushing them to close the gaps between the ottomans. It was slightly longer than the loveseat, yet (with bent knees) I would make it work. Besides, as tired as I was, I could sleep on the floor and it wouldn't matter.

"It was supposed to be a two bedroom unit." He didn't sound angry, just exhausted. "You take the bed I've got the—the chairs."

"No," I replied firmly. "You drove the whole way here, you take the…" He had maneuvered around to the other side of the chairs and was climbing on top of my makeshift bed.

"I'll fix this in the morning," he said, plopping himself awkwardly onto my arrangement; the ottomans trying to part beneath him.

"Your butt will be on the floor the first time you wiggle. You're too big for this."

He was closing his eyes and trying to look comfortable as he ignored me.

I walked away, too exhausted to argue. I went back to the bedroom, reassessing the problem. The bed was a king. He had been able to sleep with me last night under far worse conditions, and I'd just leave my clothes on tonight. I heard the sound of moving furniture. I peeked from the doorway and noticed he had put an ottoman on one end of the loveseat and was trying to lay down with his legs draped over the small couch's arm, resting his feet on the ottoman.

"That looks really comfortable," I said with unmasked sarcasm.

He was lying on his back at this point. "Well at least, as you put it, my butt won't be hitting the floor in a few minutes."

"No, now both your legs are going to fall asleep.

"We only have four or five hours until dawn, I can take it."

"It's really gallant of you to sacrifice yourself this way, but after last night…"

His eyes popped open at the mention of our very long night.

"I think we could share the bed—it's plenty big enough—and I promise to stay dressed."

"You're probably thinking I did this on purpose, aren't you?" he stated, clearly just as uncomfortable on the loveseat as he had been in the chairs.

I went over to him and knelt beside the loveseat, leaned over and slowly kissed his cheek. I let my hand brush gently across the red marks I had put on his neck in the darkness last night, and then I looked into those eyes. "Last night was on purpose..." I watched his lips part to rebut, but I put my fingers against them to let him know I wanted to finish what I had to say. "It wasn't my fault or yours, but someone did it purposely to us. Everything happens for a reason. If you can be a gentleman when I'm undressed, then I think I can trust you to be one when I've got my clothes on. Come on to bed; we'll fix this in the morning." I got up and went back to the bedroom; he'd have to make the decision if he could handle another night with me.

I turned on the bathroom light and turned off the bedroom light, crawled between the sheets and closed my eyes. It didn't take long for my mind to start to drift, I was so tired and still feeling a few crappy leftover effects from my near overdose, but as I started to let my mind slip into the deep fog that was filling it, I felt the bed sink slightly.

"Good night, Annalisa." Were the last words I heard before falling off into nothingness.

CHAPTER FOURTEEN

I had given no thought to drawing the drapery over the sliding glass doors or the bedroom windows in the wee hours last night and now the sun was rising over the Atlantic and, judging from the brightness, seemed to be sitting inches away from the back of the cottage. I rolled over to turn away from the blinding light and met his gaze as he lay less than a foot away.

"Hi," I said, trying to stay still enough not to disturb the remnants of sleep still inside my brain. He didn't answer; he just brushed his palm across my cheek, letting his index finger trail my jaw line as he withdrew his hand. He rolled out of bed and went to the window and blocked out the offending light. The room wasn't dark of course, but it was mercifully darker than it had been seconds earlier. He came back to bed, yawning and stretching as he landed amongst the cool sheets.

"What time is it?" I questioned, since I couldn't see the clock on his side of the bed.

"Seven."

"I've gotta get ready to go see Mom," I mumbled, sitting up in the bed. I felt a strong hand on my shoulder pulling me back down to the mattress.

"I checked the visiting hours when I was on the computer making our reservations. You can't see her before three p.m."

I shivered and pulled the comforter back over myself. The ceiling fan was blowing at top speed and evidently the air conditioner had been on a low setting when we went to sleep. Without all the sunshine heating the room, it was beginning to cool once again. I inched my body backward to steal a little of the warmth that I knew was behind me.

He guessed my intentions and his arm wrapped around my waist and pulled me closer to himself.

Now I was warm and comfortable, the problem was that there was no way I could be drowsy with that firm body softly pressed against my own. My arm lay across his arm and I let my fingers lace between his. I could tell by his breathing that he also wasn't going back to sleep in this position.

"This cottage is okay," I whispered, wondering if he heard me. "I don't think we need to get a different one."

He withdrew his arm from my waist and moved my hair, exposing my neck. Then his mouth found its way to the bared area, tenderly nuzzling and kissing at my skin.

I should have known better, but it felt absolutely wonderful as it sent tingles and tremors through me. Unthinkingly, I arched my neck to give him easier access. That was a serious error in judgment.

His arm pulled and held me hard against his body as his breath immediately became quick and shallow. His warm nuzzle became hot, full kisses using his teeth to bite gently into my exposed skin. Suddenly everything became a full blown 'I just forgot where the brakes are' kind of passionate.

"Whoa! Sorry," I said as I struggled away from him. I rolled off on to the floor with a light thud and then scrambled up on my feet.

He propped himself up on one elbow, his eyes still wild from what he was thinking, "Do you enjoy teasing me or is it that you really don't have a clue what you do to me?"

"I'm sorry, I didn't' mean to… I just like being close to you." I was trying to regain my composure.

He fell back against the pillows, staring up at the ceiling. "I like being close to you, too. I can't understand why you and I—I'd like to be the one…"

"Aaah!" I vented, the frustration level rising inside me. "Don't you think I would like to say yes to you? Don't you realize that you are the person I want to give myself to?" The stupid tears were rising and I hated the fact that I couldn't argue with him without being overcome emotionally. "But this can't be right between us, not this way; it'd just be like you proved your brother's point."

I marched toward the bathroom and closed the door. I grabbed the hair brush and straightened out my tangled hair. "Is that the honest truth," I asked through the closed door, "What he said? Once a guy gets what he wants then he loses interest?" I didn't hear any reply. I brushed my teeth and gargled, wishing I had brought my duffel into the bathroom so I could change clothes. I washed my teary face, trying to not look upset. When I opened the bathroom door, he was still lying in bed, but this time propped on his other elbow facing toward the bathroom.

"Come here." He patted the side of the bed. My expression must have told him I wasn't completely ready to trust him again. "Please, come here."

He no longer had the wild look in his eyes; he simply looked concerned about what I was thinking. I sat down gingerly on the edge, but he was reaching for me, drawing me toward him. I tensed, not sure what to expect.

"Please, I'm not going to hurt you, Leese." That was not the best choice of words and we both knew it. He shook his head at the blunder. "I'm not going to try to force you to do something, but I want you close to me—I want to ask you something."

I relaxed as those powerful arms pulled me against his chest. He pressed his lips to my hair and whispered, "Is that what you're afraid of? If something happens between us, then I won't care anymore?"

My throat was tingling, trying to form a lump, "I used to think that love meant something—if you gave your heart to someone, then it was forever—but..." The lump had formed and I knew the only way to continue the conversation would be to let my tears fall. I turned and looked into his eyes, his face so close. I reached my fingers up to touch his cheek. "I'm having trouble believing it means anything to a man," I said, as I looked away.

"Leese, that's the difference between needs and love. Everyone has needs. When I kissed your neck, you had a physical reaction. You showed me a need to feel more, to want more. I've never known anything else besides the need. David knows that. He's in the same trap that I was in before I met you. He can satisfy his needs, but he's never been in love. He knows respect, Dad taught him that, but not love." He made sure that I turned back to look at him as he spoke. "If I hadn't felt something different for you, David's plan would have worked perfectly. But, as much as I had the need that night, I knew I could never do something like that to you unless I knew you wanted me to, not just a drug talking.

"You don't know how many times that night while you were lying there begging me to be physical with you that I told myself it was okay, because you were saying yes. But every time the thought crossed my mind, I realized I'd never be able to face you the next morning." Very slowly and deliberately he lowered his face across my breast and placed his ear to listen to my racing heart. It wasn't sexual, but it was sensual. As fast as it had been beating, it felt as if it had taken flight with him so close. I cradled his head in my arms, wishing this moment would not end.

"He's wrong, Leese. If anything had happened between us, it wouldn't have made this easier. Even without anything happening physically, it just keeps getting harder every single second. I'm in totally new territory and what I know is that I keep expecting the only other step that I do understand."

"I want to take that next step because I love you, but it can't be this way. Call me a Christian freak, but I've got to have forever."

He rose up, his face became very serious, "I'd never call you that. I love how much faith you have in God, but we don't have forever and by the time today is over, we may not even have tonight."

A pang of fear coursed through me.

His voice dropped low and hoarse, "When you go out the door today, the whole world is going to know where you are. You will be on every news broadcast from here to Canada. I don't know if I can manage to get you back here without a news crew following us—and they'll lead the rogue right to our door."

We lay together for a long while, just being still and holding each other. I looked at the clock and it was nine-fifteen. I rose up and went to the sliding doors, looking out on the private white sand beach on the calm inlet. My stomach rumbled. "Do they serve any kind of breakfast?"

He was already up and coming through the bedroom door. "Yeah, donuts and coffee, I think. I'll go up to the office and bring something back."

I unlatched the door and slid it over letting the balmy salted breeze come into the room. "They have hammocks under the palms. I'll wait for you outside.

He went out the front door; I stepped out the back. There was a nice double-size hammock close to the water and I went down to try it out. Sitting there I turned over what would happen today when I got to the hospital. I was sure Robert would be there at some point and, if he were, what would I say to him? Was it possible that he and I could sit down and work out this mess? Perhaps I could offer him whatever money he needed to clear his debts and get out of our family and leave us alone. I could tell him that I knew about the hit and maybe I could convince him to call it off or I would produce evidence to put him in jail. Of course, I wouldn't tell him that what I had didn't amount to quite enough, but… The possibility of having him call off the hit, should free Evan from his obligations. Maybe we might have a chance, a real chance together.

"I hope you like cherry." His voice startled me. He was carrying two cups of coffee with a Danish balanced on top of each. I took one from his hand and smiled.

"Sure, I'm so hungry, I think you could have dropped it in the dirt and I'd still eat it."

He laughed, "No, I didn't drop it, but I could if you…"

I smacked his shoulder with my free hand as he joined me on the hammock. After our tiny breakfast, I went inside for a shower and to get ready for my debut back into public life. All my clothes had been crammed into the duffle, so I had to spend time ironing. He called his attorney and the document was faxed to the motel office. I folded it up and placed it in my purse.

The only thing left to do was to wait until I could see my mother. At 11:30, his personal cell went off. It was his father. He stepped out the back of the unit, closing the sliding door behind him. He motioned me to stay inside as he discovered what information his father could offer. I watched him through the glass as he paced along the beach. I could see nothing positive in his facial expression. He seemed to grow darker, angrier, and more agitated as he talked. I watched as he finally plopped down on the sand, his knees drawn up and parted, his head hanging forward, his hand cradling his temple. I watched him close the phone, but I had a feeling it wasn't a good idea to approach him.

I would have to be patient and wait for him to come to me. I watched the clock tick by. After five minutes he returned, but he didn't say anything. He went out the front door and returned moments later carrying his gun cases.

I followed him to the bedroom as he opened them on the bed. He looked at me and handed me my holster. "Put it on," he ordered.

I took it from his hand, "Are you going to tell me what he said?" I asked it gently, but he still gave me a hard look. He picked up my baby Glock and dropped the magazine into the handle. He actually scared me when he chambered the first round; he had told me I wasn't allowed to carry it chambered. He clicked on the safety and handed it to me. I hesitated.

"Take it," he snapped.

I put it in the holster and fastened the strap around the butt to secure it. I slipped my arms through the straps and clipped it to the waist of my skirt. I found my hoodie and put it on, zipping it half way.

He put on his dual holster, chambered a bullet into each gun and secured them in place. He had brought a jacket, which was going to be very uncomfortable since the temperature today was predicted to be in the low eighties. He chambered bullets in both his rifles, closed the case and slid it under the bed.

I reached out my hand to rest it on his arm as he stood up, "Please tell me what he said. I can tell it's not good, but I'd still like to know."

He still looked so angry, but I could tell he was trying to keep it under control. "Let's go sit in the living room." As soon as we sat down, he began, "It's not one rogue,"

I know my mouth opened, but he continued before I could say anything.

"It's two brothers."

"You know them?"

"They did some work for a friend of one of my dad's business partners two years ago. They haven't had any regular contract work for our side of—from our clients because they were a little too bloody."

"What happened?" I didn't know if he'd tell me, and I truly didn't want to know.

"They were supposed to take out a rival warehouse boss, who had been siphoning off business from one of the local mob members. The guy had refused to join the union of businesses when he was given the opportunity. Jack and Ricky got a little over zealous and ended up not only killing the guy, but his wife and three warehouse workers. They burned the building to the ground just to be sure there was no evidence left behind. It really pissed them off that the mob didn't care for their tactics.

"There is more than one group to work for in this business, so they have been doing work for an east coast group, but mostly private jobs since then and, by all accounts, they haven't mellowed, they've gotten worse. They're particularly good at one brother causing a scene, like the shooting at the school, and when the victim tries to get away the other brother either picks them off or has their car rigged to blow. I was right that day at the school to be extra cautious on getting away. They work cheap, dirty and quick."

I could tell there was more coming as I watched his facial expression change. " Now, would you like the bad news?"

I must have had a little catatonic look to me, as he gave a bitter laugh and continued.

"The word is out that they know you're already under a contract. Evidently Sharon Norton told them they would be stealing a mark from one of the southern mob's best if they pull it off. That would be an ultimate high for them to show our cliental that they made a mistake in writing them off years ago. They are just waiting for you to pop your head up and then they'll do their best to finish you first."

I had no tears inside me, no emotions welling to the center of my throat, just the bleak truth that what he said this morning was probably correct. Last night was the last night we would be together. I felt him reach around me and draw me against his side.

"Now that you know, are you okay?"

I nodded. "We need another car." I know that wasn't a response he was expecting, but the chances of something happening to him would be much greater if we traveled in one vehicle. I didn't want anything to happen to him. "I would think it would make it easier for you to stay back and see if anyone is following me."

He sighed, obviously believing my logic, "We'll pick up a rental at…" he started to say.

But I had something better in mind. "Are you ready to see your new car? It should only take us ten or fifteen minutes to get there from here."

"You mean your Porsche?" He seemed a little surprised.

"No, it's your car. I'm just storing it for you, remember?"

"Leese, we can't get anywhere near your house."

"I told you it is in storage. It's a big storage company off Teak Street. I'm the only one with the combo and I locked the keys inside with the car."

"We'll check the area out first. But, if I see anything I don't like, it stays in storage and you get a rental."

"And the bungalow," I added. "Would it be better to have two? You can watch me from…"

He held up another room key. "I decided that this morning. I had even decided on a rental car, but…" And then he gave me the oddest expression, "One thing worries me?"

I looked at him expectantly.

"Why are *you* thinking like *me*?"

Okay, the look made sense now; he was suspicious about my motives. "It's just—just logical, I guess."

"You never could lie worth a crap," he stated bluntly. "Why are you…"

I had heard the term about a 'light bulb' coming on, but I'd never actually seen it until that moment.

His head cocked sideways, and his eyes narrowed. "You're trying to keep me far enough away so *I* won't get hurt."

I was so busted. I was shaking my head no, but I could tell there was no doubt in him. "Leese, you're crazy. They're tough, but I'm better than both of them. I'm the sure thing that's going to end your life. I *should* give them a clear shot—at me!"

"Stop it," I snapped, clamping my hand against his mouth. "You made me promise you something the other morning, and now you're going to promise the same thing for me. Neither one of us is going to try to make this easier on the other. I'm yours until the time comes, and you're mine, no martyrs."

He reached out and held my face in both of his hands, his thumbs caressing my cheeks. "You've been a martyr since the day you figured this out. Maybe I should learn a little something about sacrifice…"

"Promise me," my voice was quivering. "Please, make it the most honest promise you've ever made," I said, repeating what he had asked of me.

The kiss came only slightly away from my lips; it was getting closer every time. "I promise," he whispered in my ear. We hung the 'Do Not Disturb' sign on our unit, and then left.

Teak Street Storage is a massive place where the rich tuck away their toys. We circled the area twice before he agreed that it was safe enough to enter. He pulled up to the closed iron gates and I had to lean completely across him to punch in my gate code. I could hear him sigh as I was stretched in front of him, my shirt pulled out of my skirt, exposing my midriff. The gates opened and we drove inside. Once we reached the unit, he made another inspection and gave me the okay to enter the code.

As the garage door went up, so did my smile. A fresh cool blast of air rushed from the building. My baby sat there gleaming the way it did when I parked it nearly nine months ago.

"Air conditioned," he scoffed slightly. "You kept your car in air conditioned storage?"

I just smiled and headed for the driver's door.

"Wait," he cautioned, as he pulled me back by the arm.

"Evan it's fine," I stated as I watched him lay down on the floor and look up under the car. "I don't think Robert ever had a clue where I stored it." My words had no effect as he popped the hood and checked the engine. He finally said okay and I brought the engine awake after it's long beauty rest.

It was like someone had stuck a syringe full of happy juice right into my veins. I looked at him and gave him a smoldering stare, "Wanna race?"

The smile fell completely off his face. "Leese..."

"I know, I know, 'be good,' right?"

He leaned into the car from the driver's window. "Yes, but I need to tell you something. I'll be in the hospital lot for a little while, looking for anything out of the ordinary, but don't expect to see me when you come out. I know it's hard but try to keep the visit with your mom short so the news media doesn't have time to get there."

I started to ask why he wouldn't be there when I came out, but he wouldn't let me.

"Drive back to the motel, but only if you are certain that you aren't being followed. If you are followed," he let his hand smack down on the window frame. "Well, I'm pretty confident you can out drive anyone to give them the slip, but be careful. I'll be back, but it might be after dark. Stay in our room, lights off and draperies closed. Anybody gets in there, you shoot."

"But…"

"No buts."

"But what if it's you?" That was a mistake I didn't want to make.

He sighed and smiled at the same time, "If it's me, I'll be speaking French, fair enough?"

"Yes."

I waited as he moved the Trans Am out of the way and I backed out. The garage door closed and we were on our way. I was going to make it to the hospital a few minutes before three which was perfect, but I still wondered what I'd do if Robert was there. We pulled into the lot and I immediately began looking for a spot closest to the entrance doors. He was no longer behind me, but I could see glimpses of the Trans Am as it traveled up and down the rows. I parked, further away than I wanted, but it would have to do. I hadn't been afraid until the moment when I opened my car door. I wasn't afraid of a sniper, I was suddenly afraid of what I would see when I entered my mother's room. It was time to find out just how bad everything had gone since I left.

I stopped at the main desk and got her room number and headed up to the third floor. The elevator doors opened to the psychiatric unit, and right in front of the doors sat a large reception desk. Evidently they didn't let just anyone traipse into the ward.

"May I help you," a young nurse asked.

"Yes, I'm here to see my mother, Nadia Winslett."

I could read a look of confusion on her face. "And you said you are—you're her daughter? I'll need some identification." She was asking, but her hand was on the telephone and dialing a number. I wondered if Robert had given instructions that no one see her unless he knew, but instead she was calling the hospital administrator. "Yes, Sir. She says she's her daughter." I snapped my driver's license down on the counter in front of her. She picked it up. "Yes, Sir, that's right, Annalisa Winslett. Yes, Sir." She hung up the phone and handed me back my driver's license. Your mother is in 378, down the hall to the end, make a left and you'll see it, a few rooms down on the right."

It was the longest walk of my life. Her door was closed and I tentatively pushed it open. It was a private room, yet there was a curtain drawn around the side of the bed. My heart was in my throat as I slowly moved it to the side. I couldn't accept what I was seeing. Her wrists were bandaged, IVs in both arms, her face was drawn and pale, and there were restraints on her arms and legs. She was asleep and I was so grateful because I wouldn't have wanted her to see my face. It would take me a minute to compose.

I went to the foot of her bed and picked up the chart. What heartless monster could Robert have talked into helping him do this? I looked in disbelief as the name of our family physician, Doctor Figarrio, was written in as the attending physician. I shuffled through the papers and found her list of meds; the list was too long.

I reached out and gently put her hand in mine, knowing that Evan said I was supposed to keep this short, but how was I going to leave her like this?

Her eyes opened at the contact of my hand. She studied me unemotionally as the seconds ticked by, and then she recognized me. "Oh, Leese, Leese..." She began to weep. "Thank God. I was starting to believe I'd never see you again."

"It's okay Mom, I'm here. What happened? The news said you— you tried to hurt yourself."

"I—I don't know. I didn't do this, Leese. Someone's got to believe me," she cried. "The last thing I remember was going to sleep and then I woke here in the hospital."

"It's okay, Mom. I'm going to do everything I can to help you."

"I want to go home," she whined.

I knew she was still going to ask me that same thing when I had to walk out the door and leave her behind. I sat there holding her hand, the straps keeping her immobile. Her eyes were watery and wild. She kept licking at her chapped lips. I looked to the yellow water pitcher and cup that sat on a table out of her reach; they were both empty. I went into her bathroom and filled the pitcher and brought it back to her bed, pouring her a small amount in the tiny cup. She sipped it eagerly, glancing around the room as if, every few seconds, it became a brand new place.

She looked up when she finished the water and cried again, "I want to go home now. Tell them it's okay to let me out of here. Oh God, Leese, I'm never going to escape. I can't find the way out. It's like my mind is filled with doors but they are all entrances, there are no exits. Every time I go through another door, I go deeper. It's like I'm trapped inside my own head. Somebody has to know the way out. I need someone to get me out."

"They have you on a lot of meds; that's why you're feeling this way. I'm going to help you, Mom. Please, just hang on, okay? I'll find a way. Doctor Figarrio will just have to listen to me." If it hadn't been Sunday, his office would have been my next stop.

She nodded her head furiously, her unbrushed hair like a tangle of wild weeds around her face. "I'll wait, but don't make it too long."

"I've got to go, but I love you Mom and *I will be back.*"

Reluctantly, she released my hand. As I was closing the door behind me the only thing I heard was the sound of her weeping uncontrollably. I hope I didn't make things worse for her by upsetting her this way.

There was a heavyset, gray-haired gentleman in a suit walking from the opposite direction as I was leaving.

"Excuse me, Ms. Winslett, correct?"

I knew he wasn't a threat, but he might be trying to hold me long enough for a threat to appear. I kept walking toward the elevator as I responded that he assumed correctly.

"I'd like to talk to you for a minute. Would you come down to my office?"

"Is this concerning my mother's poor treatment in your hospital?" I pushed the elevator button.

"Ah—pardon, me? Your mother is receiving the best..."

"My mother is being over-medicated, tied to her bed and your staff hasn't even paused to brush her hair or bring her a drink of water. I believe you and I have little to nothing to say to each other, but perhaps you will have plenty to say to my attorney. Good day." I punched the button for the first floor. I watched as his stunned face disappeared between the closing doors.

I was pulling out as I saw a news van pulling in. I smiled knowing that I had slipped out just in time.

I watched the rearview mirror the whole way back. I took a couple side streets just to make sure that no car ever popped up behind me twice. Once confident that it was safe, I went back to our bungalow.

I wondered where Evan had gone and why whatever he was doing would take so long, but it wasn't something I could question now. I would simply have to wait for him to return. In the mean time, I was starving. The coffee and Danish from this morning had long since vanished from my stomach. I looked in the fridge and grabbed the only thing we had; vitamin water. That wouldn't help much in filling me up, nor would it help me when it came time to finally sleep tonight. I had an idea, but I didn't know if the motel did such things, but it wouldn't hurt to try. I dialed the office.

"Yes, I was wondering if you could tell me if I can place a food delivery order and have it added to my room charges?"

"You're in unit eight, Mr. and Mrs. Gavarreen, correct?"

I know she must have thought we got disconnected after my extended period of silence, but that was something I just never expected.

"Ma'am?"

"Ah—Yes, that's correct?"

"Yes, that's fine. Your husband left us with an open credit in case you folks needed anything extra. Just call wherever you'd like and tell them to deliver it to the office. We'll bring it to your room."

"Thank you," I said, still stunned that he registered us that way. "That's very nice of you to deliver it to our room, but I can..."

"No, that's all right, Mrs. Gavarreen, we make special accommodations for our newlyweds."

I hung up the phone. My hunger was still there, but the newlywed line was like being hit by a stun gun. I couldn't move and everything inside me turned to jelly.

Eventually, when my faculties returned to semi-normal, I ordered two baked spaghetti and meatball dinners, one large chef salad and bread sticks from a local pizzeria. At least I could surprise him by having some food ready. Not nearly as much as he surprised me by telling the motel staff that we were on our honeymoon, but ...

Thirty minutes later there was a knock at the door and I peeked out to see a petite, older lady standing there with a large take-out bag. I opened the door, slightly. She gave me a smile, "I hope I'm not disturbing anything, but here is your dinner."

She passed me the bag as I had the sensation to tell her that he wasn't even here, but why spoil her fun. I thanked her and closed the door.

Just before dark I heard the sound of the Trans Am pulling up to the next bungalow. I watched from the window, noticing how he took everything in before stepping from the vehicle, including the slightly open curtain in our unit. He frowned and then proceeded to the door.

He was speaking as he opened it, "When I say close the..." The aroma of dinner must have hit him. "Did you use your credit card?" He didn't sound angry that there was something available to eat, just puzzled.

"No, you told me not too." I was reminding him that I *could* follow directions. "I had it delivered to the motel and they charged it to our room."

"I'm sorry I didn't think to give you any cash so you could get something if you needed it, but you can use the charge card now that they know we're in town, just don't use it for anything that can be traced back here—like a delivery order."

"But I was careful."

"It's on the news that you were at the hospital today."

"The news crew never saw me. They were pulling into the hospital as I was pulling out."

"They don't have video of you, but they interviewed a nurse and a hospital administrator, both positively identified you. You won't be able to go see her tomorrow."

"But, I have to! She needs me and I promised." I was filled with fear that the few minutes I spent with her would be all I had and then she might think I wasn't going to help.

"Leese, I know they'll be waiting for you tomorrow. If they don't go ahead and shoot you when you're walking in, they'll wait for you to come out and do something then. I'm sorry."

"Can I at least go..." My emotions were trying to uncheck themselves, but I paused to force them back down. "Can I go see her doctor downtown?" I could see he didn't like that idea either, but I continued before he could answer. "Please. I have to see him and get him to drop all the meds he's put her on. He's been our doctor for years and I think, I hope at least, he'll listen to me. I've got to do something before she…" So much for checking my emotions, I couldn't continue.

He sighed.

I knew the sigh well. It was the one he used just before he caved into whatever it was I wanted at the moment.

"I don't cry to get my way," I defended my emotional inabilities, and then began wiping away the tears. "It's just this is really hard."

"Annalisa, if I thought for one second that the tears were fake, you wouldn't sway me. But, I've never seen so many honest tears in my life."

"Sorry," I choked, grabbing a dinner napkin and trying to stop the next downpour.

He moved beside me and pulled me into that place in his chest where it seemed I fit so perfectly. "Don't apologize. In this business I haven't seen much honesty, and I'm finding that I like it."

"So can I go?" I implored, looking up at him with my still watery eyes.

"Yeah," he laughed softly. "But we'll plan that out in a little bit. How about dinner?"

We sat at the small dinette and avoided talking business. I think we both needed doing something normal, like sharing a meal, to take a little of the stress off. But as soon as I put the leftovers in the fridge, I had to ask where he had gone today.

The 'I-don't-want-to-tell-you' face appeared.

"You might as well tell me because…" Then a horrible thought crossed my mind. I flashed back to our conversation this morning about his needs and how frustrated he had been when I stopped his advances once again. What if he… I know I went pale.

"What is it?" He was genuinely concerned.

"Unless you… Never mind, maybe I don't have to know everything."

"Annalisa," he said, his head cocking sideways slightly. "What is it? You're upset about something."

"It's nothing, I'm just being stupid. Forget I even asked." I was trying to find something distracting to do, anything to stop this conversation that I initiated. "Let's watch the news—I hear an heiress turned up today." I was trying to put a little humor back into our evening.

He caught me before I got to the television and simply picked me up in those massive arms and carried me into the bedroom. It was completely dark, not even the bathroom light was on. He laid me down softly and pulled me in close.

"You want to know where I went today. Okay, let's discuss it."

My heart felt as if it was going into defibrillation and I had to catch my breath. This sounded like a hideous confession coming and I really didn't want to hear it. I knew I wasn't the first young woman to be in his arms, but somehow if he was to tell me what I suspected, everything would change for me and I'd never be in these arms again. "Please don't. There are some things I'd rather be ignorant about."

"What is going on inside that brain of yours? I got Sharon's address and went to scope out her house."

The oxygen returned to my system. "Oh, I thought—I thought there was something you didn't want to tell me."

He was quiet in the darkness, and I knew there was more. "You're right. There are some things that I don't want to tell you."

Okay, now I'm back to feeling like I could pass out on this internal coaster ride. It didn't take all afternoon to find the woman's house. I was picturing Sharon and the fact that she was a beautiful blonde, far too young for Robert, but not for… "I'm gonna be sick," I said trying to rise up.

"You don't need to know every…"

"Yeah, okay. I get that. Just let me up and…" He was still holding me as I began to tremble. I needed to get away.

"She's using Robert to get to your families fortune."

"Duh. I didn't figure a woman that looked like that was really interested in him." I snapped.

"I found out that she and I are a lot alike…"

That was all I could take of this confession. "Stop it! Let me up!" I was struggling hard against him now, but he had decided I wasn't going anywhere. He rolled on top of me, pinning my arms above my head and stopping my thrashing legs with his own. I felt almost crushed as his full weight came down on me.

"What the hell is wrong with you, Leese? Stop it, and be still."

"I don't want to know what you did with her today," I struggled to get out. "Next you're gonna tell me she just has a lot of *needs*—just like you." I was sobbing at this point and I knew if he gave me a second of freedom, I would be out the door and I really didn't care who was waiting beyond it.

He paused so long on top of me that I wondered if he was trying to crush me. "Ah, Leese—I didn't mean for it to come out sounding like... *You think I went over there and slept with her?* No, I found out she's a mob princess. Like me, her family is all mob—she's... My God, Leese, why would you think—how could you think that I would do that to you?"

"After this morning you said—you talked about your needs—and then you were gone all afternoon—and you didn't want to tell me— you and I can't..." I was on the edge of hysterics at this point.

"Leese," he crooned, his hand released my arms and cradled my face. "I haven't even been able to think about another woman that way since I met you. My needs are for one person, and that's you." His body relaxed and he positioned himself to take the weight off me. "I didn't want you to know she was mob. And that I think she's sleeping with either Ricky or Jack— they're staying together. I'm pretty sure she is waiting for Robert to get sole control of the money and then she's going to take it from him and give her daddy a big financial boost. I'm certain she'd be happy to have all of you dead, Robert included."

"I'm sorry," I whimpered. "I just didn't want to know if you had..."

His face descended in the darkness, his cheek rubbing slowly in the soft pile of my hair by my earlobe. "You may ruin this for me for life," he breathed quietly. "Nothing has ever felt this way. I've never had a need like you before." His mouth found its way to my neck, his body provocatively pressed against my own, and his hands beginning to slide down where there had always been breaks before.

I heard him whisper something urgent to me, but I couldn't hear anything except the roar of my pulse in my ears. With trembling fingers, I began undoing the buttons on his shirt, feeling the hot muscled skin beneath. He moaned at the touch of my hand. The voice came again, clearer and frantic, surprising me with his request.

"Tell me to stop, Baby. Tell me before it's too late."

"I love you, Micah," I replied. "I can't hurt you this way anymore. Make love to me."

It was as if I could feel him coming undone. Passion descended like fire. I knew he needed me the same way I felt the night he pulled me out of the pool; more than anything, more than air, more than a beating heart, more than life.

"You didn't want it this way, Leese." His body pressed firmly against my own as if two pieces of a puzzle were about to come together. "You said it had to be forever." His mouth was now in the hollow of my throat and moving lower.

"We don't have forever, Micah—tonight will have to be forever."

He stopped, his head resting against my breast. His breathing was being reigned in and control was returning. "No. You aren't doing this for yourself, you're doing it for me. I can't let you give up on forever. I can't let you change that part of your beliefs because you want to satisfy me. You said this morning that you had a hard time believing it means anything to a man. I want you to know that it means something to me."

"You've been waiting for a yes." I swallowed hard. "I'm giving it to you."

"And I'm giving it back. I'm saying no."

With that he rose from the bed and went into the shower. I lay there and tried to let the magnitude of what just happened work its way through me. I was relieved and yet I was still aching for his touch, the feel of his lips on my skin, and the feeling of a consuming passion. Would I have regretted it in the morning? I know I would have, but as far as tonight my only regret was that he was the one who said no.

I wondered when he came out of the shower if he'd get anywhere near me; we came too close this time. But he surprised me, crawling into the bed and putting me securely in his arms. "Now we can talk about my day."

"I thought we did talk about your day."

"We got distracted—at least I was distracted and..."

"Me too," I added, snuggling against his chest.

He wrapped me tighter in his hold. "When I left to get our breakfast this morning, Mom called and gave me the low down on Sharon. I didn't want to tell you because you had enough on your mind about your mom. When she was checking up on her, she found that Norton was her married name."

"She was married?"

"She was twenty-two at the time and her husband was fifty-seven. He had several million in the bank, but, mysteriously enough, he had a serious car accident three months after they were married and died."

"Funny how that happens, isn't it?

"Her maiden name is Moretti. Her family works the east coast. That's where she got connected with Jack and Ricky several years ago. Evidently she has hired them more than once. She's sloppy when she does something or else that bank withdrawal would have never shown. I guess she figures her daddy will get her out of any fix she gets into."

"So you think she's got her sights on Mom's money so that she can give it to her father?"

"Actually the extra money that has been keeping Robert afloat has been coming from the mob like we suspected, but particularly from the Moretti clan. I guess she figured they would be getting back their investment when she gets finished with him."

"So why did you say you think she's sleeping with one of the brothers?"

"Did I tell you that?"

"You really were distracted, weren't you?" I was smiling in the dark, letting my hand trace the pattern of his abdominal muscles through his cotton tank.

He squeezed my shoulders. "Don't derail me. When I left the hospital, I drove down to check out a rental in her name by the beach. The house next door is for sale so I called the realtor and asked her to show it to me."

"Wasn't it obvious to the realtor that you spent most of your time looking at the house next door?"

I could actually hear the smile appear on his face. "I didn't keep the realtor there long. But I spent plenty of time in the house."

That wasn't making sense. "But..."

His fingers found my lips to hush me. "Most people don't check to see if the person beside them is watching when they enter a combination or a code. It was easy to see her enter the lockbox code, 9-3-9-7. The realtor left and I let myself back inside. The key is now in my pocket."

I was considering how he easily remembered the size of my clothes, undergarments and shoes. "Do you have a photographic memory?" I simply had to know.

"Pretty much, but usually only if I'm interested in what's going on." He seamlessly moved on to the next detail. "They were all three there at the house. I watched until about four o'clock, I think that was when the news broke that you had been at the hospital. They must have been getting ready to go out and see what they could find when I saw her lip-lock with one of the guys before they left. She may have paid to get rid of you, but I wouldn't be surprised if one of those guys is itching to get rid of Robert for free."

"Kimmy!" I stated, suddenly sitting upright. "I've got to find out if he took her back from Bev and Matt!" Panic like a wave of nausea washed over me. "If she's here, those guys won't care…"

"Slow down, Leese. Nothing is going to happen until Robert has Power of Attorney. And I'm sure Sharon won't try anything for a few months, at least not until she can worm her way into the finances."

"I've got to call them and ask…"

"You can call them, just not tonight. It's getting late. It'll be okay. I wouldn't be surprised if Robert had decided to at least let her finish the school year there. And I'm sure with all this messy business with your mom, he didn't want her around to see it."

"So what now?" I asked resting my head against his chest. "I didn't think we'd get to have tonight together."

"Me neither. I assumed I'd be in the other bungalow pulling an all-night surveillance—there are two beds in the other unit if you'd rather spend the night in it."

"I told you this morning that this one was okay. By the way," I said remembering something that I wanted to bring up. "When I called the office for the delivery I found out how you registered us."

"You didn't like the idea of me nearly ruining your reputation at the high school, so I assumed you would be more comfortable as my—my wife while we're here."

I wanted to tell him that I'd be comfortable as his wife anywhere. I would be comfortable in his arms every night. What would it be like to spend a wedding night with him? I had nearly found out, if he hadn't been the one to come back to reality before we vanished into passion. "Yeah, I think it's better this way." I sighed as I nestled deeply against him, "Micah, are you comfortable?"

He had been propped against the head board when I asked him, but now he was sliding down to a full recline with his head on the pillows. He moved my body effortlessly as he moved his own. "I am now," he answered.

"Could we sleep this way tonight? It's not going to cause a problem, is it? I just want to fall asleep in your arms."

His lips pressed to my forehead and stayed there for a long moment. "Good-night, Baby. I..." There was nothing now but silence. Whatever he had started to say, he decided to stop himself.

"Good-night, Micah. I love you."

"Leese," came a whisper in the dark.

"Yeah?"

"I can't help but notice, you aren't calling me Evan anymore."

"Evan was a dream," I said softly, sleep starting to invade the warm corners of my mind. "You're my reality, Micah. I guess I just want you to realize I love you no matter who you are, or what you've done."

"Good-night."

CHAPTER FIFTEEN

Morning wasn't quite as harsh as yesterday. The curtains were all drawn, but the sunlight filtered in through every available crack and crevice. I was so very, very comfortable. I was still against him, his arm wrapped around my waist and the sound of his peaceful breathing on my shoulder. I lifted his hand to my mouth and tenderly kissed each scarred knuckle, the back of his hand and then his wrist. I heard him take a deep moaning breath as his arm slipped from my grasp and he rolled to his back and stretched on the bed.

"What time is it?" I asked quietly.

"Almost eight."

"The doctor's office opens at nine," I said wearily, rising up from where I had been so comfortable. I went to the bathroom for my morning routine and returned to find him up, dressed, holstered and slipping on his jacket.

I had ironed my clothes yesterday and had set them out, ready to put on. I couldn't see any reason to go to the bathroom to change; after all he'd seen me in bathing suits skimpier than my bra and underwear so I simply stood at the dresser and dropped my skirt and slipped into my jeans. Off came one top and on went the next. I had brushed my hair once, but changing shirts necessitated messing it up. I turned to go back to the bathroom to brush it when I found him standing there staring at me.

"What?" I asked as I side-stepped around him and went into the bathroom.

He followed me. "You just changed clothes right in front of me." He sounded a bit dazed.

"My bikini is tinier than my underclothes, that and the fact that you have, unfortunately, seen me butt-naked as well doesn't leave much reason for me to run and hide."

He smiled. "So now I get to change in front of you, too?"

"I've seen you in your board shorts. You do wear underwear right?"

He smiled.

"You're already dressed, but if you don't wear anything under that gun belt, cowboy, keep your pants on in front of me."

He pulled down slightly on the top of his jeans and a pair of boxers became visible.

"Well, that answers that question." I stated.

"About whether I wear underwear or not?" He winked.

"No, the boxers or briefs question," I laughed.

I used his personal cell to make a long awaited call to Bev and Matt's house. They didn't usually leave the house until eight-thirty so I knew they should be home. Bev answered, her tone was cautious because she didn't recognize the phone number, but when she heard my voice she began to cry.

"Are you okay? Where are you? I heard on the news you were back in Palm Beach. *Are you with Evan?*" Her questions were in rapid fire order, but she put the most emphasis on her last one.

"Calm down, Bev. I'm fine and I am in Palm Beach—with Evan." It was funny, but after last night, calling him Evan was now odd to me. "There are a million things I'd like to tell you, but I've got to know if Kimmy is with you or did Robert come get her?"

"She's still here with us. You're dad said things were still crazy down there. How is your mom?"

"Things are pretty bad right now and I can't talk long, but could you do me a favor if he calls and wants her to come home; give him an excuse. Any excuse that he'll believe will do. It's really, really important that she doesn't come back here until this mess is straightened out."

"Ah—Leese—if you're dad wants her..."

"Bev, he's not my dad. You know that and I've found that he is at the root of all these problems, especially Mom's. Please keep her away from here if you possibly can."

"Do you want to talk to her?" she asked quietly.

"I want to but I can't. I've got to go see Mom's doctor. If everything works out down here, I'll call you when we can talk longer. And Bev, would you tell her I love her and I miss her."

"Of course, I will. Bye, Leese."

That was a big worry off my mind. The next phone call I made was to doctor Figarrio's office to find out if he was in this morning. Once I got my answer, I was ready to go.

"Are you following me today or are you disappearing again?" I smiled to let him know I was okay with whatever decision he made.

"You may not see me, but I won't be far away. Try not to be in the doctor's office very long. The faster we move from one place to the other, the less chance we have of a news van pulling up."

"I'll try," I sighed. "It's been a while since I've seen Doctor Figarrio. I hope he'll listen to me."

Driving toward downtown, I glanced up every few minutes to see if the Trans Am was visible. He was very good at staying hidden because I only saw him twice, and that is a car that wasn't easily blended into traffic. I spent the remainder of my drive time thinking what I would say when I faced Doctor Figarrio. I usually could control my temper, but the closer I came, the hotter my anger kindled. How could he have been so ignorant, or worse, how could he have done this knowing what was going on?

I pulled into the doctor's complex and went inside. The receptionist was someone new to me. "I need to speak with Doctor Figarrio."

His cliental were the social elite and I could tell that the woman was assessing me by the clothes I was wearing. Her nose seemed to up turn as she asked, doubtfully, if I had an appointment.

"That isn't what I asked you, now is it?" I'd never tried to be a social snob, but she was picking the wrong day to piss me off.

"Well," she gave a snobbish sigh, still believing I was someone she could walk over, "He is in today, but his appointment schedule is full and we're not accepting new..."

I leaned into the glassed opening and narrowed my eyes, "Get off your cushioned chair and go tell him that Annalisa Winslett is here to see him. I don't care if he's in the middle of examining the president. Do it now!" I growled out.

The chair was empty before you could say one-thousand-one.

There were plenty of open seats in the waiting room, but I was so infuriated I just stood there as patients stared. I folded my arms, waiting for the door to the hallway to open. If I was correct, it would open quickly.

The door jerked open as Doctor Figarrio's startled face appeared. "Annalisa? Good Lord, where have you been? Your mother…"

I pushed my way passed him and headed straight back to his office.

He followed without further comment and closed the door behind us. "Annalisa, you've worried your mother into a…"

"That's a lie and you know it. My mother knew where I was." That wasn't completely true, but she and I had talked before I vanished. "What have you been doing to her?!" My voice was bordering on out-of-control as my fury mounted.

"I don't know what you're talking about…"

"Don't play stupid with me. You have been prescribing sleeping pills, anti-depressants, anti-anxiety and who knows what else. And, what makes it worse is that I know she didn't ask you for all this, Robert did."

"Robert has been concerned about your mother's…"

"Bull-crap! Robert has been feeding her all possible combinations of the garbage you've been prescribing to screw up her mind, not to help her. He's after her money and that is it."

"Annalisa, I've been your doctor since you were five, and I've never done anything to harm you or your mother."

"Well then you need to wake up, because that isn't my mother tied up in the hospital. She has a list of meds as long as my arm. She is freaked out, and if you don't drop off the drugs, she's going to really lose her mind."

"Annalisa," he said, sounding stern and almost chastising. "Your mother attempted suicide. Robert is concerned for her well-being. She has to be taken care of in the proper…"

"She didn't try suicide! How do you know Robert didn't dope her up and slit her wrist for her? I imagine the only thing he's upset about is that he didn't cut deep enough! She told me she only remembered going to sleep and waking up tied like a dog in the hospital."

"I'm treating what I know and what I see, Annalisa," he seemed more sincere. I could tell I was wearing on his defenses.

"Doctor Figarrio, you aren't helping her," I stated, cooling my temper and realizing that Robert may have been manipulating more people than Mom and me. "You know my mom. This isn't her. You've got to take her off all the drugs. Robert is the one behind all her problems, and I've all but got the proof in my hands. You're the only one who can help her. I know right now she is like your billion dollar baby and maybe you're thinking she's gonna be your fricken retirement plan, but she is my mom!" I took a breath to stop my anger from rising back up. "You took an oath to help people, not just collect a fat paycheck while you watch them waste away. Do this for her, do it for me—do it for yourself because I know your conscience is about to eat you alive. You know this is wrong."

"You're father will..."

"Robert isn't my father and after all he's done he certainly isn't my 'dad' anymore either. You don't have to tell him; just make the medical decision yourself to let your patient surface from under all the drugs. You're going to ruin her mind if you don't. Give her a chance and see if I'm right. If she is just as crazy without all the meds, then you can do what you have to, but give her a chance."

He patted my shoulder as he stood there, deep concentration etched across his face. "I'll call the hospital right now and I'll start reducing everything this morning. We'll see what happens. Within three days I should have her off most of it. But," he paused, looking very serious, "if Robert notices the reduction and doesn't like it, he'll just fire me and get someone else to do what he wants."

"I know that's a risk, but I promise you, after everything is cleared up, you'll still be our family doctor."

"If you're right, then I won't hold you to that promise; I never meant to hurt your mother."

"I think I know that now. Thank you. You don't know how much this means to me," I choked.

"I know you love your mother, Annalisa. I'll do what I can." He opened the office door and we began the short trek to the reception area. "Is there some where I can reach you to keep you updated on her progress?"

This posed a problem. I didn't actually know Micah's phone number, but I desperately wanted to be able to be kept abreast on mom's condition. "How seriously do you take your patient confidentiality?" I asked, watching the surprised look on his face.

"What I mean is that no one—*no one*—can know where I'm staying.
"

"I can assure you, Annalisa, the only person who will see your information will be me."

I had serious reservations, and I knew Micah would be furious, but should Robert pull something stupid, I wanted the doctor to tell me. He handed me a small slip of paper and I wrote down the name of our motel and bungalow unit eight. "Just call the motel office and they'll let me know to get in touch with you. I'm using a different last name, Gavarreen. Do you have a business card?"

He returned with a business card. "I've written my number on the back. Feel free to call me at home if you have any questions." He reached out and gave me a firm hug. "I didn't know the two of them were having problems or I'd have never..."

I laughed remorsefully, "Don't feel bad, I didn't realize how terrible things were myself until about a week ago. Thank you, again."

I walked out into the lobby and started for the door, but came quickly to a stop. There were two television news crews sitting out in the parking lot. I grabbed my key and steeled myself for the onslaught.

"Miss Winslett, where have you been since August last year?"

"Were you involved in the shooting in Pensacola?"

"Did your mother ask you to come home?" On, and on they came.

Questions pelted me like rocks as I pushed my way through the crowd. I could hardly pull the door to my car open for the press of reporters pushing their microphones and cameras in my face. I turned the key and edged my way passed the bodies and hit the street. I looked in the rearview and noticed one of the news vans was in pursuit. I could see a black Trans Am closing to cut between us and run interference for me, but (as much as I loved him) I really didn't need him for this adventure.

I dropped the gears and made a right turn, hit the gas and took the next left. By the time I was out of the city limits, I lost the news van and Micah. The big problem now was my car. There were plenty of Porsches in Palm Beach, but seldom did you find one with my unique paint job—I called it gun metal gray, but it was such a superior high glossed paint that it was closer to chrome. I was going to stick out like a sore thumb and, once Sharon's 'boys' watched the news, I might as well be driving a bulls-eye.

I made it to the bungalow, glad that the unit was far enough in the back that my car wouldn't be noticed from the road. I closed the drapes and waited for Micah. An hour later, I heard the deep rumble of a familiar engine.

I peeped through the curtains when he didn't come through the door after a couple minutes; it was immediately apparent what he'd bought in his extra hour. He was stretching a car cover over my Porsche; another was still wrapped and waiting on the hood of the Trans Am. As he worked to cover our vehicles, I warmed last night's left over spaghetti and set the table for lunch. When he stepped through the front door, the first thing he said was, "I don't think you needed me today, even I couldn't keep up with you!"

I wanted a humble expression, but the smile had more muscle. I went over to him and wrapped my arms around his waist. "I *do* need you; I can just out drive you."

His mouth opened, but then he paused. "I've got nothing, you're right."

After lunch, we relaxed on the loveseat waiting for the twelve o'clock news. "You realize driving your car now is probably not the best idea? I need to pick up a rental for you, but I really don't want you going anywhere else."

I snuggled into him, curling my legs onto the seat. "The doctor said he's going to start dropping Mom off her meds this morning."

He kissed the top of my head, "So he listened to you. Did you tell him your suspicions about Robert?"

I nodded. "He said he didn't realize they'd been having trouble." I wondered if I should tell him about giving Doctor Figarrio our motel information and his last name, but that was an angry argument that I would rather not have today or ever, if possible. Robert wasn't stupid and, if he was stopping by to observe her state of mind, he would notice that she was becoming lucid. I would be hearing from the good doctor, and then Micah would have reason to question how he knew how to get in touch with me.

The twelve o'clock news began and I was the top story. It was odd watching as I came out of the doctor's office, dodging reporters and driving away in my car. The news van had footage as they tried, unsuccessfully, to follow me. I felt Micah stiffen when a good picture of him appeared as he cut in front of them in the Trans Am. To anyone else watching the broadcast, it would just appear as if a car in traffic managed to get in the middle, but to Sharon and her hired killers, that shot would be very significant, not to mention how very significant it would be to a group of individuals in Louisiana.

I looked up at his face and I could see how much it bothered him; his jaw line was tight and the muscles on his neck were showing. There was nothing I could say because what was done was done. I slipped my arms around his waist and squeezed gently. I put my head against his chest as the news continued discussing my family's recent troubles.

"I'm sorry that I'm turning out to be such a problem for you." I didn't say it very loud, but I could tell that it stirred him from his state of aggravation. I felt his chin come to rest on the top of my head.

"I'm never careless, and that was a stupid mistake. I can't believe I…"

I could hear his heart rate increasing and felt his body becoming hard like stone as the muscles tensed, and he left his sentence unfinished. Then I felt his arm circle around me and he began to relax, the breathing slowed and the muscles softened.

"It's not your fault, none of this is. Leese, you realize, now that I know where Jack and Ricky are staying, I need to take care of them as soon as possible and I'll have to leave you for a while when I do."

"I want to go with you," I said, pulling back and looking at him.

"NO!"

"But what if you need me?"

No, Leese, this is what I do. I just have to make sure I get them when Sharon isn't around. I can't take a chance of her getting in the cross-fire. That would be a serious mistake to take out someone in another family."

I pushed myself upright, "Then why can this D'Angelo guy put a hit on you?"

He gave a long slow sigh and began explaining that he would be considered as being insubordinate. He accepted a job and was obligated to complete it. "You don't go back to the mob and say you changed your mind. But, they guard everyone under their umbrella of protection. We aren't allowed to simply pickoff someone in the family because we want to—it's got to be ordered from higher up."

"So you're saying that even though you're criminals, you still have a code or rules that you go by."

"Right. Every organization has to have rules and consequences for not following those rules."

"Can you ever get out?"

"Sure, it's easy; just get killed." He was being sarcastic and yet I could tell there was an underlying serious note.

"Without getting killed, can you get out?" I was hoping he would say yes, because, besides helping my family, I wanted to know I had helped him change his life.

"It's not easy and they make it so lucrative that most people stay to keep up their lifestyle."

"But it isn't impossible."

"Why are you grilling me on this, Leese?" He was starting to get that annoyed tone.

"I was just hoping, I mean after everything is finished, you could start over."

"When this is over, for once, I don't know what I'm going to do."

"If you didn't have to do this… If you could choose a new life, would you stay here—with me?"

"It's like you said, I'm too old for you. We're two different worlds."

I wasn't prepared for him to use what I said to his parents against me. "I didn't mean that, I just didn't want you to know what I was feeling for you. You're not too old for me and you can choose, if you want to."

"You don't want someone like me, Leese."

I started to rebut his statement, when he asked me to let him finish.

"You and I have been acting like a pair of kids playing house. This isn't me, Leese. I'm not this way. The things I've done would make you sick."

"But you want to change. You said you wouldn't let me give up on forever; you wanted to prove…"

His hand clamped over my mouth. "Stop it. I would like you to get a chance at forever, but I can't be the guy. I've figured that much out."

I couldn't hold back when he said that, and the tears began to silently slip down my cheeks onto his hand. He took it away from my mouth to wipe my tears.

"You," I choked, "are the one. I really am in love with you. Can't you believe that? Can't you understand that what I feel for you is the truth?"

"I should have never let us get this far," he said just above a whisper. "I just keep making the wrong choices with you."

I wondered where those choices began and I had to know the answer, but I couldn't look at him when I asked. I placed my head back against his chest.

"If I hadn't run away that first night," I asked, remembering the expression on his face the night that he stood in the living room buttoning his shirt over his freshly bandaged wound. "What would have happened?"

"It didn't happen, that's all that matters."

I could hear the pain in his response and I knew he didn't want to continue, but I had to know. "We wouldn't be here right now, would we Micah? You wouldn't have all these problems if I hadn't left that night."

"I don't think of you as a problem."

"But I am. Would you have killed me if I hadn't gotten away?"

"Are you sure you want to know this?"

I nodded and slowly looked up into the beautiful, disturbing face. He pushed me back against the arm of the love seat, his hand gripping at the base of my throat with the slightest pressure. The eyes were getting that empty stare as he held me there. I suddenly felt so small and frail as his mass dwarfed me.

"If I had gotten my hands back around your slender neck, I decided to choke you until you passed out, again. I would have raped you and then put a gun to your temple and killed you. You would have died that night if you hadn't stolen my car. Now do you understand the kind of person you keep saying you're in love with?"

"Yes," came my whispered reply.

"Good," he answered with a blank expression.

"But, I still love you, Micah."

His whole body slumped. "You're crazy…"

"I know that, but I can't change the way I feel; *you are the one.* If we, by some miracle of God, make it out of this, I want you to be my forever."

He laughed bitterly and shook his head as if there was no way that could ever, under any circumstances, happen. "If something changes, you'd be better off to completely forget about me and find someone else."

"Close your eyes," I asked.

"Why?"

"Please, just for a minute, I want you to do something for me."

"Don't kiss me, Leese."

That stung. "I'm not going to kiss you; just close your eyes."

Reluctantly he obeyed.

"For just a minute, I want you to think about someone else. Ryan is the only man I can think to use for this…"

He gave a light laugh, eyes still closed, "He's a boy, not a man."

"Well he'll just have to do. I promised him a date when I return his car and…"

The eyes came open. "You didn't tell me that. You said he didn't want you sleeping with me."

"That's because we never got to finish that conversation, now close your eyes."

He gave me an annoyed look and reclosed his eyes.

"Just for a moment I want you to think that this is over, for both of us. Robert has had a change of heart and calls off the hit, Jack and Ricky are gone. It's just me—and Ryan now." I could already see him tensing. "I return his car to Pensacola and he takes me on the date I promised him." His breathing was starting to get a little harder. "After the date, I find myself feeling vulnerable because you're gone and I end up in his bed."

The eyes opened, the veins were coming out on his neck and the jaw was clenching. He grabbed both my arms and pushed me back and stared at me. "You wouldn't do that. You're not that kind of girl…" he was grinding out the words.

"But I might. I already told you yes. What would keep me from…"

"Leese, you can't. I won't let you…"

His grip on my arms was starting to become painful and I was afraid I was going to end up with a pair of bruises like the one that had only recently faded away. "Tell me what you're feeling right now, Micah? Tell me the truth. Are you the only man you can see me with? Would you want any other man to put a hand on me?"

"I—I don't want—I'm just selfish, that's all."

"You are the one, and you know it. There is no other man out there I want. Please don't ever tell me that if this works out, you won't be here for me."

"That's a promise I will not make to you. But you're right, I can't even think about someone else touching you." He pulled me in close to that warm chest and whispered that this was just too damn hard to figure out.

"We belong to each other for however long we have," I said, my hand finding the remote and turning off the television. "We'll figure the rest out if we get the chance." This whole conversation had been too hard on both of us and I decided it was time to back off. "Can I go outside to the hammock?"

"Sorry," he whispered. "I can't take that chance."

I looked up and gave him a weak smile, "Fine, then I guess a shower will have to do." I kissed his cheek and left the room.

When I came out of the shower, I was surprised to find that he was gone. There was a note on the coffee table that said he had left to get a rental car, and a reminder to stay indoors.

Both cars were still in place so I wondered how he was getting to the rental lot. Surely he didn't take off walking, unless he wanted a chance to clear his head.

I straightened up the bungalow and made the bed, rearranged the furniture slightly, dug the disposable dishes out of the trash and washed them simply for something to do. But, once I had done every possible thing inside, the only thing left to do was to sit and think. Think about what we'd said to each other.

What it would mean to be free from the ugly curse that Robert had hanging over my head. What it would really mean to be with Micah when this was over. I couldn't tell him that there were times when he truly frightened me, but there was a part inside him that was coming to the surface that I loved more than anything I'd ever known. I knew the frightening part would remain with the total package. Someday, if we got a shot at someday, the unemotional, void and scary part of his personality would surface and I'd have to learn how to handle it without turning away. I could only hope I'd survive this and get the chance.

I heard the sound of a vehicle. I opened a sliver of the curtain to see a white, four door Taurus pull up in front of the other unit with Micah climbing out of the driver's side.

When he came through the front door, he had his unemotional face back on. "Grab your stuff. I'm moving you over to the other unit."

I was going to rebut, but I could tell he was in no mood for it. I packed up my items, wondering if he was going to bring his things as well. When he didn't make a move to get his stuff, I asked. "Do you want me to pack your clothes for you?"

"I haven't decided yet if I'll stay here or in the other unit with you."

"There isn't any reason to stay in here. I mean you can watch this unit…"

"There are plenty of reasons to stay here, alone. I just want to think it over first."

"If you stay here," I challenged him, angry that he might be thinking of putting some distance between us, "then how are you going to make sure I stay in the other unit?"

His eyes narrowed and I could tell he was not happy with my implied threat to escape. "I suppose I could tie you up, if you make me take that step."

I crossed my arms and stood there defiantly.

He walked past me and grabbed his duffle.

I relaxed.

He was going to get his things. But, when he turned around, he had something metallic and shiny in his hands; handcuffs.

"I told you, you don't know what kind of person I am," he stated, grabbing my arms and pulling them out in front of me.

He was wide open. I knew the weakest point in a person's grip and I could have twisted away. His groin was exposed for me to plant my knee, and there were a hundred different points I could pick to strike him, but I couldn't do it. I simply caved inside. I handed him my life the day I had guessed what was happening and I was utterly unable to do anything to resist whatever he wanted to do with it.

He let go to open the handcuffs, and I just stood there offering my wrists. His eyes never softened as he accepted my offered arms. The metal clipped down so tightly that I winced. For an instant, I saw the regret flash across his face, then it was gone. He picked up my duffle and threw it over his shoulder and pushed me toward the sliding door. He opened it and looked out before proceeding to pull me toward the back door of the other unit.

He had already unlocked the other sliding door and he moved me to the single bedroom, but this unit had two beds. He unclipped one side of the handcuffs and placed the open end securely around the pole on the headboard. He walked away and never looked back. I lay down on my back, unable to roll onto my stomach because of my handcuffed arm, and just cried. I heard the Taurus crank up and pull away. I couldn't believe he'd actually left me this way. The conversation that I had hoped would make him realize that we belonged together had apparently had the wrong effect.

I don't know how much time passed before I finally sat up and assessed my situation. The handcuff was too tight and my hand was paying the price. My wrist was trying to swell and my fingers had begun to tingle. I rubbed my arm to keep the blood flowing and pulled the red-marked skin out from under the metal and tried to slip the cuff to the smallest part of my wrist. I checked the headboard to see if I could free the other end, but it was firmly bolted to the wall. I pulled the bar that ran horizontally, blocking me from sliding my handcuff directly over the top of the post. It wiggled slightly as I pulled it toward me. I began rocking it back and forth, each time it became a little more pliable. I kept it up until it finally broke off in my hand. I lifted the handcuff over the top and was free. Now the only problem was what was I going to do with this freedom?

I had packed my Porsche keys in my duffle and they were still there. I could drive away and, even if he came back as I was pulling out, he'd never catch my car in that crappy rental. I laughed sardonically to myself, he wouldn't catch me even if he had his Vet.

I wondered which unit he would enter first. Would he check on me or would he simply avoid me by going back to our old bungalow? I made my decision, wrote him a note and grabbed my car keys.

It was after dark when I woke to feel his arms around me. He was kissing my neck and asking if I could forgive him for what he'd done.

"Turn on the light," I whispered. He reached the bedside lamp and his distraught face came into view. I was back where he'd left me. I replaced the handcuff back over the top of the post so I couldn't wrap my arms around him, but that was when I felt the pain shooting in my right wrist. When I had fallen asleep my arm had slid down, pulling the cuff back to where it was too tight.

I winced and tried to move it. My hand had a purplish cast.

As soon as he looked at what was causing me pain, I watched the mortified expression take over. "Damn it," he growled out, but I knew it was directed toward himself instead of me. He quickly fished the key from his jeans and released me, rubbing and forcing the blood flow back to my hand.

I cried out, but tried to muffle it by clamping my free hand over my mouth. It stung so badly, a million different pin-pricks began to assault the once numb limb and the red marks where the cuff had bit into my wrist burned like fire. He just kept rubbing it until the color returned. My eyes were watery, both from pain and emotion. He pulled me against his chest and asked me why I didn't run when he'd given me the perfect reason to do it.

"There's no place else I'd want to be," was my choked reply.

"Come on," he said, turning away from me and wiping his eyes.

"Where are we going?"

"I need to get you something to eat. We'll go for a ride." He still wasn't turning around to face me and I realized he didn't want me to see just how emotional he was at the moment. We slipped into the Taurus and drove away from the motel. "There is a drive through Chinese take-out up here on the right, or we could get a burger or a little seafood."

"I'm not really hungry," I stated, just glad to be out of the bungalow. It had been hours since I'd eaten anything, but my emotions overruled my need for food earlier in the evening.

"Please eat something, Leese. You've got to be hungry."

"Why did you do that to me? Did I piss you off for some reason? Was it something I said?"

"If you'll eat something, we'll talk." He gave me a pleading glance.

I pointed to the Chinese restaurant and he pulled up to the speaker box and looked at me expectantly. "Just some pork fried rice and an ice tea, if they have it."

He ordered the same for both of us. Once we pulled away he headed toward the public beach. It was open until midnight and it wasn't even ten. There were a few other cars parked but he drove down to the deserted end and pulled into a spot. He grabbed the bag of food and opened the door.

"Don't you want to stay in the car," I asked, as I reached for his arm.

"Nah, I was out here earlier today and there are some tables under the pines, we'll eat there."

I followed silently as we walked through the shadows of Australian pines down to an area just before it opened into a wide section of moonlit beach.

We sat down and he opened the bag and handed me a small white box and a plastic fork.

"So tell me what happened today. Why did you decide to..." I knew it was partly my fault for asking how he would keep me from leaving, but there had to be more to it than that.

"You made me think about what I was feeling for you, Leese. You made me think long and hard about it. You're right..."

I waited for something more, but he was silent. Was he admitting that we belonged together forever? Was he admitting that he was the one for me and I was the one for him? I had a feeling that wasn't what he was about to say. "Go on, Micah. What am I right about?"

"I told you I'm a selfish person. When I left to get the rental, I kept thinking about you and—and someone else. I couldn't handle it and I realized I can't let someone else have you—ever."

I reached my hand over to rest on his in the semi-darkness. The trees blocked much of the moonlight, but I could still make out the pain-filled expression on his face.

He pulled his hand away from my touch. "Don't think it's love, Leese. That's not what was running through my mind. I was relieved..." His voice choked up and I could tell he was on an emotional edge. He was looking at me now and I could see the tears starting to run down his face. I wanted so badly to reach out and stop them, but I knew he needed a minute to finish saying what was hurting him so much. "I was relieved that when this is over, no one is ever going to touch you." He stopped to wipe away the tears, "God, that is so wrong to know I'd rather have you dead than to have you with another man. You're so unselfish and giving and all I'm doing is taking everything away from you."

"No, Micah…"

"Gwen was right when she had you sing that song in the restaurant. She knows me and she knows what I'm capable of doing. I'm worse than David. At least he would have just shot you. But me? No, I've got to torture you first and make you think you're in love."

"I think you're wrong," I said softly. "There are two people inside you and they are ripping you apart. One is the person you've been raised to be and the other is the person you've always been, but never let exist until now."

He was shaking his head, looking down.

"You're punishing yourself for jealous thoughts, but if you had the choice you would never hurt me."

The head raised and the eyes flashed even in the dim surroundings, "I left you tied up like an animal. I was satisfied with what I'd done until I went into our old bungalow to go to sleep and found your note with the car keys on top of it telling me that you were staying of your own free will. That was why I went back over there, to make sure you were still there and that you hadn't changed your mind and run away. When I saw what I did to you…"

"You mean when Evan saw what Micah had done."

"You're gonna have me believing pretty soon that I'm a freak show and there are two guys living inside me, aren't you?"

"No, it's just one guy with the good and the bad taking sides."

"I have never been confused in my life. Everything has always been simple. I do my job, collect my pay, invest my money, manage my businesses and wait for the next job to come along. I had a weird feeling about this job when I took it, and from the minute I met you, I knew my life was going to change if I got close at all."

I opened my little box of dinner and took a small bite. I could tell that it pleased him that I actually ate something. "If I'm going to eat then you have to too," I said, hoping our night was finally going to lighten up.

He shook his head as if he had no interest in the food he insisted we buy. I dug my fork into my container and held a bite out for him to taste. He gave me an odd look, but he finally opened his mouth and accepted the small amount of rice. "I didn't feel like eating either," I confessed. "But, taking that first bite can change everything. It's good, right?"

He nodded and then gave a small smile. "That sounds kind of prophetic."

I moved from where I sat across from him to sitting beside him. We shared my container of rice, and by the time we were done, his arm was around me and we were as close as we had been before our afternoon had been overshadowed by his jealous revelation. Did it worry me what he said about the fact that he'd rather I was dead than in another man's arms? Yes. Was it going to change how I felt about him? No. He was working through emotions he'd never dealt with, and I had to believe that he didn't really mean what he'd said; he simply didn't know how to handle the emotion when it hit him.

We got back to the bungalow by eleven and went into the new unit. "There isn't any reason, at least not tonight, for us to be in separate units, is there?" I asked.

"No, but even under the car covers, those two vehicles are like neon signs going right to the front door of bungalow eight."

"Well, then, I'm glad we're in nine, Mr. Gavarreen," I smiled.

"I have to slip over there and grab a few things tonight, but I'll be back. He handed me his key to unit nine, but I didn't understand why.

"Just a precaution," he explained. "If someone is waiting for me inside there, I don't want them to have a key to get in here with you."

"Oh. That makes sense, but ..."

"I'll knock at the door and I'll say something in French so you'll know it's okay to open it."

The other unit was completely dark, we had drawn all the drapery and now I was worried that it was a perfect place for someone to hide undetected. "Be careful," I whispered as he left me. I locked the door behind him and waited impatiently.

When the knock came at the door, it was followed by, "Si vous m'aimez, ouvrez la porte."

I opened it immediately.

CHAPTER SIXTEEN

We went to sleep in two separate beds because he said it was better for us, for now. But, when morning came, I felt that familiar weight of his arm wrapped around me. I snuggled deeper into his grip and felt it tighten; I knew he was awake without looking. "You changed your mind," I whispered, still facing away.

His glorious mouth found my neck and my ear, "I woke up around two a.m. and you were crying. I thought you were awake, but when I got next to you, I realized you were dreaming."

I was silent, trying hard to recall anything from my dream state, but I couldn't. I was so exhausted that all I remembered doing was going to sleep. "Did I say anything?" I finally asked.

"I could only make out a couple things, one was 'I love you,' you said it several times."

"And?"

He was pausing, so I had to assume he didn't like the other thing he was able to understand. I gave him a soft nudge with the back of my elbow to let him know I'd like for him to continue.

He pulled back my hair and kissed the bared skin. Every time he put his lips directly to my neck, I felt little shock waves through my system. "You asked…" his voice getting that deep husky quality as if he was trying to keep his emotions in check, "You were asking me to kiss you, and to please not hurt you."

"Oh," I was afraid to say more. A true kiss had been taboo between us because I had made it my last request, but there was

247

more than that to the kiss. I knew, and I think he did too, that if it hadn't been off-limits, we wouldn't have been able to stop ourselves when logic and morals told us we must. "So what do we do today?" I asked, changing the subject.

"I've got to get to Jack and Ricky soon. I spent part of yesterday afternoon tracking them down, but the problem is that they're staking out the hospital. They're certain you're going to show up there to see your mom, but I wasn't able to get any clean shots. They know I'm around so they are being extra cautious."

"That's what you were doing yesterday?"

"Yeah, I've got my rifle with the silencer, but I just didn't get the right opportunity."

"How..." I couldn't imagine him with that big rifle and no one seeing him and calling the cops.

His face buried deeper into my neck and I was losing my train of thought.

"What?" he whispered.

"How do you keep from someone seeing you?"

"Experience and training," was all he would say.

"And Jack and Ricky? Are they smart enough not to get noticed?"

"No they're pretty stupid when it comes to shooting someone. They aren't carrying silencers on their pistols, so they'll either have to shoot you at close range and run, or drag you off somewhere to finish the job without an audience."

"What about Sharon? Have you been able to find out what she's been up to?"

"Yeah, she is dividing her time between sacking Robert and Jack. Robert's just too ignorant to figure out he's being used."

"Serves him right, I guess," I said, unable to keep the bitterness out of my words. "He is using my mom in the worst way possible."

"I got a call from my attorney yesterday. I've had him checking on how Robert is doing with his Power of Attorney and he thinks it may only be another day or two before the judge grants his request."

"Doesn't her doctor have to say she's incompetent?"

"It's usually a panel of doctors but yes, her doctor would be the most influential in the case."

"Then he won't get what he wants. Doctor Figarrio should be able to see a difference..."

"If he truly did what you asked and it isn't some ploy to placate you until Robert has what he needs."

"No," I said, rolling over and looking into those beautiful eyes. "He was serious, I could tell. I've got to call this morning and ask if he's starting to see a change. She's had twenty four hours to start clearing out her system."

He had that intent stare going on and I was wondering what it was he was thinking, but I was also learning that if I pressed him for things that he wasn't ready to tackle, I could end up with a problem—a problem like the handcuffs yesterday.

At that moment, my stomach gave a rolling growl. I laughed and apologized. "I'm hungry."

He pulled me in close and buried that gorgeous face into the base of my throat, planting a kiss on my chest. "Me too," he replied, but it didn't sound like he was speaking of food. He sighed and rolled out of bed. That was when I noticed he was in his boxers.

"Ah…" I turned away and pushed my face down in the pillow. I hadn't expected my internal reaction and I knew I couldn't handle the view. I could feel the flush of heat sweep from the center of my solar plexus outward head to toe. The board shorts had been hard enough to handle, but the boxers were just a little too revealing.

I felt his hand on my back. "What?" he asked, but his mirth was evident in the tiny question.

"Nothing," came my words, almost completely muffled by the pillow. "Just get some pants on."

"You said as long as I had…"

"I know what I said but—but I can't—can't handle it. Please," I said raising my head off the pillow, but not opening my eyes or turning to look at him. "You're very—exposed—and I… Wow—does this ecstasy stuff say in your system for a while?"

I could feel him coming closer.

His amusement seemed to be growing deeper as he nuzzled the back of my neck. "It seems you and I have similar needs, Annalisa."

"Yeah well right now, I *need* you to have pants on!"

"Oh, Baby," he crooned in that sexy, soft voice.

That was all I could take. I'm not even sure how I got out of the covers and onto my feet as fast as I did but I made a bee-line for the shower. I could hear him laughing as I flung my clothes from inside the shower over the top. I grabbed the handle for the cold water and turned it on, taking away my breath when it met my excessively heated skin.

"Do you want some help in there?" he asked, just to vex me a little more.

"Go away, Micah," I snapped.

I could hear him laughing, and then I could hear it fade as he left the room. I don't know how long I spent under the cold water, but I finally understood his frustration level when I had caused him to run for the shower. I wondered how, if the physical needs are really this consuming, he survived the night I was out of my proper mind—and my clothes.

When I exited the shower I could smell the coffee; he was evidently back with our breakfast. I wrapped the towel tightly around me, since I hadn't bothered to close the bathroom door when I went charging for the shower, and glanced into the bedroom. Thankfully he wasn't in there. I closed the door, and locked it—he was still laughing at me.

I dressed and gave my wet, tangled hair a quick touch with the brush and then went out to where he sat at the dining table. I was trying not to return the big smile on his face, but I couldn't help it. "Don't say a word," I warned.

The eyebrows went up, but he was still grinning. He had brought four Danishes this time and I was so hungry I could have eaten them all, but would have to show I was satisfied with half. I had inhaled both of them and finished my coffee in a matter of moments.

"Wow," he exclaimed as he watched me rise from the table. "Just thinking about sex gives you quite an appetite."

"I wasn't thinking about—ugh!" I groaned as I snatched up his cell phone. "I've got to call…"

"Whoa, Baby," he was saying trying to take the phone out of my hand.

I was so flustered I was ready to fight him for it when he simply told me I had the wrong phone. "Oh," I said, quickly putting it in his hand as if it was too hot to touch. "Sorry. I didn't mean…"

He handed me his personal phone, but he didn't release it immediately when I tried to take it. "You have no idea," he began, "what kind of a turn on it is to watch you turn on. The shower didn't seem to help you, did it?" He finally released the phone.

"Not really," I whimpered. "I never understood when friends that I've known said they couldn't wait for marriage. It still seems so wrong, but I never knew it could be so—so hard. If we had—you know the other day—would this be easier now?"

He pulled me into those arms and the heat began to rise once more. "For us?" he whispered, "I'm starting to believe this must be what happens when love and needs mix—and I'm afraid it would be even stronger if we had slipped."

"Good grief," I stated, pulling away and burying my face in my hands. "It can't get stronger than this. Is this normal? I mean you've been with other..." I couldn't even say the word. I couldn't even imagine the thought, and I could feel that jealousness that must have speared him yesterday piercing my own heart.

"I told you before this isn't something I've ever been through. I hate to admit it, but I'm just about as virgin as you are when it comes to what's happening between us. I know one side to this coin, but I've never had them together—and you," he said, tipping my face up to his and resuming the embrace I had pulled away from. "You are dealing with both issues at once."

"Micah," I swallowed, "You've got to let go of me. I can't take this right now."

His smile tugged at the corners of his mouth. His mouth at the moment was the only thing my eyes were focusing on. I wanted that forbidden kiss like a moth seeking the light, but dancing too close to the flame.

"Please," I asked when he didn't respond.

"I'll be outside for a little while to give you some time."

"Thanks, I really do need that right now."

He turned me loose and went out the door.

I pulled Doctor Figarrio's card from my purse and, with unsteady fingers, dialed the number to his office. The receptionist answered.

"Hello, I need to speak with Doctor Figarrio, please."

"I'm sorry he isn't in right now, he was called to the hospital for an emergency. I could have him call you when he gets back in."

My heart was picking up the pace, "Emergency? Did he say what kind of emergency?"

"I'm not allowed to discuss..."

"I'm Annalisa Winslett; my mother is one of his patients at Columbia Hospital. Does this concern her?"

"Really, Ms. Winslett, I'm not allowed to discuss what kind of call he's on, but I'll get in touch with him and let him know you want to speak with him. I have your number on our caller-ID. Is this how he can reach you if necessary?" Then she repeated Micah's cell number to me and I told her yes, he could reach me at this number.

I hung up and called information for the number to the hospital. She had me worried with the tone she used when she knew who I was, and it left me thinking Doctor Figarrio was there because Mom was in trouble.

"Third floor reception," I said when the switchboard operator picked up.

"Psychiatric Care, may I help you," came a friendly female voice.

"Hello, I'm calling to check on my mother, Nadia Winslett. Is everything okay?"

"And your name?"

"Annalisa Winslett, I stopped by to see her Sunday, but I was just wondering how she's doing?"

"She's fine, Ms. Winslett. She has made marked improvements since yesterday morning. Doctor Figarrio has ordered the removal of her restraints and she's off almost all of her meds. By the way, she has been asking for you."

"Could I speak with her?" I wanted so desperately to talk with her, especially since now I was pretty certain that she wasn't the emergency that he was called to the hospital for.

"I'll see if she'll pick up. One moment, please."

The phone rang twice and then mom's voice came through as clear and slur free as I had ever heard.

"Mom, wow, you sound terrific."

"Annalisa? Honey, where have you been? I was starting to think I imagined the whole thing about you coming by the hospital."

"No, Mom, I was there, they just had you really sedated. So, you must be feeling better?"

"Oh, I can't tell you how much better I'm feeling. I'm actually starting to get a sense of normalcy. They took off those awful restraints this morning and I finally got to brush my hair."

I had to laugh. Mom was one of those people who liked to look her best no matter what, so having her hair a wreck must have been pretty traumatic by itself.

"Are you going to be by today?" she asked, hopefulness permeating the question.

"I—I wish I could Mom, but I'm still having some—some issues with Robert."

"He's got a lot of explaining to do..." she started to say.

"Mom, don't even talk with him. I'm telling you he's been behind all of this. He's even..." I wasn't sure if I should tell her about his affair.

"What, Honey? It's okay, you can tell me, I can handle it."

"He's—well, he's having an affair with Sharon Norton."

"Sharon Norton! Ah! She is nothing more than a gold-digging, bubble-headed, spoil-brat tramp..."

I let Mom vent. I had a feeling from the way she exploded that there must have been some kind of suspicion there all along. But, quite honestly, it was so awesome to hear her put together a coherent sentence that I just listened and smiled.

" Mom, I'll come see you as soon as it's sa... As soon as I can work it out, but for now you just keep getting better and I'll have you out of there in no time. And, when you are finally home, if everything works out, I've got someone I'd really like you to meet."

There was a long pause. "Would this someone be a boy?"

I was thinking about Micah in his boxers this morning and couldn't possibly classify him as a boy. "How about we just call him a guy?"

"Um, I see. A nice looking guy?"

"Gorgeous is a more worthy term—and I'm so in love with him." I knew I shouldn't be telling her all this. If things didn't get resolved this guy would be the literal death of me, but I wouldn't give her anything she could use to identify him later on.

She wanted to know more, but I told her I had to go, that I loved her and would see her as soon as I could manage it.

I was on a natural high and I couldn't wait to tell Micah. I turned to go for the front door and he was standing right there, I hadn't heard him come in and I didn't know how long he had been listening, but at least he was smiling. I made a running jump and landed with my legs wrapped around his waist and my arms around his neck. Even though I think I surprised him, he caught me effortlessly and held me as I let out a shriek and a few tears of joy. "She's sooo much better," I said muffling my face into that thick muscled neck. He wouldn't let me down as he carried me to the loveseat and sat, still keeping me on his lap.

"I heard most of it," he said gently. "So you'd like the chance to introduce us?"

"Only if everything works out," I corrected him. "We still have the Robert issue to contend with. If I shoot him, does that cancel the hit?" I was teasing, but I just couldn't help it because at the moment I was simply overjoyed. He didn't say anything and I was starting to wonder if he had taken me seriously. That was when I became keenly aware of the positions of our bodies as I straddled his lap. I was ready to move, but those steel hands gripped my thighs and held me in place.

"So you not only love me, but you told your mother that I'm gorgeous. You really think that?"

"Micah, you know that I find you beautiful."

"I just didn't realize how much I liked hearing it, especially when I know you didn't know I was listening."

"That's called eavesdropping," I said trying to wiggle free.

The expression on his face was either ecstasy or panic. "Don't move like that, Baby," he said in a low gasp, as his grip tightened and his hips lifted harder against my body.

The heat was starting to flood my senses and I knew this could get very dangerous. "Let go of my legs, Micah. I've got to get up."

The hands never softened and I could see the wild starting to fill his eyes. If both of us were on an edge this would be a train wreck that neither one of us could control.

"Please, Micah—please let me up before..."

The grip released and he lifted me by my waist and stood me on my feet. "I'm glad your mom is doing better," he finally managed to say as he also stood.

We were only inches away from each other. "Me, too," I whispered as his mouth descended and this time there was very little of the cheek touched as the edges of our mouths brushed against each other.

"I think I need another shower," I replied, close enough for my lips to touch his skin when I spoke the words.

"Me, too," was the reply. "We could take one together."

The cell phone rang and startled us both. It wasn't his personal phone, it was his contact phone. It was on the third ring by the time our heads cleared enough to realize he had to answer it. He moved to the sliding doors and slipped out the back of the unit before flipping the phone open.

I didn't know why his contact would call him, but I doubted it could be for anything good. I watched his face grow fearfully dark, anger, pain, hatred, disgust mingled in one expression. He closed the phone and stood there for a moment looking out at the inlet. Suddenly his arm came back and the small black phone was hurled almost to the opposite shore. I jumped when it hit the water and vanished below the surface. What could D'Angelo have possibly told him to make him so angry? We still had time. There were weeks left before the deadline.

Micah returned closing and locking the sliding door and then drawing the curtains. I didn't like the methodical way he was acting.

"What is it, Micah? Tell me what he said. Please, tell me because you're scaring me."

He turned, his eyes so different from any expression I've ever tried to read on his face. Then he said four words that felt like a jolt of lightening, "Your time is up."

"But we have four…"

"I'm sorry, Annalisa. He told me he got a call from his contact. Robert is giving me twelve hours to finish the job. He said there would be no more playing games. Your body is supposed to be dumped on the steps of—of a church here in Palm Beach."

When he told me which one, he wanted to know why that particular church.

"It's my church, the one I attended before they sent me to Pensacola."

"I've got to get out of here and think, at least for a little while. If you run, Annalisa, I won't blame you."

"I can't do that to you," I said, the knot forming in my throat.

"Then I'll have to kill you." And he walked out the door, cranked the Taurus and drove away.

I broke down and collapsed onto the floor, sobbing and crying harder than I'd ever known in my life. Our chance for happiness had ended. Even if I could get to Robert, I knew he wanted me out of the picture and he would stop at nothing now until it was over.

I must have stayed of the floor ten or fifteen minutes when Micah's personal cell phone rang. I was guessing it was his parents or, perhaps David, but when I looked at it I was surprised that it was a Palm Beach number. I dried my eyes and answered the phone, wondering if it was Micah.

"Hello," I said, my voice still shaking.

"Annalisa?"

"Yes, Doctor Figarrio?"

"We have a problem. I need you to come to the hospital right now."

"What? I just spoke to Mom no more than a half an hour ago—she was doing great."

"Robert is here and he has told the Administration that he is firing me and has another doctor who is going to put her back on *everything*. If you don't get here and convince them that you should be in charge of her health care, she's going to be in just as bad shape as before, if not worse."

"He doesn't have power of attorney, yet. How can he…"

"Because he's her husband. You are the only one who can stop this, but you have to convince the hospital board that you are more responsible and have her best interest in mind. He's here now and if you and I don't make a case in the next fifteen to twenty minutes, we lose her again. I got here this morning when he found out that she was lucid. I've been arguing with him and this new doctor he's trying to bring in for hours. I've done all I can do. You are her last hope." He sounded genuinely exasperated.

"I'll—I'll be there in ten. Where do I go when I get there?" I closed the phone and grabbed a pen and paper. I didn't want Micah to think I was running away; although I'm sure he would rather that I was running anywhere besides the hospital. I knew who was waiting for me. I was confident I could get in, but I doubted I'd make it out—alive anyway. I simply wrote that I had to go to the hospital and that I loved him and that I was sorry but maybe it was better this way.

I jerked off the Porsche's car cover and threw it to the ground. I made the twenty minute drive in eight. I couldn't take the chance of Ricky or Jack getting to me before I could help my mother, so I pulled right up to the entrance doors and jumped out and ran inside.

"You can't park there," someone was saying.

I ran past him to the reception desk. "I need to know how to get to the Administrative board office—quickly, please."

"End of the hallway, turn right and follow the signs for Finance. They'll direct you when…"

I was back in motion before she could finish getting out the last words. I was on pure adrenaline by the time I reached the proper door. I pushed it open and the first face I saw was Robert's. He looked extremely surprised to see me. Doctor Figarrio was there as well as another physician seated next to Robert, and the hospital board which consisted of two men and one woman. The one gentleman I recognized as being the person I threatened with a visit from my non-existent attorney if my mother didn't received better care. I wasn't sure at the moment if that was going to be a help or a hindrance to my case.

This was no time to look like someone who didn't have her act together. "Hello," I said, trying to rein in my breathing. "I'm Nadia Winslett's daughter. I got here as quickly as I could."

"She has nothing to do with this," Robert began.

"She is my mother," I said turning to face him. "I have every right to be involved where her health is concerned."

"Please, Ms. Winslett, have a seat," the older administrator spoke up, indicating a chair beside Doctor Figarrio. "Ms. Winslett we've heard from Doctor Figarrio that he changed your mother's medications after having a conversation with you on Monday morning, is that correct?"

"Yes, I was here Sunday, as I'm sure you recall, Doctor…"

"Doctor Phillips," the man responded.

"Doctor Phillips, I was very upset that she was being heavily medicated, when…"

"The patient attempted suicide," the doctor beside Robert spoke up. "This necessitates…"

"Excuse me," I said turning to him. "What is your name?"

"Doctor Williamson," he responded with that smug attitude that told me he thought he was much more intelligent than I was.

"Well, Doctor Williamson, I wasn't finished when you so rudely interrupted me. Do they teach you any type of manners in medical school?"

He gave an annoyed sigh and rolled his eyes at me. "How old are you, *young* lady?"

"Old enough to know an over-paid, jackass puppet when I meet one!" I replied. I turned to Doctor Phillps, "May I continue? Or, should Doctor Williamson be allowed to cut me off mid-sentence?"

"Doctor Williamson, please refrain from making comments until Ms. Winslett is finished."

"If she's a minor," he continued, ignoring Doctor Phillips, "the whole point of her argument is void anyway and she is just wasting everyone's time." Evidently Robert had already informed him I was.

"Although it's true that I am a few months away from my eighteenth birthday..." I could see Robert and Doctor Williamson starting to smile. "I am an emancipated minor, recognized by a court of law to be an adult." I produced the papers from my purse and handed them to Doctor Phillips. He shared it with the other two members of the board and they returned it to me.

Robert's eyes narrowed. "You're a liar!"

"Oh, I can assure you, *Dad*, that the liar in this room isn't me."

"You are nothing but a spoiled, runaround whore who hasn't even been home for nine months!" He spat the words out as if they were gospel.

I turned to face the board members, "I would like an opportunity to address the three of you privately, and then you can make your decision. I'm not going to be able to speak without interruption as long as Mr. Winslett and Doctor Williamson are present."

"This meeting," Doctor Williamson spoke up before the board members could respond, "isn't private."

"Really, Doctor Williamson?" This jerk was starting to get under my skin and I knew there was no way I was letting him get anywhere near my mother. "You've been here for the last two hours or so trying to convince the board, privately, that my mother doesn't belong under Doctor Figarrio's care any longer. I think that should entitle me to an equal share of the same privacy."

"I for one," the female administrator spoke up, "would like to hear what Ms. Winslett has to say without interruption. I believe you two gentleman should step out," she said looking to Robert and his crony.

"I agree," Doctor Phillips added, and the other gentleman nodded as well. "Please, wait out in the hall and we'll call you back in when we are finished."

If looks could kill, Robert wouldn't have needed to hire a hitman.

Once they were outside the room, I began to explain what had been happening to my family over the last few years, beginning with my grandfather's supposed suicide, up until the recent incident at the Pensacola High School.

"I've hired an expert in this field and he has uncovered plenty of documentation to show me that Robert has been having an affair for quite some time. He also uncovered that Robert has squandered most of his own family's fortune, and now he's trying to take my mother's away to cover his losses. Doctor Phillips, I'm sure you noted the condition in which my mother was in when she arrived here. Have you spoken with her today?"

"Yes, I have, we all have," he stated, motioning to the other two board members.

"Then you had to have notice the extreme difference in her mental state. She's not crazy, not even close; she was simply over medicated."

"Well, it is a very serious matter," spoke the second gentleman, "to take a patient's well-being and place it in the hands of a minor..."

"It's more serious," I asserted, leveling my eyes at him, "to put a patient at risk when they are showing significant improvement by sending them back to a drug induced state of stupor."

"She attempted suicide," the gentleman continued.

"That remains to be seen. She went to sleep and woke here in the hospital—Robert could have been the one to cut her wrists, hoping it would help his Power of Attorney request. Please," I implored, giving myself a moment to pause and gaze into each person's eyes, "give her a chance to prove her intelligence and stability—she's not a suicide risk, nor is she crazy."

They spoke quietly for a few moments and then said they would like me to go out into the hallway and to have Doctor Williamson join Doctor Figarrio for one final conference.

I did as I was asked, but there was no way I was sitting beside the traitorous Robert. I stood on the opposite side of the hallway as he glared at me. Suddenly I had the notion that I needed to sit beside him; I wanted to tell him something that I hoped would stick inside him and eat away at his very tiny conscience.

"What's wrong with you, Leese?" he began immediately when I came closer. "You know I have your mother's best interest..."

"I know about Sharon," I simply stated, causing him to become silent. "I know about everything, including the hit you placed on my life."

"You're as crazy as your mother," he said dismissively.

"Did you know Sharon put a contract on me too, dear old Dad?"

He gave me a confused look.

"That was where the Pensacola shooting came in. When she's finished with me and Mom, you and Kimmy are next on her list. I may end up dead before this day is over, but I've left enough evidence for the police that you will go to prison for the rest of your miserable life. You're a stupid fool who never thought to ask the woman whose life you're preparing to destroy if she would get you out of your financial hole; instead you've dug yourself a grave."

The door opened and we were asked to return into the room. Robert followed me inside, apparently still digesting what I'd said to him.

"We've decided," Doctor Phillips began, "that, barring legal intervention by either party, we believe Doctor Figarrio and Miss Winslett have the patient's best interest at heart. Mrs. Winslett will continue on her reduced drug therapy until we are instructed to do otherwise by a court of law. I recommend, if either of you," he said directing his remark to Robert and me, "wish to keep or discard this ruling, you do so through the courts as soon as possible."

"Thank you," I said, reaching out to shake each of their hands. When I turned, Robert was already out of the room.

Doctor Figarrio put his arm around my shoulders and walked me out into the hallway. "Leese, you're going to need a lawyer as soon as possible."

"Doctor Figarrio, I may not have time to get an attorney. I can't explain right now, but get my mother checked out of here as soon as possible. And, one more thing, please tell her I said she'll need to hire twenty-four hour police protection for a while until this whole situation with Robert is exposed."

"Aren't you coming up to see her?" He seemed very surprised that I wouldn't take this opportunity to visit her.

I knew I couldn't. I might have Jack and Ricky following me right at this very moment and I certainly didn't want to endanger her any further. "I wish I could but I've got to take care of some—some business before today is over."

I could see the worry in his face. He didn't know what I was up against, but somehow he understood that I was in some type of peril. "Be careful, Leese. You're mother and your sister will both need you if you're right about Robert."

I gave him a hug and told him goodbye.

It was going to be a long walk back to the entrance. Every step I took was difficult. I imagined how it would feel when the bullet hit me. Would they be so bold to shoot me and run, right here in front of everyone? Each face that came into view as I got closer was suspect. I gripped my keys tightly in trembling fingers.

I turned the last corner before the exit doors when I saw that my car was gone. I felt a stab of panic wash through me. I turned to the receptionist, but she was on a call. I didn't want to go outside the relative safety of the hospital doors to look for it. I'd have to call for a cab. I had left Micah's phone at the motel and I didn't carry change.

The receptionist hung up and looked up smiling, "Can I help you?"

"My car was parked by the doors."

"Yes, Ma'am. You can't park there, but someone rolled it out of the way before the towing service was called. I believe it's at the bottom of the ramp to the right."

"Oh—thank you." It would be a foolish gamble to try to make it that far and the only chance I'd have would be to wait for a taxi. "Could I use your phone, I need..."

"No, Ma'am, I'm sorry but this phone is for hospital use only. If you go down to the waiting area behind me and down on the left, you'll see a bank of pay phones for public use."

"I didn't bring any change." I tried a smile, but it was weak. I was hoping she could make out the desperation in my face and have a change of heart.

"They take Visa and MasterCard," she stated.

That I did have. "Thank you." I turned the corner behind the large desk and started toward the waiting area. I was almost there when I felt a steel grip on my arm. I turned, expecting to see Micah standing there but it was someone I didn't know, but I was certain within two guesses I'd get it right.

CHAPTER SEVENTEEN

"There you are," he stated gruffly. "I've been looking all over hell and back for you."

I opened my mouth to scream when I felt the gun barrel shove against my ribs.

"Let's have a little talk, shall we," he hissed, pushing me into one of their small chapel rooms.

The door closed behind us and I had to speak and try to keep him distracted from what was about to happen. "The hospital is a pretty crowded place for a shooting, don't you think—Jack, or are you Ricky?" I was trying to sound calm, but I could feel my knees turning to jelly.

He looked mildly surprised that I had their names. "Your boyfriend has kept you well informed, hasn't he?" he smiled, pulling a brightly polished, nickel-plated barrel around from my side and placing it between my breasts.

"So which one are you?" I continued to ask, ignoring the pain as he pressed the barrel too hard into my chest.

He was older, perhaps in his forties. He was a little taller than me but not quite six foot. His eyes were chocolate brown and blood shot. He wasn't an ugly man, but he was a man who wore his hard living on the outside of his demeanor. "Jack," finally came his one word reply.

"Sharon's lover," I uttered as if I had no doubts.

He seemed to be enjoying the fact that I knew so much about him. He smiled and then he began to look at me, really look at me. He had me pushed against a kneeling bench with my back against a large wooden cross on the wall. He was making a slow assessment from top to bottom.

"At least I can see why the idiot hasn't killed you yet. You must be pretty good if you can get that far with a Gavarreen."

Just the mention of his name sent a spike through my system.

He pressed himself against me, sliding the gun back to my side. I turned my face and my stomach rolled as I felt the pressure of his body on mine. Micah had been the only man I had allowed to be this close to me; unfortunately, there was little I could do to stop Jack.

"I can't see much reason to kill you right here," he concluded, his hips thrusting into mine. I was trying to keep my tears from forming, but this wasn't the ending I had expected and I knew I'd rather be shot.

"Where's your boyfriend?" he breathed the words into my ear. "Answer me!," he snarled, jerking my head backward with a handful of my hair.

"I—I don't know. He..."

"Liar," he spewed. "Tell me where he is or I'll shoot you right here."

The hand had released my hair and I tipped my head back to look him in the eyes. "Go ahead," I said firmly.

"You think you're a tough little girl, don't you?" He licked his lips and smiled. "You can tell me where he's at or I can knock you out and go upstairs and finish what I started with your momma; too bad she'll be awake this time."

I had no room to strike him; he was hard against me, and his legs were too close together to knee his groin. "You..."

"Yeah, me. I went there to speed up the job for Sharon. She had a date with your poppa so he doped her up as usual and left her. I cut her wrists and was going to watch her bleed to death when he came back for his phone. It's too bad really, but it just helped him make her look like the crazy woman he's been creating for a while. The stupid bastard really thinks she cut her own wrists." He gave a sluggish laugh, as if the joke was actually starting to become funny to him. "Now, are you going to tell me where he's at or do I have to get rid of your mother?"

I let the tears roll down my cheeks; I didn't want him to think I wasn't telling the truth. "He left for a while before I got the call to come to the hospital. He doesn't know I'm here and I don't know where he went."

"Well, I guess you're just gonna have to come with me then," he said, the smile returning to his face. "Don't do anything stupid," he warned, pulling a cell phone from his pocket. He hit one button and I heard it speed dialing through the speaker. He didn't have to raise it to his ear; he just kept me pressed against the wall.

"What?" came the voice over the phone.

"I've got her. I'm taking her back to Sharon's."

"Just shoot her and get it over with," was the response.

"Ah, be patient, little brother, you haven't seen the close up yet. No sense in taking all the fun out of our job."

I heard a laugh and the phone was snapped shut.

Jack dropped the phone back into his pocket. "Now we're going to walk out of here just like we're two peas in a pod. If you make me shoot before we get out of here—well, there is no telling who else will get hit in the process. Do you want that on your conscience?"

I shook my head, no.

"Good, let's go get that Porsche of yours. Hand me the keys."

I gave him the keys, but I knew as soon as we were clear from all the people in the hospital I was going to fight him, and I was already sizing up the best way to knock the gun from his hand. We walked out of the room, his arm around my waist, guiding me to the front entrance. I wondered if Micah had returned to the bungalow and found my note. Would he be waiting, hidden somewhere with his rifle and silencer?

I felt the breeze hit my face as the doors opened. There was a stiff east wind and I could smell the Atlantic. My car was at the end of the ramp and I had decided to make my move when I opened the passenger door. I turned, but it was too late, apparently Jack had plans of his own. The gun hurled toward my face with a hard, painful thud and I blacked out.

I came around to the sound of a high performance sports engine being down shifted and then climbing up a slow rise. A pair of hands pulled roughly at me, dragging me from the car as I struggled to open my eyes. I was in a garage. I heard Jack's voice saying to tie me up. I was flat on the concrete, the coolness of it feeling good against my throbbing head. A younger man was pulling my arms behind me and binding them together, then he rolled me over and moved to my ankles. I resisted feebly as he held my feet together and finished the job.

I was finally able to focus as I watched them standing there discussing what plans they had for me.

"Are you sure Sharon won't be back until after four?"

"Yeah, but I told her I'd meet her and let her know what was happening. She's paying the guy to get rid of Gavarreen, but it can't look like a hit."

"She should just let us finish him off."

"She has her reasons, but we'll have enough fun while she's occupied. You think you can handle keeping our mark secure until I get back?"

"Oh, she'll be secure. I don't know if I'm going to wait for you, but I'll save you a little."

"Don't do anything stupid, Ricky. Wait until there are two of us to make sure the little princess doesn't get loose."

Ricky looked at me, noticing I was awake. "Well, good morning little princess," he turned back to Jack. "Don't be gone too long. You've had Sharon to keep you satisfied. I'm ready for some satisfaction of my own."

Jack smiled, got into a small white car and pulled out of the garage. The door came down as I felt Ricky pick me up off the floor and carry me upstairs. My head was still trying to come out of the fog that had filled it when Jack hit my temple with the gun. I looked at Ricky. He was brown eyed like Jack, but at least ten years younger. His hair was a curly, dirty blond, his features were finer than Jack's, and he was taller and, apparently, as strong as Micah because my weight didn't seem to faze him as he walked up to the second floor.

The house was large and I could only assume it was the beach house that Micah already knew about. He carried me into a wide, open living room. I could hear the sound of the waves in the Atlantic hitting the shore and I could smell the salted air.

He laid me down on the couch and seemed to study me for a moment. "You've been a real pain in the ass," he finally spoke. Then he squatted down on his haunches to get close to me. He moved my hair away from my shoulders and neck, exposing my cleavage. I'd seen that look in a man's eyes before and at the moment he wasn't thinking about killing me. He smiled as he began lowering his face.

"Don't you listen to what your brother tells you?" I managed to say. My voice was soft and trembling because I had no defenses with my feet and hands tied.

The smile got bigger, flashing surprisingly white teeth. "So you're going to talk to me, now?"

"Yeah, well it isn't easy after being clubbed with a pistol."

His hand reached up and softly touched the tender area on the side of my head. "Jack can get pretty rough."

"And you?" I asked. I had to keep this conversation going.

"I can be gentle, for the right person. Now you need to ask yourself if you're the right person because if you piss me off," he pulled out a gun from the back of the waistband of his jeans. "I have a really short fuse, and I don't have to have you while you're breathing."

That caused my stomach to roll. I looked at the gun; it was a Glock-17.

"Do you like it?" he questioned, a funny expression on his face. He seemed to understand that the look on my face wasn't fear, but recognition of the kind of weapon he was holding.

"Glock-17," I said, closing my eyes for a moment to slow the throbbing that was expanding from my temple down to my cheek bone.

"You know, I think I'm starting to like you."

I opened my eyes and smiled at him. "You'd like me a lot better if I could wrap my arms and legs around you."

The surprise hit him and his eyebrows went up.

"I'm not stupid," I continued my daring plan. "Why do you think Gavarreen has kept me alive this long? He said I'm the best he's ever had. I guess I can be the best for anyone who's willing to give me a little more time, besides I enjoy a good thrill ride. Didn't I hear you say that Jack's had Sharon and you've had to do without?" I could see my words were taking a firm hold on him. "Why is she sleeping with Jack anyway? You've certainly got a lot more to offer than he does." I gave him a thorough look over to let him know I approved of his physique.

He placed the pistol on the coffee table and then his face descended to my exposed skin, more direct than Micah had ever been. His hands moving over places I didn't want him touching, but I continued to pretend that I was enjoying his caress.

His mouth moved toward mine, but I carefully turned my head to whisper in his ear. "You aren't afraid of me are you? I know you're stronger than Micah," I lied. "You and I shouldn't have any trouble spending a little time together."

The look in his eyes was telling me he was over the edge. If he didn't untie me then I was in big trouble. I put my teeth to his neck and I felt him stiffen, but when my tongue touched his skin he lost all ability to refuse me.

"Yeah, you and I are going to get along just fine," he panted, grabbing me, roughly this time and rolling me onto my stomach. Now my heart was pounding with a fury that I'd never known. I had in no way ever imagined that I would have to fight a man in hand to hand combat, but as long as the gun wasn't involved, I felt I had a chance. My arms were free now and he was frantically sliding his hands up the sides of my shirt trying to remove it.

I stopped him and smiled, reaching down as if to undo the top of my jeans. "I can't take these off with my legs tied together."

He was obeying my every request at this point and I was almost free. As quickly as he untied my legs, I moved to an upright position. I could tell he was going to try to force me to lie down on the couch, but I stood, crossing my arms and gripping the bottom of my shirt. I pulled it off as he remained wide-eyed watching with eager anticipation.

He fairly collided with me, his muscled arms wrapping around me. My hand slipped down to his pants and his legs parted to give me access to what he was certain I wanted. And I did want exactly that as I slammed my knee as hard and high as I could into his most vulnerable area.

I heard the air leave him as he doubled over in agony. I swung my fist into his windpipe and then grabbed two handfuls of his curly hair, pulling downward, and brought my knee up to crack his nose with all the force I possessed. He hit the floor writhing in pain, blood splattered across my jeans. I grabbed his Glock and my shirt and took off running.

I flew downstairs to the garage, grabbing at a door that was locked with a keyed dead-bolt. My Porsche was there, but Jack had taken my keys. I could hear Ricky swearing upstairs and I knew I was trapped. I dropped the magazine from the gun and made sure it had bullets and then slammed it back into the handle. I ripped the top of it back and chambered the first round, safety off. My hands were shaking so hard that I knew I'd never be able to hit my target, even if he stood perfectly still. I was slipping into a strange type of fear, an animal and instinctive kind of state, and it frightened me more than the man I was trying to escape from.

He was coming down the stairs and I took aim. I'd never shot at anything other than a paper target and I didn't know if I could fire on someone who didn't have a weapon. He saw me when he was half way down the staircase, blood staining his face and shirt. He was still bent forward in pain from our last encounter, and then he tripped and tumbled down the stairs landing in a heap several feet from the base. I seized the opportunity and charged back upstairs, frantic to find the closest exit. The sliding doors to the second floor patio were right there and I made my choice, I'd jump.

I could hear him once again, the profanity worse than before, the anger hotter and more vicious. I heard a loud cracking sound of wood being splintered and hitting the wall. I pulled at the sliding doors. A pin at the top was lodged tight, preventing me from opening it.

"Damn it!" I pulled at the pin and it didn't move. There was no choice. I spun around with the Glock and would simply start firing until I hit him. Something was in the opposing hall and was moving toward me from my right and I guessed that Jack had returned.

"Où êtes-vous? Annalisa, où êtes-vous?"

I couldn't believe what I was hearing; it wasn't Jack, it was Micah. I didn't believe my eyes when he came around the corner. The gun was still clenched in my fists and pointed out in front of me.

He had his hands open in front of him, looking directly into my eyes, *"Ne tirez pas, mon amour."* He was walking toward me slowly, as I was backing up, "Stop, Annalisa," he was crooning.

I could hear Ricky coming up the stairs. Micah put his finger to his lips to tell me to be quiet, motioning me to step into the closest room down the bedroom hallway. It appeared to be the master bedroom. I went to the left of the bed and Micah went right, but just inside the doorway.

When Ricky walked into the room, he evidently had no idea that Micah was standing there because he was intently focused on me. He was still swearing about what he was going to do to me when he got his hands on me. I raised the gun his direction, but before I could take aim Micah simply called his name and Ricky turned to face him. Micah drew both pistols and blew Ricky's chest completely apart. He never knew what hit him, death was instantaneous. I looked at Micah's face and it was absolutely expressionless as he re-holstered his guns. I crumpled to the floor. I heard a sound of someone wailing and realized it was coming from me. Micah was at my side, taking the gun from my hands.

"Are you okay?" he kept repeating over and over. "Did he hurt you?"

I couldn't answer, I couldn't speak. All I could do was stare at the body lying a few feet away. Blood splattered in a wide pattern over the bedroom wall. He was pulling a piece of fabric from my hand when I realized it was my shirt. He was putting it back over my head, dressing me like a parent getting a small child ready to go somewhere.

His hands were cupping my face, forcing me to look at him. "Leese, did he hurt you?" He asked very slowly this time. Once his question finally sunk in, I shook my head no. And I crumbled into those strong arms, the place that had been both my safe-haven and my death sentence. I was crying and he was shushing me, telling me we had to get out.

"I have to get you out of here before Jack returns. I'm taking you next door." His arms were scooping me up and I felt like a rag doll.

"Sha—Sharon," I finally managed to say. "I heard them talking. She's going to pay someone to kill you."

His forward motion stopped. "She can't do that, Leese. If she decides that on her own, she'll not only start a war, but her own family will turn on her. You must have heard them wrong."

"No, I didn't. She wants you dead, too." I wrapped my arms tightly around his neck, burying my face against it. "I couldn't take it if something happened to you, Micah."

He didn't say anything else as he continued into the hallway; that was when we heard the sound of a car pulling in. Micah was swearing. He turned and went back down the hall, past the bedroom where the body was lying, and down to the next room. He put me into a large closet and placed Ricky's Glock beside me on the floor.

I watched the emotions wash out of him like the tide pulling away from the shore. His eyes were frightening, keen, yet void and heartless. Even the movement of his eyes had become mechanical. And for the first time in what seemed like an eternity, I was overcome by the sheer terror of him. When Ricky had made the mistake of trying to get to me, I watched Micah draw and fire without blinking an eye. His aim had been deadly even when it happened at lightening pace. He pulled out both of his weapons and checked them and then placed them back into the holsters. He checked my weapon and put the safety back on when he realized I had already chambered a bullet.

"Stay hidden. I'll take care of Jack."

My stupor was dissolving. "Take me with you…"

"No—I'll come back for you when it's done. Don't move."

"Be careful," I whispered, but he was already gone.

I listened as Jack was cursing and coming up from the garage. He was calling Ricky's name and I knew there would be no response. I could hear him heading toward the hallway where the bedrooms were located. I heard a choked sound as he must have come upon Ricky's body. There were some mournful sounds and a stifled sob. That was when I remembered Micah saying they were brothers, not just partners. I heard the sound of his gun chambering a bullet and then all was silent.

It seemed that I had waited for such a long time in the closet. I was afraid to leave it, but yet again, the house felt vacant because it was so utterly quiet. I pulled off my shoes to make sure that I could move undetected. I picked up the gun and pushed off the safety with a hand that was still trembling from the last battle. The gun was like a live grenade, one gentle squeeze, one accidental squeeze, one split second of decision or indecision could alter everything.

If I truly believed everything I told Micah, then I knew none of this was simply chance. God knew all along that I would be facing this battle. I only wish that I knew how it was going to end. I was glad that he hadn't hidden me in the main bedroom; I didn't want to have to walk around the gruesome body. But he must have guessed it was better that way so that I didn't dwell on what would happen to me before this day was over. There were only hours left of my life and I knew it would end just as fast.

Every movement was agonizing as I looked and listened carefully before advancing. I turned the next corner into the hall and caught my breath. Across the living room, now moving from a shadow into a sliver of light, I saw the unmistakable flash of a small refraction off a nickel plated barrel. It was Jack coming down the hall from the front door, taking aim toward the garage stairway. Jack and Micah were locked in a deadly game of cat and mouse. They had moved silently around the house and now were about to come face to face.

I watched as his arms became visible, then his shoulders and finally his evil face appeared. He was nervous to be facing Micah; even though the house was cool, I could see the beads of perspiration on his face. I repositioned myself low on the wall and slid around the corner behind the leather sofa. His chest was still hidden behind the wall and I knew better than to try for the shot.

Then I saw what he saw. A silent shadow was moving up the stairwell. I knew from the tiny amount that I could see, it was Micah. He was working his way back to where he had left me and now, if he made it to the top and took that fateful quick step through the short open space between the top of the stairwell and the gallery wall, Jack would shoot him, and a war would begin.

Jack was no longer moving, and there was only one place for me to aim with any hope of hitting him at this distance; his head came forward by another fraction of an inch as he was taking aim and preparing to fire. If I stood, he would see me and he would have to come around the corner of the wall to get a clean shot. He would have to make a rapid decision to either get rid of me and face Micah as he flew into the room, or retreat. Either way, Micah should be out of the line of fire.

With no more time, and Micah getting too close to taking that one exposed step, I had no choice. My gun would have to be lowered or he would not try for the shot. I stood up.

What happened was so fast it didn't even seem possible. Jack made his choice and swung out into the living room, readjusting his aim at me as I turned sideways and raised my arm from behind the couch with Ricky's Glock leveling at him in the same moment. My only saving grace was that I believe it surprised him to see the gun in my hand. All this occurred within a hundredth of a second and I had no choice, but to fire before he did. I watched the shell fly out the top of the gun, the blast causing my hand to sting and my ears to vibrate. He fired, but my bullet had already struck in his upper left shoulder causing his aim to be too high.

It was as if Micah had ghosted into the scene when he had heard the swish of fabric as we drew on each other. Jack was down, writhing in pain. His gun had fallen from his hand. I hadn't killed him, but I must have broken through the clavicle and shoulder blade. Micah was on him, kicking the gun away and before I could say anything, he pumped one more round without thought, without mercy, without flinching into Jack's heart ending his life immediately.

He turned and looked at me, almost as if he was seeing a stranger. I had begun to tremble, the gun in my hand feeling like burning steel. I reached down with my left hand to push the safety back on before I dropped it and caused a misfire. It was as if when I moved to bring my hands together on the weapon, his reaction was automatic. His guns came up. I squeezed my eyes shut. I couldn't watch what he was going to do. I couldn't watch the uncaring, inhuman, untouchable Micah fire at me.

"Annalisa," came my name whispered from across the room. I still couldn't open them. I heard his footsteps and then the feel of his hands carefully removing the gun from my own. Those warm hands cupping my face, "Annalisa, open your eyes."

I took a breath and opened them; his face was right there, his eyes still void yet struggling. "You shouldn't have stood up, he could have killed you."

"How—how did you know?"

"I heard the noise from my right. I knew where he was, but I didn't know where you were. And then I realized you were trying to draw his fire." Micah was coming back to me, the void was disappearing. "You shouldn't have had a chance to fire. Why wasn't your gun raised?"

"I..." I couldn't speak. Somehow he knew what was happening in the room and had moved so quickly that he was able to see it unfold.

"You were fast. One instant your hand was down and the next taking aim. You shouldn't have put yourself in danger for..." His voice cracked. The emotions were coming back to him full force, stronger than anything I think he had ever experienced.

I watched his eyes filling with tears, his face so sorrow-filled and tender.

"I was afraid," I began, "that he would shoot you when you got to the top of the stairs. It was the only way."

"Baby," he crooned softly, that voice once again like a warm blanket wrapping me in his emotion when he spoke it, "I..." He couldn't finish it, but there would be no need. His face descended to mine, and I was ready to turn away but he would not allow it.

For the first time, his mouth met mine. My eyes closed just as I saw a tear slide down his cheek. I'd never felt something so exquisite as his lips enveloped mine with warmth and gentleness. His mouth was opening, showing me to do the same. As I responded, the kiss became deeper and more passionate than I ever thought could exist. It was as if the most private parts of my mind, heart and soul were exposed to him.

He had told me once that he had wanted to teach me how to respond to a man's kiss, and now he was the teacher and I had never been a more eager student. He had begun to pull away from me, but I had to have more. He responded to my need; this time the passion was hotter because I now understood what he meant about needs. I needed him desperately at the moment. It was as if I could spend my entire lifetime in that one kiss.

And then I did.

He was the best at his job, so when the bullet ripped through me there was no reason for remorse. It was, as he described for me once, as if red-hot steel had been shoved completely through me. I had no reason to open my eyes before the rapid blackness enveloped me. I didn't want to see his expression. He had kept my last request as I asked because I never knew that it was coming. There was no air inside me. As fast as the bullet made its mark, I felt my life leave me and my last thought was, "It's over."

CHAPTER EIGHTEEN

Pain. It is such a small word, but it was my entire being. It radiated seemingly from everywhere. I was nauseous and floating in a sea of misery. There were flashes of light, a cacophony of noises— strange noises; beeps, swishes, sounds of compression, distant unfamiliar voices. I wanted to see where I was, but my eyes were difficult to control. It was as if when I tried to open them, they rolled unconsciously toward the back of my head. My chest screamed at me over the most infinitesimal movement and I was trying to remember how I ended up feeling this way.

There was something warm pressed to my hand, familiar and strong like a band of steel—Micah. Just the thought of his name forced me to try harder to come out of my suspended state. I tried whispering his name. The pain screamed louder, threatening me with every movement. "M—Mi—cah," I had managed the word as the pain sharpened.

"Baby," came the velvety voice to my ears.

I willed my eyes to open, but the room swirled in my vision. His face was there, but it wasn't clear yet. I wanted so badly to see his face. Slowly the spinning and swirling stopped; his face was above me looking relieved.

"Thank you, God," I heard him say, and I knew at that moment he was truly addressing God. "Do you know where you're at?"

I didn't dare move my head—it would have to be eyes only as I took in the surroundings. There were machines all around me, IV's and lines running to my body. "Hospital," I said, wincing at how difficult it was to say the word.

There was someone else standing beside Micah, I didn't know who he was but I knew what he was; it was a police officer.

"You got what you wanted," I heard the unfamiliar voice say. "She's awake…"

"Please," his voice sounding so desperate. "Please give me just a minute to talk with her—privately—please, I only need a few minutes." There were tears on Micah's face but I couldn't raise my hand to wipe them away.

The officer looked at me. "Do you want to talk with this man, Miss Winslett?"

I couldn't nod, that was out of the question. "Yes—I love him," I whispered out the words.

A look of disgust came over the officer's face and he turned and walked away.

"Annalisa, I've never prayed so hard in all my life. I begged God to pull you through this. Do you know why you're in here?"

I was thinking back through the fog. I watched Ricky die and then Jack. The kiss—the final kiss. "You shot me." I barely spoke; the pain more focused now through my chest where I knew a bullet had traveled.

"I didn't shoot you, Baby. I begged them to let me wait for you to come out of this so I could tell you. I couldn't leave with you thinking I'd done this to you."

"Leave?" That pain was worse than the physical. Tears were moving down my cheeks, distorting my view of his beautiful face. "Don't leave." I begged.

"I kissed you, Annalisa. Do you remember the kiss?"

"Yes," I whispered.

"I didn't know that Sharon had gotten there. She walked in on the kiss and shot you through the back. The doctors say you're a miracle. It went completely through you and hit me in the chest."

I felt panic wash through me, drowning the pain as I tried to look at his chest. I could see the blood soaked bandage. "Are you okay?" I cried.

"You slowed it down or it would have killed me. The bullet is in my sternum. They wanted to take it out when I got here, but I told them it was going to have to wait until I could see you."

"Let them take it out," I tried to say, but it seemed I was running out of oxygen.

"Don't talk too much, Leese. Your lung collapsed and it's really weak right now. Save your air, Baby."

"Sharon?" I whispered.

"I shot her…"

My eyes went wide in panic. He had told me he had to be very careful that she didn't end up in the crossfire.

"I didn't kill her, Leese, but I had no choice. When she shot us, I was knocked backward and she was taking aim again. I shot her through the shoulder before she could fire. She's in a lot of trouble for what she's been up to. You won't have any more problems from her."

"Robert—are you in troub…" I couldn't breathe. The numbers on the machine beside me were dropping low as I struggled.

"Promise me you won't try to talk and I'll tell you," he asked. "The mob thinks I tried to kill you, so I'm not sure what's going to happen—especially when they find out that I didn't shoot you. I'm worried he might still try to hurt you, Baby."

"I'll be okay," I mouthed, trying to conserve my breath. I started to open my mouth again, but his fingers came to rest across my lips.

"I told you I was selfish and I'd never allow any man to touch you. I found out how wrong I was. When that bullet went through you, it passed so close to your heart that it stopped beating. I'm not very good at CPR. I hope I didn't crack too many of your ribs."

I smiled weakly.

"But I realized I would give you to Ryan a thousand times over rather than to watch you die. All I could think was that I'd do anything, give up anything, change everything, if your heart would just start beating again," he swallowed hard, tears coursing down his face. "I've never actually told you, Leese, because I just didn't believe it could be real, but I love you—I love you enough that I don't have to be selfish. I want you to have a long and happy life with someone who'll love you always."

"You're my forever," I said, from under the light touch of his fingers.

"I've got to go, Leese. The police know who I am. I'm being extradited back to Louisiana. I won't be here for you. But I had to tell you that I didn't hurt you. I know now I could never hurt you. You've changed me, and I love you just that much more for it."

I couldn't find the words to say, but I didn't need them. His mouth came down on mine in the softest, most tender kiss humanly possible.

The officer returned and I watched him take away my reason for breathing.

CHAPTER NINETEEN

The next several days were bad enough to make me wish for death. There was the physical pain, but it didn't match the ache of knowing Micah was gone. I had to give my statements to the police about Jack and Ricky's deaths and Sharon's injuries. And, what I could tell them about Micah Gavarreen.

"You're a very lucky young lady," the officer stated, sitting beside my bed and writing down everything I told him.

"So they tell me," I winced. It was still painful to do anything other than to speak and even that was difficult.

"I don't mean medically," he corrected. "Although the doctors have said that your wound was one in a million to miss your spine and your heart, but I mean with this guy that you said was keeping you safe. He is a very dangerous man."

"Not to me," I replied.

"Well, it appears Florida won't have any claim to him," he stated, flipping his notebook closed. "These appear to be clear cut cases of self-defense. Seven years on the force and this was the biggest, bloody mess I've ever seen."

"You were there?"

"I wasn't too far away when the calls started coming in about shots being fired. My partner and I were the first to arrive."

"Tell me." I had lived through the nightmare, but at times it was only that and I wanted to hear it from someone else.

"I really shouldn't," he began.

I carefully reached my hand through the side rail on my bed and touched his arm, "Please, officer..."

"Tidewell." He sighed, "Since you were there, I guess it is okay. When we got there," he began, "we could see the front door had been kicked in—actually more like torn completely from the hinges. I thought this was a home invasion by another doped-up crack-head or a meth freak, but when we walked in the first thing we found was a guy lying dead, shot through his heart, and blood splattered everywhere."

"Jack," I whispered.

Officer Tidewell nodded, "Then we saw Ms. Norton passed out in a huge pool of blood—those hollow points he used do maximum damage and her shoulder was ripped apart. We could see him on the other side of the couch apparently doing CPR, but we couldn't see you. We had our guns drawn and we told him to freeze, but it was like we weren't even in the room to him.

"He had pretty much lost it. He was bleeding from his chest wound, crying over you and begging God to help him get your heart started. Then we saw you on the floor—hell, we knew who you were right away; everybody's been trying to find you, and the reports were ranging from a runaway to a kidnap victim."

"He was protecting me," I whispered.

"Yes, Ma'am, I believe you now, but that apparently isn't his normal line of work." He gave me a concerned look that seemed to say he thought my perception might be skewed. "My partner called for the medical unit, and was trying to help him keep you alive when I saw what looked like another body in the bedroom."

I knew that was Ricky, but my lungs were so tired I just listened.

"I've never seen that much damage from two bullets. It was like he didn't have a chest—until I looked at the bedroom wall and saw where most of it had landed."

I could see him visibly shudder. I remembered that it had been horrific when he killed Ricky, but seeing the officer's reaction confirmed the memory for me.

"Anyway, the ambulance crew tried to take over, Gavarreen had your heart beating by the time they arrived, but he didn't want to let go of you. We finally convinced him by telling him that he could ride with you in the back of the ambulance. He wouldn't let any one touch his wound, other than put some gauze over it, until you either pulled through or died. He just kept telling us he had to stay with you until you came to. We thought about jumping him and letting the doctors hit him with a sedative so they could dig that bullet out, but he's a pretty big guy."

I laughed—that was painful.

"While we were waiting to find out if you were going to make it, he gave us his statements. We searched him and took his wallet, finding out he had been using an alias of Evan Lewis but was really Micah Gavarreen. The reports were coming back as mafia and that Louisiana had him as being suspect in multiple murders. They were already flying a group of officers down here to extradite him. As far as we could tell what happened in the beach house wasn't murder so we told them as soon as the doctors gave him the okay to be released, they could take him."

"Did they," I paused for a breath, "Get the bullet out?"

"On him? Yeah, after you finally came around and he got the chance to talk with you, he was gentle as a kitten. He didn't take any anesthetic or any pain killers; he just told the doctor to dig it out. They cleaned it up and he left peacefully with the police."

I thought about the night I sealed his knife wound and saw all his other scars; no anesthetic didn't surprise me. But I couldn't stand the idea of him sitting in a prison for the rest of his life, especially when I needed him so desperately.

"Do you know what's happening with him in Louisiana?"

"No, but I know the FBI was here for him, but he was already on a plane out of here. It seems that everyone in that house was connected to the mob, except for you, of course. Are you certain he was just trying to protect you?"

"I told you—Sharon Norton and my step-father were having an affair," I didn't want to go through this again, it was difficult to say it all the first time, but I didn't want them to have any suspicions about Micah's motives. "She put out a contract on me..."

"You said you think your step-father had done the same thing. Maybe that was how Gavarreen got involved in this whole thing; maybe he was hired to kill you."

Officer Tidewell wasn't stupid and I realized I had a hole in my story as to why Micah and I met in the first place. "If he was the one who was hired to kill me," I began carefully, "Then he changed his mind. We are very much in love with each other."

"Miss Winslett, I know you aren't going to want to hear what I'm going to say, but please just hear me out. You are very beautiful and any man wouldn't have a problem falling for you, but someone like him? I'd be suspicious that he may have pretended to like you—for the money. Stockholm syndrome can..."

"I know what Stockholm syndrome is, and I know what love is."

"You're very young..."

"I am in love with him and I'm going to do everything I can to help him when I get out of here."

"All I'm saying is for you to be very cautious. Give yourself a little time to sort out your emotions."

I could tell this was genuine concern and it wasn't my feelings for Micah he doubted, but more so Micah's motives for staying close to me. "Thank you," I touched his arm again. "I plan on being very careful after this is over, especially since my step-dad hasn't been arrested."

He looked exasperated, "I'm sorry, we just aren't finding any evidence to support your suspicions, but we do have you and your mother under twenty-four hour guard."

I smiled and squeezed his hand. I was exhausted from the conversation and ready to drift back to sleep.

One week later Officer Tidewell and another detective came to my room. I was finally out of ICU and able to sit up in a bed. They were both smiling and I wondered what prompted this visit.

"I just wanted to stop by and be the first to tell you, we got him," Tidewell stated.

My heart painfully thudded as I wondered what he was talking about? Was this something to do with Micah? "Who?" I asked.

"Your step father," he stated simply.

It took me a few seconds to let it sink in and when it did, my tears began flowing even before my emotions could catch up to them.

"It's going to be the top story for the twelve o'clock news. I just thought you'd like to hear it before you see it."

I motioned to him to turn on the television. The newscast was just beginning. There was video of Robert being taken into custody as they played a clip from a taped request he'd made to have me killed.

"…the last guy screwed this up, but I can get in there to her, if you still want her dead?" The voice was so familiar to me, but I couldn't think where I'd heard it before.

"You can have the million dollar pay off if you get rid of her. Can you make it look like a hospital error, too much morphine, maybe?" That voice I knew was Robert's.

"Don't worry. I can handle the little wildcat…" That was when I knew whose voice I was hearing. He'd called me that once before after attempting to shoot me; it was David Gavarreen.

I could still hear Gwen's words that night in the bar, "He's your best ally when he's sober and when the chips are down. You never know, he might find a way to help you straighten out this mess for Leese." I'd never thought those words would have ever rung true, but he did it. He must have gone to the police and worn a wire for them, getting Robert to admit that he was behind this all along.

"David contacted you," I stated.

Both officers gave me an odd look, "Who?"

"The man who recorded him, wasn't he…" I had a feeling I'd better stop right there. They both had tuned in very sharply when I tried to identify the voice. "Didn't I hear that name just now on the news? David, Donald, Daniel, wasn't it something like that?" I wasn't sure they believed my attempt to cover what I knew.

"No, they never said his name. His first name is Nick, but we have to protect his identity."

"Oh, no, that's okay. I understand. I'm just glad this might finally be over. I had a feeling he wasn't going to be happy until I was dead."

"Well that won't be a concern for you anymore; he's staying in jail. The judge denied him bail."

A nurse entered the room, "Miss Winslett you have more visitors, if you're feeling up to it."

"We'll leave you alone. We just wanted to share the good news."

We shook hands and they left.

I wondered who was visiting me. There had been so many of the old Palm Beach crowd stop by and I guessed this was more of the same, but when the door opened the first person through was tall with extremely black hair—Ryan, followed by Jewels, Carlie, and Kevin.

"Ah, I don't believe it," I said, a smile filling my face. "What are you guys doing down here during a weekday?"

"Spring break, Leese," came Jewels' reply as she bounded to my bedside. "Wow, you like almost bit the big one, girlfriend," she continued.

"Yeah, that's what they keep telling me. I'm a medical miracle. I keep telling them God is still in the miracle business and He wasn't ready for me yet. So the four of you came down here, just for the day or what?"

"Their staying at my house," Ryan finally spoke, after staring at me for a moment.

I looked at Jewels, "Your dad was cool with that?"

"No, of course not. Not until Ryan's mother agreed to play chaperone."

"Oh," I smiled.

"So, OMG, you've been like hanging with big time gangsters," Jewels began. "They're saying Evan, Micah or whatever his name is, is like some big time hitman..."

She was prattling on not noticing that her words were hitting me pretty hard. Ryan picked up on it though.

"Jewels, she might not want to talk about him right now," he interrupted her, trying to bring her feet back to the planet earth.

"Oh, yeah, right. Was he the one who..." She let her sentence trail off.

I knew most of the stories on the news were keeping everyone in suspense as to 'who shot the heiress.'

"No," I said, swallowing to keep my emotions down. "He got shot when I did."

"How?" Kevin asked. Somehow it didn't surprise me that his analytical mind would be immediately drawn to that puzzling statement.

"Oh my God, I didn't know he got shot, too!" Jewels exclaimed. I could tell she had some concern for him in her voice, but it was mostly the excitement of a deepening story that she wanted to know more about.

Ryan seemed ready to stop the group discussion about Micah, when I reached out and touched his arm.

"It's okay," I simply stated. I proceeded to tell them about Sharon, Jack and Ricky. How she'd hired them, and that Micah was trying to protect me. How I had been grabbed by Jack at the hospital. My tale about what happened between me and Ricky was greatly abbreviated. I told them that Micah showed up and ended up killing them both. "But when it was over, and he was kissing me..." I watched Ryan's face go dark with anger, but I continued. "Sharon walked in on us and put a bullet through my back; a bullet which traveled completely through me and buried itself into his chest."

"It's amazing you both aren't dead," Kevin said with surprise. I could tell he was running anatomy through that mental marvel that he called his brain. "You're lucky she didn't use hollow points."

I rolled my eyes and gave a small laugh. My chest didn't hurt quite as bad, and laughter was becoming possible, when I could find reasons for it. I almost told them that was what Micah used, but I didn't think that would be appropriate. "Yeah, you're absolutely right."

We talked a little more and then Ryan asked if he could have a few minutes alone with me. There was a small pang of something that crossed Jewels' face, and I knew she was starting to consider Ryan differently from her other male friends. But, they agreed and left us alone.

I had to tell him as soon as the door closed. "Jewels is starting to think of you as more than just a friend, you know that right?"

"We're working through that," he sighed. "Neither one of us is really ready for a relationship, together anyway." He pulled up a nearby chair and lowered my bedrail so that he could be closer to me. He reached out and put my hand between both of his.

It felt so good, because they kept the hospital freezing cold and warmth was a rare commodity in here.

"So when do you get to go home?"

"My doctors are arguing over that, but it looks like it could be this week if I agree to a live in nurse for a few weeks. I hate being in here..."

"I missed you," he added, quietly stopping me from speaking. He must have decided a different subject would be better. "What happened to my car?"

"Ah, crap!" I had forgotten about his car, and the last place it had been at was the Inlet Motel. "We—I left it at the motel we were staying at so probably on a wrecker lot somewhere. I'm sorry."

He gave a little laugh, "Leese, I'm not worried about my car, I was just curious." Then his face became serious again. "You didn't forget about your promise did you?"

"Well I might not be up for a date for a..."

"Not that one."

"Oh." That was when I remembered what he'd asked me not to do. My skin flushed pink with just the memory of how very close I'd come to breaking that one just before the call came in shortening my life span to twelve hours. "No."

He gave me a hard look. He evidently took the pink flush to my skin a different way.

"Honestly, no—we didn't." But I couldn't help feeling like he needed to know that Micah was the only man in my heart and on my mind. "Ryan, I don't know what's going to happen to him, but you've got to understand that I'm really and truly in love with him. I don't want you to think I'm available when I get out of here."

Disappointment was written all over his face, but he attempted to smile. "You still owe me at least one date. Then you can tell me if you're really off the market."

"I'm off the market," I confirmed. "But I do owe you that date. I just don't know how much longer this healing process is going to take."

"You can move around okay, right? She didn't damage your spine or..."

"No. There isn't much room between the shoulder blade and the spine, but she managed to miss them both—it's my lung and chest that are slow healing." I lower my gown slightly and pulled away the gauze from the place where the bullet exited. I watched him wince. "Yeah, it's pretty gross. I've got a good plastic surgeon who says after the lung is completely healed and they take out the chest tube, he'll make it look almost like it never happened."

"Don't think I'm gonna let you forget about our date. As soon as the doctor says you can do some ground flying, we're going for that drive."

I laughed and then cringed in pain.

He instantly looked worried.

"It's okay. It just really hurts to laugh."

He stood up and leaned over me, planting a very slow kiss on my forehead. "You rest and get better. I met your mom downstairs in the lobby and gave her my number and my parent's number so you can get a hold of me when you're ready."

My eyes had begun to tear. He was so sweet and so sincere. "Sounds good," I said, swallowing and trying to keep myself from letting them spill down my cheeks.

CHAPTER TWENTY

I was out of the hospital three days later, but home became my new hospital—infinitely more preferable, but still similar. Four weeks later, I was cleared to resume normal activities. I still had plastic surgeries to face, but they would wait.

Mom, Kimmy, and I were happy together. Life was almost normal. It had been difficult to explain what happened with Robert to Kimmy, but Mom was incredibly sensitive. Kimmy came to understand that he had done some things against the law, and when that happens you have to pay for what you did by staying with the police.

I had been trying my best to contact anyone in Louisiana to find out what was happening with Micah. I'd called his father's restaurant, but no one from his family would return my calls. I hired a new attorney who was trying to get information for me, but had been running into the proverbial stone wall when it came to the Louisiana officials. The only thing we were both pretty certain about was that he was not being held in any jail or federal facility. I tried contacting Gwen through law enforcement, but she wouldn't respond.

Two and a half months after the last moment I had seen his face, I hired a private jet to take me to New Orleans. I rented a car and drove to Giorgio's Italian Bar and Grill, but no one from his family was there and the employees were absolutely no help.

I drove the familiar road out of town down I-10 to the exit that would eventually lead me to his house. I was so afraid; afraid I wouldn't find him there, afraid I would find him there but he would tell me to go away, afraid of my own emotions, but I was becoming so desperate.

When his house came into view, my heart soared. Memories hit me so hard I could feel physical pain in my chest; swimming with Micah, jumping out a window with David in pursuit, shooting lessons and quiet dinners shared between the two of us, a night of learning that Micah could keep his promises no matter how difficult they were.

I pulled into the circle drive, noticing that there was a Lexus parked around the side by the garage door. Someone was here and I was going to get some answers.

I was a bundle of nerves and anticipation. If he opened that door, I had no clue what I would do. I rang the door bell and simply held my breath. I heard a distant male voice, but it was muffled and hard to hear; my heartbeat jumped higher. Then I heard a female voice laughing and getting closer to the front door. That scared me—Dear God, don't let him be here with another woman. Now my heart was beating so rapidly my scar was hurting.

The door opened and a beautiful young woman, older than me but still in her twenties, stood there looking surprised. She was red haired and fair skinned, wearing a bikini top and a pair of shorts. "Hi," she finally said. "Can I help you?" But something told me she recognized me. "You're Annalisa Winslett, aren't you?"

My picture had been on television so much over the last several months that it wasn't unusual for people to recognize me—but she was in Micah's house! Without a whole lot of clothing on!

"Yes—I'm—I'm trying to find Micah…"

"Oh, Mr. Gavarreen." she stated.

The way she said it gave me a moment of relief. She evidently wasn't here as his—guest.

"Yes, is he here?"

"Oh, no. We bought this house from him," she stated as a man came up behind her and said hello.

"He sold his house?" That just didn't seem possible. This was the only place in the world where I knew I could find him. He couldn't cut the tie to the one place I had counted on to secure his memory to the planet.

"Yeah, we closed last week."

"Do you know how I can get in touch with him?"

"No, I'm sorry. We only met his attorney at the closing. I have his attorney's number."

"Yes, please—if you don't mind."

She invited me in as she went to retrieve it. He had sold the house with all the furnishings and a flood of emotions hit me.

She gave me his number and I thanked her and left. I dialed it before I pulled out of the driveway and got a receptionist. I didn't identify myself, but simply told her it was a matter of extreme urgency that I speak with him. When I got him on the line, and he discovered who I was, he didn't want to talk to me. I was begging for all I was worth for him to please at least tell Micah that I needed to find him. He reluctantly took my phone number and then hung up on me.

I was almost back to New Orleans when my phone rang. I pulled off on the side of I-10 because if it was him, I knew I wouldn't be able to drive. But it wasn't Micah; it was Celeste.

I was sobbing and crying asking her to please tell me what was going on and that I *had* to see him.

"Where are you, Leese?"

"I'm on I-10, almost back to New Orleans."

"I'll meet you at the restaurant in twenty minutes and we'll talk."

It didn't take me twenty minutes to get there, but I waited outside for her car to pull in. We never made it inside. When she saw me she came over and sat in my car. I was trying to keep it together, but I was failing miserably.

"Is he in jail?" I managed for my first question, mopping the tears off my face.

"No," was her short response.

"Can I see him? Can I meet him somewhere?"

"Leese, he's going through something that is very difficult for him."

"Well, it certainly isn't easy for me!" I was trying not to snap at her, since this was the closest I'd gotten to him since he left the hospital.

"Leese, did you ever think that it might be wrong for you to come chasing after him? Did you ever think that if he wanted to, he would find you?"

The words were like she had slapped me in the face. They had the same effect and I felt my composure coming back to me. "Celeste, I love him and I…"

"Stop it! I thought you were someone who was unselfish and caring. Don't do this. Stop looking for him. Call off your attorney and leave him alone."

"Couldn't he at least tell me himself to leave him alone?"

"No, he can't! You're going to kill my son if you don't back off. Do you understand me, Leese?"

She was truly angry with me, and I still couldn't understand why I had to stop.

"If you love him," she took a breath, sounding as if her anger was softening. "And I mean *really* love him, then forget that you ever knew him."

I opened my mouth, but I was so desolate inside from her words, I couldn't speak.

"You don't know anything about our lives and the people we deal with. You two got too close, and that isn't good for someone who…" Her frustration level went back up as she attempted to find the right words. "You were together because he was supposed to kill you! Don't you understand that? Leave him alone. Don't come back here to New Orleans. Stop bothering Gwen and end this, now."

"I'm not trying to hurt him or any of you, Celeste."

"Good, then you'll listen to me and do as I ask. Go home. I'm sorry." She was moving from anger to tears.

I wrapped my arms around her and told her that, even though I didn't understand, I trusted her enough to do as she asked.

She cried on my shoulder and thanked me, and then got out of the car.

I flew home. It was all over now; my search had ended. I had never been so hollow, so empty, and so barren as when that plane touched down in Florida.

CHAPTER TWENTY-ONE

Mom was concerned over how depressed I was, but I couldn't snap out of it. I'd come so close and he was now out of my life forever. My eighteenth birthday was coming up on Wednesday and I had decided, rather than living with Mom and Kimmy, I'd take my inheritance and find some place quiet to buy a house and spend some time in seclusion.

Ryan had called me several times and left messages, asking about our date. I finally relented and returned his call. He was in Palm Beach for the summer and he openly told me that, if nothing else, he could be a good distraction for a little while. He wanted to know what I was going to do for my senior year, and I said I was finishing up my credits online because I just wasn't ready to dive back into public life.

I agreed that we would celebrate my birthday together the following weekend; just me and him, the Trans Am and my new car, and a big stretch of desolate airstrip on the north end of Lake Okeechobee.

Sunday morning we left for church, traveling in separate vehicles because I needed my private drive time. I had traded in my Porsche for an Aston Martin Volente. It was the only time I really didn't think about Micah, when I was traveling too fast for the memories to catch me.

I was back to being someone who exuded the fact that I had money. I was back in my designer clothes and had my good jewelry and expensive Louis Vuitton purse, and Prada shoes, but it was window dressing and on the inside I was painfully empty. I'd give it all up to be just any other eighteen-year-old girl who had the man she was truly in love with, the man of her dreams.

I pulled into the tree covered lot of the Baptist church. As much as I loved the little church in Pensacola, this was my home church. I'd learned to sing my heart out for God standing on their stage; I'd praised, danced and worshiped inside these walls most of my life. I believe that nothing is chance. God has His hand in everything, even in my deepest pain. He had a reason for what I was going through. I didn't like it, but I accepted it as His will and that was the only thing left to keep me moving forward.

I stood outside, leaning against my car in the shade, early as usual because of my driving. I'd pulled my long brown hair back into a pony tail with just a couple strips loose by each ear and waited for Mom and Kimmy to show. A few people were arriving, but they knew I hadn't been in much of a mood for being social lately, so they simply smiled at me and went inside. I watched a postal truck pull into the parking lot and a young man took a package and went inside the office. I thought that was a little odd. I knew they advertised that they would deliver on Sunday, but I'd never seen one actually do it. The pastor stepped out of the office and pointed my direction.

The man approached me smiling, carrying a small box. "Are you Annalisa Winslett?"

"Yes, I am," I replied cautiously.

"I have a package that I need you to sign for."

"Addressed here—to the church?"

"Yeah, that's what it says and it was specifically noted to be delivered here at nine a.m." He handed me the box with the green signature card attached to the top. I signed. He removed the card and told me to have a nice day and left.

Okay, I don't know what anyone else would do, but lately my life had been on the crazy side so I shook it and then listened to it, looked for wires sticking out—yeah, I couldn't help but wonder if I was getting a mail order bomb.

I cautiously opened it and lifted the lid. Inside was a sleek new iPod. I lifted it out and underneath the iPod was a note that read,

"Happy Birthday, It was the only song that could possibly say how I feel about you. Love, M."

I almost dropped it. I knew the handwriting and I knew who M was. My hands immediately began to shake. I opened my car door and sat down, before I fell down. I plugged it into my stereo system and found the single song that had been downloaded on the player. I didn't recognize it. It was titled *The Reason* by Hoobastank. I hit the play button. The first words sung were, "I'm not a perfect person..." and I started crying.

He might as well have written the lyrics himself, because it ripped straight to the bottom of my heart. "...I'm sorry that I hurt you. It's something I must live with everyday. And all the pain I put you through, I wish that I could take it all away and be the one who catches all your tears. That's why I need you to hear...I've found a reason for me to change who I used to be. A reason to start over new...and the reason is you..."

I couldn't stop shaking, I couldn't breathe. All this time I had been aching for him, needing him, wanting to know if I had dreamed that he had told me he loved me. And then I had sealed him up inside my heart when Celeste told me that I had to let it go, for his sake.

I felt a warm hand touch my arm. I turned and, just like a dream, he was kneeling there beside my car. I don't remember going into those marvelous steel bands that he uses for arms, but I knew I never wanted to leave them. I was sobbing, just about to shake into a million pieces and all I could say was his name, over and over.

"Baby," came the voice that was like a piece of heaven.

God, I missed that voice.

He was using his thumbs to try to dry my tears as he cradled my face. "You switched to waterproof mascara?" He choked out, his eyes filled with tears that threatened to overrun his lashes.

I laughed. "Where have you been? I thought I was going to lose my mind completely."

"I told you getting out of the mob isn't easy."

I stopped breathing. "You—you're..."

"Yeah, Baby, that's all in my past now and I was wondering if you still were interested in forever?"

"Oh, Micah, do you really mean it?"

"I didn't know if you still wanted me..."

I couldn't let him finish that sentence, as I laced my fingers through his hair and raised my lips to meet his. I wanted to have the kiss, the kiss I didn't think I would ever have enough time in this lifetime to finish. There would be no painful ending to this one; this would be the beginning of so much more. This kiss was warm and gentle, sensual and long. I could feel that familiar heat burning through my veins and I knew I was flushed with color by the time our lips parted.

"I guess I'll take that as a yes," he whispered and then kissed me again. This time a little stronger, a little hotter and building with all the need we had for each other. "Oh, Baby, I can't tell you how much I've missed you."

I moved to kiss him again. I knew I was never going to get enough of this. But now he was smiling and putting his fingers to my lips.

"We are in the church parking lot," he grinned. "I'd like to keep doing this but—well, if this is your church then I don't want them to have a bad impression about me."

I laughed. There were going to be a lot of impressions that people would take away from the two of us being together and most of them I knew were going to be bad, but I also knew that God had brought us together for a reason.

"I love you, Micah," I whispered, hungry for another kiss, but knew he was right. We needed discretion and restraint. "You're really out?"

"My whole family has gone through hell to get me to this point—and I know this is where I want to be. Gwen got me out of Florida before the Fed's arrived. She's put her job on the line to see that all the evidence in Louisiana has been destroyed. Dad and Mom both faced the local family to stand up for me when I said I wanted out, and David..." he choked on the words. "Well let's just say he's in the most trouble of all of us."

"Why?" I had to know. "Because of getting Robert put away?"

"Leese, it's like a cardinal sin. No one in the family works with the police; it's a death sentence. I didn't even know the crazy bastard did it until it was too late. Dad is still trying to save his ass."

My hand went to my mouth, shock, surprise and fear filled me. "Why would he risk that?"

"He figured it out. He knew it was real for me. He's never been in love, but after I had to leave you and he saw what it did to me, he knew he couldn't chance Robert putting another hit out there on you. He knew it would have killed me. I guess Gwen had been right about him all along."

"What can we do to help him?"

He gave a weak smile, "Let my family handle it and be happy that we're together."

I wrapped my arms around that glorious neck and held on tight. "I can do that."

"I want to make a bigger change in my life, Leese. I believe in what you believe, I know God does everything for a reason now. I trust Him completely. I want to come forward in church."

That was more than I could take and my knees buckled. He caught me and sat me on the hood of my car. "Don't pass out, Baby."

"What changed it for you? Tell me how you finally figured it out?"

"When Sharon shot us, it was a miracle that neither one of us was killed. The bullet came through you and if it had an ounce more thrust it would have pierced my heart, but it didn't. But it did take something away. Unbutton my shirt," he said softly.

With trembling fingers I began to expose his skin, when I got to his heart, I saw the nasty scar, similar to my own, but it was what was missing that took my breath away. The bullet had pierced through the side of his tattoo, removing the first two letters. He knew when he saw it that I had been right all along, God has a reason for everything—no matter what it is.

He pulled his hand out of his pocket and opened a black velvet box; a beautiful diamond solitaire sparkled from within. Kneeling on the ground, he simply asked me to share forever with him.

That was when I realized my mother and sister were in the parking lot watching everything that was happening, as well as my pastor and a few dozen other church friends.

I nodded and said, yes. The parking lot erupted into cheers.

He put the ring on my finger, stood and pulled me into his arms. "Well," he whispered, "At least they sound happy for us."

I dried my tears as we turned toward the group and began to walk, "Yeah, the only person that I know who will be really upset is my date for next Saturday."

He stopped and looked down at me. He wasn't angry or even jealous, but he was extremely surprised. "Have you started dating someone?"

"No, it's a first date and it was to celebrate my birthday—and to do a little wild driving."

"Ryan," he said it as if he had known it all along.

"Yeah, I was finally going to make good on my promise, but…"

"You're keeping your date," he stated as we resumed walking toward the crowd.

"No, I can't." I was ready to protest, but he finished his statement.

"You're just going to have your fiancé as your chaperone, and he isn't allowed to touch. And you, Mrs. Gavarreen will remain untouchable, until the moment you say, I do."

"I only have one question," I said as I reached out and grabbed my mother's hand. Kimmy was already hugging Micah's waist.

"Mom, this is Micah, the man I love."

She smiled and hugged his neck, "Hello, Micah. It seems I owe quite a bit to you."

"I actually owe your daughter my life, but I'd like to ask if you would allow me to marry her?"

"Only if I want her to be happy; she has never spoken of anyone like she does about you. What's your question, Honey?" she asked

I looked from Mom to Micah and back. "How soon can we put a wedding together?"

PREVIEW OF UNFORGIVEABLE

Prologue

I was running away, but I didn't know where I was headed. It was dark and frightening. Everywhere I turned was another dead end. I wanted to scream his name; I wanted to see his face, but I couldn't go back. I had to keep running. I wanted to turn around, but there was a force that was taking me away, and like a strong current in deep water, I was being pulled further out. The tears were coursing down my cheeks and I knew my life was over; he was gone and I'd never see him again.

I was holding something in my hands, and, as I struggled to see what it was, I knew what I had to do with it. The knife was as dark as my surroundings, but the blade was razor sharp and I felt it bite into my palms as I traced the curve of it. It was over; there was no need to go on. What use is a heart that has lost its reason for beating? I gripped the handle and placed the tip of the blade against my chest.

Then I saw his face like a light in the darkness. His beautiful face was filled with love. I watched him come closer, his face changing, growing dimmer and angrier. He was right in front of me, close enough to reach out and touch me, but he wouldn't.

His hands took the place of mine over the dagger's handle and then he looked at me and asked, "Why did you throw my love away?"

I couldn't answer; I could only cry. I felt rain pouring down on me as thunder and lightning rolled.

Suddenly, fury exploded across his face as he jammed the blade into me.

The pain was unlike anything I'd known. It was like ice on fire as it plunged through my dying heart. I collapsed. The rain washed into a river of blood, and the last word I whispered was his name, "Micah."

ABOUT THE AUTHOR

Lindsay lives in Florida on the west coast. She is married and has three children. Although she holds a degree in technology, writing full-time (someday) is her dream job. She enjoys different genres, but always comes back to writing romance.

Novels:
Heart of the Diamond (published)
Untouchable Trilogy:
Untouchable (published) Book 1
Unforgiveable (coming soon) Book 2
Untraceable (in progress) Book 3

Lindsay enjoys hearing from her readers.
Feel free to contact her at:
Delagair@gmail.com

17070895R00177

Made in the USA
Lexington, KY
23 August 2012